I dedicate this book to my children, Victoria and Christiaan.
You both inspire me every day. Keep up the good fights.
And I'll try to not embarrass you.

SECRETS OF A MIDLIFE WITCH

J.C. YEAMANS

RSP

REED SHORE PRESS

Published by Reed Shore Press under the Imprint Broomstick & Lace.

Lewes, DE 19958

ISBN: 979-8-88652-002-6

For content elements, visit the J.C. Yeamans website: https://jcyeamans.com/content-elements/. Please visit the link if you would like more information on the contents before reading this book. There are spoilers.

Cover: Charles W. Clark, Reed Shore Press.
The cover design uses Rosarivo font (designed by Pablo Ugerman) and Photoshop brushes by Brusheezy.com.

Editors: Christopher Barnes & Amy Cissell of Cissell Ink

PRONUNCIATION GUIDE

Gwynedd: GWYN-eth
Crwth: KROOTH
Hywel Dda: HOO-il Tha
Bryn Cader Faner: BRIN CAH-dar Vah-ner
Pentre Ifan: PEN-tra EE-van
Lammas: LAM-uhz
Lugnasadh: loo-NAH-sah
Elfriche: EL-free-chay
Nain: NINE
Taid: TIDE
Bean Nighe: BIN NEE-ah

CONTENTS

CHAPTER ONE

FIRST CLASS

THE IMAGE IS SEARED into my memory—a bare, brawny butt with a strange tattoo of a crescent moon and a circle, screwing a woman from behind! Shit! I slam the door as quickly as I'd opened it and inhale until my lungs are full. The student I passed in the hallway earlier gave me awful directions. Clearly, my Celtic Studies grad class isn't in there.

I close the door before the couple has time to see who opened it on their lovefest. "I thought you locked the door?!" the woman squeals. At least I didn't ruin their morning romp. But really? Having sex in a study room where anyone could walk in at 8:45 a.m.? Have the decency to check the lock for fuck's sake.

I leave the lascivious sounds and roam around the basement corridors of Stewart Hall with butterflies in my stomach. It's been so long since I was a student at Delaware University at Bearsden, a second-tier college in the small, suburban town where I grew up. Known for engineering and the sciences, it's not surprising the Celtic Studies department is relegated to the musty basement.

The university, or DUB as we call it, boasts Georgian buildings of red brick, sitting in flawless alignment on either side of lush squares of grass called the Green. Divided into North and

South Campuses, it has mazes of paved walkways guarded by the Old Men oak trees, nicknamed for their appearance sans leaves.

A week ago, an email had announced Dr. Archibald Cockburn, the Celtic Studies chair, would be a guest speaker for the first week of classes. An Edinburgh native, he studied and taught in London before accepting a position at DUB. I can't get past his unfortunate surname of Cockburn. I envision an old man smoking a pipe with a scruffy, white beard. Of course, I'm stereotyping, and DUB has a smoke-free campus—no pipes permitted.

I pass a banner with the words *Go Highlanders* and a Scotty dog wearing a kilt and playing bagpipes in itty-bitty boots. Right after, I arrive at classroom 005. I'm still rattled, but the chatter on the other side of the door allays my fears, and I enter. Students near my son Tyler's age crowd the room, and they're wearing t-shirts and jeans with flip-flops. I've overdressed in a teal blouse and white Capri pants with heeled sandals.

I dart to an empty seat at a back table and set my backpack on the floor. A flood of students pours in, finding space against the walls or sitting on the edges of tables—violating fire codes, I'm sure. The young man to my right leans toward me. "Is this the first time you've attended one of Archie's presentations?"

"Actually, this is my first class since I graduated in the eighties," I say with wide eyes.

"Wooow. Well, it's fire," he says in a surfer-dude accent. "Though I'm here for the class. My name is Spencer Huxley, but my fam calls me Spence."

Fire? "Are all of these students in the grad class?"

He moves his hands with every word like he's directing traffic. "Nah. They came for Archie's first-day presentation. He's covering the first two classes for Dr. Hughes this week. She's not back from Britain yet."

Spence is lean with jet black hair cropped on the sides and longer on the top with a deep purple streak swimming through it. His pale complexion contrasts with his thick eyebrows and black eyeliner, and he's in a dark magenta t-shirt and ripped, faded blue jeans.

"I'm taking the class, too. My name is Gwynedd Crowther. Most people call me Gwyn," I say, offering him my hand.

Spence gently gives it a peck. "Awesome to meet you, Gwynedd." What a well-mannered young man he is.

Students trickle in until the clock strikes nine, but the chair of the Celtic Studies department has yet to show. A few minutes later, the door flings open, and a young, blond woman runs into the room, adjusting her clothes. I recognize her as the guide who led the summer campus tour I'd attended to refresh my memory. She went on and on about the chair. But I missed his name at the time—distracted by the overwhelming changes to the campus.

I check the time on my cell phone. "It's been almost fifteen minutes. Do you think the chair forgot?"

"Nah. Archie probably had to change his clothes. Why are you taking the class? Thirty-some years is a looong time." Spence pulls his hands apart in slow motion.

"I know. The campus is barely recognizable. I thought I'd try a graduate-level class before applying for a degree. My parents were Welsh and attended DUB years ago when Celtic Studies was a fledgling department."

Spence nods. "So, you probably know a lot about it?"

"You can fit what I know about Celtic anything on one pinky. My parents never shared much about their heritage, and they've been gone a few years now."

"Sorry to hear your parents are gone. Family is important. I don't get to visit mine often. They live in California." The door creaks open, and Spence opens his palm toward the door. "Prepare yourself for the prose of Scotland."

Dr. Cockburn is striking. At first glance, I would guess he's in his mid-forties, but he exudes a youthful air because of his muscular physique and sculpted face. He stands at an impressive height of over six feet and has wavy, ash-blond hair with strands of silver meandering through it. His eyes gleam with icy-blue irises above a chiseled nose and a neatly trimmed goatee. He's wearing mostly eighteenth-century Scottish garb, and the AC/DC t-shirt looks comical with his kilt and black boots. But he's damn attractive.

He enters the room with confident strides, reciting a poem in a Scottish brogue. Spence and the other students can't take their eyes off the man—mesmerized by his recitation. I, too, find myself spellbound by the man while he recites the Robert Burns poem "Tam o' Shanter."

Dr. Cockburn looks past the students as if speaking to a far-off land. His bicep flexes, stretching the arm of his t-shirt when he reaches into the air for an unseen object—perhaps an entity in a dimension only he can see. The heightened passion in his words highlights his handsome face as he finishes the prose.

No, wha this tale o' truth shall read,
Ilk man and mother's son, take heed;
Whene'er to drink you are inclin'd,
Or cutty-sarks run in your mind,
Think! Ye may buy joys o'er dear;
Remember Tam o' Shanter's mare.

The students burst into cheers and applause for Dr. Cockburn's performance. He bows, accepting their praise with a cocky smile. "Thank you all for attending my annual kick-off to the semester and school year. I'm not permitted to wear the dirk anymore due to safety rules, so it's destined to hang on my wall at home. As always, it's my pleasure to give you a wee taste a country where Celtic history originated? I guess I'll never know.

When class ends, most of the students pack up, throw their tech in backpacks, and rush to the door. While I put away my laptop, the tour guide from the summer flirts with the chair. "Thank you, Dr. Cock-burn." The blonde throws me a glare on the way out. How rude.

Spence takes out his cell phone and gives me his number. "You should always have the contact info of other grad students. I should have yours, too, in case you can't make it to class or need a drinking buddy." He lifts an imaginary shot glass to his mouth and chugs it. He waves goodbye and heads to the door.

As I zip my backpack, the professor ambles toward me—his boot buckles clanking with each step. "Blessed crwth player." He sets the clicker on the table next to me.

I look at Dr. Cockburn with a puzzled brow.

"It's the meaning of your name," he says. "Gwynedd Crowther. Blessed crwth player."

My forehead crinkles. "What's a crwth?"

"It's a bowed string instrument. The Welsh bards played them at court as far back as the sixth century, singing stories and poems of tribal-war bravery and family lineage. According to the Laws of Hywel Dda from around 900 CE, the bard was a member of the royal household. You come from a highly respected ancestry, no doubt."

"I don't think so, but it's a nice thought." I pull on my blouse and smooth it out.

"Don't be so humble." He leans into me. "Your ancestors may be more important than you realize."

He's so close, I get a whiff of his cologne. "I want to apologize for mispronouncing your name earlier, Dr. Co-burn." I fiddle with an earring.

"Don't trouble yourself. And you needn't be so formal. All the graduate students call me Archie."

"All right—Archie," I say with tight lips.

Dr. Cockburn leans against the edge of the table and knocks the clicker to the floor. I squat to pick it up for him, but his hand reaches for it first, brushing the side of my hand. An intense heat shoots up my arm, overwhelming me with a tingling sensation. I must be hallucinating because I swear my hand is glowing, the color of fossilized amber, and my head spins like one of those ballerinas inside a little girl's jewelry box. I lose my balance and grab the side of the table.

Archie reaches for me. "Are you all right, Gwynedd?"

"I don't know what happened. Maybe it's the heat." I touch my flushed face.

"I could fetch you some water? We have a water cooler in the office."

"No, I'm fine now." I massage my temples. "I'll see you on Thursday."

I stroll with care to the door and glance back. Archie raises a corner of his mouth and winks. On the walk home, I wonder, do other women have hot flashes like this?

I enter through the mudroom and kick off my heeled sandals. Fretting a disheveled appearance could spark worry in Tyler, I smooth my frizzy, chestnut-brown hair and futz with the fringe of bangs. I can't do anything about the dark circles under my hazel eyes or the lifeless pallor of my skin. Sleep deprivation is a youth killer.

I prepare a cup of Earl Grey and settle into my home office until lunch. A remote, part-time job for a local insurance company helps pay the bills and provides health insurance while

I experiment with grad school. Thank the stars I convinced my husband Richard to purchase a high-value life insurance policy, a purchase he deemed completely unnecessary—the irony.

I check the fridge for hummus and discover I forgot to buy it again. Sleep deprivation has zapped my brain cells, too. "Damn, I wish there were hummus in there." A hot, tingling sensation overtakes my hand, gripping the fridge door. "These hot flashes are getting weird."

"Hey, Mom," Tyler says, entering the mudroom in jeans and a polo shirt.

He gives me a bear hug and bends about a foot to place a peck on my forehead. A devoted and intelligent son, he inherited my husband's good looks, along with my chestnut hair and hazel eyes, and my level-headedness. His last name is Wolfe, my husband's surname.

"How's work?" I ask.

"Things are going great. My team hopes to purge the bugs in the software by December before the update gets launched."

"That's good. What would you like to eat?" I retrieve lunch plates from the cabinet.

"Why don't I make us something? Tell me about your week while I make you a hummus wrap." He opens the fridge while I collapse into a kitchen chair.

"Sure, but I forgot to buy hummus." I lean back in my seat, annoyed by my forgetfulness.

Tyler peers over the fridge door at me. "There's an enormous tub in here."

I go to the fridge to prove him wrong, and a tub of hummus sits on the second shelf in plain sight. "You put that in there."

"I didn't, Mom. You really need to get more sleep. You're having trouble with object permanence."

I snap at my son. "I swear. THAT tub of hummus was NOT in there."

"It's OK, Mom." He hugs me and pats my back. "Relax while I make our sandwiches."

"My first class was wonderful. You were so right about taking a course. I got a little lost looking for the room, though." The couple screwing in the study room isn't appropriate lunch conversation, so I keep it to myself. "I made a friend. His name is Spence. He's younger than you!"

"Awesome." Tyler sets our sandwiches on the table and plops into a chair next to me.

"Spence used a word I've never heard you use. What does fire mean?"

He bites into his cheese sandwich. "Fire means great, you know, cool, awesome. We also say lit. I'm sure you'll pick up the slang in no time."

"That's what I thought." I take a bite out of my tasty wrap. "Dr. Archie Cockburn, the Scottish department chair, recited a Robert Burns poem in Highlander garb. At the end of class, he mentioned my name in Welsh means 'blessed crwth player.' It's an old Welsh stringed instrument. Kinda cool, or lit. So, tell me what's happening in your life. Dating anyone?"

Tyler looks at his plate in silence. I get the message, scoop the crumb-laden plates, and place them in the kitchen sink, noticing the worn drain. One more repair Richard failed to get to.

"You know we should start working on the house." He eyes a crack in the plaster ceiling. "March will be here sooner than you think. You can always live with me until you figure out what you wanna do."

I know he's right, but my motivation must be hiding in the garbage disposal. I curse Richard for leaving this all to me. There's a sudden, thunder-like pounding on the back door to the kitchen.

Tyler turns his head toward the knocking, and a woman with red hair enters. "O.M.G. It's Ms. Baldwin."

"Good morning!" My best friend Veronica prefers to be called Ronnie and has a disposition as bouncy as her ringlets of crimson hair. Tall with sexy curves in all the right places, her hair isn't the only body part bobbing as she kicks off her sandals and tramps into the kitchen in her tight t-shirt and jeans.

"Hi, Ronnie. What's up?" I ask.

"Hey, Tyler! Oh, my gods, Gwyn. I have to tell you about my date last night." She fills the teapot and places it on the burner. "I wish you would buy a freaking coffee pot. This guy was amazing. Hung like a horse, and what a body!"

Ronnie shimmies back and forth as she babbles on about her sexcapades. Her azure-blue eyes twinkle with the zest of life above a straight, dainty nose on a heart-shaped face dotted with freckles. A man magnet, I've lost count of the number she's dated since her divorce two years ago.

Tyler rolls his eyes. "Time for me to return to work."

"Stick around, Tyler. You might learn something!" Ronnie cackles.

"As usual, it's been enlightening to see you, Ms. Baldwin." Tyler hugs me goodbye. "Have a great day, Mom." He puts his sneakers on in record time and pulls the door shut with a whoosh.

The teapot whistles, and Ronnie collects a cup from a cabinet. "Want another Earl Grey?"

"Absolutely." I sit back and enjoy her attention while she fills me in on her new man.

"His name is Derek Young," she says, pouring steaming water into our cups. "He loves oral sex. My god, he must have stayed down there for half an hour."

Mind-blowing, satiating oral sex. I wouldn't know. Richard rarely did it. I'm blushing like a naïve schoolgirl, but this isn't the first time she's narrated Tales from the Redhead's Boudoir.

We've been friends since our first yoga class together—eight years of amusement.

"We screwed for hours. Best exercise ever." She stretches her arms over her head and twists her spine back and forth.

"Ronnie, I get the impression this guy is a little younger than you?" I sip my Earl Grey.

A mischievous grin sprouts on her face. "Yeah, he's thirty-one."

"He's thirteen years younger than you!" Immediately, I regret the words slipping out.

"Oh, who cares?! I don't know where it will go, but he wants to go out again." Ronnie radiates with a glow in her cheeks I've not seen since she signed her divorce papers. Harold, her ex, accused her of cheating when she devoted her life to him. She left at the first sign of abuse.

This guy could be different from the others. "What does Derek do?"

"He's a fitness trainer. Runs his own gym. Explains his virility." She guffaws, banging her hand on the table. "I crack myself up."

I crack up, too, laughing more at Ronnie's behavior than her attempt at a lame joke. "Young's Fitness Center? The new place on Main Street?"

"Yep, that's the place. I met him there last Saturday, using a Daily Pass. He came over, all sexy in his logo t-shirt, and offered to help me get oriented. I told him I wasn't interested in a membership, and he offered me dinner. He was so sweet and courteous. When he dropped me off, he gave me a peck on the cheek."

I blink twice. "But Ronnie, you said you had sex?"

"I couldn't help myself. After the peck on my cheek, I planted one on those sweet lips, and the rest you know." She finishes the last of her green tea.

"You've gotta learn to control yourself," I say.

"I figured he was cruising for a one-night stand. When he said he wanted to see me again, I was stunned."

"You shouldn't be. You're so funny and pretty. I wish I had your looks."

"What a sweet thing to say. I don't know why you put yourself down like that. You're an attractive woman, Gwyn. You're just a little rough around the edges right now. You've been through a lot."

"I suppose." Months of anger and grief left tread marks on my face.

"Damn, I didn't mean to stay this long. Gotta get to the café."

Ronnie owns a trendy restaurant on Main Street called Sunshine Garden Café, a tie-dye explosion of color with hanging blown glass lighting. DUB students hang out there, including students in the Fellowship of Associated Pagans, a group she joined as a community member not long after her divorce.

"Are you sure you won't attend the Fellowship open house with me?" she asks. "Great people and a couple are probably taking class with you."

"I know you're really into your FAP group, but I don't think I'd fit in."

Ronnie bursts out laughing. "Gwyn, you can't call it that. Fap means to masturbate, so we don't use it."

"Oh." I clench my teeth, thinking I should brush up on more slang. "I attended my first Celtic Studies class today. The department chair is a guest speaker this week. He's not what I expected. His name is Dr. Archie Cockburn."

"I know Archie! He's an academic sponsor for the Fellowship, and he's hot," she says in a husky voice.

"I didn't notice." But I absolutely had. "I mispronounced his name as Cock-burn in class."

Ronnie cackles. "That is so you. He's funny and amiable too. I've really gotta go now. Text me if you change your mind." The door slams with a whoosh.

Maybe I will?

CHAPTER TWO

THE DREAM

NIGHTMARES, HOT FLASHES, THROWING sheets. I can't escape them. It didn't help I left a window open, and the neighbor's dog barked all night. I have a long day of Welsh research, so I drag myself out of bed and make a cup of tea.

I imagined going back to school at my age would be stressful, but this course is fun and way more interesting than the catalog description. While investigating stories of fairies, brownies, and dragons, I stumble on pagan and modern-day witchcraft sites. They display simple symbols of various shapes and intricate works of art, like Celtic knots, the Eye of Ra, and the Tree of Life.

Click, click, scroll. Click, scroll. Click, scroll. STOP. I gape at the circle with a crescent moon called the Horned God symbol. I found it!

I'd nearly forgotten about the tattoo and the incident in the study room. The Celtic Horned God symbol represents masculine energy and rules over fertility, sex, and virility—the origination of the term horny. I snicker. "An appropriate tattoo, at least." By the time I've finished my long day of research, it's time for dinner and the monotonous cleaning after.

I slip on a cotton chemise and lie in bed, waiting for the nightmares. Unrelenting. Unabating. Persistent. A rerun dream produced by *The Trauma Network*. I fixate on the jagged crack in the ceiling above me, sharp with splintery edges. Another repair.

Nauseating recollections slip in like a sharp dagger with toothed edges, twisting back and forth, leaving me shredded. The memories seep in with a gut-wrenching sting. Richard was on his way to meet a colleague to show a house, talking on his cell phone. Police think he skidded on black ice. I'll never know, but it's what happened at the house after the funeral that needles me. And I can't get past it.

I should count pagan symbols tonight instead of sheep. Actually, counting sheep would be appropriate for Wales. "Damn hot flashes." I throw the covers off in desperation with flaming cheeks and a body dripping with sweat. The sheep fade as my weary eyes win the battle for slumber.

A mixture of mist and fog turned to snow. Having buried Richard in the morning, family and friends gathered at the house. I hadn't slept, so I took a nap. As I lay in the cherry, four-poster bed Richard's father built, I stared at the yellowed ceiling, eyeing the start of a crack in the plaster.

"Gwyn? Are you awake?" Ronnie asked, entering the room. "A few people want to say goodbye."

I slid out of the big-ass bed onto the floor. "I need to get rid of this bed."

She laid her head against mine. "Probably a good idea. Shall we go down?"

Downstairs, Blanche, Richard's elderly mother, sat in the living room with my sister-in-law, Sammy. Blanche never considered me elegant enough for Richard and relished pointing out my flaws. Sammy's husband Drew sat secluded in a corner of the living room, answering work emails. Tyler played video games with a couple of friends from his college days, a mind-numbing distraction to help him forget the day's event. He stopped and looked at me with wet eyes.

In another corner of the room, Cassandra Parnell blotted tears with a tissue. A fellow realtor Richard complained about so much, the sound of her name grated like her pink-lacquered nails scraping a chalkboard. A slender woman in her 40s, she had a diamond-shaped face and bleach-blond hair. She consoled David Berkovich, Richard's best friend since high school, while he wiped his face with a shirt sleeve. I always confused his name with the Son of Sam serial killer from the late '70s.

"I need to get rid of the four-poster bed," I said. "Sammy, if you and Drew would be interested in it, Richard would want you to take it. If not, I'll sell it."

"Why would you ever sell your bed? His father built the bed for the two of you!" Blanche sobbed, plucking her last straw.

I massaged my temples. "Blanche, I've always hated the four-poster bed. It's too high off the floor."

"Well, I would like the bed if no one else wants it," Cassandra said through sniffles.

I stared at Cassandra, perplexed. "Why would I give you the bed? Frankly, Richard barely tolerated you."

Apparently, Cassandra was on her last straw, too. Crying through a flood of tears and uncontrollable gasping, she spewed the words that would alter my life forever. "It's not true! Richard loved me! He planned on leaving you and said the bed would be ours!"

Sorrow turned to shock, to disbelief, to heartache, ending in rage. In a haze of fury, I pulled on boots and marched outside coatless into the freezing night. I rummaged through the shed, tossing shovels and rakes until I found the tree axe. Back in the house, I passed by everyone and made my way upstairs on a mission.

The muttering of voices followed me up the stairs. "What is she doing?" "She's lost her mind."

I swung the axe, slice after slice, with a boundless rage. Tyler and Ronnie entered the bedroom, pleading with me to stop. Chop. Cleave. Split. Crack.

"That bitch can use you as toothpicks now!" I stepped back, sporting a wicked smile, as the bedpost hit the floor with a thump.

Ronnie whispered in Tyler's ear, and he left. She stood, her head cocked and arms crossed, while tapping a black heel on the wooden floor. "Are you done?"

"I think so." I laughed, gasping for air. Starting with a whimper, cries escalated into full-blown blubbering. I collapsed to the floor, axe in hand. "For three years, he lied to me. I figured he avoided touching me because he was too depressed to make love. He just didn't want to make love to me."

Ronnie sat beside me on the dusty wooden floor and squeezed my hand. "Gwyn, you let it out, honey."

"How did I not see it? I'm one of those oblivious wives who missed the signs, but they were right there glaring at me. Thinking back, I saw it in his face the morning he died."

All the questions bombarded my overloaded brain. When did the affair with Cassandra begin? Where did they meet? How many people knew about their affair? David Berkovich? Damn straight Son of Sam knew, and he probably covered for him.

"You loved and trusted him. His failings aren't yours." Ronnie brushed my hair to the side as I wiped the tears from my bloodshot eyes.

Instantly, I was in a dark room with a glimmer of light shining through a doorway. A tall man sauntered toward me, taking my hand. I couldn't make out his face, only the outline of his body. He led me to a bed, pressing his lips to mine. I was receptive and returned the advances. He leaned forward, causing me to fall onto the bed.

The full weight of his muscular body pressed against my nakedness, and his warm lips planted soft kisses on my neck, breasts, and belly. My heart fluttered when the back of his hand brushed across my nipples, making them erect. Beep, beep, beep. I turned my head to the sound but looked back as he slid further down my torso. Beep, beep, beep. Floating like a living, dark shadow, my lover placed a wet kiss on my pubic bone. My body quivered as he moved further. I raised my pelvis to meet him when he positioned his open mouth on my...beep, beep, beep.

Beep, beep, beep, beep.

The blare of the alarm wakes me with my heart racing like a bullet train. What a bizarre dream! Shit! I set the alarm wrong. No time for a shower. I wash up and throw on a thin sports bra, a DUB t-shirt, and jean shorts, slipping into my flip-flops on the way out the door.

Fifteen minutes of the class has passed by the time I arrive with sore skin between my toes. The old door hinges grind as I enter. It's cold enough to preserve slabs of beef and smells like it, too. I rub the goosebumps on my arms, thinking a hot flash would be welcome right now. Spence sits at the back table, talking with a young woman with wavy, fire-red hair, and motions with his hand to join them. Archie is busy helping a group of students and doesn't notice me.

"Hi. I'm Skye McGowan," she says in a husky voice. "I missed the first class. Overslept." A younger version of Ronnie, her hair radiates like the flames of a fire, falling to her shoulders in soft waves and framing her oblong face. Sunburnt skin suggests a recent visit to Rehoboth Beach.

I offer my hand with a friendly smile, noticing the obvious influence on her given name—sky-blue eyes. "Nice to meet a friend of Spence's. I'm glad you're both willing to work with this old woman."

"I think experience should be valued, and you're not old. Dr. Hughes is old," Skye chuckles. "But we love her." She must be freezing in her loose camisole top, struggling to reach the top of her jean shorts.

"We're searching for sites about stone circles and cromlechs throughout Wales. What did you research yesterday?" Spence asks while he types.

"I started a general search for Wales but ended up on pagan sites," I say. "Fascinating stuff."

"Yeah, we pagans have awesome symbols. I have a tat of the Tree of Life." Spence lifts his t-shirt to display an elaborate tattoo on his stomach, a tree decorated with curved branches and leaves.

This glacial classroom has my legs shaking like a jackhammer. "The tree is beautiful. You must have lain still a long time to have it inked."

"It was a gift from my boyfriend Tanner for my twenty-first birthday. Gwyn, are you cold?" Spence snickers, rubbing my arms like a flint to start a fire.

I'm enjoying the impromptu heat massage from Spence. "I'm freezing. Do you attend the Fellowship of Associated Pagans meetings?"

"Absolutely," Spence replies. "Skye is in the Fellowship, too. We've been pagans since our undergrad days."

"Students on campus give us a hard time. They think we're weird potheads and Satanists." Skye rolls her eyes. "It's so ignorant. Satan is a Christian construct. We do shit for the community, too."

"I discovered a bunch of pagan symbols on there, one I saw recently." I display the picture of the tattoo on my laptop screen. "A Horned God symbol with a pentagram in the circle."

Spence tilts his head. "Where did you see that tat?"

"On the first day of class. I was searching for this room and walked in on a couple doing it. I didn't glimpse their faces, but I saw that tattoo on the right cheek of a very toned butt."

My Zillennial friends guffaw out loud. Spence smacks the table with a hand, and Skye knocks a large textbook to the floor with a whomp, prompting Archie to turn around and glower with heavy eyebrows. The man even looks attractive with a scowl.

"Lots of guys get Horned God tats," Spence whispers. "They think it represents the whole 'horny' thing. So immature."

Skye whispers, "It represents male virility, but also great power. Most men don't deserve that power or the tat, but you should absolutely get one, Spence."

"Maybe I already do?" Spence wiggles his eyebrows.

I chuckle at his silliness. "Please, tell me it's not on your butt."

"I'm playing. I don't need a Horned God tat. I have all the virility I need."

Skye and I snort, trying to stay under the chair's radar. Students flash frowns in our direction. "My best friend Ronnie is in the Fellowship. She's been trying to convince me to attend meetings since last spring. You must know her."

"We know Ronnie," Spence says. "She's the other redhead in the Fellowship. We call Ronnie and Skye the Fire Twins."

I bite my lip. "Well, maybe I'll go. The first meeting of the semester is tonight, right?"

"It's an open house for students and townies. We haven't had a full meeting since spring semester. No chants or charms and no nudity. Someone started a rumor, saying we run around bonfires naked." Skye rolls her eyes.

Our constant chatter draws Archie's attention, and he meanders around empty tables toward us. Instead of the kilt and boots, he's wearing jeans and athletic shoes with a black Radiohead t-shirt. A department chair would have dressed more formally in my day.

"I see you dedicated students are working diligently on your research," Archie says, sarcasm bringing out his Scottish brogue. "Ahh, the Bryn Cader Faner stone circle is unique, but I would suggest you include Scotland in your search as well."

Using Spence's laptop, Archie brings up an image of enormous stone megaliths, a circle within a circle. "The Callanish Stones were built before Stonehenge and are more impressive, in my opinion. Being a Scot, I may be a wee bit biased. However, this Welsh American may disagree." He glances at me with a lopsided smile.

Squirming in my seat, I bow my head to break the awkward gaze and freeze. The frigid AC in the room has turned my nipples into mini mountain peaks, poking through my thin sports bra and t-shirt. Mortified, I snap my arms across my chest. When I lift my head, he's gone.

Skye teases, raising her ginger eyebrows. "Hey, it looks like the chair noticed someone. Are you available?"

"What? No." I'm more than a little embarrassed. "I mean, I am, but he must be reacting to my disheveled appearance today." And unfortunately, maybe the peaks of Crowther Mountains. Who am I kidding? More like Crowther Hills.

"FACTS. He eyed you like a snack." Spence pretends to chew.

I don't appreciate the snack metaphor. "You're both being ridiculous." Having buried Richard seven months ago, dating hasn't even crossed my mind. "It wouldn't be appropriate. He's the chair."

"Dating students is frowned upon, but technically, it's not against the rules," Skye says. "He's not your professor, anyway."

"Don't you think we should stop gossiping and work?" I'm not liking the path this discussion is taking.

As Archie makes the rounds, the blond grad student from the summer tour corners him away from any eavesdropping. Anger builds in her eyes while she talks, and Archie shakes his head, mouthing a clear "no." She huffs as he walks away.

I crouch over the table. "What was that about?"

"The blonde is Courtney Davies. Rumors say they had a fling over the summer. She looks pissed." Skye covers her mouth and snickers. "Courtney's a member of the Fellowship, too. I think she joined to get close to Archie. Don't know why she stays."

"Oof, he walked right into that one. She was so thirsty for him. Comes from a rich family on Long Island." Spence rubs his money fingers together.

Skye continues to type. "Archie made a mistake. He should've been clearer about ending things with her."

Archie takes a break and props his feet on the desk, glancing in our direction periodically to monitor our lax work ethic, I'm sure. I try to avoid eye contact, but those icy blues pull at me like magnets, and I swear I catch him staring. Self-conscious and paranoid, I focus on my work.

"Which cromlech are you researching?" Archie's Scottish voice makes me jump in my seat. "So sorry. Thought you knew I was standing here."

"It's OK. I'm a bit jumpy since I'm so sleep-deprived." Skye and Spence pretend to work, but their prying eyes and ears hang on every word while I talk with the chair.

"Why are you having trouble sleeping?" Archie asks. "I have trouble myself occasionally."

"Recurring nightmares due to stress, but it's getting better."

"I'm sorry to hear that." Archie moves his eyes from me to my laptop screen.

"I found the Pentre Ifan Cromlech, a Neolithic burial chamber and dolman in Pembrokeshire. It's so big."

"Ah, yes. Pentre Ifan means Ivan's village. It's the largest cromlech in Wales. Folklore says the friendly fairies who lived in the nearby woods lifted the stones in place because they were too heavy for men. According to legend, their song on the night of a full moon would encourage you to dance so they could carry you off into their world."

I shudder. "That's both enchanting and terrifying."

"Aye. Most folklore is. I'll leave you three to your research." He glances at me one more time and walks to another group.

Spence gets nosy. "You can tell us. What's stressing you out?"

"Yeah, I'm awesome at interpreting dreams. Try me," Skye says.

"Nothing to interpret. I'm reliving a bad day I had in January. My husband passed away, and the day of the funeral was difficult." My new friends stare at me with weepy eyes, and I glance at my laptop. "Please don't feel sorry for me. I'm OK." It's what I keep telling myself, but the nightmares tell a different story.

"You can count on us to help you with classwork or anything," Spence says.

"The Fellowship is full of people like us. Please come and meet the other members." Skye sways back and forth. "Most of us are pretty chill."

"And get free food." Spence rubs his stomach.

I send Ronnie a text: *Will attend Fellowship mtg.*

She texts back: *So excited! See you there!*

Class ends with an announcement from Archie. "It was delightful to monitor the course this week, but unfortunately, my time has come to an end. Enjoy the remainder of your day and the semester."

The students thank Dr. Cockburn as they leave, and I make my way to the door. Courtney Davies dawdles, filling her backpack, and the chair addresses me. "Wait, Gwynedd. I'll walk out with you."

While I wait, my eyes hop from the dust-laden baseboard to the humming air conditioner to the outdated chalkboard, landing on Courtney Davies, who's glaring at me. What is her problem? Archie flings his satchel over a shoulder and opens the door for me. It's been ages since a man held a door for me.

"Thank you." The humid warmth of the hallway warms me like a thick, fuzzy blanket on a winter's night.

"I want to apologize for prying. Insomnia plagues me sometimes. I hoped my remedies might be of help." Archie's warm baritone voice softens his intimidating height and muscular build.

"They're more of a nuisance now," I say, twisting an earring.

Arriving at the stairs, several students rush past us for the next class. "Hi, Dr. Cock-burn!" an undergrad student says. He sighs, his shoulders deflating like tires on nails. "You see, you're not the only student who mispronounces my most unfortunate surname. So, will I see you tonight?"

"You mean the Fellowship open house? My friend Ronnie mentioned you were an academic sponsor. Yeah, I'm going."

"Of course, I know Ronnie. I'll see you tonight then." He winks and strolls to his office a few feet down the hallway, and I ascend the steps for home.

CHAPTER THREE

MEET THE PAGANS

A NAP AFTER WORK leaves no time for dinner, so I throw on a teal halter dress and white sandals for the sultry weather. For the first time in months, my skin exudes a peachy glow.

Forced to park in the South Campus parking lot, I dread the hike in heels to Victorian Row—historical homes DUB uses for overflow. The Fellowship meets in the Pumpkin House, the Victorian with dark-orange siding and ornate gingerbread trim. A warm breeze flits through my hair while I walk, but the humidity is thick as mud.

"Yes, you came!" Ronnie dances on the porch. She's a stunner in a low-cut, apple-red dress and black pumps.

Grasping my hand, she pulls me inside the foyer, which divides a large parlor on the right and a formal dining room on the left. Curiosity seekers fill the rooms, while some students come for the food. There's a grand oak fireplace mantel centered on a parlor wall. Purple banners hang on either side of it, displaying pagan symbols of the Celtic Tree of Life and the Wheel of the Year.

Ronnie glimpses a familiar face and drags me to meet one of the community members. Maybe a decade older than me, the man has white, frizzy hair pulled back into a short ponytail and a wiry beard that ends at a bit of a paunch. Bushy eyebrows sprout above emerald-green eyes. He reminds me of a hippie nutcracker I once saw in a department store, complete with a Hawaiian print shirt, cargo shorts, and sandals.

Ronnie introduces me to the hippie. "Gwyn, meet Shane Murphy. He owns Mystical Sage, the store across the street from my café. He's from North Carolina and is one of my favorite people."

"Welcome to the Fellowship." His firm handshake rattles my entire arm.

I smile timidly. "Thank you. I look forward to learning about paganism."

"Skye needs help with the food trays. Gwyn, why don't you stay here and chat with Shane." Ronnie rushes over to the dining room to help, leaving me with the hippie.

"I admit I've never shopped at your store," I say. "I know little about paganism and the occult." Or any other religion, thanks to my upbringing.

"We sell the typical pagan and witchy stuff, but we also stock dried herbs for homeopathic remedies. Even puzzles, magic tricks, and the like. You should stop in next time you're on Main Street. It's so busy, I posted another part-time job."

"Your store sounds intriguing." And so does the job.

A formidable Black man who looks to be in his 40s parts the crowd, towering over everyone in the room. His arm and chest muscles stretch the material of his white polo shirt and his thighs strain the seams of his jeans. He has a broad nose with cropped dark hair and light-brown eyes that are almost electric. "How you doing, Shane?" the Black man asks.

Shane bumps fists with the giant. "I'm finer than a frog hair split four ways. This is Gwyn, the friend Ronnie told us about."

"Hello, Gwyn. I'm Elijah Jackson," he says in a deep, cavernous voice. "I hear you may join our small but powerful group." Reaching for my hand, I worry it might break off, but he has a gentle grasp.

"Nice to meet you." His hand swallows mine, but it's warm and soft.

Shane has a twinkle in his eyes while he pets his long beard. "Elijah is a social worker and runs the Bearsden homeless shelter."

"It must be a rewarding job," I say, lifting my head a bit to talk with him.

Elijah closes his eyes for a moment. "It is. Can be heartbreaking as well."

"I imagine, but you're trying to make a difference in their lives." My stomach growls, reminding me I skipped dinner.

I glance over at the dining room, where students and locals have lined up at the refreshment tables. Spence has arrived with a slim, attractive man. I assume it's Tanner. A young woman with wavy brown hair dressed in a white shirt, plaid skirt, and red flats stands behind the beverage table. She places an ice scoop into a bowl of cubes and adjusts it when the scoop slides—three times. Who knew there was a proper way to place an ice scoop?

"Who's the young woman in the plaid skirt?" I ask.

"Audrey Kenilworth," Shane says. "She's here on a post-graduate fellowship in physics."

Elijah crosses his bulging arms. "I kinda hoped she'd moved on. Never took to her. Rich, white girl trying to do good? Awful fake to me."

"I think she's got gumption." Shane pushes his lower lip up. "Growing up in a rich family, no question she was raised with privilege, but she's had it tough since her parents disowned her. She's trying."

"Well, she's gotta try a lot harder." Elijah grimaces in her direction.

Animalistic rumblings rise from my stomach again. "Please, excuse me. I didn't eat dinner and need to check out the refreshments before they're all gone. It was a pleasure meeting you both."

I say my goodbyes and push through the throng of people to find the food. Eager to avoid the scourge of a hot flash in this stuffy room, I snap up a tiny plate and fan myself.

While perusing the food on the table, a familiar Scottish voice fills my ear. "Are you looking for something in particular?"

I turn to find Archie dressed in more appropriate attire: dark jeans and a blue dress shirt. The heat in the room increases my frustration as I fan myself. "I'm looking for veggies and fruit."

"Maybe you're looking in the wrong place?" He gestures to a table on the far side of the packed dining room.

Archie follows me to the table, and I'm tempted to scarf down my food, but I'm self-conscious. Instead, I bombard him with questions while I nibble at my food. "How long have you been the sponsor of the Fellowship of Associated Pagans? Are you a practicing pagan?"

"Nice to hear you're so interested. I've been the sponsor since I came to DUB about seven years ago. To the second question, I try, but I'm not a very good pagan." He pours himself a glass of iced tea. "Would you like a glass of tea?"

"Yes, thank you. My parents raised me without religion. Taught me to be a good and kind person. I wasn't sure about joining this group, but I like the members I've met. They seem like a friendly bunch."

"They are. We would love to have you." He lifts a corner of his mouth and hands me the glass.

Between sips of iced tea, Archie shares stories of his hometown of Edinburgh, and I tell him about my looming house repairs and living alone since Tyler moved out. His eyes wander over my dress. "You look wonderful this evening. A bonnie dress you're wearing."

The compliment makes me blush. "Thank you. A nap invigorated me." I scan the room for familiar faces. When I return my gaze to him, his icy-blue eyes haven't budged. The air has the consistency of gelatin, and I fan my flush face with the paper plate. "I've enjoyed talking with you, but I should find Ronnie. I've barely spoken to her this evening." Ronnie motions to me to join her in the parlor.

"My pleasure. We should chat again soon." Archie grins with a glimmer in his eyes.

I return the smile. "I would like that."

Archie winks at me as I squeeze through the crowd to join Ronnie, Spence, and Tanner in the parlor. Tanner has a swimmer's body and a tanned, rectangular face with a narrow nose. He's wearing charcoal trousers with a salmon dress shirt and tie.

Spence motions to his boyfriend. "Gwyn, this is my boyfriend, Tanner Jones. I told him all about you." He wraps an arm around Tanner.

"Nice to meet you, Tanner," I say, shaking his hand. "Spence has spoken highly of you."

"He better have, or he'll be driving himself home." Tanner glares at Spence with midnight-blue eyes.

Spence plants a kiss on his cheek. "Don't sass me, hon. You know I love you more than my tattoos."

Ronnie slaps Spence with the back of her hand and cackles. "And he *loves* his tattoos!"

"My tats tell my story." Spence bares his shoulder, revealing a tattoo with Tanner's name, and gestures to others. "When I die, my ink will be my epitaph."

"Quite an epitaph you'll have," Ronnie says.

The banter between Tanner and Spence warms my heart, and I long to have a love like that. "Tanner, Spence said you're a financial advisor. Do you enjoy it?"

Tanner wrinkles his nose. "It can be stressful, but I love numbers. Numbers don't lie and always have possibilities."

"Oh, please. Don't let him fool you." Spence rolls his eyes. "He could talk your ears off about Dow futures for hours."

Ronnie clears her throat. "Gwyn is thinking of joining the Fellowship." She looks at me with a pleased smile.

"We could use another member," Tanner says. "To expand our community work."

Spence hugs me. "And Gwyn plays well with others."

"Thank you, Spence." I notice Skye helping Archie fill the trays with the last of the food in the dining room.

Ronnie catches me eyeing them. "So, what did you and Archie chat about?"

"Yes, spill the tea," Spence says.

My eyebrows collapse, and I throw them a dirty look. "Small talk. Nothing of consequence." Skye joins us in the parlor, but I don't see Archie.

"Gwyn, his face lit up, talking to you." Ronnie crosses her arms and grimaces.

I love my friends, but they're working too hard to make something out of nothing. Skye adds her comments on the matter. "They had a moment in class, too. FYI, Audrey had to leave. Early start at the lab tomorrow. And Zoe never showed. Probably forgot to enter the date on her phone again."

Spence throws his hands up and gestures with each word. "One of us should schedule a reminder on our phone to remind her."

"Ronnie's right," Tanner says, using an analytical eye. "Archie's eyes were glued to you during the conversation." He picks lint off Spence's magenta tee and kneads his shoulder. Such a sweet display of affection. It's clear they have a deep love and respect for each other, a balance that never existed in my marriage.

"I appreciate all your advice," I say, "but you're all reading too much into it. I just met the man."

Ronnie spins her eyes. "Suit yourself, friend. Skye, why don't you show Gwyn how we set up for meetings and celebrations?"

"Sure! Follow me to the altar." Skye motions with an index finger and a playful eye, and I follow her into the parlor, where a small oak table serves as an altar in front of the fireplace. It's decorated with several candles, an iron sickle, and a bowl with dried corn on the cob.

"The altar is still set up for Lammas, also called Lughnasadh," Skye says. "Meetings take place on Thursdays and begin at 7:00 p.m., but we get here a few minutes early to set up twelve chairs for the circle. It would be amazeballs if you joined. Thirteen would be a better number."

"Why stop at thirteen?" I ask. "Wouldn't more members solidify the group? Especially with students graduating and leaving."

Skye rearranges the items on the altar while she explains. "True, but more than thirteen makes the training more difficult."

"Training for what?" I ask. Ronnie never mentioned I'd have to train to be a pagan.

Skye's eyes grow big and white with sky-blue dots. "Uh, rituals. Yeah, you have to train to learn the rituals."

I tip my head. It's like she said something she shouldn't. "When do I start?"

"Not this year." Skye fiddles with the sickle on the table. "You should spend this year observing."

By the time Skye finishes my impromptu orientation, the open house has whittled down to a few stragglers listening to Archie tout the Fellowship's food collection program. Ronnie

and I chat on the porch about the wonderful evening, waiting
for Derek, when a sudden urge overtakes my bladder, and I
rush inside. Coming out of the bathroom, I notice the house
is dimly lit and vacant. Archie is waiting to lock the front door.

"Thank you for not locking me in," I say, stepping on the
porch.

Archie locks the door and moves close to me. "Not a problem. Ronnie told me you were in the bathroom. Do you have
far to walk?"

I take a step back. "Yes. I had to park in the South Campus
lot. The parking sucks here. Hasn't changed in the thirty years
since I graduated." I don't know why I'm so nervous, but I
can't stop tapping the heel of my sandal.

"I agree. Would you like me to walk with you to your car?"
He leans toward me to speak. "It's sort of on my way home."

I smile at his icy-blue eyes, tugging at me. "I appreciate the
offer. The Green is like a graveyard late at night."

The gleaming moon illuminates the Green, and the lampposts emit a hazy glow. We stroll for a few minutes without
conversation, listening instead to the sound of crickets chirping and the flutter of moths attacking the lampposts. As we
approach the set of red brick archways separating the Green
from South Campus, he stops and turns toward me.

The glow from the nearby lamppost spotlights Archie's
eyes. "You attended DUB as an undergrad, no?"

"Yes. I loved my college days here." I lean back on the arch
opposite him to give my feet a brief reprieve.

"Students have told me this is called the *Kissing Arch*. Do
you remember it from your days here?" Strands of hair fall
to one side of his chiseled face, and full lips peek through his
neatly trimmed goatee.

I collect my hair behind my head, enjoying the breeze. "I
remember friends joking about the arch story."

"A young man would kiss his date goodnight under this arch." He ambles toward me with a shimmer in his eyes. "Before the young woman returned to her dorm on the other side."

He places an arm on the coarse brick and leans into me. Placing a soft peck upon my blushing cheek, the soft whiskers of his goatee tickle. The heat appears to ignite my cheek, spreading throughout my head, neck, and beyond. I become light-headed like the time his hand brushed against me in class, and the red brick buildings spin around and around. What is happening to me?

"Do you think that's what they did?" Archie's breathy voice is distant. "Or is it a university folk tale?"

When the whirling stops and my head clears, my heart pounds with the weight of a sledgehammer. I feel the heat of his skin as he towers over me. What a handsome man he is. "Archie, are you flirting with me?"

He stands with a blank face and runs his fingers through his fallen hair. "Ms. Crowther, I do not flirt. I was merely...demonstrating."

"Riiight." Applying pressure on my right sandal, the heel breaks off. "Shit." I bend over to pick up my damaged heel.

"That is unfortunate." Archie turns his lips inward, suppressing a laugh.

I'm not amused and squash my lips together. "The parking lot is on the other side of the arches next to the South Campus dorms." Removing my sandals, I proceed in my bare feet on the rough cool pavement. When we arrive at my metallic-blue Prius, he opens the door for me to get in, and I lower the driver's side window. "Thank you for walking with me. It's a safe campus, but you never know what's waiting for you in the dark. Goodnight, Archie."

He lifts a corner of his mouth. "Sleep well, Gwynedd."

I watch Archie saunter back under the light of the moon through the *Kissing Arch* and drive home.

My droopy eyes glare at the dagger-like crack in the ceiling. Another consecutive night of bad dreams seems inevitable, but I try thinking of something else. I met a few nice pagans tonight. Nothing strange about that at all. Try breathing exercises the psychologist suggested. Breathe in. Hold for five, four, three, two, one. Breathe out. Breathe in. Hold for five. Breathe out...

In a misty haze, I float, suspended in the air. Men and women chant in a circle. An old woman cloaked in black extends her vein-wrinkled hand to me, her face obscured by the hood of the cape. I extend my hand to grasp it, but the room swirls. "Gwyn? Are you OK?" a friend with wild, red hair asks. Holding a wooden staff in one hand, the old woman seizes my hand and pulls me to her.

"Gwyn!" Ronnie grabs my shoulders and shakes my upper body. "Wake up, woman! Are you OK?!"

"What?" I'm in a daze. The intense sun burns through the curtain, stinging my squinting eyes. A veil of crimson waves hangs over my face. Is it already morning?

She punches my arm. "You scared the shit out of me! Good thing I found the hidden key to the front door."

"I'm sorry. Dead to the world, I guess." I sit against the headboard and rub my eyes.

"You need to get better sleep. Derek got me into lifting weights. He swears it helps people sleep more soundly. I don't know yet, 'cause I never sleep when I'm at his place." She howls with laughter. "You can use DUB's fitness center as a student. Right?"

"Yeah. I'd have to work out with all those young students, but I'll try it tomorrow." Procrastination for the win. I recap the prior night's walk with Archie, and what happened under the *Kissing Arch*.

"No one on campus believes the *Kissing Arch* story." Ronnie's mouth morphs into a tooth-filled semi-circle. "He was flirting, but is it bad if he likes you?"

"He says he wasn't." My eyes are blurry, and it hurts to focus without my contacts. "I won't see him in class, anyway. Dr. Hughes returns next week."

"Dr. Hughes co-sponsors the Fellowship. She's way past retirement age and was chair before Archie. You'll like her. She has an old-school presence. You still wanna go shopping?"

I massage my temples in little circles. "I forgot. Damn menopause. Migraines, memory lapses, hot flashes, hormonal shifts." My eyes bug out. "And weird sex dreams."

"Oh, do tell?" Ronnie's ginger eyebrows arch above curious eyes.

I grin from ear to ear. "Not. A. Chance."

Ronnie taps my arm and cackles. "If you ever want to share, I'm all ears!"

"I'm sure." I place my hand on hers. "You know, I couldn't have survived all these months without you and Tyler. I love you, friend."

"You did the same for me." Ronnie strokes my arm. "Now shower and brush your teeth, because your breath stinks!"

After shopping and the much-needed time hanging out with my friend, work sucks up the remainder of the afternoon until it's time for dinner. While I'm eating, I make a list of repairs needed to sell my banal, colonial home. I hate the stress of moving, but at some point, I have to leave this neighborhood of friendly people and white picket fences. This house devours me daily, one bite at a time.

I take a brisk walk after dinner through my neighborhood, the west section of Old Town Bearsden. Old Town has tree-lined streets of mature oaks and maples with leaves of emerald and forest greens. The massive trunks and exposed roots displace the sidewalks, creating a roller-coaster walk. September has brought cool evening temps, and I regret not carrying a hoodie.

Suddenly, the pungent odor of a neighbor's rotten garbage makes me gag, and the air turns icy cold. Droplets of white mist erupt from my mouth, and tree limbs snap, falling to the sidewalk and missing me by inches. Within seconds, I'm overcome with intense heat, sweating like a marathon runner. Damn these hot flashes, but where did the frigid air come from?

Back at the house, I'm wrapped in my bed quilt like a mummy and glare at the crack in the ceiling, clenching my teeth. A glance at the nightstand reminds me of the pagan book collecting dust, a gift from Ronnie. Flipping through the pages, I fall upon a picture of the Horned God symbol and chuckle.

Chapter Four

DR. HUGHES, I PRESUME?

I BROWSE THROUGH THE social media feed on my phone while I'm eating my eggs and sipping tea. While I'm chewing, I stop mid-bite. I have no recollection of dreams. FINALLY. A night of respite from nightmares.

A good night's sleep gives me energy for my first day of weightlifting. Wearing purple leggings and a sleeveless, lavender top, at least I look the part, and I make the long walk to the fitness center on North Campus.

The fitness center has an area for everything, including a weight room with separate areas for the machines and free weights. I start with the weight machines, figuring I'm less likely to make a fool of myself or get hurt. Ten pounds on the bicep curl machine is lame, but my muscles have atrophied to gelatin-like masses.

I experiment with a few machines and peer at the bench press, gargantuan and intimidating as the muscular men using it. Screw it. I came here to build strength. How hard can it be? I lie flat on the bench, placing my hands on the bar above, and push up, but nothing moves. Clearly, it's broken, but to be sure, I attempt one more time, grunting like a pig.

"You think you can push 150 pounds with your wee frame, do you?" a Scottish, male voice asks.

I bend my head to find Archie upside down in black gym shorts and a red wicking shirt. His toned shoulders and arms glisten under the bright ceiling lights.

"What do you mean?" I'm so embarrassed he's seeing me in athletic wear. It exposes my flabby arms.

Archie smirks. "You have 150 pounds on the bar. Did you plan on pushing that?"

"Oh, I didn't check the weight. I feel stupid." Even upside down, those icy blues sparkle.

"Would you like me to adjust the weights for you? You should start with an empty bar. It's forty pounds. I can spot you if you like."

"I wouldn't want to delay you from your workout." Don't let those bulging muscles deflate on my account.

"I finished." Archie removes the heavyweight plates and stores them on the rack while I lie on the bench, kneading my fingers.

"Sure, if you don't mind?" I'm relieved he offered to help me.

"Not at all." He stands behind my head and molds my hands around the bar. "If you set up wrong, you could hurt yourself, especially being a little older."

Ouch. That remark hit me in the pit of my stomach. I'm anxious his touch might spark another strange heat surge, but his gentle hands only prompt a bit of nervousness. As I push up on the bar, I grunt and contort my face, sweating by the third set, but Archie motivates me with words of encouragement like "outstanding" and "brilliant." When I've finished, he reaches for my hand to pull me off the bench.

"So nice of you to coach me," I say. "This is the first time I've done this."

"I don't mind at all. Weightlifting builds great strength. If you like, I could coach you twice a week. I'm here anyway."

A shy smile slips onto my lips. "I'd like that. Ronnie thinks the lifting will help me sleep."

"Aye, it should. It will tire you out. I wish I could help more, but I'd need to know why you're having trouble sleeping."

I hesitate. "My husband passed away several months ago. It's been hard. I think the exercise will help."

"Ronnie mentioned he passed. I'm sorry. I imagine it's been difficult." Archie rolls his lips inward. "I can certainly help you with exercise." He checks his phone. "I'm sorry. I have a meeting in thirty minutes and need to shower. Can I have your cell number? I'll text you later with times to meet."

I didn't expect to end up with Archie as a weightlifting coach, but I do like his company. On the ride home, I have a new sense of purpose. What would my Zillennial friends say? #goals

Tuesday, I wake to a text from Archie giving me times to meet him at the fitness center. With only one night of poor sleep and no strange dreams, I face the day with renewed vigor. And I get to meet Dr. Hughes. Skye sits in the back, dressed in her usual skimpy clothes and flip-flops already typing on her laptop, and Courtney has a spot alone at a far table. The oppressive heat has returned and stretches August into September—sticky like taffy.

"How was your weekend, Skye? Did you do anything fun?" I take out my laptop and set it on the table.

"Went to a party with a small live band in the backyard." Skye stops typing and raises a hand with her fingers spread out. "It was fire!"

I truly hope "fire" is Zillennial lingo and didn't require a visit from the Bearsden Fire Department. Soon after, Spence dashes in and plops into a chair at our table. He has on a black V-neck tee with ripped jeans and flip-flops, but no eyeliner. His hair is sticking up at random.

"I got out of bed like fifteen minutes ago. I bet you can tell!" He guffaws, pointing at his punk-like hair. "So glad I got here before Dr. Hughes arrived. What's the tea?"

"What's the tea?" I ask. Spence used this phrase at the open house.

"You know. What's happening?" Spence motions down with his fingers. "Wassup? What's the tea?"

"Oh, I'm a quick learner," I say. "Spence, to answer your question, what's the tea? I started lifting weights at the fitness center. Made a fool of myself, and Archie was right there to witness it."

Skye's eyes grow big. "Oh, no."

"What did you do?" Spence asks in a low voice.

I give them a synopsis of my lifting session and Archie's offer to coach me twice a week. Courtney turns her head in our direction. I guess we're too loud.

"Well, wasn't it nice of him to offer?" Spence snickers and waggles his eyebrows.

Air passes through my lips. "It was completely platonic. I'm grateful he showed up when he did."

"It's impressive you're trying to get in shape," Spence says. "I run a few times a week and sleep like a baby. Archie knows how to lift. He'll be an awesome coach."

"I think it's fantastic you'll get to spend time with... How do I put this without being offensive?" Skye clenches her teeth.

"Someone closer to my age?" I purse my lips. "He's still many years younger than me."

My Zillennial friends grin with emoji tooth smiles, kidding this Gen Xer. Most people their age would have tossed me aside like a dated cell phone—too old and not enough memory.

A spindly, older woman in her mid-70s enters the room wearing an orange blouse and a black mid-length skirt, hinting at the coming of fall—Dr. Hughes, I presume. She carries a weathered satchel on her shoulder, clutched by a knobby hand. After placing a binder on the podium, she clears her throat and drinks from a DUB travel mug as the murmur of voices dissipates.

"Good morning. I trust Dr. Cockburn conducted class wisely, and you have a head start on the semester presentation. His annual recitation of Robert Burns to kick off the fall semester is always delightful. He performs recitations of other Scottish poems throughout the academic year. Please, take advantage of them."

Possessing a snowy complexion withered with wrinkles, Dr. Hughes has applied brow pencil, black mascara, and dark-red lipstick on pencil-thin lips. She has shoulder-length, silver hair that cuts across her face, covering one of her copper-brown eyes. "If you have questions about the syllabus, please send them in an email. I will respond promptly. We begin today with the Welsh bards and poets."

Her lecture style is reminiscent of my undergrad years, fitting like a worn leather glove, and she displays a video with a tenor performing in Welsh on the wall monitor. The bard accompanies his hypnotic singing with a crwth, a six-string wooden instrument played with a bow, the instrument Archie spoke of. After a divisive discussion on the authentic performance of the crwth, the class quickly packs up and departs, except for Courtney. She's moving at a glacial pace to pack her bag. I stand to leave.

"Gwynedd Crowther, yes?" Dr. Hughes asks from her desk.

"Yes." How did she guess who I am?

"I knew your parents, Gwynedd. We used to be good friends right here at DU, Bearsden. I lost touch with them after I left to work on my doctorate. When I returned to take a professorship here, we never reconnected. I was sad to hear of their passing seven years ago. Such a loss."

Well, that explains it. Growing up, everyone always said I looked like my mom. "I miss them terribly. They were the only Welsh family I had in the states, and my husband passed away in January." I don't remember her. She didn't attend my parents' funeral. I would remember her silver hair and stature.

"I read about your husband in the newspaper. So much loss for you to bear." She lays her cold, fragile hands on mine.

I flinch at the chill of her hands and pull mine back. "It's not been easy."

She buckles the flaps on her leather bag. "Well, I'm overjoyed to have you in class. I remember you as a small child, maybe three years old. I can't believe that child is the woman in front of me now."

Courtney interrupts as she exits. "See you on Thursday, Dr. Hughes."

"Indeed." Lugging her packed satchel on her shoulder, Dr. Hughes walks toward the door of the classroom with me by her side and stops.

"Gwynedd, I'm on the way home for lunch. It's only a couple of blocks from campus. Would you like to join me? I have a private collection of Celtic resources in my home office. We could eat lunch, get acquainted, and you could browse them after."

"Sounds wonderful, but I'll need to send my son a text. He usually comes for lunch on Tuesdays." I take out my phone to send Tyler a text.

Leslie waves a hand. "Please, don't relinquish your family time."

"It's not a problem. I think he does it to check on me." I wrinkle my nose.

Tyler sends a smiley emoji when I cancel lunch. He will never admit our weekly lunches allowed him to monitor my emotional state, but I get it. Finding out Richard cheated on me with Cassandra invoked a catatonic state for weeks. He fumed over his dad's infidelity, and part of me relished it.

The stroll to Dr. Hughes's house on Drummond Lane takes about fifteen minutes. We reminisce about the thirty years of changes on the DUB campus meandering through the Green, and I talk excessively about Tyler. Dr. Hughes takes long but steady strides with labored breathing, and I struggle to hold back my brisk pace.

As we approach her home on Drummond Lane, I discover she owns the miniature Tudor house I've admired on my power walks east of campus. The red-brick exterior has an arch around the wooden entry door with a brown-stone fireplace to the left. We stroll up the cracked, concrete driveway to a side entry door covered in thick layers of barn-red paint. She unlocks the door and nudges it with her hip.

"This door has stuck like this for years," Dr. Hughes says. "I planned on replacing it with an energy-efficient door when I first bought this house, yet here we are."

"I know exactly how you feel. There are so many little things to update in my house, I don't know where to begin." I follow her into a tiny laundry room.

"Indeed." Dr. Hughes hangs her house key and sits on a small stool to remove her pumps and put on black slippers. I remove my sneakers. "The kitchen is through here."

The compact kitchen has the original pine cabinets and daffodil-yellow walls. An oak, drop-leaf table with chairs for two hugs the outside wall under a window.

She opens her fridge door. "Would you like a sandwich?"

"I'm a vegetarian. Do you have cheese or hummus?" I hope I'm not being a bother.

"I do, Gwynedd." Dr. Hughes removes a block of cheese and deli meat from the fridge and finds a sharp knife in a utensil drawer.

I pull out a chair and place my backpack on the floor. "That would be wonderful, Dr. Hughes."

"Please call me Leslie. We don't need to be formal here. Relax at the table while I make our sandwiches."

Leslie prepares our delicious, no-fuss lunch, and we chat. The lively, unpretentious stories of her Welsh travels contrast with her dignified presentation in class. She shares narratives of hidden beaches covered in soft sand and cerulean, clear water surrounded by grassy cliffs, and her love of the Welsh language.

After lunch, Leslie leads me to an office in the back of her house, knocking into several framed pictures lining the narrow hallway. I glimpse a section of a cozy living room with an overstuffed, green-plaid chair and ottoman watching over the stone fireplace—a warm, inviting spot to read or rest with a snuggly throw.

I'm taken aback when I enter her tiny office. Packed wall to wall with various items, it qualifies for an episode of a hoarder's reality TV show. I'm struck by the aroma of decaying leather books and dried sage, hanging from a set of iron hooks. Floor-to-ceiling, built-in shelves blanket a wall behind an old desk. Shelves hold books, old photographs, and an assortment of candles and crystals.

Leslie invites me to join her behind the desk. "Please, feel free to search. They're not in any order. I planned to organize them, but the piles grew taller. I keep telling myself, 'This is the last one I'll buy,' yet can one ever have enough books?"

Yes, Leslie. Yes, you can. There are book piles on the desk, next to the desk, and on top of the industrial filing cabinet. I try not to judge, rolling my eyes out of her line of vision.

To reach the higher shelves, I grab a chair and turn around to glassy eyes—yellow on the left and powder-blue on the right, staring into mine. "Agh!" I yelp.

Leslie glances at me. "Oh, you've met Mr. Yeats."

"I didn't know you had a cat. He has such peculiar coloring." With a split fur coat of jet black and burned ginger, Mr. Yeats is the first chimera cat I've encountered outside of pictures. He purrs, rumbling on top of the filing cabinet, and swings his tail back and forth in a friendly gesture with an odd flicker in his mismatched eyes. "You named him after the Irish poet?"

"He was a stray in the area who tried to mate with female cats on the street. They kept rejecting him, hence I rescued the poor soul and called him Mr. Yeats." She laughs with a deep, raspy voice, and her copper eyes flicker like her cat's.

"I get it. Because the woman Yeats proposed to rejected him over and over." I wrinkle my nose. "Clever."

"I considered it an apt name for a poor rejected and dejected male," Leslie says.

Not knowing where to start, my eyes roam, starting with the bottom shelf. I scan books on UK travel, British cookbooks, and books with obvious Welsh titles: Hanes Cymru, Meini Hirion Cymreig, and Gwrachod Cymru.

"Those are in Welsh, my dear. Do you speak Welsh?" she asks.

"Not a word. My mom explained why the two DDs in my name have a TH sound. That's it." I open a book to observe written Welsh. The words resemble a cryptic word puzzle, so I place it back on the shelf.

Faded photographs detailing Leslie's substantial life litter the shelves. Perched against the back of the top shelf, a color photograph has aged in a tarnished metal frame. The clothing and haircuts of college-age students point to the '60s. Two women and a man are sitting on a brick wall in front of Urquhart Hall.

I climb on the chair and push up on my toes to snatch the dated photo. Wiping away the years of accumulated dust with the underside of my yoga shirt, I examine the youthful faces.

Leslie points to the photo. "Your parents, Rhys and Lowri—and me. I regret not connecting with them when I returned to Bearsden. They were my closest friends in college. I was so excited for them when your mother became pregnant with you. I'm sure you don't remember, but I babysat occasionally. You were no more than three years old when I left for my doctorate."

"You all seem so happy. It's sad you never reconnected. My parents didn't socialize much, but they would've enjoyed spending time with an old friend." I scrutinize the picture to find Leslie's face in the young woman next to my mom. "You are pretty in this picture with your bob."

Leslie's hair had been dark brown, a beautiful coloring to pair with her copper irises. The young coed in the picture appears fit and full of vivacity, unlike the time-worn woman before me.

"Oh, here it is!" Leslie hands me a thick, leather-bound tome on the standing stones of Great Britain. Pulling the tome from the shelf leaves a gaping space, and my arms drop from the weight. "If the standing stones are not in there, they do not matter."

"This is amazing, Leslie. Thank you so much." Checking the time on my phone, I discover I'm running out of time to change and meet Archie at the fitness center. "Seeing this picture of my parents from college tugs at my heart." I place the picture back on her desk and lift the heavy tome. "See you on Thursday."

Leslie blinks once. "My pleasure. See you in class."

As I carry the tome of stones back to my car, I think it's such a coincidence I would end up taking a class with an old college friend of my mom's. But it's odd Leslie would return to Bearsden and never speak with her. Why?

CHAPTER FIVE

SAVING
MITCHELL HALL

FALL SNEAKS IN WITH leaves turning shades of sunset and brings cool evening temperatures. My muscles hurt like a bitch from workouts with Archie, but the nightmares have subsided. I haven't had this much energy in over a year.

I throw on a coat sweater over my loose blouse and skinny jeans and head out early, but I get stuck parking in the South Campus parking lot again, anyway. And I regret wearing high heels as I pass the Old Men oak trees—majestic and too selfish to relinquish their leaves. When I arrive, Ronnie's boyfriend has dropped her off, and she motions for me to join them at his car.

"Gwyn, this is Derek Young. Derek, this is my best friend in the world, Gwynedd Crowther."

Burly as Ronnie described him, he's a handsome man with tousled, dark-brown hair and a rugged, tanned face with a nose that turns up at the tip. I glimpse dark eyes and a kind-hearted grin. I wave and return the smile. "It's so nice to meet you!"

"It's great to meet you, too." Derek reaches through the open window to shake my hand. "We should meet for dinner sometime. At the Sunshine Garden Café?"

Derek has a firm handshake, and I sense an air of confidence. "Sounds like a fabulous idea."

"See ya later, honey." She blows him a kiss through the car window. "And thanks for the ride!" Derek puckers and returns the kiss before driving off. "I think I love that man! He treats me so well. I'm so afraid I'm gonna screw it up."

"Why would you think you'd screw it up? He appears to like you a lot!" I haven't seen her this concerned about a guy returning her affections.

Ronnie raises her shoulders. "I think he may not like me so much if he ever learns everything about me."

"What the hell are you talking about?" I ask.

Entering the Pumpkin House, we find the young members chatting in the far-left corner of the parlor. I spy Courtney and wonder if the rumors about her dating Archie are true? Ronnie tells me to chill while she helps the students set up the chairs in a circle.

Deep in conversation, Archie and Leslie talk on the far-right side of the room, and a statuesque, curvy Black woman in a flowing yellow dress joins them, ranting without stopping to breathe. Her black stilettos have her standing eye to eye with Archie, and she has long, burgundy hair and a velvet-like complexion.

Shane and Elijah enter together, but Elijah's unforgettable belly laugh arrives before he steps into the parlor. I wave in his direction. "Wonderful to meet you again. Crystal clear night, isn't it?"

"Yeah, it surely is." Elijah unzips his loose-fitting DUB hoodie and hooks his thumbs in the pockets of his blue jeans.

"It's getting chilly at night finally," Shane says in his drawn-out, southern accent. "I love fall weather, but in Delaware, September doesn't know whether to spit, blow, chill, or burn." His black hoodie has a colorful Tree of Life logo on the back.

I gesture to the Black woman in the yellow dress. "Is that Trinity Johnson speaking with Dr. Hughes and Archie?"

Elijah peers over at them. "Yeah. She's the head of the LGBTQ support group Family for All. She sure looks pissed about something."

"For sure, you don't want to cross her. You'll lose!" Shane roars with laughter.

Elijah snickers and waves his hand back and forth. "Never won an argument with her yet."

Archie, Leslie, and Trinity finish their heated discussion and move toward the circle of chairs in the center of the room. The rest of us shuffle to find a seat. The one next to me is empty.

Leslie clears her throat, but it does little to remove the raspy quality of her voice. "It's so wonderful to visit with all of you after our summer break. I look forward to the Autumnal Equinox and Samhain celebrations, and we should plan for them tonight. Many of you have already met our newest aspiring member, Gwynedd Crowther. Please give her a warm welcome. If any of you have not introduced yourself, please do so now in our circle."

A sudden clap of the wooden screen on the front door resonates in the foyer off the parlor. A young, petite woman runs in with clipped, black hair sticking out in all directions and flopping around like a bobblehead. She stops near the circle.

"Oh, snap! Am I late? I'm sorry! Must have set the time wrong!" Her small round face has a golden hue with a cute button nose, wide-set eyes with long black eyelashes, and a tiny mouth with plump lips. She shimmies into the circle in her jeans and lavender tee, bearing the words *Bite Me* with an image of a black cat's open jaw.

Spence flings his hands up. "Girl, do you ever double-check the time you set on your phone?"

A few of the members chuckle while the feisty young woman scowls at Spence and points at her shirt. She plops into the empty seat and grins at me before slinging a sneer at Spence. He blows an air kiss to her, and several members crack up, including me.

Leslie casts a disapproving stare at the woman and Spence. "We began introductions for Ms. Gwynedd Crowther. Since you have captured our attention, Ms. Wu, why don't you go first?"

The lively young woman pops out of her chair like a jack-in-the-box and rattles off her words with such speed, I struggle to process them. "Hi! I'm Zoe Wu! I'm excited you want to join the Fellowship! I have Celtic ancestry on my mother's side and love being a pagan and following nature's way!"

Such a perky pagan! Beaming with an enthusiastic smile and shiny, brown eyes, I want to steal some of her energy. Zoe plops back into her chair and grimaces at Spence.

Courtney Davies introduces herself, but her voice is too soft for me to hear. Drop-dead gorgeous in a lady's tee, jeans, and clean, white sneakers, I can imagine how a man would find her irresistible.

Audrey Kenilworth stands with a stiff back. She has coal-black eyes and a face with picture-perfect makeup. Preppy but casual in a navy-blue blazer over her white shirt and jeans, she gazes directly at me. "My name is Audrey Kenilworth of the New Jersey Kenilworths. I think I speak for all of us when I say it's an honor to have you seek membership in our group. Welcome." I love her sincerity, but part of me wishes she'd loosen up.

With introductions finished, Archie takes over the meeting but relaxes in his chair. He peers at me with warm eyes. "As a sponsor of the Fellowship, I want to welcome Ms. Crowther. It's always a joy to add a new member to our organization. We have many activities to plan for the Autumnal Equinox and Samhain celebrations. Perhaps we could split into three smaller groups, but first, we must discuss the next Bearsden City Council meeting."

Members shift in their seats as Archie continues. "Trinity informed Dr. Hughes and me of a new agenda item added to Monday's City Council meeting. As you are aware, downtown parking is a major issue for our town, and the expansion of DUB has not improved the situation. To address the paucity of parking, one council member has recommended the city buy Mitchell Hall. Once purchased, the city plans to condemn the old mansion, tear it down, and build a multi-level parking garage."

The Fellowship erupts with outrage, starting with Elijah. "My grandmother knew the Mitchells well. She managed one of their local art foundations. Would be a damn shame for it to be demolished."

Tanner chimes in. "I like the idea of finding some land to build a parking garage, but tearing down the old mansion would change the entire appearance of that end of Main Street."

"The city needs to address the parking situation," Shane says, "but the administration of DUB needs to be part of the solution. Student parking has spilled over into the city like a river at high tide."

"The new council members are schemers." Ronnie shakes a finger as she rants. "Lots of corrupt decisions since the last election. Do you remember how no one wanted a big modern hotel built, and it got rammed through by one vote? We know who the slimeballs are."

Audrey raises her hand, pleading for a turn to speak. "I heard the current owners can't afford the necessary renovations. My family had to have an old family home condemned for the same reason." Unlike Audrey's pessimistic view, the other grad students share memories of celebrations at Mitchell

Hall—Halloween open houses, spring garden parties, and DUB mixers.

Trinity cuts in with a resonant voice to divert the morbid turn of the conversation. "The passing of Alistair and Rose Mitchell saddens all of us. They were stalwarts of our community, especially the LGBTQ community. Unfortunately, they had no children, and the nephews and nieces aren't interested in keeping the place. I'm inclined to agree with Audrey. We may not be able to do much about this one."

This one? Has the Fellowship fought other city agendas? Admittedly, I did not keep on top of city politics. I'd concentrated on raising my son and my career, so I don't share the consternation over the mansion. "I shouldn't express an opinion, considering I've never been inside the mansion, but you have to admit, it's in terrible shape from the outside. Maybe it's too late to save it. Too expensive, like Audrey said." I glimpse her smile.

As I scan the other faces in the circle, I observe Archie's puzzled eyes, and the others have faces of hovering insects with bug eyes. And in a flash, I'm the poop emoji.

"What a stupid thing to say, friend," Ronnie whispers to me as I sink in my seat.

"We all have our opinions." Archie gazes at me. "And as always, the group should respect all of them. We never all agree on how we should proceed when these things occur. It's important to consider all solutions."

"Remember, Gwyn's new and doesn't know all the good we've done. Give her a chance." Elijah reaches around Zoe to give me a fist bump.

"How is it you never visited the Mitchell's mansion?" Shane asks.

"It wouldn't be a surprise if you had known my late husband. He hated parties." I fidget with the edges of my sweater and regret mentioning him.

"That blows," Spence says. "You missed out on some hella awesome parties." He shimmies in his seat.

"Apparently." I ruminate on an alternative to offer while the others talk among themselves and consider other options. "You know what? If we can't stop the sale of the mansion to the city, the property still has to be condemned. Right?"

Archie cocks his head. "What are you hinting at, Gwyn?"

"City council will have to vote on its demolition." I straighten my back and smooth out my sweater. "What if they can't condemn it because of historical significance?"

"I worked for a historical property's nonprofit one summer as an undergrad," Skye says. "I could call them for help with the paperwork."

Leslie breaks her silence. "A magnificent idea, Gwynedd, but the city could sell the building to someone else, an outside buyer most likely, who would bypass any paperwork. I've seen the city council win fights like this time and time again."

"Lots of corruption on the council." Tanner leans forward on his legs and rubs his hands together.

A light bulb clicks on. "What if they didn't sell it? We could lobby them to make it a community center."

"Great save," Ronnie whispers in my ear.

A rumble of chatter ensues with the Fellowship's renewed energy, exhilarated by the possibilities. A community center should be an easy sell. The gardens could accommodate an area for kids to play outside. The city could rent it out for weddings, parties, and meetings. It's a sustainable solution that would provide jobs, too. And the students mention the creation of an annual open house in memory of Alistair and Rose Mitchell.

"That's brilliant, Gwyn." Trinity smiles, turning her thumbs up. "I've been searching for a better place to house our organization, and this could be a solution. So many possibilities for the entire community."

Archie delegates the plan. "A show of hands if you think the group should pursue this project for the year?" Every member raises a hand. "It's unanimous. Are there any volunteers to attend the first council meeting to observe and report?"

"I'll go since I attend most of them anyway," Shane says. "Perhaps one of the younger members would like to attend with me?"

Audrey shoots her hand in the air. "I would love to go with you, Shane."

"Audrey and Shane will attend and report back to us next week." Archie stands with a hand in his jeans pocket. "Let's break up into small groups and do our planning for the fall festivals. Thank you all for taking on this fight for our community."

I have so much fun planning festivities for the Autumnal Equinox. Ronnie was right. I should've joined sooner. When the meeting disbands, Trinity walks over to me, clicking in her stilettos. Her face glows with a wide-toothed grin and jade-green eyes. "I'm over the moon Ronnie convinced you to join us. You know your parents used to attend our meetings. I was fifteen at the time. You are the spitting image of your mom."

"My parents were pagans in college? They never mentioned it to me." I'm stunned, and the idea of my parents attending Fellowship meetings makes me chuckle inside.

"Oh, it was a long time ago." Trinity puts her hands on her hips and laughs. "You know, we don't always tell our children everything."

I grin at her jovial behavior. "You're all so friendly. I'm glad I came."

Trinity moves closer and wraps me in an awkward embrace. "I am, too. Know you are welcome here." She releases her grip and exits through the front door.

Archie and Leslie discuss the upcoming council meeting with Shane and Audrey in the parlor. They don't seem close to finishing, and I'm exhausted. I should have asked Tanner and Spence to walk with me at least part of the way to the parking lot. Hindsight—my favorite plan.

Black lampposts dot the empty Green with balls of light, casting a hazy glow. A welcome break from the stifling heat, a cool breeze clutches strands of my hair while I inhale nature's perfume from the chrysanthemum beds of gold, russet, and white pom-poms, a vision of tiny snowballs.

As I approach the Old Men oak trees, I crunch with each stamp of my sandals in the roller rink of tan and umber marbles. The lamppost flickers and buzzes with an increasing, grating hum, and the bulb explodes with a pop, spewing pieces of glass on the pavers and grass! I shriek, slapping my chest to assuage my spastic heart and jump to avoid the sharp, knife-like slivers.

I squint at the Old Men oaks, menacing in the dark with arm-like branches, and notice unexpecting victims lured into their lair. Bags of loose trash flap relentlessly against the bark, scaring the shit out of me, and I snatch a pocket of air.

Forced to take methodical steps to avoid the rink of tree marbles, I stop when a putrid smell permeates the area, decaying flesh from an animal perhaps, but it's eerily familiar. When an unexpected, icy chill erupts, I spy a burst of white fog slinking through the inky air—my breath. In my peripheral vision, I discern the swinging of an arm-like branch, and my feet collapse underneath me, sending my body backward in slow motion as an amber glow shoots two feet out of my hand.

CHAPTER SIX

INHERENTLY DENSE

I BLINK. TWICE. AND flinch at the face of Audrey Kenilworth. Loose strands of brown hair dangle in my face, and I puff to spit them from my mouth.

"Ms. Crowther?" Audrey has a hand on my neck. "Are you OK?!"

I detect a sore spot on the back of my head, and my veins throb with every pulse of my heart. "I think so. It's a little tender. Was I unconscious?"

"I don't know. I was too far away." She offers to help me up.

In the distance, rapid footsteps increase in volume until they stop at us. "Naw! Don't stand!" Archie pants, trying to catch his breath. "You could have hurt yourself."

"I'm fine. I have a tender spot on my head, but my tailbone? Entirely different story." I rub my butt, wincing and wriggling from the pain.

Archie kneels to check the back of my head. A heightened concern shows in his crinkled brow. "You should go to the emergency room and get evaluated. You hit your head and could have a concussion. Maybe call your son?"

"No!" I press on my aching temples, and the whiff of his cologne makes me dizzy. "Tyler will think I can't take care of myself. I'm a grown woman and know if I need an emergency room visit." Audrey stares with her deadpan face, tapping her shoe incessantly as I justify my decision. "The wait at the local emergency room could take hours. Follow with hours of tests, only to tell me to go home and rest." I squish my face like a two-year-old with my heels dug in. Well, not my heels—just my ass.

Archies glares at me while a zephyr sweeps wisps of hair back and forth like a pendulum across his forehead. My heart sinks, recognizing the distress on his face. He breathes in, holding the night's air captive, refusing to break his unwavering glare. His breath escapes as he brushes the loose strands of hair back and rolls his eyes. Gwynedd: 1. Archie: 0.

"Help me up?" I ask, sporting a winner's smirk. He helps me stand, and I moan like a wounded soldier. My head spins a few times. "Yeah, my butt took the brunt of the fall." I flick bits of crushed acorns, sticking to my sweater like Velcro.

"What caused you to fall?" Archie asks.

"Uh—" I try to answer, but Audrey interrupts me.

"From a distance, she appeared to slide backward." She's still tapping her shoe. Does she have to pee?

I shake my throbbing head. "The lamppost bulb burst, throwing glass everywhere." I edit my story a bit. "It was too dark for me to see these damn acorns. Must have stepped on one and rolled on it. My head landed on the soft grass." Archie strokes the tip of his goatee, staring, and Audrey continues her foot tapping. I force a smile and twist my spine. "Seriously, I'm OK."

"I don't live far from campus," he says. "Will you at least come to my house and ice your head? You should stay awake for a while."

"Oh, fine," I say, having lost the second round. "Can we at least drive to your house? My car is in the South Campus parking lot."

Archie smirks as he looks away. "It's settled then. Audrey, it's opportune you passed by."

"I know! I was on my way to the library to pick up a book." Audrey gasps, placing a hand over her heart. "Gwyn, will you send me a text in the morning? Let me know how you're feeling?"

"Sure." I think she's being overly dramatic.

She curls her mouth in an odd *I-don't-know-how-to-smile* way and sprints into the halos of light. That upper-class upbringing branded her with quirky behaviors.

Archie cups my left elbow to assist me while we walk, but I'm not having it. "I have legs. I can walk, you know."

He stops and glares at me, pinching his lips. "Sure. And how has that gone so far?"

I roll my hazel peepers. "FINE." My head hurts too much to argue with him.

After a brief argument over who will drive my Prius, Archie drives us the short distance to his house. He turns onto Duncan Street, one street over from Dr. Hughes's home. Student renters have inundated the neighborhood of two- and three-bedroom cottages and bungalows to the dismay of the faculty and townies, but I doubt they bother Archie.

A cute cottage with a long center dormer of square windows, Archie's house has a gray-stone facade with a small front porch and a single detached garage. He parks my Prius in front of his house and helps me out of the passenger seat. Carrying my shoes, I tiptoe barefoot on the chilly flagstone walkway. A few tan and yellow moths flit around the entry light while I wait for him to unlock the front door.

The *wee* foyer, as Archie referred to it, has an exquisite oak hall tree to the right of the door and a narrow staircase. There is a dining room on the left and a living room on the right. The walls have a warm, peachy hue. It's a nice compact house for a single professor. I stash my hoodie, purse, and sandals on the hall tree.

He flips the light switch in the living room. "Why don't you sit while I get the ice packs?" The worn leather chair is a russet color, and I groan with a mixture of pain and pleasure as the cushion swallows my bruised bottom.

A collection of Celtic artifacts hangs on a long wall—an impressive display of swords, small knives, and flintlock pistols. There's a matching leather loveseat with antique walnut tables flanking it. A stone fireplace hearth invites a fire, and a painting rests on the mantel.

Archie returns with a gift of ice packs, placing one under my butt and the other behind my head. "Hold them in place for ten minutes or so and wait a wee bit to ice again. Can I get you something to drink?"

"No, thank you." I regret the way I reacted earlier, and the corners of my mouth droop like wilted flowers. "This was kind of you. I'm sorry I snapped at you earlier. I'll ice and be on my way."

He lowers his eyebrows. "You don't make it easy to help you."

"I know. Not making excuses, but the last eight months have been a challenge. I haven't found my footing, so to speak."

Archie laughs, shaking a finger at me. "That's for sure."

"Very. Funny." That damned contractor hammers away in my head.

He settles his body against the doorway next to me, and strands of hair tumble onto his forehead, itching him to brush them back. The ticking of an antique clock on the fireplace mantel seizes the silence, seeming to grow in decibels with each tick, tick, tick.

"I notice you have several antiques." The walnut tables and chairs are lovely and unusual for a bachelor's pad. "I wouldn't have imagined you had a house full of them."

He locks his eyes on mine. "I appreciate bonny, old things."

I shift in my seat. "I assume your car is in the garage. What do you drive?"

"I own a Tesla." He gestures to the garage side of the house. "It's charging in there."

"A luxury car seems like an extravagance on an academic's salary. How do you afford it?" I regret the question immediately. I observe his gaping mouth and veer my gaze toward the clock, ticking like a time bomb on the mantel. Having failed at my quest to make small talk, I welcome its timely explosion, but alas...

He shoves his hands in the pockets of his jeans, and his nostrils flare. "Not that it's YOUR concern, but I receive a supplement for filling the chair of the department, and I'm rather frugal. And EVs help the environment. I bought a small home that costs a pittance to keep up, and I have no wife or child to support."

"Or a girlfriend?" Figuring I've already annoyed him with my frankness, why not continue? We're friends now, right? "I heard you dated a grad student over the summer. Or is it a rumor?"

Archie's eyes roll from one side of his face to the other, drawing the perfect semicircle. Noticing a sword has fallen off its hanger, he moves to the wall display. "Naw. It's not a rumor. I hoped few knew about it. We dated for a couple of months. It was a miscalculation." He adjusts the sword back into the hanger.

"A miscalculation? Maybe she was too young for you?" I'm surprised he isn't reacting more negatively.

He peers at me out of the corner of his eyes. "I've dated women of different ages. Age isn't important. It's the person you are with who matters."

"I think I've iced long enough," I say, handing him the ice packs. "Thank you so much. I know this took time away from your evening."

"I'll take these to the kitchen and will be back right quick."

I long for fluffy sheets and a plump pillow to cradle my aching head. I push out of the chair and view the painting over the fireplace at a better angle. It features a woman with long, brown hair, blowing in the wind, and her open hand reaches toward a stormy sky in a field sprinkled with wildflowers. I can't make out the lady's face, so I drag my bare feet and sore ass to the stone fireplace to get a closer look.

"This painting on the mantel. It's mysterious, isn't it? The lady reaches for something in the approaching storm." The scent of herbs passes my nose, the burned remains of a tiny bundle in the hearth—a trace of lavender, cinnamon, and sage.

I stagger closer, massaging my aching butt, and the blurred features of the woman come into focus. She has a pale complexion with a squarish jawline and a straight nose. Her irises have a mixture of gray and green, with a ring of brown in the center above rosy cheeks. Her blown hair splits into hand-like fingers, latching onto tufts of air. So real, I imagine a gust of wind and pull my hair back. "Hey! She's gorgeous! What do you say? Bonny?"

"Aye, she is."

I jump with a yelp. "Oh! I didn't know you were in here." Archie's collar-length hair brushes my neck, soft like the pass of a cat's tail, raising the hair on my arms. Returning my focus to the mysterious woman, I scrutinize the lady's face. He hovers so close the heat of his body warms with an invisible touch. I squint my eyes at the women's face. "Wait. The lady in the painting looks a little like—"

"You," Archie says with a boyish smile. "More than a wee bit, in my opinion."

I cross my arms. "Huh. You WERE staring at me in class that day." My head bends to speak with him this close, or I'd be having a conversation with his chest—not an unpleasant alternative.

"I'm sorry. I hoped you didn't notice. My eyes wandered while everyone was working, and I saw you turn your head just so." He gestures to the painting. "The more I examined your profile, the more I saw how uncanny it was."

"It's kinda eerie," I say, fiddling with an earring.

Archie displays a haughty grin as he examines the painting. "A bit, but in my life experiences, I've found these occurrences are rarely a coincidence."

This close, I notice silver strands wiggling through his wavy hair. His irises appear translucent, like crystal-clear water, and I'm drowning in them. "Well, now I know." I glance back at the painting to compose my jitters. "And it explains the misunderstandings." Archie listens with wide eyes and an occasional nod, while I blabber about the times others had suggested he was attracted to me. "Skye and Spence were certain you had a romantic interest, despite any of my explanations. Even Ronnie was egging it on. People only see what they want to see. Isn't that funny?"

Archie moves closer, but I step back and trip over my own bare feet. He grasps my arm before I crash into the woodpile. I grab the mantle to balance and chuckle. "You must think I'm such a klutz."

"Not so much, but let's not add to your existing injuries," he says, smiling. Still clutching one arm, Archie wraps his remaining hand around the other, massaging my bicep with a thumb. My brow crinkles. Did I complain about a sore arm? His slight smile melts from his face as he sucks in his bottom lip, a failed attempt to keep the words from escaping their captivity. "It would be funny if they were wrong."

My mouth hangs open while I process what he said. "I, um, what?"

He smiles. "Ms. Crowther, I believe this is the first time I've found you at a loss for words." His cologne has a subtle, woodsy aroma, tugging at me with tiny tentacles to move closer.

"I'm confused. You must think I'm dense." Short puffs of air replace my breathing, and heat builds in my torso, creeping up.

"Hmph, maybe a wee bit." He gestures with his thumb and index finger. "At first, your likeness to the lady in my painting intrigued me, but I spent time with you and wanted more. Compliments and flirting garnered no response. I resolved you must not be ready and let it be. Tonight, when I saw you were hurt. My heart skipped a few beats."

"You were overly concerned." I wring my hands. "Since Richard died, I've moved with the motivation of a sloth. You'd have to hit me with a brick."

He strokes the underside of my chin. "I understand. That's why I backed away. You've been through enough trauma. I didn't want to add stress to your life, but you brought up the subject."

Blinking several times, I find myself short of breath. "I never imagined you'd be attracted to a woman my age. I mean, look at me."

"I am looking at you. You have a bonny face." He shrugs and strokes a finger across my cheek. "Lots of women do, but they don't have your smile. Or your candor. Or your brazen opinions and obstinance." He presses his lips together. "To be honest, I don't know whether to growl...or kiss you."

Archie's icy-blue gaze never falters while embers ignite in my stomach. I bite my upper lip, blushing like a naïve schoolgirl, and search for a response in my dizzy head. He moves closer and strokes my arm as the burning slinks toward my neck. Tiny beads of sweat sprout on my chest. "I don't possess the perky body of a grad student. I've got lumps and wrinkles, not always in the right places."

He lays a palm on my cheek, setting his thumb on a laugh line, and fondles it. "Lines of experience." He presses his soft lips on mine, and his whiskers titillate my skin.

Archie pulls me tighter against the firmness of his chest, and I lose my balance, grasping at his t-shirt to keep from falling. His mouth parts, inviting me to do the same. The beads of sweat pilling above my lips no longer matter—our mouths already wet with tongues interlocking. How am I kissing this man when ten minutes before, I'd berated him for owning an expensive car?

A hand falls to my lower back, crushing me even closer to his body. My thermostat rises everywhere, and my face flushes. I snatch pockets of cool air between unyielding kisses and drifting hands as sweat trickles down my neck toward my breasts. But nothing stops the combustion of Crowther. In a panic, I thrust him back, breaking the lingering kiss.

Archie steps back, consternation plastered on his face. "I'm sorry! I've offended you." His chest rises and falls with jerky movements.

"No! It's not your fault!" I laugh, fanning myself with the futility of my hands. "Well, technically, it's your fault. Hot flash. It happens if I get overheated. You could retrieve one of those ice packs?!"

His shoulders relax, and his breathing calms. "Oh! Right away." He darts into the kitchen, returning with a fresh kitchen towel and an ice pack.

I slap the ice pack under my chin and close my eyes, basking in the icy respite while cool water rolls between my breasts.

"Ahh—" I open my eyes to Archie's sweet smile and wipe the drips of dignity off my chest. "That was humiliating."

"It's fine." He blots my face with the towel and an ounce of apprehension. "I wonder, though. Will this happen every time I kiss you?"

"I don't know. This is the first time a man has kissed me since I hit menopause. I hope not." Does he plan on doing this again?

A crease indents between his eyes. "You hit menopause after your husband passed, then?"

"No." My eyes fall to the floor. "Menopause started about a year before he passed."

"Oh." Archie swallows and glances at the dinging clock. It's 9:30 p.m.

"Here, I think I'm done with the ice pack for the evening." I dry my hands on the towel and pass it to him. "I should get home. This day extended way past my expiration."

"I'd like to kiss you again before you leave." He strokes his goatee. "If you think it's safe?"

I'm drawn to his full lips, peeking through his goatee. "I think so."

As Archie moves closer, I'm not sure how I feel about him. I want him to kiss me, but is it because it's been so long since I've been with a man? He's so gentle and funny. Why wouldn't I want him? But I'm scared it's too soon for me to handle this. He barely touches his lips to mine, and a hand roams my back, stopping at my bottom. "Your bum is wet."

I laugh. "From the ice pack."

As Archie walks with me to my car, I recall the incident at the Old Men oaks. Should I tell him what really happened? No, he'll never believe me. But maybe he will? Oh, hell. "I need to tell you something about my fall, and it's gonna sound strange."

He listens with a piqued interest. His eyebrows draw together as I share the bizarre incidence of the cold pocket of air and the putrid smell of decaying flesh that occurred before the lamppost bulb exploded. "I know it was dark, but I turned my head and could swear I saw the limbs of the tree swipe my feet. Please, don't think I've lost my marbles." I keep the hallucination of the shooting amber light to myself or he might think I've lost it completely.

"Curious." Archie slides his hands into his pockets.

He regrets those kisses now, I'm sure. "I must have imagined it. Has to be my body temperature fluctuations and the darkness playing tricks on me. Thinking back, I experienced something similar on a walk a couple of weeks ago."

Archie's eyes widen. "Did you smell anything rotten the first time?"

"No. I smelled someone's garbage, or that's what I thought it was." The door to my Prius unlocks with a beep-beep. "Right after, a large branch fell and missed my head by inches. I know. I'm a magnet for calamity."

"Seems like a coincidence, no?" He rubs his jaw.

I throw my purse into the car, and he helps me into the driver's seat. "You said there are no coincidences."

"I did. Please, text me when you arrive home? And I'll meet you on Saturday at the gym."

I wave goodbye to Archie and head for home. After the Bluetooth connects my phone with the car, I call Ronnie.

She answers with a muffled voice. "Hello."

I rattle off the events of the evening following our meeting, spitting words like an auctioneer. "And he kissed me deep and long." I wait for a response, but the audible sounds of heavy breathing and sensuous pecks resound on my car speakers. "Ronnie? Are you having sex?"

After a brief silence, Ronnie replies. "I'm sorry, Gwyn. What did you say?"

"Why did you answer the phone?" I shake my head.

She chuckles in a husky voice. "You never call this late. I figured you had an accident."

"Did you hear anything I said?"

Ronnie's heavy breathing fills the car speakers. "No, I'm sorry."

"Never mind. I'll talk to you tomorrow." I chuckle under my breath and end the call.

Ronnie goes back to copulating while I drive home to an empty bed. I send Archie a text, and he sends me goodnight wishes. While lying in the toasty cocoon of my blankets and quilt, I mull over the missed signals of Archie's affections and the years of Richard's cheating. Am I that dense? I stare at the ominous crack in the ceiling, and the dagger with craggy splinters threatens to drop on me at any moment.

"Screw you."

CHAPTER SEVEN

DATING GAMES

I SMILE WHEN I view the text from Archie waiting on my cell. He hopes I have a "wonderful but restful day." I know exactly what he means. Take it easy. Nearly forgetting about Audrey, I send her a text, too. Archie's confession of his affections fills me with elation, yet the strange hallucinations at the Old Men oaks leave me unsettled.

On the long walk to meet Ronnie for lunch, I pass Mitchell Hall. In its current state, the mansion appears dreary, covered in snake-like ivy slithering over the red brick. In contrast, the nineteenth-century Raven Pub looks remarkable after the sandblasting and construction of a two-story, wrap-around porch. The original owners based its name on the premise that Edgar Allan Poe had slept there and put a curse on it. I'm sure Mitchell Hall would shine as brightly with the same care, minus the curse.

Rhea, a bubbly undergrad with flawless, sienna skin, has been a fabulous hostess for Ronnie, and we'll be sad not to see her after she graduates. "Hi, Ms. Crowther. Ronnie told me to seat you. Follow me." Rhea picks up a menu and shows me to a booth in the back, hidden from the crowds. The classic rock playing in the background masks the noise of the clientele enjoying their meals.

Ronnie struts over to my booth and drops onto the seat with a thump. "I've been on pins and needles. Derek will be late. What happened last night?"

"I don't know where to start." I give her a synopsis of the incident, leaving out the strange parts.

"Geez, Gwyn. Are you OK?" Ronnie asks, worry straining her eyes. "Did you go to the emergency room?"

"Uh—" I squeeze my eyes shut and brace for the scolding.

"Gwyn, you stubborn bitch. You could have a concussion." She slaps my hand.

"I know. Archie was pissed. He asked me to go to his house and ice it, and before you yell at me again, yes, I went. My butt shines with all the shades of black and blue and hurts like a bitch." I massage my backside. "Something happened before I left." Ronnie raises her flaming eyebrows while I share my uncanny resemblance to the woman in his painting.

She cackles, exposing her pearly whites. "Creepy, huh?"

"Yeah, but it's what happened next that threw me for a loop." I roll my eyes, and a silly smile emerges. "Apparently, you and the others were right. Archie is attracted to me. He kissed me, long and hard. Richard never kissed me like that. Ever."

Ronnie grins as wicked a grin as I've ever seen on her face and wiggles her eyebrows. "How was he?"

"What do you mean?" I'm perplexed. I told her what happened.

"You know? How *was* he?" She shimmies her hips back and forth in her booth seat.

I lean over the table and lower my voice. "For fuck's sake, I didn't sleep with him. It was only a kiss."

"Oh, what a missed opportunity." She pulls her legs apart under the table, moving her hips up and down.

"I can't hop into bed with a man I barely know after being married for almost thirty years. And Richard hasn't even been gone a year. What would people say? Especially Tyler."

"Gwyn, you owe that bastard Richard nothing. And Tyler would understand. He wants you to be happy."

"Besides, I had a hot flash at the most heated moment. It involved humiliation and a lot of dripping. He sent a text this morning, asking how I was. So sweet."

"Gwyn, please tell me you'll give this man a chance. I've known Archie for a couple of years. He's been involved with a few women in the time I've known him, but those relationships went nowhere. And he seems to like you a lot."

I turn my head, and the smile fades. "I'm going to tell you something else. Please don't think I'm off my rocker." After coming clean about the weird phenomenon of the sudden cold and putrid smell, Ronnie stares at me with no reaction.

"Did you tell Archie?" she asks.

I peer over the menu at her. "I did. Should I order the falafel salad or the Thai wrap? He didn't say much."

"The Thai wrap is fabulous." Ronnie has a noticeable crease between her eyes, but soon after, her face lights up like an incandescent light bulb. Derek has arrived, and she stands to welcome him with a kiss and a hug. It melts my heart to see her so happy.

"Nice to see you again, Gwyn." Derek sits across from me in the booth, and Ronnie shoves in next to him with enough space for a sheet of paper. Once the waiter takes our orders, Derek shares recent news. "I usually run through campus in the morning before breakfast."

"Unless he's stayed at my place the night before." Ronnie winks with an open mouth.

He nudges her and chuckles. "Stop interrupting, babe." His face turns grim. "I hate to break the mood, but they found a dead body on the Green this morning."

Ronnie gasps. "Oh, dear gods. Do they know who it is?"

"Some homeless guy who strolled campus spewing non-sense," he says. "The DUB security and Bearsden Police are all over campus. I overheard them talking. They found the body crushed with his eyes removed and are worried it might be a serial killer."

"Where did they find the body?" My mouth hangs open, panting with shallow breaths.

"Not sure. The body bag was lying near the Old Men oak trees." Derek stops, noticing my reaction. "Are you OK, Gwyn?"

Acrobats do somersaults in my stomach. "I was there last night and smelled something nasty, like rotting flesh."

Ronnie sinks in her seat, and her skin turns the color of a marshmallow. "You don't know that smell was from a body. Gwyn fell there, but she's OK."

Derek warns with ominous eyes. "The both of you shouldn't walk on the Green alone after dark, not until they're done investigating."

Our food has arrived, but I've lost my appetite.

By Saturday, the news of the murder has spread throughout Bearsden and beyond. Even major network news stations from Philadelphia have arrived. A murder like this in Wilmington would barely get a mention in the news, but Bearsden? Bearsden has a murder rate of zero, so a deluge of media has inundated our small college town.

I send Archie a text canceling our workout, and my phone rings. I swipe the green button on the screen as my heart thumps. "Hello."

"Good morning. How are you feeling?" he asks.

My insides turn warm and mushy, hearing his voice. "My butt hurts, but that's the worst of it."

"You should rest." Archie remains silent for a few seconds. "You heard about the murder, I assume?"

Way to ruin my mood. "Yeah. Ronnie's boyfriend Derek told us yesterday at lunch. I'm freaking out a little." More than a little. I was there.

"We'll talk about this at the next Fellowship meeting, but I'd like to get together before that. Come by for dinner on Tuesday?"

An eager smile slips onto my lips. "I'd love to."

"Wonderful. Come around 6:00."

Hot water beats on my bruised bottom as I moan, but the shower relaxes me. After towel drying, I peek at the artistry on my ass. Oof. I should have iced more. I scrutinize my changing body while I comb my sopping hair and observe firmer muscles. The WWE won't knock on my door anytime soon, but I'm pleased with my progress. I slide on my favorite pair of skinny jeans and a deep V-neck shirt, forgoing heels for flats, and apply minimal makeup. I pass for sexy, midlife sexy, but my wide grin fades quickly. Maybe sexy isn't a good idea?

When I arrive at Archie's, the front door is open, allowing the cool evening breeze to enter the house. A light knock on the screen door brings him rushing with an enthusiastic smile stretching his goatee.

"So glad you came." Planting a soft kiss on my cheek, I get a whiff of his woodsy cologne, and the fragrance calms me. He appears relaxed in his worn jeans and navy-blue Henley shirt. "It's getting a wee bit nippy out now." He closes and locks the door, and I feel a *wee* bit trapped. "Find a seat in the living room and chill, as the students would say. Your favorite ice-packing chair is available." He chuckles and returns to the kitchen.

"Ha. Ha. I think I'll try the loveseat." I place my purse on the hall tree, kick off my flats, and find a comfy cushion waiting for my bruised bottom on the leather loveseat in the living room. Whatever he's cooking in there has an amazing aroma, like fresh-baked bread, and instantaneously, my stomach rumbles.

The stained-glass chandelier in the dining room suddenly emits a soft glow across the foyer. Archie sets a salad on the oak table. "Gwyn, dinner is served."

I hurry into the dining room barefooted, and he pulls out a chair for me, choosing the head of the table for himself. He's dimmed the chandelier and lit candles. While I use tongs to place salad into my bowl, he pours wine into my glass. Setting the stage? "How was school?"

"Actually, not productive." Archie fills his salad bowl. "I spent most of it explaining to four sets of parents why I can't discuss the grades of their adult children with them. Two threatened to sue. Let them. Reminds me why I miss teaching. And you?"

"I had class with Leslie. It was an entertaining lecture on the legends of King Arthur. It got me thinking of my Welsh roots a bit more, too. My parents never talked about their childhoods in Wales, and after both sets of their parents died, they had little reason to return. I think I still have an eccentric great aunt living there, but I've never met her." I take a sip of wine. "Then, of course, I had lunch with Tyler like I do every Tuesday before work in my home office."

"It must comfort you to have his support." His eyes catch mine while he sips his wine.

I look at my salad and jab my fork into a clump of lettuce and cucumber. "It is, but I've gotten so busy, I told him we should stop."

"Am I part of the busy?" he asks.

I blush and shift in my seat. "Maybe? But I need to exercise, too."

Our salads finished, Archie takes our bowls into the kitchen and returns with what appears to be a flattened loaf of bread topped with crusty knots. I blink several times, and he smirks. "Not everything is always as it seems." He cuts through the bread. It's full of mushrooms and veggies. It looks delectable. The man can cook. Richard's idea of cooking was ordering a pizza. Dinner conversation allows us to discover more about each other. We discuss our college days, mine at DUB, and his in Edinburgh and London.

"Is that why your Scottish accent isn't so thick? Because you lived in London for so long?" I ask.

"Yeah. Spent quite a lot of time in London for graduate studies. And got a teaching position after. Lived there for fourteen years." He takes another sip of wine.

"Don't you miss your family?" I ask, stuffing my mouth. "I assume you must have some there."

"I do. My father, Harris. He's in his early 70s but is strong as an ox. He lives in Edinburgh with my older brother, Quinn, and his family. I have some aunts, uncles, cousins—strewn all over Scotland. I try to visit once a year."

"And your mother?" I take another bite of dinner, thinking it was an intrusive question I shouldn't have asked.

Archie pauses his next bite. "Sadly, I never knew my mother. She died giving birth to me. Her name was Elspeth."

"Such a beautiful name," I say, holding his gaze.

"A beautiful name for a beautiful woman. Wish I had known her." Archie pushes from the table. "Can I get you anything else? More wine?"

"No, thank you." I pat my stomach. "It was so good."

"In that case, I'll carry these into the kitchen." He collects some plates and stacks them, placing the utensils on top.

I lay my napkin on the table and stand. "Let me help."

"No need. I'm going to set them on the counter and load the dishwasher later." Archie carries the plates and utensils into the kitchen, and I'm right behind him with the rest of the Mushroom Wellington. He frowns when he turns to find me behind him. "Ms. Crowther, you'll be the death of me with your stubbornness."

I return Archie's displeasure with a spirited smile and play Tetris with the food containers in the fridge. Returning to the loveseat in the living room, I expect him to join me. The sexual tension is lurking like a thief, hidden in passing glances and fortuitous touches. I'm not relishing a repeat of hot flashes, interrupting passionate kisses.

"Would you be interested in a game of checkers?" he asks.

My eyes scan the room and settle on his cheerful face. "Sure?" Is he serious?

Archie retrieves a wooden board with checkers and sets it on the wooden steamer trunk in front of the loveseat, pulling a walnut side chair to the trunk for himself. He smirks and rubs his hands together. "I'll warn you. I play a mean game of checkers."

I peer into his eyes with a simper. "We'll see, won't we?" Leaning over the trunk, my hair falls, and he pushes it behind my ear, holding my eyes captive.

"Your eyes have a unique coloring." Archie tilts his head and examines them like an academic. "Eldritch eyes."

My brow creases. I don't have a recollection of the word. "Eldritch?"

"Aye, it means eerie, odd." Archie leans back and sets up the checkers on the board. "Historically, it comes from the Middle English word *elfriche* meaning fairyland."

"That's interesting." It's also an odd compliment, and I'm not sure how to react. I examine the antique furniture and weaponry on the wall while we share stories of our childhoods and play checkers. I love his home. It's warm and inviting with worn and cherished items. Several checker games later, I've won four out of seven.

Archie sits back in the walnut chair and emits a drawn-out sigh. "I'm done. I've met my match."

"Stop." I chuckle as I stack the checkers. "You let me win all those games."

"I did NOT let you win. You cheated." He winks at me.

I lean over the trunk and stare into his shimmering eyes. "I'm not cheating."

"I know you're not." Archie crouches over the checkerboard. He kisses me, and his goatee tickles my chin. The obnoxious ticking of the antique clock interrupts the rhythm of our breathing, and he withdraws his lips, an unfulfilled desire burning in his eyes. He returns the checkerboard to its place on the shelf while my hand presses against my chest. Who would think checkers could be so passionate?

He sits on the loveseat next to me and leans back, propping his bare feet on the steamer trunk, and clasps his hands behind his head. I put my bare feet next to his on the trunk and rest my head on the loveseat cushion to admire the weapons collection on the wall. He prods me like a child playing footsie.

I roll my head to the right to find him staring. There is no exchange of words, only unspoken gazes of desire. He turns his head to meet mine and kisses me, offering his tongue, and his cologne entices me to go further. I want him, but the practical voice in my head urges me to wait until I know him better.

Archie lifts his mouth, snatching an amorous breath, and nuzzles my nose. "I want you, Gwynedd, but I know it's too soon. I will wait as long as you need."

"I told you Richard hadn't kissed me for a long time? There's more." My eyes tear up. The tugging in my heart pulls, ripping open my most vulnerable self.

Archie's hand cups my face. "It's all right," he whispers.

"Richard hadn't made love to me in over three years. He was cheating on me, but I didn't find out until the day I buried him. When the skank told me, it made me feel unattractive and unwanted on top of my grief."

"Oh, Gwyn. You know none of that is true. I desire you." He pulls me onto his lap and strokes my face. "Richard was a fool."

He kisses me with an open mouth as I run my fingers through his silky blond waves, and the swelling in his jeans confirms the truth in his words. A coy smile sneaks into my wet mouth. I want to stay but know it's time to go, so I wriggle off his lap. "I should go."

Archie pushes off the loveseat, planting a kiss on my flushed cheek. "I'll walk you to your car."

"Don't bother," I say, stroking his arm. "You'd have to put shoes on. I'm parked right in front."

"I'll not argue with you, Gwyn. Better to save that for more important matters later."

I slip on my shoes and collect my purse from the hall tree. "I had a fabulous time. Thank you for dinner and everything."

Archie lays a warm hand on my cheek and kisses me good-bye.

CHAPTER EIGHT

CRYSTALS, SAGE, AND PHANTASMS

THE NEXT DAY, I walk to the Sunshine Garden Café for lunch with Ronnie and fill her ears with the Tuesday Tales of Gwynedd Crowther. Excited for me, she suggests we double date some evening, but I haven't told Tyler yet. She understands but stresses I should spill the tea.

Following lunch, I cross the street to Shane's store, Mystical Sage, to investigate the job he posted. The part-time job at Jones and Davies Agency allows me to keep my health insurance, but I want to get out of the house. The store has a red brick front like so many others on Main Street and a large display window with a bright, fuchsia sign—CRYSTALS, TAROT, MAGIC.

Entering the shop with a ding of a bell, I'm immediately struck with a bouquet of scents—a concoction of eucalyptus, vanilla, lavender, cinnamon, sage, and rosemary. A few whiffs send me into a sneezing fit.

"Deosil." Shane pops his head from behind the counter. "It's Irish, for may it go right with you." He's such a hippie, but in this store, I'm the one who looks out of place in my red polo shirt and khaki shorts.

"Thank you, Shane. The fragrances are too much for my feeble nose, I guess. I want to browse the store, but I'm also here to inquire about the part-time job."

"The job pays more than minimum wage, but it's not a lot of hours. I expected a student might want it. Are you sure you wouldn't want a job with more hours?" He takes out an application for me to fill out and pulls a pen out of the skull mug on the counter.

"I have a regular part-time job with an insurance agency I've been with for years, but it's so boring working from home. A few hours in a store would get me out of the house."

"You can fill out the application back here at the Tarot Card reading table, but first let me show you around."

Shane shows me incense, Tarot Cards, bottles of herbs for spells, homemade soaps, and oils for healing—tools for people practicing the occult or taking a bath. There's a kitchen corner stocked with tools for grinding herbs and wooden bowls for mixing spells. I can't believe people buy this stuff.

A customer enters the store asking for witch herbs, and Shane excuses himself while I fill out the application. When I'm finished, I roam around and end up in the crystals room. I pass my hand over a few of the large pieces of quartz, and a vibration occurs. Another pass triggers a more intense vibration, and they light up. Shane must have them connected to electricity, but I don't observe any cords.

"They're as pretty as a picture, aren't they?" Shane asks. "Still interested?"

"Absolutely. Here's the application." I hand him the completed paperwork and glance at the crystals. I can't believe Shane would resort to such a sham, but who am I to judge?

"You're obviously overqualified, but it would be great to have you here. After the background check, I'll ring you."

"That sounds great. Do you believe crystals can heal and spells work?" I'm not doing much to support my application by bashing his wares.

"Darling, many things exist in this world beyond our basic understanding. The mind is a powerful entity. Who's to say what is and isn't real?"

"True. I can start whenever you like." I open the door with a ding. "See you at the meeting tomorrow night."

"Will do, Gwyn. Have a glorious afternoon."

The Fellowship meeting starts with Shane and Audrey's report on the Monday Bearsden Council Meeting. I'm sitting between Ronnie and Skye, flanked by fire, and burning from the ray-gun eyes Courtney is firing at me.

Audrey stands wearing the face of the grim reaper and reads her notes. "The Council unanimously voted to pursue the purchase of the property, intending to have the building condemned. It's what we expected." She sits with a stiff back and folds her hands.

"I think we can proceed as planned." Shane props a sandaled foot on one leg and leans back in the metal chair.

The student members want to protest on campus, and we all agree that it's worth the time to bring attention to the matter. And Archie delegates our work. "Let's start with a small group to investigate getting Mitchell Hall declared a historical site."

Skye waves her hand in the air. "I can work on the historical stuff, but it would be awesome to have two members help with the paperwork."

Audrey shoots her hand up in the air like she's got a spring in her shoulder. "I can help." Her response appears so awkward, but maybe she's eager, as Shane suggested.

"I could be of help, too." This is a fantastic opportunity for me to spend more time mentoring this young woman who needs family. "I've worked for an insurance company for many years."

"Tanner, would you organize the student protests?" Trinity asks.

"Sure." Tanner slides back and throws Spence a don't-give-me-any-trouble kind of smirk.

Ronnie waves her hand. "Can I suggest we get ahead by forming another group to work on the community center angle?"

"Good idea, Ronnie. You, Elijah, and I could start on that." Trinity gestures to Dr. Hughes. "Leslie, you should probably add to this. You've lived here longer than most of us."

"I have." Leslie rarely comments more than this at meetings and when she does, her emotionless face shares no hints of what she's feeling or thinking. I prefer the Leslie-at-home version.

Archie stands and waits for minor chatter to subside. "Before we dismiss early to enjoy the unusually warm weather, I want to remind everyone to please be careful. The Bearsden police are still investigating the murder of the homeless man found on the Green."

Tanner and the students gather on the porch to gossip about the horrid murder, speculating about the cause of death. Logically, to have a serial killer, there have to be more murders—not a pleasant notion. They dawdle down the steps, and Courtney scowls in my direction. She can't possibly know about Archie and me. We've been nothing but platonic in public.

Leslie and Archie exit the Pumpkin House together, and he suggests I join them on the walk back to her house and my car. On the walk to Drummond Lane, we chat about Leslie's summer research on the bards at the National Library of Wales in Aberystwyth, until we arrive at her house. "Thank you for the escort. Gwynedd, do you park your car at Archie's every Thursday?" she asks.

"Yes, I do. It saves me a little money not having to park on campus." I'm not lying.

"That is most convenient for you." She glares at us before walking to her side door. Halfway up the driveway, she turns to address me. "Gwynedd, please call soon to set a time for dinner with me."

On the way to Archie's house, he elaborates on Leslie's dinner plans. "You know that wasn't a question, don't you? Leslie has a way of making a demand seem like an invitation, but the gods help you if you don't accept."

"I figured that out the first day I met her. Were you aware she knew my parents?"

Archie has a twitch in his eye as he shoves a hand in his pocket. "Aye, she mentioned it to me in an email, before I met you. She was excited when your name showed on her class roster."

"You never mentioned you knew." I stare at his icy blues, waiting for a response.

He hesitates and smiles. "You never asked." We end our stroll at my car, and he gazes at me with those magnetic eyes. "It's early. Would you like to come in for a few minutes?"

A glance at my cell tells me I should leave, and I bite my lower lip. "I don't think so. I've been going since class this morning. An early bedtime would be best."

Archie slides both hands into his pockets and nods. "I'll see you on Saturday at the gym then." He helps me into my car, and I drive home.

As I get ready for bed, an incessant knocking on the bedroom window calls me to it. Limbs of the full-grown oak tree whip the glass with sudden gusts of wind, and I worry the windowpanes will crack. I turn off the light to get a better view and shriek at the image of a strange creature on the massive tree trunk! I flip the light switch on faster than you can scream, "aghhh," and palpitations snatch the tranquil moment.

I turn the light out again and peep through the window at the trunk—only odd swirls decorating the bark. Gray limbs have grown into mangled, arm-like protrusions, taking root against the edges of the window with finger-like hands. Now I need to call an arborist.

The intense glare and blinding rays of unwelcome sunshine cut through the bedroom curtain, slicing with precision across my face. The late-night research with Spence and Skye lasted way past my bedtime. I have a hangover like I'd been on a college bender at The Raven Pub, but I've awakened before my alarm.

Squinting is the most I can muster, so I remain in the comfort of my bed, reliving the weekend I spent with Archie. Working out, hikes in the local park, and dinner at his house included fervent necking that tested not only my will but assuredly the constraints of his pants zipper. I would love to cook him dinner at my house, but Tyler might happen by. I'm not ready to tell him yet.

The Indian Summer continues, but I'm ready for it to end. Let fall take its rightful place with cool, crisp air and crunchy, fallen leaves. When I get to the basement of Stewart Hall, Archie is standing outside the Celtic Studies office, arguing with Courtney Davies. Not aware I'm there, he turns and walks into the office. Courtney follows me into class with the expression of a woman rejected etched on her face.

Leslie strolls in and sets her satchel on the desk. "Good morning to you, Gwynedd," she says with a placid demeanor.

"Good morning, Dr. Hughes." I take out my laptop and avoid making eye contact with her.

Spence and Skye come in together, dashing back to our table in their flip-flops, and Leslie delivers a disapproving scowl. "We both overslept." Skye swallows, trying to catch her breath as she removes her laptop from her backpack.

"How did you make it here on time?" Spence huffs and puffs while he sets up his laptop. "You were up as late as us?"

I shrug and open a web browser to finish last-minute research from the night before. "I woke before my alarm today."

Skye slides her hands across her face, which has lost its sunburnt hue. "I hate being late for class."

"Dear, you're not late. You had a minute to spare." I wish she wouldn't stress so much over it. She's a dedicated student.

Spence wipes his forehead. "We don't want to experience the wrath of Dr. Hughes."

Our professor stands to make an announcement. "A reminder that class is canceled on Thursday due to the preparation for the pagan festival of Mabon." She displays a picture of dancing fairies on the large monitor. "Fairies appear in Welsh, Scottish, and Irish literature and art. I would like you to split into groups and research the lore of one country."

We begin our research with Scottish folklore. I land on a website discussing the fairies of the Seelie and Unseelie Courts. The Seelie Court fairies, benevolent but sometimes mischievous, are mild compared to the Unseelie. A click on the name Sluagh takes me to a dedicated page, and I'm paralyzed by the picture on my screen. It resembles the image I saw on the tree trunk in my backyard.

The large raven shadow figure threatens with a gnarled face, clutching the body of a child and lifting him to the sky. The frightening Sluagh uses the raven shadow as a host fairy, and some folklore calls it the Host of the Unforgiven Dead. I shudder at the thought.

"Gwyn," Spence whispers. "Gwyn." He taps my arm to bring me out of my catatonic state.

"Yeah?" My eyes drift over to my friends, and they're staring at me.

Spence places a hand on my arm. "We've been calling your name. Are you OK? You're shaking."

"Yeah." I force a smile on my rigid mouth. "It's so cold in here. I've entered some links of what I found. It's a little unsettling. I expected stories about fairies to be all sweet, cute stuff. This is disturbing."

Spence clicks on my link in our shared document, and the two of them sift through the article on Spence's laptop screen. "Gross," Skye says with a husky laugh.

"Hey. It's an evil Sluagh in the form of a raven. It could be Poe." Spence snorts, prompting an annoyed gaze from Dr. Hughes.

He's right to clown around. It's made-up nonsense. So, why do I feel dread? In my peripheral vision, I swear I notice Courtney curling her upper lip. Comparing our research fills the rest of class, and we pack up, but the vision of the Sluagh haunts me.

I follow Skye and Spence toward the door. "I guess I'll see you both at Mabon. It's my first official pagan celebration."

"It's a good one to start with," Skye says. "Eating and watching the sunset. It's a fun time, and you're welcome to bring family members. My boyfriend is coming."

I grin at the surprising news. "You never mentioned you had a boyfriend."

Skye smirks and bats her lashes. "Who said I only have one?"

Spence shakes a finger at me. "Don't forget to bring the food you signed up for. Dr. Hughes gets snippy if you forget."

Don't I know it, but Leslie is more flexible with me. I wonder why?

CHAPTER NINE

MABON

WHEN I ARRIVE AT the Pumpkin House, most of the older community members are setting up for the festivities in the parlor, except for Elijah. He's delivering our food donations to the shelter. The students arrange the food in the dining room with Ronnie's help.

"Hey, Gwyn. I haven't heard from you in a while. You must've been busy." Ronnie's eyebrows spring up and down.

I throw her a dirty look. "I have been." Busy wondering if I need a psychiatrist. The image on my backyard tree was identical to the illustration I found in class.

"She's been hanging with us. Drill Sergeant Hughes over there loaded us with work." Spence tosses bottled waters into an ice-filled cooler.

"It wasn't so bad." Skye plugs in a slow cooker and pours in soup. "Dr. Hughes is thorough."

"But lack of sleep makes me fidgety." Spence stretches his arms all around him, shuffling his feet.

I cross my arms and grimace. "We're supposed to notice a difference?"

Spence's jaw snaps open. "Oh, my gods! Aren't you getting saucy? You're like one of the fam now, Gwyn. You can't be a member without sauciness and sarcasm."

Ronnie smiles, sending me a look of I-told-you-so. In a short time, I have a sense of belonging to this diverse group of people. Tanner has arrived, and a Black woman with cropped, black hair chats with Trinity. It must be her wife, Charlie.

Elijah walks in with Zoe trailing behind. "I'm here on time!" Zoe dances in the foyer, eliciting cheers and laughter from everyone, and joins Tanner and Spence in the parlor.

Archie strolls over to us, smiling coyly at me. "Are we ready? I'd like to start the ritual, so we can eat." He rubs his hands together in a sinister but humorous fashion.

Shane pats his belly as he eyes the dessert table. "Yes, let's get started."

Archie invites everyone into the parlor. There are about twenty chairs to accommodate the family and friends joining in our little celebration, and the scent of cinnamon candles permeates. He directs us to hold hands. "I want to welcome everyone to this joyous celebration of Mabon. We want to thank Mother Earth for the harvest she has provided and acknowledge the light we have enjoyed. Dr. Hughes will lead in the sharing."

"Sharing?" I whisper to Ronnie. "You didn't tell me about this."

Ronnie pats my leg. "Shh, you'll think of something."

"I invite you to share one item you will shed from your life," Leslie says. "An albatross that has been holding you back from a successful life."

Archie presses his palms together. "I'll go first. I've got a second fridge in the garage that would be useful to the shelter."

"I'm donating clothes to Family for All," Skye says. "They've had an increased need recently. It's the least I can do."

"I'm letting go of my ex's friends." Ronnie throws an invisible object and lets her arm fall slowly. "They're full of so much negativity. Shocker."

"Tanner and I canceled our cable subscription. We're donating the money to Family for All. Who needs cable, anyway?" He flings the fake cable over his shoulder.

"I'm donating a portion of my antiquarian books to the university library," Leslie says. "They'll be more useful there." Who could argue with that one?

Ronnie elbows me. "I'm going to donate furniture I don't use to the shelter." Immense grief and anger still gnaw at my insides, and I decide to let those go, too.

When we've finished sharing, Leslie stands, a look of satisfaction suffusing her face. "Marvelous choices, everyone. May you go in peace."

Dinner allows time for conversations, especially discussions concerning Mitchell Hall. I join Tanner, Shane, Ronnie, Derek, and the students who are joking about the Death Metal band that played at the Raven Pub, commenting on the poor musicianship and the over-the-top costumes. Bored by the discussion, I walk over to join Leslie, Archie, Trinity, Charlie, and Elijah.

"Gwyn, you haven't met Charlie," Trinity says with a mouth full of apple rum cake. "I've told her all about you."

"It's always nice to meet new members. Trinity cherishes this group. I almost wish I were part of it sometimes." Charlie hugs Trinity and lays her head on an arm. Trinity kisses her on the top of the head. Charlie has a dark complexion with a short nose, cute dimples, and a contagious smile.

"It's wonderful to meet you, Charlie," I say, shaking her hand. "I'm enjoying it."

Archie shoves his hands in his pockets. "Did you know the victim, Elijah?"

"Not well. His mental health was questionable. We tried to convince him to live at the shelter." Elijah kneads his jaw.

"You always do your best," Leslie says. "We are fortunate to have you in our community."

Elijah casts his eyes to the floor. "Unfortunately, one's best isn't always enough."

"You have saved so many of our youth from the streets." Trinity's eyes bounce from one member to another. "We should all be careful going forward."

Finished with the morbid conversation, we all gather on the Green to view the changing hues of a powder-blue sky with streaks of pink and yellow. Ronnie introduces Derek to Archie, covertly planning a future double date, I'm certain. Archie sends me yearning glances, making me self-conscious. As the shadows fade, so do the members of the Fellowship and their guests. I have to admit it's a bit of a letdown for it to end.

Archie suggests we escort Leslie back to her house. It's still dusk when the streetlights cycle on. The drone of mowers purrs in the distance, and the fresh-cut grass latches onto the evening breeze, tickling my nostrils. Leslie stops in front of her house. "Thank you for accompanying me. In all my years living in Bearsden, I've never felt as unsafe as I do now."

"We'll always look out for you, Dr. Hughes." Archie places a hand on hers.

"Thank you, Archie. I wish you both a pleasant evening." Leslie hobbles up her driveway to the side door and nudges it with her hip.

"I've seen the expressions on her face," he says. "I don't think she's fooled by our guise of a platonic friendship."

"She may have a suspicion, but that's all she has." We arrive at his house, and I veer toward my car.

Archie grasps my hand. "Why don't you come in for a glass of wine to cap our celebration of Mabon?" He entrances me with his transparent-blue eyes, shimmering in the moon-light—the flicker of a spell cast upon me. "I only want to spend time with you, Gwyn. You know, you haven't seen my dirk?" He lifts his eyebrows and flashes a mischievous smile.

I wrinkle my nose and chuckle. "I've seen your dirks on the wall in the living room."

"Ahh, not my special dirk. It's a family heirloom I keep locked in a case. Passed down for generations. Seriously, it's special to me." Archie offers his hand. I accept, and he leads me up the driveway to the back door. It's a small entryway to his kitchen. He removes his shoes and socks, and I slip off my sandals. "Hang your jacket on the hall tree. I'll get the wine."

Archie brings me a small glass of white wine with a sweet aroma, perfect for after dinner. He sips the wine, savoring every blast of flavor while I drink mine in two tips of the glass. He sets his wineglass on the hall tree. "Ready to view a relic of Scotland?"

"Sure. That's why I came in," I say, tipping my head.

He turns with his hand on the oak newel and puts a foot on the stairs. "Are you coming?"

"The dirk is upstairs? In your bedroom?" I roll my eyes to the hall tree and glimpse my hoodie.

"Aye, in a locked display case." Archie takes his foot off the step. "Being a priceless antique, I wouldn't trust it anywhere else while I sleep." The mantle clock in the living room ticks while I clink my polished nails on my wineglass, and he runs a hand through his ash-blond locks. "Gwynedd, I promise you, I have no ulterior motive. I can show it to you another time if you like, or I can lock my hands in my pants." He shoves his lecherous hands into the pockets of his jeans.

Archie has never given me a reason to doubt his word. I set my empty wineglass on the hall tree next to his and follow him up the creaking oak stairs. An immaculate guest bedroom sits alone at the top of the stairs with a daybed and desk. We pass a hall bathroom on the way to a larger bedroom. He flips the light switch. "After you," he says, shoving his hand back into its pocket.

The first thing I notice is his magnificent bed and gasp. "Wow! Where did you find it?" The Victorian walnut bed has a headboard so high it nearly reaches the ceiling. A satin comforter the color of a midnight sky decorates the bed with a mound of pillows.

His eyebrows leap. "In the rubbish. Can you believe it?" He shuffles to the other side of the bed.

"It's exquisite. Richard never wanted old furniture. His father was a carpenter and built our queen bed." My eyes dance around his face. "I'm sorry. I don't know why I brought his name up."

"You were married for a long time, even if the last few years weren't the best. It's all right." Archie motions to come where he's standing, in front of a glass case. The glare on the case dissipates to reveal a long dirk with a blade of swirls and an aged wooden handle with a shiny aqua gemstone. Not a dirk of beauty, but it must be valuable if he's taken the time to screw a locking, tempered glass case to the wall to protect it.

Shifting closer to him to view the heirloom up close, the bare skin of my arm brushes against his, and it tickles. "The dirk has a dark blade. That's unusual, isn't it?"

Archie touches the glass case with his fingertips, and the aqua gem appears to sparkle. "It's iron. Part of the reason it's so valuable. It has a special purpose in my family."

"And what is that?" I ask with a flirtatious grin.

Archie's eyes lock on mine. "A complicated explanation for another day, I'm afraid."

We're so close, I have to bend my head to stare into his icy-blue eyes, so transparent at this proximity I expect to see into his soul. The sound of our slow, deep breathing fills the endless, silent moment. He blinks only once, not wanting to break his hypnotic gaze. The yearning builds, and the heat of his skin reaches out to me with invisible fingers, caressing without touching.

My lips part, and I fear he'll consider it an open invitation to enter me, yet he doesn't move—not a flinch, nor a twitch, standing with a promise in his pockets.

It started with a kiss. A passionate, magnetic kiss. Lying naked with my tousled hair draped across the satin pillowcase, I inspect the outline of Archie's rounded shoulder, the firmness of his torso, and the curve of his upper thigh. A sprinkling of wavy strands softens the definition in his jawline, and the slight scar on his cheek hints at an untold story—perhaps etched by the tip of a dirk in a past life.

Archie's chest rises and falls as his eyelids twitch, having succumbed to the call of dreamland while I lie in the afterglow of the most fulfilling sex of my life. A gentle smile rests on his mouth as he sleeps. Unable to find my path to slumber, my body quivers, thinking back on how I ended up naked and spent next to this enchanting man.

It started with a kiss. A wet, hungry kiss. Not able to balance, we fell on the magnificent bed, and Archie crushed me, emptying my lungs like deflated balloons. As we gasped for air, our tongues played and hands roamed, feeding the impulse of the monster lust. Breaking the kiss, he grasped my cheek and gazed into my eyes with the hunger of a starved beast. "Do you want me to stop?" He panted with guttural breaths.

I purred with inviting eyes. "No. I want you."

Archie pushed off the bed and unbuttoned his Henley shirt, never removing his eyes from me. I sat up and placed a hand on his shirt. "Let me help." I pulled his shirt off, and my hands explored his chest, caressing his nipples and springy chest hairs. Sliding my hands over his rippling torso, I reached for his belt, sporting a sexy smirk, and unbuckled it, taking my time like a reverse striptease. He whipped it out, chuckling, while I pulled the zipper down in slow motion.

After removing my shirt, he stood back, admiring the package he'd unwrapped. I'm relieved I wore a black lace bra and panties—anything to accentuate my small breasts and cover the ripples of cellulite on my butt.

Archie threw the linens toward the footboard and crawled onto the bed with his jeans unzipped and hanging open. I laid back on the mountain of pillows, and he moved toward me, resembling a panther on the prowl. Outlining the edges of my mouth with his finger, he barely touched the hot skin of my lips. My bra clasp came undone, and Archie slipped it off, dropping it to the floor.

His warm lips brushed my neck and nuzzled my ear. I shook uncontrollably, but wrapped my hands around his shoulders, urging him to continue. "Are you all right?" Archie whispered in a husky voice. "You're shaking. I can stop."

"I'm a little nervous. I haven't done this for a long time." My lips parted as my chest pushed out.

Archie cupped the side of my face. "Tell me to stop at any moment. I won't be upset." He entered my mouth as if to consume me while I fingered his soft curls. His mischievous smile returned, prompting the flutter of butterflies in my stomach. His lips continued their journey lower until reaching a nipple, eliciting a soft moan from my shivering body. I glanced at my breasts to find him kneading my other nipple with his fingers, making it erect, and my back arched to his touch. "You have a beautiful body, Gwyn," he said, unzipping my jeans. "I can't wait to see the rest of it."

"I hope you aren't disappointed." I trembled as he tugged at my jeans and glimpsed his hungry eyes. He kissed my belly and parted my legs. Instantly, the memory of my dream with the mysterious lover popped into my head. I panicked. "STOP!"

Archie raised his head with wide eyes, a look of disappointment plastered on his face, as if I'd canceled the loan on his Tesla. "I should stop."

"No." I stroked the side of his chiseled face, smiling coyly. "Just checking."

"Trust me." He lowered his gaze on the path to my upper thigh.

I laid my head back, shutting my eyes so tight the Jaws of Life couldn't pry them open. At some point, Archie removed my panties. His lips grazed the skin on my inner thighs. Plump kisses. A roving tongue. When he found me, my legs stiffened. You'd have sworn I was in severe pain. The bristle of his goatee chafed my skin, but it didn't matter. Pleasure won that competition.

The mixture of ecstasy and pain increased in intensity with every passing minute. Quivering, trembling, writhing. I existed outside myself like in the dream, distracted by the passing voice of a woman shouting outside. Beginning as a muffled sound, it grew until I heard the woman screaming at the top of her lungs. Orgasmic fulfillment seized my body at that moment—the screaming woman was me.

It started with a kiss. A lustful, inviting kiss. The velvet touch of Archie's lips on mine returned me to reality while my hands clenched the edgings of the throw pillows. The silkiness of damp sheets caressed my body underneath. My eyes opened to his satisfied smile, and he laid his palm on my upper chest as I continued to quiver. "Are you all right?"

"That was me screaming, wasn't it?" Of course, it was me. Why did I even ask?

Archie held back a chuckle and stroked my skin. "You don't know?"

"Aghh." I covered my face with my hands. "Was I loud?"

Archie pointed to the window, and the chuckle broke free. "There may be a few houses on the street who mightn't have heard." He brought his hand back and slid it across my breast, teasing my areola with a finger.

"I'm so embarrassed." But I craved for him to do it again.

"Why? I wanted so much for you to enjoy it. With all that's happened to you, you deserve the pleasure of it."

Archie's jeans had a noticeable bulge forcing the fly to hang open. I tugged the belt loop of the soft denim. "I'm lying here, naked, and you still have your pants on."

"I can remedy that in a jiff." He removed his jeans and underwear, tossing them onto the wooden floor.

I ogled his body. "Sit against the headboard." The sheet fell when I shifted to my knees, waiting for him to comply.

Archie cocked his head. "Ahh, you're giving orders now, are you?" He shifted back against the walnut headboard onto the pillows.

"Yes," I said with a devilish smile. Climbing on top of him, I inserted my slender fingers into his silken blond waves and kissed his open mouth. He wrapped his muscular arms around my torso and crushed my breasts against his firm chest. I wanted to devour him and never stop. He lifted my petite body, weightless as a feather in his grasp, enough to find the slippery entrance he had intimately explored moments before, filling my emptiness with desire and need.

It started with a kiss. A tender, loving kiss. Sifting through the memories of the eventful evening, I think back to its innocent beginning. We stared at each other with an eagerness to act, but Archie stood steadfast with his hands in his pockets. And an overwhelming impulse came over me. I grabbed the front of his shirt and kissed his hungry lips, prompting him to free his hands as we fell back on the bed.

My eyes droop as if two little Welsh brownies are pulling the lashes shut. The smile has relaxed on Archie's handsome face, a shadow image in the darkness, while I fight to focus through the slits of my blurry eyes. Floating between dream state and awareness, I glimpse the dirk in the glass case. The aqua gemstone appears to radiate, calling out to me with a pulsating glow as I sink into sleep.

I roll my head and flinch when I find Archie staring at me. The musky scent of frolicking permeates the air, inviting us to play again. He's lying on his side with his head propped on an arm as the other relaxes against his toned abdomen. I try not to compare him to Richard in the daylight, but the contrast between them is like comparing a finely sculpted statue to a gelatin mold.

"Good morning." Archie places a warm kiss on my dry lips. "Did I scare you?"

"No," I say with a shy smile. "Forgot where I was, and I had a hard time falling asleep." I fiddle with the patch of curly hair on his chest. "I was a little revved up."

"That, you were." A satiated grin forms on his luscious mouth. "I hope you're happy you stayed. I worried it might be the wine."

"It wasn't the wine. I don't know what came over me. I've never done anything like that in my life. Sorry if it worried you." Rolling onto my stomach lessens the aching in my bruised butt. My long hair slips, sending a chill down my naked back, and I shiver.

Archie pulls the sheet and comforter over me. "I was a bit shocked, but I had a wonderful time. Chuffed to bits you stayed. I hope you enjoyed it as well?"

I give him a light push. "As if you didn't notice. What does chuffed to bits mean?"

"I noticed." He's grinning from ear to ear. "Chuffed to bits means very happy." He rubs the tip of his warm nose on mine.

"I hope I'm not sounding over the top, but I've never felt that good." I'm embarrassed to talk about my lackluster sex with Richard in recent years and decide I shouldn't.

"It was incredible for me as well." Archie kisses me again and reaches under the sheet to cup a bruised butt cheek, and I wince. "I'm sorry. Your bum's still bruised? I hadn't noticed."

"I'm glad you didn't. It's in full bloom now." My ass is far from sexy under normal circumstances.

"Let's have a look, shall we?" He lifts the sheet and examines my bouquet of bruises. "I would say your bum has delightful shades of chartreuse and indigo."

I grimace and blink twice. "Well, at least it's camouflaging the ripples of cellulite."

Archie laughs with a twinkle in his eyes. "I'd love to stay and chat all morning about your bruised arse and cellulite, but I have to shower and get to school for a short meeting. You're welcome to stay until I get back. I could make brunch?"

"Sure," I say, smiling coyly.

Archie plants a quick smooch on my mouth and rushes to take a shower. With my contacts out, his figure blurs to an out-of-focus blob of flesh. I notice something stuck on his butt as he disappears into the bathroom. "Hmph. How can he not feel that?"

Water is running, but he returns through the door. "Forgot my cell. I like to play music while I shower."

As he walks toward me, I yell, "Stop!"

Archie freezes, wide-eyed and bemused.

Good thing I got my glasses from my purse. I retrieve them from the nightstand and slide them on. "I want to ogle you in focus." A naughty smile sneaks onto my lips.

He poses like a statue of Adonis and jumps onto the bed. "Ms. Crowther, you have no shame." He gives me a quick peck, grabs his cell phone, and returns to the shower with his muscles glistening in all their defined glory.

And I see it. Can't unsee it. The mysterious object stuck to his toned ass isn't an object at all. It's the Horned God tattoo!

"Shit!" I hop out of bed. I'm hyperventilating, and my heart pounds so hard I'm expecting it to break through my ribcage like a scene from the movie *Alien*. I collect my clothes in a panic. Bra. Jeans. Shirt. "Where the hell are my panties?" I flip back the comforter to find them shoved next to the footboard and slip them on and nearly jump into my jeans. On the way down the stairs, I stumble, putting on my bra and shirt. Archie yells my name, and I rush to slip into my sandals and snatch my purse. I'm unlocking the front door when footsteps echo in the hallway upstairs.

He hurries down the steps wrapped in a towel, droplets trickling down his chest. "Gwyn? Why are you leaving?"

I squeeze my eyes shut and rest against the door. When I open my hazel peepers, he's standing in front of me with a hand on the door.

Archie's icy-blue glare paralyzes me. "Why are you so upset, you would run out like this?" He's out of breath and waiting for the deafening silence to end. "Talk to me, Gwynedd."

I bite my lower lip. "I saw your tattoo." The smell of tea tree and sandalwood passes my nose.

"Tattoos offend you, do they?" He rolls his eyes. "Many of the Fellowship have tattoos, as you well know."

"No. It's the type of tattoo." I gaze into his eyes, hoping for any explanation other than the one living rent-free in my head.

"The pagan tattoo? I'm embarrassed it's even there, but I had little say when I got it. I was at a pub with a bunch of mates in college. Drank more than a wee too much Scotch whisky, and they dragged me to a tattoo parlor. Woke up with that piece of artwork on my arse. Why does it bother you so much?"

Staring into those eyes is like looking into the abyss, and I'm worried I won't have the will to crawl out. "You know the first day of class you monitored for Leslie?"

"Aye." Goosebumps sprout on his toned arms.

"Searching the basement hallways, I had a hard time finding the classroom and heard voices behind a door. I opened it and a couple was screwing. All I saw was a bare butt with that tattoo." I point to his tattoo in an accusatory manner.

Archie's eyes fall to the dampened spot at his feet. "I won't lie to you, Gwyn. It was me. Not one of my prouder moments."

"It was Courtney, I assume? I understood your relationship ended in the summer?"

He lifts his gaze to me. "I ended it in the summer, but Courtney can be very persuasive. It was the last time I was with her."

"Really?" I ask in a judgmental tone.

Archie rubs the nape of his neck. "I'm not a perfect man, Gwyn. I've made more than my share of mistakes. And I've already told you she was a—"

"Miscalculation?" I glare at him, pinching my lips.

"I made it perfectly clear to Courtney it was over, but she was obsessive. It's why I ended it." He moves closer to me, and his scent captures my sensibilities. "And do you know why it was the last time?"

"No. Why?" I ask.

He places a finger under my chin. "I met you that day. When you called me Dr. Cock-burn and turned red in the face, I said to myself. A woman who blushes. How refreshing."

I shake my head. "But screwing in a schoolroom in a public building? What were you thinking?"

"That's the issue. I wasn't thinking with my head. I've no excuse for my behavior, but I understand why it upsets you." He presses his forehead to mine and cups the back of my head with his cool, damp hand. "Please stay. I don't want you to go." A rigid protrusion under the towel resembles the handle of a dirk—sexy and dangerous.

"I left my contact lenses on the nightstand. At the least, I have to get those."

He kisses me tenderly. "Shall we go up and get them?"

"I thought you had a meeting with a student?" My brow crinkles.

"I think I've missed it. I'll apologize later." He drops his towel. "Tell him I was distracted."

CHAPTER TEN

THE SPIRIT OF SAMHAIN

I'VE SPENT MANY NIGHTS with Archie, a good portion of it tainting his satin sheets. I want to tell Ronnie, but I'm ashamed I razzed her so much about sleeping around. Leslie accepts my offer to organize her books for the donation, and the gods know she needs the help. And I've canceled Tuesday lunches with Tyler. Relieved I've had no more strange experiences, I assume it was stress. Since Mabon, I'm floating on a cloud of happiness.

My first Wednesday working at Shane's store, Mystical Sage, proves to be uneventful. I decorate with various Samhain and Halloween themes, concentrating on the witch theme to sell more products. It works like a charm, pun intended, as I sell a few crystals, candles, and herbs for spells.

While Shane is at dinner, I inspect the crystals room for his secret electricity feeding the crystal display but find nothing. He's a sneaky son of a gun. I have to suppress snickering when the self-professed witch in town stops by and argues with me over the quality of the herbs. When she leaves, another customer enters.

"Hey, Gwyn. I heard you were working here," Elijah says. "Shane around?"

"No. He went to dinner," I say. "He'll be back soon. Can I help you?"

"One of our volunteers got sick and can't serve dinner tonight at the shelter. Could you help us out? We'll give you a free dinner."

"Sure." I point at the door. "Shane's here now, too."

Shane enters and pats Elijah's back on the way to the counter. "Hey, Elijah! Here to buy supplies?"

Elijah gives Shane a bit of a quizzical eye. "Not today, Shane. I stopped to get the names of student volunteers to help serve dinner at the shelter, but I'm good now. Gwyn's gonna help."

"Great! Gwyn, darling, any problems while I was gone?" Shane settles on a stool behind the counter.

"One customer. An older woman dressed in black who called herself a witch complained about the quality of your herbs." I snicker under my breath.

"Ahh. That would be Agnes Pritchard. She's a curmudgeon and eccentric old woman." Shane twists his long beard around a finger. "Humor her. She's a steady customer."

"Oh, I will," I say, clutching my purse. "I'm ready, Elijah. Shane, this was fun. I can't wait to work on Saturday."

Shane dusts the countertops as we leave. "You both take care."

Elijah and I arrive at the old warehouse turned shelter at the edge of town after a lengthy walk. There's a rainbow banner hanging over the entrance: *All Are Welcome Here*. The entrance dumps directly into a large dining hall with a cafeteria-style serving area. He introduces me to the kitchen crew, but I won't remember all their names.

I've served for about twenty minutes when Trinity stops in with a young man wearing a DUB hoodie who needs emergency housing. "Hey, Gwyn! How did Elijah wrangle you into serving?"

"In the right place at the right time, I guess." I throw my palms up.

Trinity directs the student to sit at a nearby dining table. "Well, they can always use the help. I hope you'll volunteer again."

Everyone welcomes me without blinking an eye while I serve potatoes on the trays passing by, except for Sebastian, a scruffy, old Black man who reeks of the Wilmington landfill and the local gin distillery. "Who the fuck are you?" he asks.

I freeze, hoping to form an appropriate response, but Elijah comes to my rescue. "Hey, Sebastian! Glad to see you back, man. This is Gwyn. She's helping us serve today. Isn't that nice of her?"

Having the face of an outsider, I spread a friendly grin on my peachy complexion. Sebastian evaluates my face with the inspection of a proctologist. "You have an enchanting face."

Elijah and the serving crew crack up, and Sebastian takes his potatoes and moves on. I get a mushy feeling in my stomach, knowing this man gave me an ounce of acceptance when confronted with fear. "You have a secret power, Elijah, relating to these people. It makes what I do seem irrelevant."

"Sebastian is a sweet old man when he's sober," Elijah says. "Gotta keep him off the streets. He needs love and support. And don't worry, you'll find your way, Gwyn. Somehow, I know you'll find the path to your secret power."

Trinity motions for Elijah to walk with her to the homeless student at the dining table to orient him. The poor young man cries, and Elijah wraps his arms around him. Trinity pats the young man on his back and comes to join me in the serving area.

"You know, I stayed here when I was in high school. Right after my momma kicked me out." Trinity dishes out ladles of peas as she reminisces. "I met your mom and dad right here at the shelter."

"Why didn't they tell me? I'm finding they kept a lot of things to themselves. Leslie said they were best friends in college."

"Yeah. I'm sure that bothers you. You discovered nothing when you rummaged through their belongings after they passed?"

"No. I didn't have it in me to go through all their stuff. Boxed things up and stored them." With Richard's passing, I have even less resolve to do it now.

Trinity pats my back. "All I can say about Leslie is people drift apart for lots of reasons."

In that instant, a disheveled, dirty, white man in tattered clothes crashes through the entry doors, spewing nonsense. "Help me! Help me!" the man yells. "The big raven shadow in the tree snatched me with its huge claw branches, trying to crush me! Tried to pluck my eyes out! It's a monster! A demon! And it's coming after you!"

I panic. My heart pounds like a hammer in my chest. The homeless man described the Unseelie Court fairy I read about in class. It has to be a coincidence, but I stand like a statue with a vision of the Sluagh in my head. I expel air in a huff, not aware I'd held it in for so long. The man runs around the dining hall, scaring the guests. Their children whimper and cry from the hysteria.

Elijah puts his arm around the frantic man. "Let me help you, Frank." He wraps his bulging arms around the homeless man and convinces Frank to sit at a table while he gets him a meal.

Trinity shakes her head, and air passes through her lips. "Poor Frank. Always spouting wild stories."

"But what about his clothes?" There's no way his clothes should have so many tears in them, and it doesn't allay my fears.

"His clothes do appear more ripped than usual, but that's some ridiculous talk about a raven shadow in a tree. He saw the Raven Pub sign and conjured that shit in his head."

I suppose she's right, but nausea has taken root in the pit of my stomach.

By the last week of October, I've settled into a routine: work, class, Fellowship meetings, working out, and spending time with Archie. Tyler is enjoying his newfound freedom, and sleeping issues are a distant memory unless you count the deprivation due to sex. If I'm going to have hot flashes and get sweaty, what better reason for it? The tenderness Archie provides fills an immense hole in my heart, hollow for so long.

I wake to the gorgeous face of my lover, finding I've fallen asleep on an open book on the loveseat, and my laptop has gone into sleep mode. "What time is it?" I lift my head from the book and massage the depressions the book left on my face.

Archie rubs my thigh and glances at the mantel clock. "About 8:00 p.m." The clock dings its first of eight.

I straighten my back and stretch my arms out, wincing at the kink in my neck. "I know you were hoping for some extracurricular activity tonight, but I'm pooped."

"Dr. Hughes has been working you all too hard." He places the palm of his hand on my cheek. "I think maybe you need sleep more than sex."

"Well, that's debatable, but you may be right tonight. I was awake until late a couple of nights this week, studying with

Spence and Skye. My age has caught up with me." The mantel clock dings its final eighth time and leaves a ringing in my ears.

"Why don't you stay tonight, anyway? I know the murder on campus appears to have been an isolated incident, but I'd prefer you not go home after sunset."

I close my book and turn off my laptop. "By the way, did Trinity or Elijah ever tell you about the man who ran into the shelter, screaming? Happened the first week of October."

He cocks his head. "No. They didn't. What happened?"

"He ran into the dining hall shouting about a monster trying to snatch him. It bothered me. He called it a raven shadow in a tree. Said it tried to crush him and poke his eyes out."

Archie widens his eyes.

"Does it mean something?" I slide my laptop into the back slot of my backpack.

Archie tenses a corner of his mouth. "Doesn't sound believable, does it?"

"Of course, not. It's still creepy as hell." I lean back on the loveseat.

Archie peers at the mantel clock, takes an intentional breath, and brings his gaze back to me. "I have to tell you something, and you won't like it."

I sit up, my eyes narrowing. "What won't I like?"

"As the head of the Fellowship, I have the unfortunate position of informing you only full members can attend the special ceremony for Samhain. I know you've been looking forward to it with all the planning, but you can't take part until next year. And that's if you remain with the group."

"Why did you wait until now to tell me? You know I was excited about it. Halloween is my favorite holiday." I'm peeved. Ronnie said nothing to me about it.

"Ah, but there's a difference. To pagans, Samhain is a serious holiday, and you're still learning. The Fellowship instituted this rule long ago. I knew you'd be disappointed, so I waited to tell you. I'm sorry."

The scowl on my face could annihilate a small village. Good thing he wasn't expecting sex tonight, because he killed the mood. "I understand, but I'm...salty."

Archie frowns and offers a conciliatory hand. "Let's turn in early. By the time we get ready for bed and chat, it will be 9:00 p.m. soon enough."

I get cleaned up, hop into bed, and scoot under the sheets. October has been the fourth warmest on record in Delaware, but the temperatures have finally dipped into the 50s at night. Archie left a window open, creating a nip in the room, so I pull the comforter around my neck.

He yells from the bathroom. "Gwyn, can you close the window? It's supposed to get cold tonight."

Ugh. Ask me now when I'm all snug under the comforter. If only I could wish the window closed. I shut my eyes tightly for a minute and open them. The lights flicker in the bedroom, and the window slams shut. The room goes dark except for the spray of light from the bathroom, and the aqua gem on the dirk in the glass case radiates with an intense luminosity. My body stiffens.

Archie turns out the bathroom light and walks to the bed, grumbling. The glow on the gem has disappeared. "Why did you turn out the light? I can't see where I'm going."

"I didn't. It flickered and went out." Truthfully, I have no fucking clue what happened, and the frogs leaping to my ribcage prove it.

"Argh. Probably a brownout triggered the breaker. Damn Bearsden City Electric. I'll flip it in the morning. Thanks for shutting the window." He kisses me and rolls on his side.

"You're welcome." My palpitating heart tells me to question my sanity or my reality.

I'm miffed Ronnie didn't tell me about Samhain. She apologizes and offers me dinner at the café to explain, and it's packed as usual. "I guess I'm being ridiculous. The Fellowship makes the rules, not me. But I wish you had told me."

"I'm sorry. The Fellowship likes to keep some rituals private. Not all newbies are serious in the rituals." Ronnie hands me a menu. "We've had some unpleasant experiences with silly students in the past, but I agree. Archie should have told you sooner."

"I can meet him after. Bob for apples." And I'm thinking a new sexy witch costume might spice things up, too.

Ronnie opens her eyes wide and flutters her lashes. "Maybe bob for something else?" She cackles, and I throw her a side-eye.

After dinner, I slip on my DUB hoodie and head for home. Passing by Mitchell Hall, I stop and inspect the exterior of the mansion. Black wood shutters are missing or hanging by a single screw. The once ornate, black iron fence has rusted from weather and oxidation, and its side gate hangs ajar, almost inviting me in. I figure, what the hell, and go in.

Overgrown and unkempt, the Celestial Gardens are dismal in the moonlight. Walking through the maze of squares, I arrive at the stone water fountain with figures of playful fairies pouring water and splashing their feet. The existence of a grassy mound is odd, but apparently, so were the Mitchells. I read the plaque nearby. "Please guard this mound, the dwelling of my children of the fae."

In the right back corner stands a full-grown hawthorn tree, providing shade with its slender, thorny branches full of parsley-colored leaves. Unexpectedly, the giggles of children emerge behind me, and I turn to catch a boy and a girl with golden-blond locks running from the mound. What type of parent lets their kids run around on Main Street after dark with a killer on the loose? "You two should not be in here. It's after dark and—" The two cherub delinquents sprint off toward the gate.

A chilly gust catches my hair, sending it flying in all directions, and the hawthorn leaves rustle behind me. I turn around to threatening limbs flailing with large, arm-like shadows, and the thorny leaves and small twigs sting the skin on my face. At moments like this, I wish I could magically stop the wind.

I raise my hand to block the debris, and it tingles and radiates with a vivid amber glow like before. Instantly, the wind stops. In the distance, there's a faint cawing of a raven, and the hawthorn tree appears to growl. I bolt out of the gardens and gasp for air! What is happening to me? I inspect the front and back of my right hand as the faint amber glow dissipates. These aren't hallucinations.

Chapter Eleven

Samhain

THE CHILL OF FALL has arrived, providing a cool, moonlit evening for Trick-or-Treating, and neighbors have decorated their homes with fake spider webs, skeletons, and carved pumpkins. The talk of a serial killer has died down, and the community enjoys a safe Halloween. But I'm scared, and knots still tighten in my stomach over the occurrence in the Celestial Gardens.

I try to put the ideas out of my head as I drop chocolate nuggets into the eco-bags of Mini-Dracula and his buddy Mini-Frankenstein. I can't attend the Samhain ritual, but I can surprise Archie after in my sexy witch costume. Wrapping myself in a black hooded cape, I drive to his house to surprise him.

The front and back doors of Archie's cottage are locked, so I walk in these four-inch heels to the Pumpkin House. I peek through the windows but see no one. Entering the foyer, faint voices trickle from the back room, and I tiptoe back to listen.

Curiosity gets the best of me, and I open the door a slit. The Fellowship members stand in a circle in the candle-lit room, dressed in black, and chant softly. The dream where I visualized people chanting replays in my head, and I get queasy. Feeling like an intruder, I decide to leave and wait for Archie in my car. While pulling the door closed, I'm relieved I've gone unnoticed—until I am.

Being over one hundred years old, a few doors in the Pumpkin House hang level, but not this one. The door groans as it opens until it hits the wall, and here I am, standing in the doorway like a deer in headlights. Leslie stands at the head of the circle holding a wooden staff, topped with a white crystal. Members gasp when they discover me, and I skedaddle out of there. I hear Dr. Hughes and Trinity shouting to stop me. I make it to the front door before Ronnie and Archie have caught up with me.

"Gwyn. Please, wait." Archie reaches out to me, but I pull away. His face has a look of oops-you-caught-me on it.

Winded and biting her upper lip, Ronnie tries to calm me. "Gwyn, it's not what it seems."

"You know what it seems to me?" My face feels so hot, it must match my red lipstick, and my heart's pounding like it's going to explode.

"I can only imagine what notions are running through your head." Archie takes in air and holds it until his chest deflates.

"I see clearly what's happening here." I pant with one hand on the front door while I rant. "You're a cult. It explains why everyone is so happy. I trusted both of you!" I shut my eyes, trying to contain the exasperation. How could my best friend and my lover betray me like this?

Archie glances at Ronnie and grimaces. "We have to tell her. No other option." His apprehensive eyes lock on mine, holding me captive.

"I'll explain it to her." Ronnie offers her hands to me and pleads. "Please? So, you know I'm telling you the truth."

I want to give Ronnie the benefit of the doubt, but my fists are super-glued to my hips. And she has no patience.

"Oh, for fuck's sake." Ronnie grabs my fists and pries them open, prompting a snicker from Archie. "Gwyn, we're not a cult."

"You're not?" My eyes swing back and forth between their distressed faces. "Then who the hell are you?"

Ronnie bites her upper lip and squeezes my hands. "We're a coven."

Archie ambles closer. "More like a community of witches who do good. You must sense our intentions."

Eyeing them back and forth with a robotic head, I guffaw so loud the other members of the Fellowship must hear me. "I understand you believe you're do-gooder witches, but I can't be part of this farce. And I don't belong here." I turn toward the door and grip the knob.

"Please, don't leave." Archie reaches for my hand on the doorknob. "You do belong here, Gwyn."

The clacking of spike heels approaches, getting louder with each ear-splitting click. Dressed head to toe in black with her burgundy hair flowing, Trinity has the mother of all scowls on her face. "Have you told her yet? I assume that's why you're still out here wasting away our limited time?"

Ronnie clasps her hands on her head and mutters. "We're trying."

"We don't have time for this pussyfooting around." Trinity pushes them aside and grabs me by the shoulders. "Here's the deal. Your parents were powerful witches, your mom from an ancestral line. They came here to help recruit and vet new members to build this coven in its infancy. We're keepers of this community. You, my dear, have inherited the skills of your parents and need to cultivate them."

She removes her hands, and my racing heart subsides a little. Memories of all the strange episodes trickle in like a leak in a dam. The odd hot flashes. The amber glow in my hands. The window shutting. And the incident in the Celestial Gardens. "If what you say is true, why did my parents leave?"

Trinity scratches the back of her head. "They didn't want to raise you with magic. Leslie agreed to never recruit you, a vow the rest of us didn't have to honor. After Ronnie joined the coven, we made her aware of your lineage. Together, we decided it was worth the risk of luring you in. Find out if the ancestral magic was still there."

Archie's face relaxes, and he peers into my doubtful eyes. "Recruits take part with the Fellowship one year before we reveal our true identity. Gives them time to absorb our energy and discover their hidden craft, if it's viable. That was the plan for you as well until this happened, but you've already had some strange experiences, no?"

He knows I have. I stand with a gaping mouth while the un- explainable incidents spin like a merry-go-round in my head. I press my hands against my nauseous stomach.

Trinity rubs my arm. "Ronnie, why don't you and I go back? Archie, I'm trusting you to fix this." Trinity gestures to Ronnie to follow her back to the room.

Archie approaches me again, but this time, I stand my ground with a look of a witch contemplating a hex. "I know you doubt all of this."

"I don't know. It explains a lot of things." I stare at my hands, recalling the amber glow. My eyes slink back to his gor- geous face. "Was pursuing me all part of your recruitment?"

He huffs, and his brow crumples. "Is that what you think? I was told flat out not to pursue you in any capacity. When you asked to keep things quiet, I was relieved."

"Then why did you?" I search his transparent eyes for any hint of truth in his words.

Archie lays a hand on my cheek, and his distraught face softens. "You know why." He swipes his thumb across my lips.

"You wanted so badly to attend this ritual. Now you can. You'll discern we aren't a cult, and maybe you'll find yourself."

I look away. "I'll take part in the Samhain ritual and make my own educated opinion. After tonight, I have to rethink all of this."

"Fair enough." Archie offers me his hand. "Shall we go? Trinity is blowing steam out of her ears by now." When we reach the backroom, he grips the doorknob. "I love your sexy witch costume." He winks and pushes on the door.

Awkward: *feeling embarrassed or causing inconvenience*—that's me.

"Come sit between me and Zoe," Ronnie says. "We'll guide you through it."

Zoe waves her hand, motioning to me. "I'm so excited you know about us." Her infectious smile comforts me, and I try to make the best of the situation.

Archie takes a seat between Elijah and Skye. I scan the faces in the candlelit room, smelling of wormwood incense. How can I remain friends with these delusional people? The members have dressed in a variety of formal and informal black clothing except for Spence. He's wearing a clown costume, complete with rainbow hair, face makeup, oversized red shoes, and a red nose. He waves at me, flashing a big, red grin, and I struggle to contain my laughter.

"Welcome, Gwynedd," Leslie says. "We are so delighted you are joining us in this ritual. You discovered the underlying reason for our existence much earlier than planned, but we hope you will consider remaining in the group after this experience. Trinity, I believe we are ready to proceed." She taps her staff on the wooden floor three times.

Everyone stands and extends their hands, palms up. Ronnie nudges me to do the same. The room has an odd presence, as if something momentous awaits. Across from me, Archie's eyes are closed, as are most of the Fellowship members. Audrey and

Courtney concentrate as if they're conjuring spirits in their private world.

"Hearken to these words, oh spirits. Hear our cry," Trinity says. "We call to you from the other side. Visit us. We welcome you here. Loved ones don't be afraid. We will not shed a tear."

"Can you feel the energy?" Spence rolls his head all around with his eyes closed.

"Spence is right." Elijah scans the ceiling, searching for something. But what? "I've never experienced this before."

Skye extends her arms and flips her hands up and down. "I'm tingling."

"With all your talking, you're gonna ruin this." Trinity huffs and moves her focus to the ceiling, extending her hands like she's summoning something in a seance.

I lean toward Ronnie. "What are they blabbing about? I feel nothing."

"Shh," Ronnie whispers. "Concentrate. Leslie said it's not happened in decades, but it could happen tonight, especially with you here, my friend."

As I stare at the ceiling, I hope to find a spot to zone out while this charade continues. A small, blue blob emerges, resembling a hologram. I scrutinize all the walls for evidence of light beams but don't discern any. The hazy blob expands with multiple arms, extending out and around the perimeter, growing exponentially while a loud machine-like whir fills the space. The members exclaim words of astonishment, reveling in its appearance.

"This is fucking awesome!" Spence shouts. "See Tanner, I told you the clown costume wouldn't make a difference. Now I don't have to change for the party after."

Skye snorts. "Maybe we'll get a visit from a clown from the past." Spence lets his middle finger break free.

Tanner grimaces. "Don't encourage him, Skye."

"Stay focused, my friends. Do not break the concentration." Archie gazes at me with those icy blues, and a hot sensation warms my upper chest. What a time for a hot flash. I pull at my shirt, trying to fan myself.

Leslie raises her voice over the loud whir. "Break the focus, and the portal may close."

Portal? I've reached my boiling point and am about to stamp out of this farcical presentation. To top it off, the obnoxious whir has triggered a splitting headache. I glance back at the so-called portal, and it's morphing into the vision of a familiar masculine face with narrow cheekbones, a straight nose, and dark-brown eyes. My hand drops from my shirt when the vision speaks. "Gwynedd, do you hear me? I so wanted to find you, and I have."

The plasma-like face morphs in and out of focus, and his warped voice reverberates throughout the room. The members all mutter words of amazement, not wanting to scare off the vision.

"Richard?" I glance at Ronnie, and her jaw has fallen so far, I'm expecting her to scrape it off the floor. "Ronnie, who is doing this? This is cruel."

"No one. I swear. It's him, Gwyn. It's Richard. He's come through the portal from the Otherworld." She grabs my arm, and a look of angst seizes her face.

Archie intercepts my anxious gaze, and his face tenses up. I can't bring myself to respond. I see Richard. It's definitely his face, albeit a see-through, shimmering version, but it can't be him. He's dead.

Leslie replies to the vision. "Why do you seek an audience with Gwynedd? Are you here to share your love and concern for her from your world?"

"Gwynedd was my wife." The members gasp and murmur while the vision continues to speak. "I seek her knowledge of the fate of Cassandra Parnell."

My anxious face collapses. In a defining instant, a nanosecond of clarity, the juncture of not knowing to *knowing*, all things become unambiguous. Only Ronnie, Archie, and Tyler knew of Cassandra. I have to trust they wouldn't betray me, so I answer the vision of Richard. "I'm here."

"Gwynedd, I must know. How is Cassandra? Is she dealing with my death well? I worry about her so much. She must be so sad." Richard's plasma-like face transitions from blue to indigo.

Anger foments in my gut. "You want to know about Cassandra? And why would she be sad? You were only colleagues, right?"

His color changes from indigo to pink. "You must know by now we were more than colleagues."

The older members glance around the room and at each other with froggy eyes, and the students gape at the vision in a daze. Ronnie grasps my hand and tightens her grip as I rant. "Damn straight, I know. How could you come from wherever the hell you came from and not ask how I'm doing? Or Tyler? He was devastated by everything."

"I knew Tyler would be OK because he has you. Cassandra only had me," he says.

Every person has a limit, the last straw, a match in the powder keg. In an eruption like Mount Vesuvius, or Mount Crowther, I spew all my rage, not caring where it lands. "I don't give a shit about Cassandra. She can rot in the skank Hall of Fame, but not asking about your son?" My face flushes with drops of sweat, and I've forgotten where I am. "I refuse to tell you anything about Cassandra, but I will tell you about me, not that you asked. I'm doing fantastic! Working part-time, taking a graduate class, making new friends. One friend is very special. He finds me attractive and has helped me grow as a person."

The members' eyes hop around the circle while I continue to rant, scorned wife, after all. Archie stands across from me, scratching his goatee. The vision of Richard bellows in a thunderous voice. "Gwyn! Tell me about Cassandra!" His voice rings throughout the room, and the younger members' bodies stiffen. But he doesn't scare me.

"I will not!" I'm so enraged, my entire body shakes like an earthquake has struck our little corner of Bearsden. The members tremble, and their eyes bounce around the room. "You see this man? This gorgeous man?" I point a finger at Archie. "I'm fucking this kind, appreciative man. All. The. Time. Better in bed than you ever were. I'm so glad I got to speak to you, but now I'm done. Go back to whatever slime hole you seeped from!"

In an instinctive action, I wrench my hand from Ronnie's tight grasp and shove my hand toward Richard's plasma face. Unexpected energy radiates from my hands, yellow like the sun with black swirls, and he disappears into the portal. I swing my hand down to shake the glow from my hand, and the portal closes with a thunderous clap. And a glistening, black shadow slithers along the ceiling until it disappears into the wall.

Silence seizes the room except for a high-pitched ringing in my ears, and the minor earthquake has stopped. I scan the circle, catching glimpses of open mouths and motionless bodies except for Leslie and Trinity. They're grinning like Cheshire cats. And Archie's standing with his arms crossed, frowning. I wait in silence for a member to move or curse me, having ruined their brief connection with the Otherworld, and my words slip out. "I'm sorry."

"That was lit!" Spence guffaws like a hyena and slaps his legs.

Everyone hoots and hollers, commenting on the amazing experience and thanking me profusely for participating. Courtney cries and runs out of the room, and my heart sinks. Audrey runs after her.

"Silence!" Leslie calls out with a jarring thud of her staff. The Fellowship quiets within seconds. "Audrey, stop! Let her go."

Trinity admonishes Archie. "Didn't your mama ever teach you not to shit where you eat, and you've dumped twice in the same kitchen!" Archie doesn't respond. You don't give Trinity a rebuttal. "I think that's the most we'll get out of this ritual tonight. Gwyn, I know this was a shock, but you got through it. And now, you know who, and what, you are."

Leslie lifts her chin with the appearance of mission accomplished stamped on her face. "Let us all remember what we accomplished here tonight, colleagues. At our next meeting, we will discuss our next steps concerning Mitchell Hall. Go in peace."

Everyone collects their belongings, and Archie glances at me with a devilish grin. Leslie motions for me to join her. "A moment, Gwyn. Archie, I would like to speak with you after." She no longer appears a fragile old woman as I approach her. "Speak your mind."

"Trinity said my parents left the Fellowship, this coven, because they wanted me to have a life without magic." I stare at her placid face, scrutinizing it for any sign of emotion. "It explains why you never reconnected with them."

"I kept my vow to Lowri. We hoped you would develop your powers organically over time and discover your true origin, yet I am overjoyed at the early revelation. You saw the power emanate from you. With time, you too will have the powers of your mother."

"Maybe," I say. "I've not decided anything. I'm saying we'll see."

Leslie raises her chin. "We certainly shall."

I turn and pass Archie as he enters Leslie's den, and he winks at me. When I walk onto the porch, I find the Fellowship members waiting for me. The young members huddle together, buzzing about the phenomenon. Elijah walks over and lifts me in a bear hug. He's speechless as he lowers me to the porch floor.

"Yaaas." Spence hugs me and sways back and forth. "It's so awesome you found out! I couldn't keep the front up for an entire year."

Tanner taps Spence's shoulder. "Enough, dude. You're gonna overwhelm her, and we have a party to attend."

"I think I'm way past that, Tanner." I examine my friends with a fresh eye—a magical eye. A couple of students stroll past the Pumpkin House porch, and I imagine being them again—not knowing about witches, covens, and supernatural beings. Everything I knew about the world has changed, and I'll never be able to view the world through those other eyes again. Ever.

"Gwyn, darling," Shane says. "I'm comforted on a supreme level you are *in the knowing*. It elevates my hopes for our community."

"Let's give Gwyn some breathing room, shall we?" Trinity corrals them off the porch. "She has a lot to think about before our next meeting. If you need to talk, you know where to find me."

The members say goodbye and depart into the chilly night, leaving Ronnie alone with me on the porch. She fidgets with the zipper on her jacket. "I should explain myself."

"No need." The air has a bite, so I wrap my witch's cape to reduce the cold air sneaking under my skirt. "I wouldn't have believed you. Even when I saw the portal open, I didn't believe it was real. Not until Richard, his spirit, whatever you want to call it, was glaring at me in the face. What did Shane mean when he said I was *in the knowing*?"

"Knowing about us. Being witches. Magic." Ronnie opens her eyes wide, splaying her hands in front of her. Abruptly, her face contorts, and the corners of her mouth fall. "It's horrible Richard was the one who crossed over. It's too cold and late to explain how I became involved. We'll meet for lunch." She chuckles through tight lips. "So, Archie? Why didn't you tell me you took the plunge? You know I wouldn't judge. I mean, it's me. And now the entire coven knows you're sleeping together, anyway. I don't think Leslie and Trinity are too happy about it."

"I was embarrassed, having given you such a hard time about sleeping around." I purse my lips. "And Leslie and Trinity have no say in the matter."

The front door opens, and Archie steps onto the porch, snapping his black leather coat. "Nippy, isn't it?" He blows on his hands, rubbing them together.

"Is Leslie gonna throw you to the wolves?" Ronnie asks.

"Naw. Got a bit of a scolding and some orders." Archie points at the front door. "She'll be out in a jiff." He grimaces at me and exhales. "You wanted to keep our relationship quiet?"

I clench my teeth and shrink while Ronnie cackles at us. "Derek's not here yet. Why don't the two of you go ahead? We'll take Leslie home."

"Sounds good to me. Shall we go?" Archie offers me his hand. "Holding hands in public shouldn't upset the order of things now that they all know our most intimate details."

I send him a frosty glare and take his hand, hot like an electric blanket. "Thanks, Ronnie."

"Don't do anything I wouldn't do!" she says as we cross the street.

On the invigorating stroll back to his house, we don't speak about the portal opening, Richard, or the fact Archie's a witch or I'm a witch. Except for the release of energy from my hand, I feel the same. No special powers flow through this body.

"I like this," Archie says, kneading my hand. "Touching you in public is sensual." He has a burning in his eyes while his thumb strokes the back of my hand.

The impromptu hand massage warms my fingers. "All the shenanigans we've done in your bed and this? Holding my hand turns you on?" I roll my eyes. "You're absurd."

"Oh, really." He brings my hand to his mouth. Starting with light pecks to the back of my hand, he progresses to open mouth canoodling, and tongues my finger.

"Archie, stop. Someone might see us." The arousal between my legs defies me. We've arrived at the Old Men oaks juncture, and I spy the alleyway between Campbell and Menzies Halls, the shortcut to Archie's neighborhood.

He licks his lower lip. "But I'm just kissing your hand."

Determined to remove us from the faint glow of the lamp-post, I drag Archie to the alleyway, where he shoves me against the red brick of Menzies Hall. Cupping my face in his hands, he gazes into the dark shadows for my eyes, and I glimpse the lustful, blue tint of his irises in the moonlight.

"When you shouted at Richard, declaring your desire for me, I wanted to take you out and fuck you right then," he says in a breathy voice. "But this will do." He presses his open mouth against mine, smothering my lusty moans. His erection pokes through the chino material in his black pants, and I lay my hand on the bulge, enjoying the warmth it radiates.

Archie unfastens his belt buckle and unzips his pants. Reaching under my witch's skirt, he finds my panties and pulls them off deftly, pocketing them in his chinos. In one swift action, he clutches my toned thighs, lifting me against the hard, cold brick, and enters me with the full force of his body. The back of my head scrapes against the rough mortar, but the pain can't compete with the pleasure between my thighs.

In the middle of our lustful act, I remember reading about a drunk couple caught fucking behind the green dumpster in the Raven parking lot and thinking "how inappropriate and low-class," yet here I am, humping in an alley against the exterior of Menzies Hall cold sober.

Archie stops, lowers me to the ground, and pushes his manhood back into his pants. "Let's finish this in a warmer, more comfortable place, shall we?"

I imagine any other place would be more comfortable than a cold, red-brick wall. Once inside his house, he locks the front door, and pieces of clothing fly off in all directions. We stumble to the stairway half-dressed and start again right there on the steps. It looks so sexy in the movies, but it's absolutely not. Hard, uneven edges of wood dig into my back, and I grunt. "This is so not working for me."

"I'm sorry." Archie gestures to the living room. "The ice packing chair?"

The worn leather chair works wonders, as does the loveseat, a kitchen chair, and ultimately the beige, plush rug near the hearth of the fireplace. Wrapped in heavy quilts like a sleeping bag, we're hot near the umber flames, flickering in the fireplace.

Archie rolls off me onto his back, and his chest rises and falls, ebbing like the tides. "I'm finished. I'll need a gallon of water after this evening," he says in a thicker, Scottish brogue. "Sleeping right here. I don't think I can stand."

My palpitating heart soothes to a steady rhythm, and I slap him playfully. "Oh, stop. You're being ridiculous." We haven't spoken one word about what happened at the Pumpkin House. "Should we discuss the elephant in the room?"

"It's a fawking big elephant." He strokes my thigh with the tips of his fingers. "Let's wait until morning."

"I don't know how I'm gonna sleep. My parents are strangers. My entire childhood was a lie." I imagine the amber glow emanating from my hand. "How do I move forward?"

Archie searches for my hand and intertwines his fingers with mine. "Look at what you've already endured. Underneath your naïve, vulnerable exterior lies a passionate, stubborn, and resilient woman. You can do it."

I lie across his firm chest, playing with the soft hairs on his pecs. "Tell me the truth. Did you pursue me because I'm supposed to be a powerful ancestral witch?"

"No, Gwyn." Archie rolls on his side and lays a hand over my heart. "I've not lied to you, and I never will."

I peer at him with a skeptical eye. "Well, you never told me you were a witch."

"You never asked." He winks.

CHAPTER TWELVE

TO BE A WITCH, OR NOT TO BE?

I WAKE TO THE clanking of dishes and the intoxicating aroma of baking. Swaddling myself in a quilt, I shuffle around the living room for the strewn garments of my witch's costume, finding everything but my lacey panties. I chuckle, thinking about the moment of indiscretion in the alley, and decide to get them from Archie before dressing. A check of my phone reveals a text notification.

Ronnie: *Hope you had fun last night. See you Thursday for lunch?*

Me: *Sure.*

The smell of blueberry pancakes permeates, and my stomach growls like a dog. "Breakfast smells so good. I'm ravenous." I'm sure I have a mop for hair, but I don't care.

Archie turns around and rushes over, sporting a beaming grin, and gives me a quick kiss. "Good morning." He's wearing the black tee and chinos from the night before.

I smirk at him. "You smile like you got laid last night after a year of celibacy."

He chuckles like a schoolboy. "I've not had sex all night like that since—I can't remember, but it's more than that. A considerable amount of stress was lifted last night." He smooths my disheveled hair and returns to the stove to flip a pancake.

A cup of tea waits for me, and its rising steam invites me to take a sip. "Because I know the pagan group is a cover for a coven? And I'm supposed to be a witch?"

"Aye. I'm never comfortable with the secrecy, but it's necessary." Archie retrieves the maple syrup from the fridge and sets it on the table with the plates and forks. "You ARE a witch, Gwyn. You saw what you did last night. Do you remember other phenomena?" He places the plate of pancakes on the kitchen table and sits next to me.

"I suppose," I say, setting the plates. "It's still not real to me. I have so many questions," I mumble with a mouth full of pancake. "The first time something happened was when I touched you after class the first day and under the arch when you kissed me on the cheek."

"I have a small confession. Those brief touches were ignitions of power. Think of it as a spark to start a fire." He clasps my hand and strokes it with his thumb. "I didn't know it would affect you so strongly and as quickly as it did, so I stopped."

I tip my head and squint at him. "So, you weren't flirting?"

His eyes turn lascivious. "Oh, I was. By then, I wanted you. Two birds, one stone." Archie slides three pancakes onto his plate and pours syrup over them. "Were there other times?"

"A few. The night I fell near the Old Men oaks, I saw the same amber glow shooting from my hand, and the night you asked me to shut the window? I didn't want to get out of bed, so I closed my eyes and wished it would shut."

"When the electricity went out?" Archie stops mid-bite and grins. "Ah, that was you! Why didn't you tell me?"

My shoulders fall as air hisses through my lips. "I worried you'd think I was losing my mind."

"Of course not, but I would have fretted you might destroy something by accident." He snickers and stuffs his mouth with a piece of pancake.

"Ha. Ha. Ha. I don't feel like a witch. Certainly not one with great power." I drink my Earl Grey, savoring the last drops.

"You'll need to train like all beginners. Your power needs cultivating. Recruits meet together and train with experienced witches. I'll try to arrange the first one for you on Friday evening here in my magic space in the basement." He gestures to the basement door.

My eyes open wide. "You have a magic space in your basement?"

"It's hidden. I'll show you on Friday." He pauses, and his face grows somber. "I'm beyond happy you're *in the knowing*, but I hated watching the hurt you endured when your husband's spirit appeared. I wish the reveal could have transpired without the confrontation."

"Me, too." I finish the last bite of pancake and drop the fork on the plate with a clink.

Archie collects our plates and sets them in the sink. "I have to shower and get to school. I'm so late. Why didn't you dress?" He wipes the counter and washes his hands.

A mischievous smile spreads across my lips. "You have my panties."

"Oh." Archie chuckles and reaches into a pocket of his chinos. It's empty. He checks the other one and rolls his lips inward. "Oops."

My eyes pop out, visualizing my lacey panties decorating the paver walkway next to Menzies Hall.

When I arrive at class on Thursday morning, Skye and Spence rag me about Archie and the Samhain event saying things like "I told you so" and "I knew it." Courtney arrives, averting her scornful eyes as she opens her laptop.

"I know the two of you don't care for Courtney," I say, "but she has feelings. I feel terrible about Samhain."

"She has to face reality. Her relationship with Archie ended before it got started. It was nada." Spence makes a zero with a hand.

"She's so extra. She threw herself at him." Skye flips her hair and bats her eyes in a mocking gesture. "I'm not making excuses for him either, though. He should have been clearer it was a casual fling."

I don't dare tell them the identities of the lustful couple in the study room. Archie certainly shoulders some of the blame. Courtney glares at us, and I change the subject. "Archie says I'll begin training on Friday. Do you think he'll ask you both to go?"

Spence replies with a cocky inflection in his voice. "Abso-fuckinglutely. I'm the only student with a level three status."

"Level three? There are levels of magic?" There's so much I don't know, and the questions pile up on Crowther Hill.

Skye grimaces at Spence. "He's bragging. And yeah. I'm at level two." Skye elaborates on the others as she opens her laptop. "Courtney is a neophyte. She's learning the basics. Audrey is level two, but nearing level three. Zoe started level two, but should have stayed on level one. She wasn't ready for spells."

"Who decides when you're ready to move on?" I ask.

"Archie, but Dr. Hughes always has the ultimate say, Supreme Elder and all. Her ears must be burning." Spence points to the door when Dr. Hughes enters. She scans the classroom with cat-like eyes to find me, sets her satchel on the desk, and prepares for class.

Skye continues. "And Trinity. She always has an opinion, whether or not you want it. From what I hear, Trinity has known Dr. Hughes since she was in high school, so she has powerful skills."

That makes sense. Trinity has great respect for Leslie. "The rest of the members have level three status?"

"Everyone except Ronnie. She's a solid level two." Spence types Friday's training into his phone calendar. "They have varying degrees of efficiency, of course, but Archie has ancestral powers like you. He's like super-duper level three."

"Riiight," I say. "I'm still unsettled from Tuesday night. Not convinced yet I'm who you all think I am." I open my laptop and prepare to take notes.

Skye and Spence glance at each other and burst out laughing. Spence shakes a finger and lectures me. "Girl, you're in so much denial. Did you see what you did with your hands on Samhain?"

"I'm not sure what happened." Something came out of my hands, but I don't have a clue how. As I wiggle my fingers, a faint glow emerges. I push my hand into my lap and cover it.

Dr. Hughes announces the Celtic Studies department, in collaboration with the English department, will present a stage performance of readings and poetry. Dr. Cockburn will recite the poetry of Robert Burns and other Scottish poets. After presenting a historical overview of the Celtic languages, she starts a tourism video narrated in the Welsh language. It resembles the language in a fantasy novel. Imagine living in a world full of dragons, fairies, and witches. Five witches exist in this room. It doesn't get more real than that.

After class, Leslie asks to speak with me but waits until the classroom has cleared. As Courtney passes, she scowls in my direction, smacking me dead in the face. Leslie inspects me. "Gwynedd, I'm happy you attended class. I expected you might withdraw from school and the Fellowship."

"Why would I?" The course cost a lot of money. Of course, I'm going to finish it. "It was a shock, but I trust Archie." I pause, trying to form the perfect sentence. "I know you're displeased with our relationship, but if it weren't for Archie and Ronnie, I would have left."

"We frown on relationships in the coven. Tanner and Spence were in a committed relationship when we recruited them. However, Archie became involved with a member, and the relationship ended badly." Leslie clears her throat. "When these sorts of things occur in a coven, it affects the entire structure and strength of all of us. Do you understand what I'm saying?"

"I do, but I've not committed to this group yet." Looking at her with a stern face, I clarify my position. "I will make my own decisions. If you can live with that, I'll move forward with my training."

"It will do for now." She tilts her head. "I would like you to come by the house on Saturday to show you something important. I am asking. It's not a command."

Hmph. What could that be? "How about first thing in the morning? I'll walk over from Archie's place."

"I wake around 6 a.m. After seven will suffice." Leslie's cat eyes have a fixed stare, waiting for my response.

"I'll knock on your side door at eight.," I say with an arrogant smirk. "And I'll see you at the meeting tonight."

Leslie purses her lips but remains silent. On the way home, it occurs to me. Maybe I shouldn't piss off an Elder witch?

Heavy banging on the back door makes me jump in my kitchen chair. Damn it, Ronnie. She dashes into the kitchen after flinging her shoes. "I'm so excited." Ronnie wraps her boa constrictor arms around me. "You have no idea how many times I wanted to tell you about the coven." She pulls out a chair and sits while I get our lunch.

"I hope you like the veggie wraps," I say, setting them on the table. "I'm not as talented a cook as your chef."

She takes a monstrous bite. "It tastes yummy. I love hummus, but I'm sure you don't wanna talk about the contents of your wraps."

"You got that right." I bite hard into my hummus wrap and chew like a horse.

"About three years ago. I saw an ad posted on the Sunshine Garden Café bulletin board for the Fellowship of Associated Pagans Open House. Spence, Zoe, and Skye were regulars at my restaurant as undergrads. They were such a jovial bunch. Never a frown or a dismal face on any of them ever. One day I asked why they were always so happy?" Ronnie's wrap has a tear, and pieces of cucumber and carrot dump into her lap. "Shit. You'd think a restaurant owner would know to eat over her plate."

A soft sigh sneaks through my lips. "You were saying."

"Oh. Spence said they were pagans. When I saw the Open House posted, I figured, why not go? Find out what it's all about."

I imagine Ronnie attending the Open House. Her vivacious personality fit right in, I'm sure. "That's when you met everyone?"

"Yeah. Everyone except Courtney." Ronnie stops to drink her iced tea. "She joined last year. Audrey recruited her."

"Interesting. I imagined Archie did all the recruiting." Perhaps Audrey felt left out and wanted a close friend in the Fellowship?

"Dr. Hughes asked Archie to come here from the UK because of his ancestral background. He's able to sense when a person has some innate powers that could make them a suitable candidate to learn the skills." She finishes the last bite of her wrap.

"Oh, he sensed you had potential?" He didn't have to sense my potential. He knew I was a dormant witch.

"Yeah. I was drawn to the group organically. He sensed my energy by staring into my eyes one night in a ritual. It was so creepy, but then I thought maybe he was interested in me. I mean, he's hot, but not my type."

I recall Archie's gaze. "Is that why he was staring at me during the Samhain ritual?"

"Probably. He never did it again, but over the year, I noticed weird things happening. I would think about moving something, and mysteriously it shifted. Or I'd have dreams where the situation came true." Ronnie slaps her hands on the table. "It freaked me out!"

"I know what you mean." It's a relief to know why the phenomena happened to me, but it's not reducing my anxiety to be *in the knowing*.

"I suspected I was going crazy. Trauma from the abuse and the divorce. I confided in Archie. We had become friends, and I hoped he wouldn't judge me. He asked me to trust him and showed me his magic space in the basement. On the way down the steps, I surmised, 'yup, he's a serial killer.' When I saw him open a secret panel, I wanted to bolt."

My eyebrows draw together as I look down at my plate. "You've been in his magic space?"

"Oh, yeah. Mind blown. He showed me a simple magic spell. He said the visions and odd occurrences happened because my skills were surfacing after spending time with the Fellowship. It had been about a year." Ronnie notices my downcast eyes.

"Don't be jealous. I mean...you've already been to his real magic space." She goggles at me and cracks up.

I smirk at her and take our plates to the sink. "And you started training after?"

"Yeah. Fantastical!" Ronnie's hands leap into the air. "I shrieked the first time a spell worked!" She observes my sullen face. "You're not saying much. Are you angry with me? You understand why I couldn't tell you, right?"

"No, I'm not mad, but so many secrets. And from you. It's hard to stomach, you know?" Ronnie averts her eyes, but I grasp her hand and smile. "I had the same sort of things happen." I tell her about all the times the amber glow radiated from my hands and my unusual dreams. "The weird sex dream I had? The one I told you about?"

"The morning I had to wake you? Yeah, I remember." She gapes at me and bangs on the table. "Oh, my gods, was Archie in the dream?"

"I don't know for sure, and I didn't tell him about it, but I think so." Should I tell him?

"I hoped the two of you would get together." Ronnie squeezes my hand. "I'm telling the truth when I say I didn't tell anyone about Cassandra."

I gaze at my best friend without a hint of doubt on my face. "I believe you."

"We're forbidden to tell anyone, Gwyn. You can't even tell Tyler." Ronnie leans back in her chair and taps her nails on the table.

Tyler. How will I ever tell him? Has he inherited my family's magic skills? "Yeah, I know. I'm gonna struggle with that. How do you do it? When it's someone you love?" I load our lunch plates into the dishwasher.

"I'm not gonna sugar coat it. It's been more difficult than I imagined. You. Now Derek. It's such a relief you're *in the knowing*, but at some point, I want to tell him. Trinity's wife, Charlie, isn't a witch, and she knows. So, why can't I?"

She's being rhetorical, because how would I know? I get iced tea from the fridge to refill my glass, and an obnoxious hum starts. Great. This entire house is falling apart.

"It's hard to have a relationship. You're the first woman Archie's been with who wasn't openly living as a witch for as long as I've known him. Elijah and Shane don't date much because of it. Skye dates several men at once, so she doesn't get too serious. The other students try to connect with witches in other covens sometimes. Most of the people Archie recruited joined other covens."

"What?" I ask with bulging eyes. "There are other covens?"

"Oh, hon. You need to sit back down."

CHAPTER THIRTEEN

WITCH IN TRAINING

WITCHES. COVENS. THROUGHOUT THE state of Delaware and everywhere. I went about my mundane life without knowledge of them, preoccupied with missing socks and Richard being late for dinner.

The Coven of Bearsden discusses the need to prepare for the next City Council meeting, where the council members will consider the demolition of Mitchell Hall. With the purchase complete, nothing stands in their way except us. The meeting is like every other meeting except for the whole we're-witches-and-we-do-magic thing. Everyone's here except Courtney.

Dr. Hughes taps her Elder staff three times to bring the meeting to order. "It will be necessary to influence their decision. I don't make that recommendation lightly. We preserve our lobbying for the most important issues."

"Normally, I would say it is what it is," Trinity says, "but it's important to preserve the Mitchell's home. They supported us. They were *in the knowing* and never outed us. We owe it to them."

A hand vote decides it. The Coven will lobby the City Council at the next meeting. Archie stands to make an announcement. "At this time, the Nine who will attend the council meeting will remain to practice our strategy."

"Please!" Zoe pops out of her chair. "Let me go this time. I promise I'm ready."

"I appreciate your enthusiasm, Zoe," Archie says with an encouraging smile. "You have made tremendous progress on your levels. In the future, we will consider you when you arrive on time."

Zoe drops into her chair, pouting. Spence gives her a quick hug and she perks up. Audrey sits upright, displaying a bright grin, and waits for her name to be called.

"These members will remain for the strategy practice," Archie says. "Dr. Hughes, Trinity, myself, Elijah, Shane, Tanner, Ronnie, Spence, and...Gwyn."

"What?" I goggle at the leaders of the coven.

Ronnie whispers, "Well, look who's the teacher's pet."

"No!" Audrey stands and roars with tight fists. "That's not fair! She's not even trained! She's a Neophyte! I worked hard, and you promised I would participate in the lobbying at the council meeting."

"Please, sit down, Audrey. I'll explain," Archie says.

I stand to bring attention to myself and interrupt him. "I agree with Audrey. Someone with experience should go. I've never been part of your lobbying efforts."

Archie glares at me and turns his head toward Audrey. "I promised you would join the Nine this time, but Gwyn needs to observe how we handle the city council for future meetings once she's along in her training. I give you my word you will join us in the future."

Audrey sits like she's got a pound of lead in her pants, and a bitter scowl puts a dent in her picture-perfect face. I cringe like the mom who's going to the prom in place of her daughter. "I know I'm new, and you want me to learn the ropes immediately, but I can't let you do this. Not if it means I go in her place. I think—"

"You. Have. No. Say." Leslie punctuates her words in an elevated, raspy voice. "The Elder and Leader decide what is best for the Coven, not the Underlings and Neophytes. It is done."

I sit down as Skye, Zoe, and Audrey leave, a little miffed at the tone of Leslie's voice. According to Ronnie, the Nine is a smaller, focused group of seasoned witches who work together. I have no business being included, but what can I do? We all stack the metal chairs and move to the back room to practice the strategy for their lobbying.

I'm confused. How do you practice lobbying? Do we need to develop talking points in a secret locked room? Once we lock the door, the Nine form a simple circle. I'm waiting for someone to take out a laptop, but they're standing and holding their palms up. Ronnie encourages me to do the same. Are they seriously going to pray for the vote to go their way?

"Gwyn," Archie says. "You don't need to do anything but be part of the energy. Focus in your head on the task at hand."

I pretend to know what the hell he means. Everyone closes their eyes, concentrating on... I have no idea. Not knowing what I'm doing, I glance at Archie, and he's sending a blue eye beam at me like the night of Samhain. I frown at him and wrinkle my nose. He mouths "stop." I try to focus, staring back at his gaze.

He sends me another ray of energy, and a tingling sensation spreads throughout my body. A warm amber glow radiates from my hands, and I stand immobile, wishing for it to end. The radiating energy intensifies, building bigger until—snap! It ends. Spence dances and bumps a hip against Tanner, and Elijah and Shane high-five. What the hell did we do?

"That should do it." Archie's face lights up. "Be careful not to let the energy light get larger than a glow around your hands. I recommend we all wear gloves."

Gloves are going to hide glowing hands? What the hell is he talking about?

"So much easier with Gwyn's energy connected," Trinity says. "Who will speak at the meeting?"

"I don't mind," Elijah says. "I can mention my grandmother's connection with the Mitchells."

"I can speak for the students. I promise I'll dress appropriately this time." Spence pretends to straighten a tie around his neck.

"Try to be early." Trinity puts a fist on her hip and shakes a finger at us. "You know the parking will be a bitch like always."

Leslie clears her throat, and her Elder eyes demand our attention. "Before we disband for the evening. I want to make an important recommendation. Gwyn's intrinsic powers allow us to operate in a more efficient and reliable capacity. From here on, she will be part of the Nine. Her training will progress rapidly. I have no doubts."

Archie shoves his hands in his pockets. "No offense to you, Dr. Hughes, but I promised Audrey she would join the Nine."

"No offense taken. The discussion has ended. Gwyn joins the Nine. See you all on Monday evening." Leslie taps her staff three times, dismissing the coven.

Archie squints at Leslie with a glare of an overruled lawyer. I question the hierarchy of power in the Coven. Archie is the leader, yet Leslie, as the Supreme Elder, gets to overrule any decision he makes.

My eyebrows meet in the middle and contemplate what happened. "Ronnie, I don't wanna sound dumb, but what was the point of that?"

Ronnie elbows me. "You don't need to know. Just come along for the ride."

Later in bed, I can't hold back the mounting questions. "Archie, when you looked at me tonight, did you send your energy to me?"

"More like trying to trigger yours," he says, kissing me on the shoulder. "And it worked."

I twirl his hair around my finger. "I'm confused by what happened. How will producing energy affect the outcome of the vote?"

Archie gawks at me, raising a corner of his mouth. "You'll see."

Tyler hammered me with questions about the Fellowship at Friday's lunch, requiring me to fabricate responses. Lying to my son leaves me nauseous with a side of bitter and sour. Ronnie is right. It's easier for your loved ones to be *in the knowing*. Tyler doesn't even know about Archie. How do I dump the news on him regarding our family history? "Hey, Tyler. So, Nain and Taid were Welsh witches in secret and never told us." He'll be on the phone with the nearest psychiatrist. Better to swallow the vinegar and lemon—and lie.

I enjoy another fabulous dinner at Archie's, but I fumble my utensils during dinner, anticipating my first training. When we're finished, he wipes the counters, and I load the dishwasher. I attempt to place a porcelain dinner plate into a slot and drop it to the floor. "Shit!" Bending over to collect the shards, I cut the palm of my hand. "I'm so sorry."

"I don't care about the plate." Archie grabs a tea towel and rushes to me. "Wrap your hand with this old towel and sit. I'll get my first aid box." The white kitchen towel has pretty peach rosebuds and turns bright red while blood seeps into the fabric. He returns with the box and cleans out the wound.

"You're shaking." He strokes my face. "You have no reason to be nervous. Ronnie will be here."

"I know, but the night of Samhain scared me, and last night, when the energy flowed through my body, I felt out of control. It's all moving too fast. I'm not sure I'm ready to jump into the deep end of the pool."

"I understand." He takes out a sterile pad and gauze from the first-aid kit.

"I've not even seen you do anything with me alone, a spell, a hex, whatever you do." I pretend to perform make-believe magic with my other hand, swirling it all around.

Archie chuckles at my fake magic as he places a sterile pad on my cut. "First of all, we swear to do no harm. We reserve hexes for necessary defense." He wraps my hand in gauze and looks for adhesive tape in the box. "Witchcraft encompasses many levels. You'll begin with divination, which will be easy for you. We only use magic when the situation calls for it."

"OK," I say, but I'm not convinced. My hands are trembling, and the wound stings like a bitch.

He lays his hand on my bandaged palm and stares into my eyes. "Remain still," he says in a monotone voice.

Archie closes his eyes and chants. The unintelligible words soothe me, sending a warm sensation through my body. Great. He's triggering a hot flash. I become dizzy, and my palm burns like I've snatched a hot pan from the stove. His hand glows with the amber energy, squeezing with the strength of a vise-grip. The dizziness worsens, and I'm sure I'll pass out and snap! The energy disappears.

He releases his tight grip and strokes the fleshy part of my palm with his thumb. "Take off the gauze."

"Shouldn't I keep the bandage on for a day or two?"

Archie stares at me with a blank face. "Humor me."

I remove the gauze but leave the blood-soaked pad. When I lift the pad, I find a dark, crusty line on my skin. My mouth drops, and a single drop of drool escapes.

"Healing magic," he says, wiping my drool with the towel. "It's healed enough to keep the bandage off while you train tonight."

My eyes draw together. "But you said you only use magic when it's absolutely necessary."

"Aye," Archie says with a kiss. A thunderous knocking on the front door interrupts our magical moment, and his face lights up. "Must be the tutors." He goes to the door, and I follow him. Spence, Skye, and Ronnie have arrived. They come in and hang their coats on the hall tree.

"I'm so excited, I'm so excited, I'm—" Spence exclaims, shimmying over to me. He attacks me with a bear hug and massages my shoulders like he's getting me ready for a boxing match.

"I get it. You're excited." I chuckle and pat his arm.

Ronnie notices my hand, and her eyes widen. "What happened, Gwyn?"

"I cut my hand on a broken plate," I say, spreading my fingers.

"Looks like someone performed a healing spell." Skye takes my hand and scrutinizes the wound. "And didn't finish." She peers at Archie with disapproving eyes.

Spence pulls at my hand. "Let me see!" After a brief inspection, he grimaces with a humph. "You should have finished it, Archie."

"I decided it was best to let it heal some on its own." He whispers something in Spence's ear out of my earshot. "Spence, get the teapot from the kitchen. If Zoe shows up, I'll send her down. I don't expect Courtney or Audrey to show up tonight. They are both...how should I put it—"

Skye sniggers. "Pissed."

"I imagine," he says, a lopsided smile twisting his mouth.

We follow Archie into the basement on narrow, worn steps. He has to bend his head near the bottom to avoid hitting it. It's damp and musty and full of old furniture pieces and boxes. He walks over to an uneven stack and pushes them aside, revealing a pine door that opens into a well-lit room.

A familiar mix of smells hits me, like Shane's store—cinnamon, rosemary, lavender, and mint. It's a cramped but adequate space for two shelves at the ends of a large worktable and a wall drying rack for hanging herbs. The shelves have bottles, candles, and lots of vintage books with crumbling spines.

"I'll leave you all to your studies." Archie turns to leave. Panic returns to me as he walks away.

"Spence, I'll be right back." I follow Archie out of the room. "You're not staying?"

"No. I don't train. Not until level three. Spence has more patience than most. I'll check in throughout the evening." He plants a quick smooch on my lips. "Stop worrying and have fun."

I return, and my fellow witches are gathering items to grind and mix their spell ingredients. Ronnie and Skye work together while Spence gets me started on divination. "Here, drink this," Spence says. "It's cinnamon tea."

I inhale its intoxicating aroma and slurp a taste. "It's so good."

"Gwyn, the way you drink tea. It's so graceful." Ronnie cackles and snorts.

I cross my arms and blink twice. "As Zoe would say, bite me."

"Oh, my gods," Spence says. "Act more serious about this. Witchcraft performed the wrong way can hurt things or people." He smacks his face and shakes his head, groaning like a frustrated teacher.

Laughing nervously, I grasp his arm. "I'm sorry. I promise I'll concentrate."

"Listen, Gen Xer." Spence crosses his arms. "You may be from this long line of powerful ancestral witches, but right now, you couldn't cast a spell to save your life. Now drink your tea like a good little Neophyte."

I finish the tea while Ronnie and Skye prepare a concoction with the mortar and pestle, grinding herbs and placing them in a round, wooden bowl.

Spence pulls out a black cloth with gold writing on it and a triangular stone hanging on a piece of twine. "Level one starts with divination. You're gonna learn how to use your mind to find answers. The cinnamon tea helps to prime your mind to enhance your psychic powers."

I chuckle and smooth out the wrinkles in my shirt. "Should I drink two?"

Spence explains the cloth has varied writings and symbols on it, but we're going to practice basic yes and no questions. He shows me how to hold the twine in the center of the gold embossed circle, allowing my psychic energy to lead the stone to the answer. I ask a few silly questions, and the stone pulls to the correct answer like the divination cloth has an invisible magnet. I gape at the cloth.

"See," he says, patting my back. "I told ya. You're a natural. Now ask something serious."

I close my mouth and concentrate for a moment, holding the twine over the cloth. "Will Zoe come tonight?" The divination stone takes a hard pull north to YES, and Zoe comes running into the room out of breath, carrying a bright-blue velveteen bag.

"I know I'm late," Zoe huffs. "But I have a good excuse this time! My car ran out of gas. I had to get a ride from one of my Unremarkable friends." Unremarkable friends? That's a terrible thing to say about a friend and not fitting her disposition.

Spence frowns and waves a hand to the floor. "I'll give you a pass, but you know you have to keep gas in your car for it to run, right?"

Zoe distorts her face like she's eaten a lemon and notices me. "Hi, Gwyn!"

"Hi, Zoe." I admire her velveteen tote. "What's in your pretty bag?"

"Lots of pre-made spells." She grins and sets the velveteen bag on the table.

At the other end, Ronnie and Skye chant with their hands over the wooden bowl, waves of amber radiating from their hands, and poof! Flames of yellow and orange burst from the bowl, flickering and reflecting light on their red hair.

"Fire!" Spence yells, but I don't think it's Zillennial slang. "What are you doing?!"

"That's amazing." I'm mesmerized by the magical flames.

"Oops!" Skye and Ronnie crack up as they cover the bowl with a worn piece of canvas.

Not long after, the screeching of the smoke alarm fills the boomy basement, and Archie comes running down the stairs with a thud, thud, thud. "Everything all right in here?" he asks, hyperventilating. "I've said before you have to be careful casting fire spells. My new smoke alarms go off with the slightest presence of smoke."

"Sorry, Archie. We forgot." Ronnie and Skye clench their teeth.

Zoe laughs and points fingers at herself. "Well, at least it wasn't me this time."

"No harm done," he says. "How is our newest recruit fairing?"

Spence pats my back. "Fantastic. Gwyn finished level one already. I suggest she start level two."

"Excellent. Start level two right away. I'm sure she can manage." A proud smile erupts on his face, and I'm filled with an overwhelming sense of joy as he leaves.

"Yo, Fire Twins." Spence glares at them, irritation clutching his face. "No more fire spells here. Work on something else, like a house protection spell or a love spell, not that either of you needs the latter." He bursts out laughing, clutching his abdomen.

"Smartass." Skye flips him the bird, flashing eyes of a serial killer.

Ronnie cackles while she gathers new ingredients. "We'll work on a house protection spell."

"Good. Zoe, come join Gwyn. We'll work on the first spell with her." Spence slides a bowl in front of us. "Why don't we work on something you've started, Zoe? Gwyn can learn the activation part next time."

Zoe dances around. "Yay!" She dashes to my side and dumps the contents of her charming bag.

Several tiny velvet pouches of black, blue, and indigo roll onto the table. None have distinguishable markings on them. Spence's dark-brown eyes are bugging out.

I pick up two bags and examine them. "Are all of those different spells?" I ask.

"Yeah! I couldn't sleep one night, so I used the time to make a bunch! I forgot what they're all for." She pushes her palms up.

I tap my puckered lips. "Not that I know much about spells, but isn't it dangerous to not know what they're for and keep them all together like that?" I stare at Zoe, and she spreads her mouth into a gargantuan, tooth-filled grin.

Spence shakes his head. "Girl, we need to have a serious discussion if you ever want to complete level two."

We spend the rest of the evening creating spell pouches and bottles, taking care to label each one. I get all the chants confused and have no success, melting all the herbs into blobs of wilted brown goop. When our lesson ends, everyone cleans up and departs while I remain in the magic room to practice more. After the fifth and final failure, I call it quits, snarling like a wolf in frustration.

"I'm glad you're so enthusiastic." Archie surprises me from the doorway. "But this was your first lesson. Think how many times you had to practice learning how to ride a bike when you were a small child."

"I'll have you know, I learned to ride on the first push off the curb on my sixth birthday. It was a cruddy blue bike with big tires." I smile, thinking of the beaming expression on my dad's face as I rode off. Would he be as proud of my magic training? I think not.

Archie exhales and checks the time on his cell phone. "All right. Poor analogy, but do you understand what I'm trying to say?"

"Yeah. I only wish I had more control over what I'm doing." I puff and stare at the mess in the wooden bowl. "It's scary, otherwise."

He raises an eyebrow and chuckles. "Scary for us, too."

"Very funny." I frown at him with the look of a failing student.

Archie saunters toward me. "Put your hands up. We're going to connect our energies. Casting spells isn't about summoning your energy. It's about intention. The intention is the heart of your magic."

I raise my hands, palms facing him, and he places his large hands against mine. His touch, always warm, triggers my heart to beat faster. I almost hear its faint thumping in the silence. "Close your eyes," he says in a calm, husky voice.

I sense the warmth of his breath on my face and the scent of Scotch whisky. I open one eye to peek and chuckle at the serious expression on his face.

"Be serious, Gwyn." Archie's shoulders fall as he mutters. "Stubborn woman." He gestures down with two fingers for me to close my eyes, and I comply. "Listen to your breathing. The pulse of your heart."

This time, I focus on the inner hissing of my breath and the beating of my heart. A warm tingling spreads from my torso through my limbs, a fever without the aches and pain. I fill my lungs and blow out, but I can't control the rhythm of it. "Archie. I've gotta stop. I'm having a hot flash."

He murmurs as his hot breath ignites my skin. "It's not a hot flash, Gwynedd. Open your eyes."

When my lids lift, a glowing amber light radiates from our hands and bodies. I'm trembling like a frightened animal ready to dart.

"Don't be frightened," he whispers in a gruff voice. "Slow your breathing. Embrace it." He slides a hand up my arm, never breaking the touch, until he arrives at my rounded shoulder. His mouth parts as he slides his hand over my breast, stroking my nipple without touching it, and the tingling turns to arousal.

My body tenses, and my legs rub together. "If this is foreplay, the orgasm is gonna kill me."

"Gwyn," he says with a breathy laugh. "Stop your nervous chatter."

His lips hover over mine with light caresses as his hand brushes my belly and slinks to my inner thigh. He guides me to amble back toward the pile of meditation pillows in the corner, and we fall, landing on a cushion of air. Taking care not to break the connection, he removes my clothing piece by piece until I'm lying naked.

Existing in a fog of warm, amber glow, his light non-touch explores every surface of my body while raising the deepest senses of my soul. The arousal multiplies until it becomes a pleasure short of torment. I'm so relieved we're in the magic room. In the basement, no one can hear me scream.

CHAPTER FOURTEEN

PRACTICING MAGIC

DRUMMOND LANE HAS MAJESTIC, mature trees with leaves of mustard and persimmon, dropping with a steady patter on the lawns and sidewalks. I shiver on Leslie's stoop as the fall gusts blow my hair. I stuff my hands in the pockets of my hoodie, and a naughty smile stretches my face when I recall the antics in Archie's secret room. If his objective was to make me comfortable with my magic, mission accomplished, and bonus points for the way he achieved it.

Leslie answers the door, her Elder witch face on display—arrogant and emotionless.

"So glad you came," Leslie says, a smile fighting to surface. She walks into the kitchen, and I follow her.

My eyes jump around the kitchen. "You said you wanted to show me something."

"Yes." Leslie's face becomes animated, like she's got a secret to tell me. "Follow me to the office."

Upon entering, I notice the room shows signs of cleaning. "Did you get someone else to organize your books?"

Leslie stares at me with a placid face. "No." She stands by the cabinet in the corner and motions to me. "You will need a space to hone your skills. Practicing at Archie's during instruction serves a function, but you need a work area without...distractions."

I don't appreciate her judgmental tone. Leslie grasps the edges of the cabinet and slides it to the left, revealing a doorway into a hidden room. "Your magic room, I assume?" I take a peek.

Leslie folds her hands. "Yes. I imagined it would be difficult for you to have one in your home with Tyler not yet *in the knowing*."

"Probably would be best." I dread the day I have to tell Tyler, but it's inevitable. "Plus, I need to sell it. I'm hoping to list the house in the spring."

"Splendid." Mr. Yeats scuttles into the office, attempting a quick slip past us into the magic room. Leslie sticks her foot out in front of him. "No! Mr. Yeats." She picks him up and turns him around. "Never let Mr. Yeats into the magic room. He makes a mess. Can you remember that?"

"Sure." I stroke my hand across Mr. Yeats's furry back. He purrs and scuttles out of the office.

I follow Leslie into the room where she practices witchcraft. From the exterior, this room is a lean-to shed off the back of her house. No one would ever know its true purpose. Like her book hoarder office, this room has an abundance of items—various size bottles, hanging baskets of dried herbs, crystals, and bones. There's a long table cluttered with wooden bowls, mortars and pestles, a cutting board with knives, a crystal ball, and an immense grimoire bound in leather.

After showing me tricks to concoct effective spells, she holds out an open palm with a house key in it. "What's the key for?" I ask.

"It's the key to my kitchen door." Leslie raises her chin. "For you to practice whenever you have the time."

I hesitate, thinking it may be another ruse to suck me further into their shrouded world, but I take it. "Thank you, Leslie."

Agnes Pritchard, Bearsden's out-of-the-closet witch, skulks around the store in her black cardigan and floor-length skirt, picking items at random. She sniffs at herbs, grumbles, and puts them back. Shane says she never steals, but being new to all this witchery, I'm inclined to not trust her. It's five minutes to closing, and she's still not come to the counter. I arrange the pens in the skull cup, waiting for Shane to arrive and kick her eccentric ass out.

"Is there anything special you're looking for, Ms. Pritchard?" I ask, tapping my fingernails on the counter.

Agnes sends a glaring stink eye in my direction. "Nooo." Her long, salt and pepper hair hangs in different lengths, with shorter strands swooping across her face. It's impossible to discern her features other than a short, narrow nose and some tattoos on her wrinkled arms. It's no surprise kids make fun of her for being a witch.

The new bamboo door chimes clank when Shane enters wearing jeans and a black hoodie showing the phases of the moon across the front. "Nice to see you, Agnes. You've got one minute before I lock you in!"

"Hmph." She throws the cinnamon sticks back in the basket. "I'll come back tomorrow." She makes her way to the door, sliding her feet, and exits.

"Aghh." Shane locks the door behind her, and I press my face into a pucker. "That woman makes me want to tear my hair out!"

Shane laughs, pulling at his beard. "She's an odd one, for sure. We've tried multiple times to invite her back to the coven.

Leslie says she's been a hermit for years after dropping out back in the late '60s. There's a history there Leslie never talks about."

"She doesn't appear to be the collaborative type," I say with a hint of sarcasm.

"For sure." He scratches the bald spot on his head. "How would you like a swift lesson on the use of crystals? We all have our specialties, and crystals and stones are a love of mine."

"Sure." I flip the sign from open to closed and follow him to the crystal room, expecting him to show me the secret to the scheme he has installed. Standing over the large, vertical crystal display, I wave my hands, and they light up as they did the first time. I snicker at Shane's sham. "At least tell me what you have connected to these."

Shane cocks his head and pets the whiskers on his face. "Nothing, Gwyn. You're lighting them, darling."

I stare at the glittering crystals. "I don't understand. My energy causes them to light up?"

"Of course. Without an intention, you're igniting them without purpose, so to speak. You must concentrate on an intentional use in a spell or ritual to be effective. I sell the large crystals mostly to Unremarkables. I charge way more than I should, but they buy them anyway. You're better off having a small box with a collection of many. They don't have to be fancy."

I lean my head. "Zoe used that term, Unremarkables. Who are they?"

Shane's yellowed teeth peek through the billows of white. "You, darling, before Samhain."

"Oh," I say when the bulb lights in my head. "People who aren't *in the knowing* like my son Tyler."

"Yes, ma'am," Shane says. "As you were a short time ago."

"Are there other non-witches who are *in the knowing* like the Mitchells were?"

"A few." He looks away and shoves his hands in the back pockets of his cargo pants. "We're gonna run out of time. Come to the storage area, and I'll give you an expeditious tutorial on crystals and stones."

In the storage area, Shane pulls out an old cigar box full of crystals and stones of various colors—rough and smooth. "Amethyst crystals aid in psychic abilities, and this yellow citrine quartz helps in the remembrance of dreams. We use the rose quartz for healing in the home or when suffering a significant loss in your life." He puts his hand on my shoulder. "You may want to start with rose quartz."

"OK." I lower my eyes, but I'm thankful for his fatherly concern.

"Oh, the clear crystal!" Shane exclaims with a clap. "This is the most important one you can own. It boosts the powers of everything else you're using. Herbs, bones, and other crystals. It's great for protection spells. The malachite provides protection, too. Carry it with you to help sense danger. The white one is Moonstone. You can use it in place of some others, but it aids in recalling dreams and intensifies intuition. So, carrying a couple of these in your purse can be very handy."

I glimpse the time on my phone. "Thanks for the short tutorial, but I better get home. It's already dark."

Shane hands me the cigar box. "Take them. You can add to the collection with your own. Discover what works for you."

"Thank you, Shane." I tear up at the gift of crystals and give him a brief hug. "I'll see you on Wednesday."

"Anytime, darling."

A storm has rolled in, and I throw on my hood to cover my hair. I walk at my usual brisk pace, hoping to arrive home by 7:00 p.m. to eat a late dinner. As I pass the Raven Pub, the front door opens, allowing the smell of fresh popcorn to escape into the night. I haven't been there in ages. Perhaps Archie and I could eat there one night? My stomach grumbles and roars as I quicken my pace until I catch sight of those damned blond-haired children sneaking into the Mitchell's gardens again. I need to talk with them and call their parents.

I search all over the gardens but can't find the delinquents. They poke their heads from behind a concrete bench, and I finally make out their faces, lit by shimmering moonbeams. They have peachy skin with pretty, mint-green eyes and delicate features. Hard to find fault with those sweet faces. They wave at me and run to the mound, giggling. By the time I rush there, they've disappeared. Damn it.

In a cold instant, a deep growl like that of a rabid dog crops up behind me, and my heart races like a sprinter breaking out in the last corner. I turn around, taking baby steps to rotate but find no dog. The arm-like limbs of the hawthorn tree flail with a sudden blast of wind, inviting me to its creepy hollow. An unexplainable foreboding permeates my entire body, and I clutch the box of crystals and stones close to my heart.

Rotting flesh enters my nostrils, reminiscent of the night I fell at the Old Men oaks, and I grapple with the urge to vomit. I walk backward, afraid to turn around. The arm-like branches swoop fallen leaves to its trunk and collect them in a pile. When I back into the water fountain, I shriek and run out through the gate to the sidewalk, slipping on the wet pavement and landing on my ass. I stand and wipe the wet leaves off my jeans as I steady my breathing. What an eerie place. It's certainly not appropriate for young children.

CHAPTER FIFTEEN

ETHICS OF A COVEN

MAYOR TRAVIS MANLEY, THE misogynistic, middle-aged turd who won the election last fall, sits at the center of the council chamber desk, his stubby fingers checking the strands of his long comb-over that's not fooling anyone. His friends on the council sit to the right of him—Patrick Rivera, Randy Palmer, and Lindsey Hope.

The mayor owns a local lumber franchise and had the backing of commercial developers in downtown Bearsden, a conflict of interest, but he still got enough votes to beat Jessica Devine, a sitting councilwoman in her 60s with a long history of commitment to the community. She sits to the left of Mayor Manley along with Corey Jones and Jeremiah Jackson, the new members elected to fight overdevelopment on Main Street.

In the historical, red brick building at the east end of Main Street, the Bearsden Council Chamber doesn't have an empty seat, and members of the community spill out into the hallway. Elijah speaks during the public comments portion of the agenda, highlighting the time his grandmother spent running the Mitchell's Art Foundation. Shane follows him, stressing the importance of preserving one of the oldest buildings in

Bearsden to honor the Mitchells, and introduces the idea of transforming Mitchell Hall into a community center. The entire room erupts into deafening applause.

Spence, the last speaker, represents the Delaware University students. He kept his promise to dress appropriately in a lavender dress shirt and tie with dress pants. As expected, his lively and humorous storytelling of past Mitchell Hall open houses had everyone in stitches, even the mayor and his cronies.

Archie signals the Nine to prepare their energy ring, except we're sitting in a row, not a circle. Leslie sits at the far end, keeping her Elder witch eye on me. We must appear odd wearing gloves inside, but the November chill provides an adequate cover. Mayor Manley thanks everyone for speaking and announces they will proceed with the vote.

"Before the council votes," Mayor Manley says. "I want to be clear. We have heard all your comments and will take them into consideration. Be aware as elected council members, we must vote our conscience to do what is best for the city of Bearsden." Sure, Mayor "buy-me-with-a-few-dollars" Manley. Jessica Devine, the former mayoral candidate, raises her hand. "Yes, Mrs. Devine?" the mayor asks.

Jessica Devine has delicate facial features with light-brown hair, a kind temperament, and a sweet voice. "Personally, I find the number of community comments this evening overwhelming and would prefer to postpone the vote on the fate of Mitchell Hall until the first meeting in December. With Thanksgiving in a couple of weeks, that would allow us time to discuss this matter in an executive meeting before a public vote." She sits straight in her chair with a confident air.

"I second the motion," Jeremiah Jackson says. A soft-spoken, Black man in his forties, he owns and runs Mickey's Diner, an icon established by his father in the '50s.

The crowd in the room bursts into a boisterous uproar, stamping their feet. Mayor Manley pushes his nose up and his mouth down, forming the frown of the century, and hammers his gavel several times in an attempt to control the crowd. "Order!" the mayor shouts. "Order!"

The gaggle of city residents calms to minimal chitter-chatter, and the mayor continues. "Because we have a motion, we will vote on whether to delay the vote on the Mitchell Hall demolition. All those who vote yes to delay the vote on the Mitchell Hall demolition raise your hand."

Jessica Devine, Corey Jones, and Jeremiah Jackson raise their hands high into the air, and the chamber deflates into moans and sighs, knowing the measure will not pass. The corners of my mouth droop.

Noticing the disappointment on my face, Archie whispers in my ear. "Don't despair. It's not over yet."

"I don't get it," I whisper to Ronnie on my other side. "Does Archie not see we've lost?"

A nefarious smile has captured Ronnie's mouth. "Wait. We are only getting started."

The Nine activate their witch energy, hiding the amber glow within their gloves. The energy from the other eight witches stimulates the surge in my body, and I'm trapped within it. People chant deep inside my head, words I can't decipher, buzzing like an invasion of an insect alien race.

Mayor Manley proceeds with the vote. "All those who vote no to delay the vote on Mitchell Hall, raise your hand." The mayor and his cronies all lift their hands except for Lindsey Hope. Her arms rest on the chamber desk with one hand bent up. "Ms. Hope?" he asks. "Are you voting no?"

Lindsey Hope struggles to speak. "I...I wanna say no, but I can't."

Everyone in the chamber leans forward in their seats, hanging onto the words of Lindsey Hope and sneering at the mayor. "What are you saying? Why can't you vote no?!" Mayor Manley asks in a gruff voice.

"I don't know." She whines, wrestling to raise her arm as if she's pushing against a stack of cinderblock. "I can't make myself do it. I guess my vote is yes."

The community explodes with squeals of joy and thunderous clapping. The mayor adjourns the meeting in a huff and announces the vote on the demolition of Mitchell Hall will be determined at the first meeting in December.

As the Council Chamber empties, the Nine witches congregate on the paver sidewalk in front of the town hall, congratulating each other on a job well done. A few of us remain to discuss the specifics of the outcome. Leslie stands, revealing a crack of a smile on her usual expressionless face. She's been silent through this entire farce.

Trinity bobs her head and motions to me. "We can thank Gwyn. Adding her energy was the winning ticket."

"It was never this easy before." Ronnie nudges me. "I'm so happy you're with us now, friend."

My eyes hop from Ronnie's face to the others, stopping at Archie. "I don't understand. What did we do?" I search his face for an honest answer.

"You really don't know?" Archie cocks his head and strands of hair slip onto his forehead.

I push my shoulders up. Sorry. I'm clueless. "No. I don't." I glare at them, wearing a for-fuck's-sake-tell-me frown. "Is someone gonna explain it to me?"

"I will," Trinity says, peering at Archie. "Someone should have told you what we were doing instead of trying to impress you with it. We used our energy as a group to cast a spell of influence. This time, on Lindsey Hope."

My mouth drops to the pavement. I lower my voice and speak so fast the words run together like one big word. "We made Lindsey Hope vote yes? That's not ethical!"

"And you think they're ethical?" Archie asks, narrowing his eyes.

Ronnie speaks up for all of them with a defensive tone in her voice. "Archie's right. They're corrupt."

"You've done this before?" I mash my teeth together. Ronnie and Archie should have told me. I had no idea their work included controlling people.

Trinity puts her fists on her hips. "Before you go getting on your high horse, you should know that corrupt crew pockets money from developers to sway their votes, only to fill their coffers. You think that's ethical?"

"Well, no," I concede. "But we should have at least tried to sway her with all the community support we had."

"And the mansion would be lost." Archie searches for approval on my disappointed face and brushes his locks back.

Breaking her silence, the Elder witch praises us. "Excellent work. You should all sleep well tonight. We will meet as usual on Thursday. Goodnight, everyone."

When we arrive at Archie's, I don't utter a word, and he lets me be mad. I get out of his Tesla and walk to my Prius.

"You're going home?" he asks, tiptoeing on eggshells—more like tiptoeing in a minefield.

I turn to face him, deciding I can't end the night on such a sour note. "I think so. You should have explained what we were doing. Give me time to process it."

"You're right." Archie breathes in a pocket of air and holds it briefly. "I anticipated the outcome would make you happy. It didn't occur to me you would find fault with our method of persuasion."

"I'm happy they're not tearing down Mitchell Hall just yet, but I don't like secrets." Richard's infidelities gnaw at me like a dog gnaws on its leash. "I've had enough of that."

"I know you have. I'm sorry." Archie caresses my hand. "Stay tonight?"

"I can't. Tyler is stopping by tomorrow for lunch. I haven't seen him much recently, and he still worries about me."

"I understand. Family is important." He plants a tender kiss on my lips, being careful not to set off any hidden bombs. "Sleep well, Gwynedd."

Having a normal conversation with Tyler presents a challenge, because I can't discuss the whole I'm-secretly-a-witch-in-a-coven thing. And keeping secrets from him requires me to be a better liar, not a skill I relish honing. I've barely touched my wrap, nibbling at it like a bunny.

"Mom, are you feeling OK? You haven't eaten much." Tyler takes a bite of his PB and J, scrutinizing my reaction. "Are you mad I didn't call recently?"

"No, I'm preoccupied." I gaze into his hazel eyes, noticing his chestnut hair has grown past the collar of his shirt. The longer hair suits him. "I have something to discuss with you."

Air escapes the sides of Tyler's mouth. "Please don't ask me about dating. When I meet a person I like, I'll let you know. I promise."

I shake my head and pat his hand. "No, it's not that. I'm thinking about dating. Get out there and move on. Be honest with me. Would it bother you?"

"You deserve to be happy. Go for it. And if you're dating, maybe you won't hound me." He gawks at me and sniggers.

"I get the hint. How does a woman even find dates at my age?" I hate this charade, but I can't tell him about Archie yet.

"Hell, if I know. I have trouble. It's all about work for now, but I'm sure you'll figure it out. You're smart and pretty, Mom. The right man will find you attractive and snatch you up."

I blush at my son's compliment. "Did you ever attend parties at Mitchell Hall during college?"

"Oh, yeah. Didn't you?" Tyler gets up from his chair, slides on his old DUB hoodie, and heads to the mudroom to put on his shoes.

I follow him to say goodbye. "No. Your dad never wanted to go."

"Wow, I don't know anyone from college who didn't attend at least one party at Mitchell Hall." He opens the door. "They were an awesome, old couple."

Yes. I bet they were.

I'm dusting the crystal display at Mystical Sage when Audrey Kenilworth enters, bundled in a navy wool pea coat with a DUB plaid scarf and mittens. She casts her gaze toward the bottled herbs when I walk into the front of the store. How do I approach her over the situation with the Nine? She has a right to be offended.

After collecting a few items, Audrey dumps them on the glass counter. She drops her eco bag, and I ring her up. "I hear Monday night's lobbying proved successful."

"Yes," I say as I place the herbs in her bag. "The community seems pretty damn happy about it, too."

She stares out the front display window at busy Main Street, already decorated for the holiday season.

"Audrey, I feel awful about Leslie's decision. Being new to all of this, I reasoned it wasn't wise to argue with her. In the future, I won't let it happen again. You should be part of the December Council Meeting." I hand the eco bag to her.

"Thank you for saying that. It still stings." She stares at the counter and sucks in her bottom lip. "I'm going to practice meditation later, using crystal energy. Why don't you stop by my apartment? It helps with stress, and I don't mind showing you."

I grin with the face of a proud mom. "That sounds great. I can come when Shane gets back."

Audrey forces a smile and leaves. It's promising she's willing to put her anger aside and work on our relationship, but I've got to have a mom-daughter talk with her about her social skills.

Shane returns a little earlier than planned, having delivered some special items to Ms. Pritchard. I poke fun at her order. "What was in her bag? Eye of newt and toe of frog, wool of bat and tongue of dog?" I snort.

"Close, darling." He gives me a friendly hug. "It contained mustard seed, buttercup petals, holly leaves, and hound's tongue plant. You know those disgusting sounding ingredients are alternative witch names for plants?"

"Oh." I roll my eyes. "I feel stupid. There's so much witch stuff I don't know."

"Nonsense, darling." He pats my arm. "You have much to learn, but I suggest you reread Macbeth." He bursts out laughing, and for a moment, resembles Santa Claus in a Hawaiian-print shirt.

"Would you mind if I left early? Audrey stopped by and invited me to practice meditation with crystals."

"That sounds wonderful. Better you get a sprinkling of training from everyone. Each witch has a unique specialty, an area of excellence, if you will."

I clutch my purse. "Thanks, Shane. I'd like to build our relationship. It's hard not having parents to support you."

"Audrey tries to belong, but it seems so forced. Maybe you can get her to—what do the young folk say—chillax?"

After a rhythmic knock on the door, Audrey invites me in. I notice she's been living with a few pieces of furniture. True to her story, her parents have done nothing to help. The perfect facade is a cover for a poor, lonely life, and I point it out. "You need a sofa." I bite my tongue immediately. It was an insensitive comment from my foot-in-mouth gaucheness.

"Yes, I do," she says, frowning, "but I have some floor pillows. They're great for meditation. Follow me. They're in the corner of my living room."

Audrey shows me how to set up and relax, allowing the muscles to loosen to piles of mush, but I'm as tight as an over-wound old clock. And it's not like she's the best role model. I find my inability to empty my head quite amusing, and I chuckle.

"Gwyn, you have to be serious," Audrey says. "What are you snickering about, anyway?"

"Oh, nothing." I close my eyes this time and concentrate on using my inner energy, enhanced by a clear crystal she loaned me. While I listen to my breathing, the crystal has a calming effect. I enjoy the floating, hypnotic trance for about ten minutes.

In the middle of this lovely calm, she insists on trying to carry on a conversation and talks in a subdued, spellbinding voice. "So, you never knew your parents were witches?"

"No. Nothing at all," I reply in a breathy voice. I'm floating inside on the ripples of waves toward a beach of white sand. I think it's Wales.

Deep in my trance, she interrupts my calm again. "What part of Wales was their homeland?"

"I don't know." How am I supposed to meditate if you keep asking me questions?

She's relentless, and the images dissipate with her intrusions. "Did you find any references to magic in their possessions?"

"No, but I haven't gone through all the boxes in storage." This conversation is bizarre when we're supposed to be concentrating on inner healing. A tendon pulls in my neck and snap! I come out of my trance-like meditation with a kink in my neck.

Audrey looks all around the room, grimacing.

"I'm sorry." As I massage my neck, I conclude I suck at meditation. "I'm having a difficult time relaxing recently, but for a few moments, I experienced a calmness. Thanks so much for trying. I'll have to practice this on my own."

"Maybe next time, you'll do better," she says, offering a sweet smile—wow, she has one.

I slip on my fleece jacket, scarf, and gloves and head to the door. "Before I go, I want you to know if you ever need the support of family, you can depend on me like a mom. I care about you."

Audrey's dark, almost demon-like eyes tear up, and I wrap my arms around her stiff body. "I'll see you tomorrow night at the Fellowship."

"You know you can call it what it is, right? It's the Coven of Bearsden." She chuckles, wiping tears from her eyes.

I roll my eyes. "Right."

CHAPTER SIXTEEN

THE
INCOMPARABLE
MR. YEATS

WITH TIME TO KILL before I meet Archie for dinner, I decide to take up Leslie's offer to practice my magic skills at her home. On the nippy walk to her house, I'm stressing over our first night out, because I haven't told Tyler about him yet. Maybe we can get a seat in the back?

Opening Leslie's side door requires the ceremonious push of the hip to jar it open. She must have office hours, which suits me fine. I'd rather not have her lurking over my shoulder. I drop my fleece jacket, scarf, and gloves into a living room chair and walk back to the magic room. Mr. Yeats greets me with a swipe of my leg, and I stroke his back, sliding my palm over his fuzzy tail. I push the cabinet to the left, and he tries to sneak past me.

"Oh, no, you don't!" I lift Mr. Yeats and turn him around, nudging him to leave the office. He scuttles up the hallway, and a faint meow echoes in the distance.

After an hour of failed spells and near mishaps, I call it quits. I don't have a clue what I'm doing and have so much to learn. If only my parents had taught me. And why didn't they? Should I even be doing this? While cleaning up, I knock a bottle of a dried, brownish herb over, and the cork falls out, emptying half the contents onto the table. "Shit."

I push the cabinet aside and hurry into the mudroom, searching for a dustpan and brush, and find them in seconds. Rushing back to the room, I flinch when Mr. Yeats hisses at me like a lion from the wooden chair in the corner. "Agh! I can't deal with you right now. I've got to clean this up. Be good and don't make a mess." But how much of a mess can Mr. Yeats make while I put the crushed herb back in its bottle? I collect most of it but have trouble with the last few granules.

"I'll have to tell Dr. Hughes you spilled her blessed mugwort."

I freeze. My heart palpitates, and air stagnates in my lungs. It's a masculine voice with a distinctive Irish accent. I turn to find a man in a dark-gray, three-piece suit. He's sitting in the corner chair with his arms and legs crossed, wearing antique spectacles. I want so badly to expel a blood-curdling scream, but I can't breathe.

He stands and straightens his fluffy, black bow tie, smoothing out the wrinkles in his antiquated coat and trousers. Walking toward me with his hands folded behind his back, he appears agitated. He leans into my face, ogling me through his spectacles, and whispers, "Boo."

The blood-curdling scream breaks free with the loudest shriek I've ever yelled. I dart out of the magic room like I'm running from a mugger and roll-slam the cabinet door closed. I fumble, trying to pull my cell phone from my jeans pocket, and call Archie. It goes to his voice mail. Damn! He must be in a faculty meeting.

"Archie! There is an Irishman in Leslie's magic room! I don't know what to do! Should I call the police? Oh, wait. I can't call the police. He might be a homeless person with dementia and wandered in here—" And it dawns on me. The doors were locked. "I don't know how he got in, but he's got on an old three-piece suit and antique glasses. So strange, and he's got odd eyes, one yellow and one blue." I pause. "Never mind. See you at dinner."

I shove my cell into my pocket and walk back to the office. Peeking through the doorway, I discern no evidence of the cat or the man. I tiptoe to the cabinet and place both of my hands on the edge of the secret cabinet door. With a swift pull, I roll it open and jump at the sight of the slender man waiting at the door for my return. I push up on my tippy toes and stare through his spectacles, glimpsing the yellow and powder-blue eyes. "Mr. Yeats?"

"Who else would I be?" Mr. Yeats adjusts the spectacles on his nose. His demeanor, stiff like his collared shirt, has the air of an elite. He wears his short, dark-brown hair parted off-center and has a narrow jawline with a pointed chin and pouty lips. A straight, pointy nose protrudes from the center of his pale face, and thick eyebrows sit atop his spectacles. The suit resembles the fashion of the 1900s.

"So, THIS is why Leslie didn't want me to let you in here. She didn't want me to know you can change into human form. You're a... What's the word?"

"Familiar, and Dr. Hughes is the proper way to refer to her, Ms. Crowther." His yellow eye twitches. "And I'm sure I don't know her motivation." He moves to the table and uses a folded piece of paper to sweep the remainder of the mugwort and deposits it in the bottle, topping it with a cork.

"I'm not sure I understand what a familiar is exactly. How does it work?" I ask.

"A familiar is a spirit helper, a witch's assistant in preparing magic." Mr. Yeats tidies up the magic table while keeping a cat eye on me. "Therefore, I am Dr. Hughes's magic assistant."

I cross my arms and send him a condescending smirk. "But you're a cat."

Mr. Yeats purses his lips. "Transforming into a cat allows me greater freedom. It's easier to sneak in and out of places. When I'm permitted, of course."

I glance at a pile of books on Leslie's desk. "Are you the one cleaning Leslie's office?"

"When she allows it. Yes." Moving to the office, he picks up books and reads their spines.

I follow him into the office with a piqued interest. "Oh, you can leave the magic room and keep a human form?"

"For a time." He blows dust off a book and glares at me through his spectacles. "You ask too many questions."

"I have a lot more, but I'll wait until the next time I come to practice the craft." With his back to me, I sneak into the magic room and snatch my purse, rolling the cabinet to close off the room.

Mr. Yeats turns around with the look of someone insulted and pissed off. "Now, why did you do that? I won't be able—"

"To get in?" I ask. "Ha! You can't move the cabinet. Can you leave the house in human form?"

He crosses his arms and presses his lips together so tight, they disappear. "No."

"Good. Then I can leave." I exhale and wipe my face. The shock of meeting Mr. Yeats has left me scatter-brained, so I check my purse and pockets, making sure I've got all my belongings. "I'm meeting someone for dinner."

"A Dr. Cockburn, I surmise." He pulls a handkerchief from his pocket, blows hot air on the glass of his spectacles, and cleans some smudges.

I frown as I examine his nosey face. "Has Leslie been talking to you about us?"

"She tells me EVERYTHING." He returns his spectacles to the bridge of his nose. "And her name is Dr. Hughes."

The walls of the Raven Pub have a mixture of exposed brick and walnut-stained wood, and I check the tables around us for people who might know me. Archie sits on the side of the booth, facing away from the entrance, while I sit opposite him, eyeing every person who enters the back room. He chuckles under his breath as I share every detail of meeting Mr. Yeats's alter ego during our meal. "Go ahead and laugh," I say, picking at my fries. "It scared the living shit out of me. I almost called the cops."

Archie smiles at me, squinting. "I'm sorry. Good, you didn't. How would you have explained it? And Leslie? There would have been hell to pay. If she believed in hell, of course."

"It's so strange. Do you know how many times I petted his back and tail? Allowed him to sit on my lap or rub against my leg? Eww." I shudder all over.

He gives the waiter his credit card. "Do not underestimate Mr. Yeats. He's a familiar and can be a wee mischievous."

"Why keep it a secret from me? One of you should have warned me, so I was prepared." I'm so annoyed at the secrecy in the coven.

"Ah, that's always a tough decision to make." Archie sways his head. "How much to reveal to a recruit and not have the person freak out?"

My eyes slump to the table. "I get that, but you should have trusted me."

"Aye. But you've had trauma and weren't supposed to know about any of this for months, giving you time to adjust." He places his soft hand on mine. "When I first met you, you weren't the vision of strength."

I gaze into his icy blues and tip my head. "And now?"

"You turned out to be a lot stronger than anyone perceived." He leans forward and stares into my eyes. "You need to have faith in yourself and your magic."

A woman with short, brown hair walks into our dining area with a drink in her hand. A huge grin emerges on her face when she glimpses Archie. He notices her and flinches. "Excuse me for a minute, Gwyn."

Archie gets up from the table and walks over to the woman. She kisses his cheek, prattles on about something, and grabs his phone, entering something into it. He notices my gaze and cuts the conversation short. The woman scowls. She strokes his goatee and struts back to her table, where another woman is waiting for her, and he returns to our booth.

"Who was she?" I ask.

Archie inhales, holding it for a moment. "A former doctoral student. Says she has some research she would like me to review."

"That's nice of you." Why am I so jealous? We've only been together for a short time.

Archie plays with the popcorn kernels in the basket, and the memories of my visits to the Celestial Gardens pop into my head. The visits trouble me, and I'm worried the experiences were more than my imagination playing tricks on me. Maybe I should tell him? He'll think I'm a worrywart for nothing, anyway.

"You're quiet. Something on your mind?" Archie slides the popcorn basket aside and reaches for my hand.

My eyes fling back and forth from my empty plate to his icy blues. "Yes. On my walks home, I snuck into the Celestial Gardens a few times. I caught a couple of small children playing around in there after dark."

"Go on." Archie scratches at the whiskers of his goatee while I recount my visit.

"I tried to run after them a few times, but they sneaked past me somehow. On Saturday after Samhain, I got a good look at them and their faces. They ran behind the mound. I ran after them, but when I got there, they had disappeared."

Archie rests back on the wooden booth, a crease developing between his eyes. "What were their features?"

"Unusual. They had blond hair, golden like the sun. Peachy skin. And this was the freaky part. Mint-green irises. I've never seen eyes like them before."

"And they disappeared into the mound," he says with an expressionless face.

"I didn't say that." His eyes wrinkle with worry, and my lips part. "No. You're saying that." I look around for our waiter. "I need a drink."

Archie crouches over the table. "There is more to explain, but not here. We can drink at my place."

"I'm not done," I say, leaning on the table. "I heard a growling like a dog, but I turned around and—no dog. Only the eerie hawthorn tree, sweeping its branches violently in the wind. It reminded me of the night I fell near the Old Men oak trees. Or was I tripped? I've lost all sense of reality since Samhain."

"You haven't." He wraps his firm hands around mine. "You should have told me about the children when it happened, especially the incident with the hawthorn tree. We should go."

"I wish my parents had told me about all of this. Maybe I wouldn't feel so lost and paranoid. I wish—" My jaw snaps open. "Shit."

Archie looks to the right and left. "What's wrong?"

My face flushes, and a hand contracts into a fist. "That bitch Cassandra walked in here with a friend. I haven't seen her since—"

"Who is Cassandra?" Archie gapes at the realization. "Oh, she's the woman your husband—"

"Fucked." I snarl, grinding my teeth. "I can't face her. She humiliated me in front of my family. I've got to get out of here without her noticing me."

Archie picks up his leather jacket and slips an arm into a sleeve. "Put on your coat, and we'll dash out of here now."

I wrap my DUB plaid scarf around my neck, covering a bit of my face. Archie grasps my hand, and we move like the wind to slip past Cassandra.

"Gwynedd Crowther?" asks the woman with a whiny, nasal voice.

Archie pleads with me, pulling at my arm. "Don't stop, Gwyn."

But I do. I turn and glare at her with the intensity of a nuclear bomb. She still looks tacky as ever. "What do you want?"

"You're here with a man?" Cassandra asks in an accusatory tone. "Richard's not even been gone a year, and you're dating? That's how you honor him?"

"Yes. I'm with this man, and I'm happier than I ever was with Richard." I grind my teeth to stop myself from ranting, choosing a few rational words instead. "Honor him? He didn't earn it."

"No wonder he was with me." Cassandra's head jerks from side to side. "You're a...you're a witch!"

I glimpse Archie, and his head quivers no, but I can't stop myself. I smirk at Cassandra and say, "Thank you."

CHAPTER SEVENTEEN

JUST A LITTLE FAE INVASION

ARCHIE SAYS THE SCOTS refer to the fairy visitors as the Seelie and Unseelie Court. The damn folklore turns out to have some teeth in its stories, but the children of Seelie Fae don't scare me. Wish I could say the same about the Unseelie. He asked me not to share my experiences with anyone. I try to act normal in class and share the discovery of Mr. Yeats's alter ego with my Zillennial friends.

"I wish I'd been a fly on the wall." Skye pretends to adjust her invisible spectacles. "He's so pompous."

Spence snorts as he packs his backpack. "I would have sold tickets."

"Shhh," I whisper. "I don't know if Dr. Hughes knows I saw him."

Skye glances at Dr. Hughes and chuckles. "Oh, she knows."

"Absofuckinglutely, she knows. Tells her everything. Probably presented her the recap in prose." Spence snickers and throws his bag over his shoulder.

Most of the students have left, including Courtney. Since Samhain, she hasn't spoken to any of us outside of class. Perhaps Audrey could talk with her friend. It can't help the coven to have an angry witch moping about. Dr. Hughes stares at me with a look of I-know-what-you-did and motions to me.

"Looks like she wants to talk to you." Skye slides her arms through the straps of her backpack. "Good luck."

Spence waves goodbye as they leave. "Have fun with that."

"Thanks." Sure. Abandon me, friends.

"Skye. Please, close the door behind you." Dr. Hughes glares at me and blinks once. "We wouldn't want Unremarkables to hear our conversation, would we?"

While slipping on my gloves, I try to apologize. "I know what you want to discuss. Mr. Yeats got into the room, and I'm very sorry about it. I should've been more careful."

A hint of a smile creeps into her mouth. "Now that you know of his more educated side, be aware Mr. Yeats can be extremely helpful when creating spells. He has been at my side for over forty years. Ask him for assistance when you need it."

"I'll keep that in mind," I say, zipping my coat.

"Archie spoke with me this morning about your experiences in the Celestial Gardens. Please, keep all of this in a box for now. We will share it with the coven tonight and discuss the implications."

"Should I be worried?" I fiddle with my earring, attempting to control the tremor in my hand.

Leslie's brow gathers into folds. "We should all be concerned."

Waiting outside Archie's office, I contemplate the sharp turn my life has taken. Three months ago, I was the widow of a dead cheating husband in a catatonic state, watching the world roll by me like a silent film. Today, I'm an ancestral witch in a coven whose hometown has a slight fae problem, but I'm working two jobs, attending grad school, and have a kind, younger man drooling after me. You can't have everything.

The door to Archie's office swings open, and a young woman walks out, tears dripping from her eyes. He follows her out with his back to me. "Don't worry, Samantha. I will talk to Dr. Hughes."

She sniffs and wipes her nose with a tissue. "Thank you, Dr. Cock-burn." Archie's chest deflates, and his head falls back.

"Do you have a minute, Dr. Cock-burn?" I ask in a girlish voice.

He turns around, his jaw clenched, until he discovers it's me, and an affectionate smile softens his mouth. "Let's go into my office."

Archie shuts the door and hugs me, bending over to kiss my cheek. His puny office doesn't shock me, since the Celtic Studies department encompasses a small area of study. Like his home, books and other items occupy the shelves in perfect order. Large stacks of papers have their own assigned space on his desk, neatly piled. A stray pen laying to the right of his computer monitor suggests the illusion of a messy desk. What will he say the first time he sees my house?

"What can I do for you, my stubborn Welsh American woman?" he asks.

"Nothing." I brush the stubble of his recently trimmed goatee. "I wanted to remind you we're eating dinner with Ronnie and her boyfriend Derek at the Sunshine Garden Café before the Fellowship meeting, or should I say coven meeting?"

"Naw. You should not. We never know who might be listening through the door. I didn't forget. I'm looking forward to it. Another night out suits me fine."

"You told Leslie about my experiences in the gardens? She seemed concerned."

"As the Elder, she needs to know." Archie strokes the tip of my chin. "There's more to tell, but you'll hear tonight. Let's get through dinner without thinking about it."

Not a chance.

We meet Ronnie and Derek at the Sunshine Garden Café around 5:30 p.m. After a quick search of the menu, Andrew, one of Ronnie's favorite waiters, takes our order. Derek and Archie hit it off immediately, discussing the nutritional challenges of building muscle on a plant-based diet. While they buzz in conversation, Ronnie and I have our own muffled conversation under the clinking of glasses and voices in the café.

"Does Derek know yet?" I ask. "I have the same reservations about Tyler."

"Hell no," Ronnie says. "He wouldn't believe me. And you understand you're gonna have to tell Tyler someday, right?"

"What are you two whispering about?" Derek sets his bulging arms on the table with a rumble.

"Tampons." Ronnie never moves a muscle on her face, but I roll my lips inward, an ill attempt at suppressing a chuckle. She stares him down and blinks.

Derek grimaces at her. "You expect me to believe you're discussing feminine hygiene at dinner?" He stares back at Ronnie and squints.

"Sure. We compare sexual positions, too." She raises her flaming eyebrows to the ceiling. "Would you like me to elaborate?"

Archie waves his hand back and forth, snickering. "Please, don't. Not on our first double date."

We all crack up, creating a bar-like ruckus in our booth at about the time Andrew delivers our dinner. As usual, the food presentation is artistic and mouth-watering.

"This looks incredible, Ronnie," Archie says. "I can't believe I've not eaten here before."

"I hope it's the first of many more." She surveys all our food like a proud mama.

Derek picks up a knife and fork and cuts through his crispy tofu. "Archie, what is your little pagan meeting about tonight?" He takes a bite, closing his eyes to savor it.

Archie glances at Ronnie and me. "Uhh, most likely the lobbying for Mitchell Hall. We want the city to make it a community center." He places a small piece of tempeh in his mouth.

"That's a great idea," Derek says. "Would take a lot of money to reno it, but I think it's better than demolishing it and erecting another modern eyesore that doesn't fit with the architecture of Main Street." It's great to know he cares about the city's progress. He brings his beer mug to his mouth and pauses. "Whatever happened with the investigation of the murder on campus?"

Archie and I lock eyes, and Ronnie notices. "I've not heard a thing. You, Ronnie?" He takes a sip of his wine.

"No." She eats a slice of eggplant, inspecting our faces like a Bearsden investigator sifting for clues.

"How about you, Gwyn?" Derek asks. "You're being awfully quiet."

"Nothing to say." I wrap rice noodles around and around my fork and stop to sip my wine. I swallow. And swallow again.

Derek takes a sip of his beer. "Well, I hope they catch the bastard and put him away."

And Derek thought tampons were inappropriate conversation for dinner?

I wring my hands in our witches' circle while Archie delivers the news of my experiences in the Mitchell's Celestial Gardens. I chime in to describe the evidence of the fae children, leaving out the bizarre details of the hawthorn tree for now. My fellow witches talk among themselves, chirping like birds expecting a storm.

"Why didn't you share that with me?" Ronnie asks. "I figured something weird was going on at dinner."

"I wasn't *in the knowing* when most of the shit happened." I wipe my face with my hands. "How was I supposed to know they were fairies?"

Leslie taps her Elder staff twice to bring a focus back to the coven. "We have known for many years the Seelie Fae can cross over into our world. The last time they appeared, I was attending school here at DUB. This may be a foreboding of more worrisome events to come."

"I agree," Trinity says. "I was a teen when it happened. The Seelie Fae children retreated into the Otherworld. I expected we'd seen the last of them."

"We had a similar incident occur in my small town in North Carolina," Shane says. "We never saw them physically, but people would come home and find their pictures and knick-knacks all cattywampus."

The younger witches gape like zombies with glassy eyes, listening to the tale of the Seelie Fae children. Like me, this is all new, but should it surprise them? They believe in conjuring spirits from the Otherworld. Why not fairies? With the flip of a switch, I turn on my "what if" mode, and the array of possibilities floods my head like a tsunami. What other stories of supernatural creatures hold a sliver of truth?

"Let me get this straight, Dr. Hughes. All the folklore we've been reading about in class is true?" Spence asks in a voice so high it sounds like someone grabbed his balls.

Archie interjects, trying to calm his fears. "Spence, the premise of the folklore holds some truth, but a lot was fabricated to cover the reality of their existence. It's a necessary explanation for the Unremarkables. There wasn't a reason to make any of you younger witches aware of their existence until necessary."

"That's so cool!" Zoe exclaims. "Can we meet them? Do they speak our language? We could learn about their world. Find out why they're here?"

"You don't engage with them, Zoe. You try not to piss them off!" Elijah warns.

"I think it's cool, but also terrifying," Skye says, her hands trembling. "What if the Unremarkables see them?"

Tanner wraps an arm around Spence to calm his jitters. "I feel the same way. It's kind of like roaches. When you find one or two, you know hundreds are hiding in the woodwork."

"Is that imagery supposed to be comforting?" Spence asks in a falsetto voice.

Leslie tries to clarify. "They don't hide in the woodwork, as you suggest. The Seelie Fae live among us. Around us. They are always with us."

"Wait. They could be in this room?" My eyes roam the walls and wooden floor for evidence of the little ones. "I'm with Spence. How do you sleep knowing they're everywhere?"

"They're not likely in this room," Archie says, "but they live among us in another dimension in the Otherworld, until they crossover, of course."

This entire time, Audrey and Courtney haven't commented at all. They sit motionless, with their eyes bouncing around the circle. I empathize. I'm a little scared, too.

Trinity glares at me with her green laser eyes. "Gwyn, don't engage with them again. At least it's only a couple of fae children. It could be worse."

Archie glances at me and Leslie. "It may be." He scans the circle for reactions.

I share the phenomena surrounding the hawthorn tree—the growling, the foul smell, and the arm-like movement of the branches. My fellow witches jibber-jabber, filling the room with a word rumble. Tanner speaks first, kneading his sweaty palms. "I think I speak for the younger witches here when I say we need to know everything. Personally, I feel a little betrayed you kept this from us."

"There's more," I say. "It happened the night I fell at the Old Men oak trees. There was a putrid smell that night and right before I fell, I imagined the limb of a tree swiping my legs. But now, it seems very real to me. And the next day, they found the dead body there."

Out of nowhere, Audrey jumps to refute my claims. "I was there when you fell, and I saw nothing like that." She taps her foot like she can't find the off button.

"Audrey, you told me you were too far away to see anything." Now she talks?

She crosses her arms in a huff. "I was close enough. I know what I saw." She must be super pissed about the council meeting. Her nonstop foot-tapping adds to the tension and noise in the room while the coven chews over the disputed claim.

Archie stands to quiet the coven and gestures to Audrey to sit. "I was there as well. Gwyn told me about it. I considered nothing about it at the time. Now, I'm inclined to believe it's an Unseelie, trying to cross over. Specifically, I think it's a Sluagh, known to use trees and other objects as a host. It would explain the crushed body of the homeless man found near the Old Men oaks."

Leslie's eyes slither around the circle while she explains. "Most know it by the name Host of the Unforgiven Dead. It would require the invitation of an ancestral witch working alone. A coven would never call on a Sluagh."

Spence grabs the top of his head with both hands. "Excuse my Celtic language, but what the fuck? We read about those in class!"

"The damn thing was terrifying," Skye says. "An enormous shadow of a raven with a gnarled face!"

Elijah rubs the side of his head. "Frank, a regular at the shelter, was spewing some nonsense about that, and we didn't believe him."

"No, we didn't!" Trinity closes her eyes and presses her lips together.

This entire time, Courtney says nothing. I guess she's too scared to talk. Sitting next to her, Audrey continues to tap her foot. Most of the older members listen, taking the news in, but the young witches explode with questions, especially Tanner. "So exactly what does this mean?" He fidgets with the buttons on his shirt. "Should we be seriously concerned this thing can cross over? I can't imagine how we could keep this from the Unremarkables. They'll notice a monstrous raven flying in the sky. How do we protect ourselves from it?"

Archie runs fingers through his hair. "So far, the Bearsden Coven has kept its work camouflaged. As for protecting ourselves? We're not sure if protection spells will work. We must be vigilant. I know of no time an Unseelie has crossed over in my lifetime, and it's disconcerting the Sluagh is trying now."

Leslie stands to join Archie. "The Bearsden Coven formed not long before I started school at DUB. We managed very well, with a few minor incidents. If the Host of the Unforgiven Dead crosses over, it will be difficult to obscure. We may need the help of witches from other covens in the county."

Audrey still hasn't found the off button for her foot. "Well, I disagree. There isn't enough evidence to prove the—what's it called again?" she asks, throwing a hand in the air.

"The Host of the Unforgiven Dead." Ronnie grimaces. "It's got a pretty nasty name, Audrey. You'd think you could remember it?"

"Hmph. I'm sorry I don't have the recollection you do." Wow! Audrey has a huge chip on her shoulder after that council meeting.

"Meanwhile," Trinity says, "I think Leslie and I should visit the Mitchell's place. Check it out."

Leslie taps her Elder staff one time. "An excellent idea. For now, Gwyn, do NOT go to the gardens again. You are a new witch on level two with a month of training. You do not have the skills to defend yourself."

"And the same goes for the rest of you." Archie swings a finger at the younger witches, and they grumble at the orders. I don't relish going back there either, not knowing what dangers float in that magical space.

"Before we dismiss," Leslie says, "let's not forget about our plans for Mitchell Hall. We'll discuss what we should do in the week approaching the vote in December." She taps her Elder staff three times to dismiss the coven.

While stacking the chairs, I ponder our last order of the meeting. With the possibility of a horrific, murderous Unseelie Court fairy sneaking into our world, does it make any sense to worry about the vote on the fate of Mitchell Hall?

CHAPTER EIGHTEEN

FAULTY MAGIC

FOR THE NEXT COUPLE of weeks, I spend my spare time at Leslie's house, practicing spells and honing my witch energy. It no longer scares me thanks to Archie's unorthodox training, but the extent of my magical ineptness heightens my anxiety to extra levels. Not enough witch-energy sex exists in the world to ease the palpitations. If this monster-fairy Sluagh crosses over, I'll need to have control of my magic. How do I develop skills in such a limited time? Part of me wishes I'd never walked into that first pagan meeting—except I got to know Archie.

The threat of the Sluagh brings seriousness to our witch training at Leslie's house. Even Zoe has attained a moderate level of organization, making huge strides in successful protection and healing spells. Zoe practices with Courtney, who has finally shown up to lessons. Ronnie and Skye pair again, leaving Audrey and me to train together. Of course, Mr. Yeats insists on supervising our spell concoctions, irritating Spence.

"Agh, Mr. Yeats!" Spence throws his hands in the air. "I need a break from you!" He pushes Mr. Yeats out of the room, rolling the door closed enough to keep his human form out but not the feline. In chimera cat presentation, Mr. Yeats slinks back in, changing into his human form in the time it took Spence to shuffle back to the worktable.

"Is that how you're going to prepare the protection spell?" Mr. Yeats inquires with a lift of his arrogant brow. "Dr. Hughes would never prepare it in that fashion."

Spence squeezes his eyes shut and shakes his head all about, causing his hair to settle in a black, disheveled ragtop, a classy one with a purple stripe. "Mr. Yeats, I know you're supposed to help, but criticizing every step of the spell is ruining my concentration. How about you help the other pairs of witches while I work with one pair? Can you handle all of them?"

"I suppose." Mr. Yeats adjusts his spectacles, wrinkling his narrow nose. "If you don't take my advice, the protection spell may have a vulnerability, allowing a small percentage of failure. Your choice, Mr. Huxley. Success or failure."

Spence bats his eyes. If the lower half of his face didn't have the scowl of an insulted man, I'd swear Spence was flirting with the feline. "Fuuu...ine. I'm sure the Fire Twins could use your help."

"Bring your tush over here, Mr. Yeats." Ronnie puckers her lips. "If you think you can handle us."

Skye shimmies with a jazzy rhythm. "I'll warn ya. I'm all fire with no brimstone."

Mr. Yeats distorts his face like a prune. "I'll have you know. I am a gentleman." He straightens his coat and joins them at the table where they grind herbs with a mortar and pestle while Spence guides Zoe and Courtney in their protection spells.

Audrey and I train alone. Once we've ground the herbs with the mortar and pestle, we dump them in the bowl and chant, channeling our witch energy to activate it. Neither of us can spark the spell, questioning our preparation. I'm unsure of the chant, but Audrey is more skilled. "This is the correct chant. I don't know why it's not working," she says. "Let's try one more time."

On the last attempt, our witch energies spark, generating beams of energy to ricochet all over the room, until coming to a stop at a stack of books, now a clump of burning flames of electric yellow! All the while, the witch apprentices drop to the floor, screaming obscenities. Mr. Yeats appears unaffected by the bouncing balls of electric energy, bending this way and that.

Spence shrieks like a small child, slapping his face. "Fuck!" He runs to the stack of books in the corner, but Mr. Yeats's swift response has him there in seconds, covering the burning books with a heavy cloth. Remnants of minuscule puffs of smoke rise from the catastrophe.

"THAT was a misfire of energy, Ms. Crowther and Ms. Kenilworth." Mr. Yeats waves at the swirls of smoke, redirecting them away from him as he coughs. "You could have incinerated Dr. Hughes's home, you know."

"Ladies." Spence lays a hand on his chest. "Skye and Ronnie are the Fire Twins!"

Audrey and I goggle at each other, but I think it's too funny to be scared by it. "I don't know enough about any of this to have a clue how that happened."

"That never happened to me before," Audrey says with tight lips.

Spence taps at his palpitating heart. "All I know is no one will trust me to do training again if you burn down Dr. Hughes's house. I'm sure I'd lose my grad funding, too, if we lit it like a box of matches. I wish I knew what caused it."

"It's so obvious." Mr. Yeats adjusts his spectacles. "Ms. Kenilworth must be an ancestral witch."

Audrey's eyes bubble out like an animated cartoon figure. "Uh, my family has no witch ancestry. In fact, they kicked me out for being a pagan."

"It's true," Ronnie says. "She told me when it happened a couple of years ago."

"Maybe they don't know?" Skye blows away the remaining swirls of smoke. "I mean, Gwyn didn't know either."

"I am NOT an ancestral witch. I would know." Audrey stamps her foot.

Mr. Yeats clears his throat. "I am rarely wrong about these things."

"Well, to be careful," Spence says, "let's switch partners. Gwyn and Courtney, you work together, and Audrey can pair with Zoe."

Courtney whines like a spoiled teenager. "I will not train with a neophyte. I want to train with Audrey."

"Courtney, you know you can't apprentice with a close friend," Spence says, sporting an I-can't-with-your-shit-today face. "Gwyn has a higher skill level than you already have. She's not a neophyte. It'll be fine."

Skye offers a solution. "Courtney could train with me, Spence. I wouldn't mind."

Spence waves both of his hands back and forth. "Ronnie can't train with Gwyn for the same reason."

Courtney isn't having it and storms out of the magic room in a huff. Her footsteps echo in the hallway, and the kitchen door slams.

Spence sighs and shakes his head. "I can't with her anymore." He picks up items from the floor and returns them to the worktable.

"Why don't I go talk to her?" Audrey asks, looking toward the office.

"Nah. She has to be an adult. I'll let Dr. Hughes and Archie deal with her." Spence arranges the spell bowls to prepare for a new spell.

Audrey crosses her arms. "Well, that is the problem. Archie dealt with her."

Everyone gets quiet, and their eyes hop from object to object, avoiding Audrey's agitated face. I'm unhappy with the path of this conversation. "Archie is the Coven leader, and Dr. Hughes is the Elder witch. It's their responsibility, not ours."

Audrey stares at the spell bowl, and her face bursts into a portrait of sheer happiness. "You're right. Now what, Spence?"

"I'll work with Gwyn. You practice with Zoe. And Mr. Yeats? If you want to be helpful, you can sweep the half-burned book pile and dump it in the trash."

"Do I look like a maid?" He puts his fists on his hips and cocks his head.

Spence snorts. "Actually, you sorta do."

How do coven members go about their lives with impending doom hovering like a burgeoning rain cloud ready to burst at any moment? I'm not cut from that mold. I wake at night again from the mounting fear. On top of everything, the dreaded Tyler-I'm-dating reveal hangs out there like a flimsy hand towel covering a naked woman—one stiff wind from exposing the goodies. Proceeding as normal appears like the best plan, but I don't have a clue what normal is anymore.

As I get dressed for Celtic Arts Night, I scrutinize my changing body, discerning what these months of lifting have done to transform it. The dainty, weak physique of my yoga days has transformed into a body full of toned muscles. The physical strength gives me a level of confidence I never had before, and it could come in handy if I have to defend myself.

When I arrive at Duncan Performance Hall, I find Archie on stage, reciting a Robert Burns poem to an empty auditorium. Wearing eighteenth-century Scottish garb like the first day I met him, I'm reminded of how stunning he looks in the plaid kilt and boots. He speaks with so much passion in his voice. I catch the last verse while he recites the poem using a pronounced Scottish brogue:

Fare thee weel, thou first and fairest!
Fare thee weel, thou best and dearest!
Thine be ilka joy and treasure,
Peace, enjoyment, love, and pleasure!
Ae fond kiss, and then we sever;
Ae fareweel, alas, forever!
Deep in heart-wrung tears I'll pledge thee,
Warring sighs and groans I'll wage thee!

After the final stanza, he bows. I clap so hard it turns my palms into a glorious shade of pink as the claps reverberate in the auditorium. "Bravo! Bravo!"

Archie notices me and bows once more. I grin at his silliness and recollect how he made me laugh before Samhain, before joining *in the knowing* and learning of the threat of the Sluagh. He runs down the side steps of the stage, clanking in those boots, and kisses me. "So happy you could get here early." He adjusts his sliding, shoulder plaid. "The only way to guarantee a well-lit parking spot close by."

"Yes," I say, fussing with my hair. "I got the last one. It's a miracle."

"Why don't you come and wait with me in the dressing room for a bit? It's a wee room but comfortable." The room is tiny. A table sits along the wall next to a rack of costumes. The room has no windows, which makes it the perfect dressing room. Archie leans back on the table, pulls me to him, and wraps his arms around me. "How is training going with Spence?"

"Not too well. I'm surprised he didn't tell you." I caress his chest, and his nipples poke through the thin cotton. "Courtney came, but got pissed and left, and some strange things happened."

Archie massages my back through my turtleneck. "We can talk about Courtney later. Remember, no matter what innate power you have, it's untrained and untamed. You'll improve."

"I hope so." I smile coyly at him. "You're sexy in your kilt."

He returns the smile and looks away, as if he's embarrassed, and that surprises me. "It may appear I'm enjoying myself up there, but I don't love reciting in front of a large audience. A classroom full of students provides me all the adulation I need."

"Or the adulation of one?" He holds me so close you'd need a pry bar to separate us. I slide my hand around and cup his firm buttocks.

"As Spence would say, absofuckinglutely."

We chuckle as I run my hands across the back of his plaid kilt, and I gape at my discovery. "Archie, you aren't wearing underwear."

A smirk slinks onto his mouth. "Scots are known for not wearing anything under the kilt, you know."

"But it's not the eighteenth century." I slap his arm and grimace.

"Good point, but I also need to do laundry." He fondles my nipples through my turtleneck and fiddles with the zipper of my jeans. "And it makes for easy access for amorous adventures."

Something stiff pushes through his thin kilt, and I doubt he has a gun in his pocket. Kilts don't have pockets. "Archie, I won't make love in here. It's a public place."

"Correct me if I'm wrong, but wasn't the brick wall of Menzies Hall a public place?" He cocks his head.

I throw him a disapproving frown and amble to the door. "I'll see you after the show, and we can continue this later in a more appropriate setting."

"Your decision. I'm ready and willing." Archie spreads his legs under the kilt and strokes his goatee.

When I get to the open door, I stop and shut it until it latches, locking the deadbolt—twice.

CHAPTER NINETEEN

FAUX DAUGHTER

"YOU'RE MIXING WITH THE wrong quantity of herbs again," Mr. Yeats says, hovering like a helicopter mom. "They aren't ground enough."

He pushes me aside and snatches the pestle from my hand, twisting and grinding against the mortar. You'd think he was grinding wheat to bake a cake. The door to the mudroom bangs open and voices babble in the kitchen. They approach the magic room.

Trinity walks in and lays her hand on my back. "Hi, lady. Whatcha working on?"

Leslie inspects my work. "Looks like a slumber spell." She touches my upper arm. "Are you having trouble sleeping, Gwynedd?"

"A little. I thought I'd try this, but Mr. Yeats doesn't have confidence I can make it." I send him a side-eye.

"Nonsense." Leslie throws him a judgmental gaze. "Mr. Yeats, I'm sure Gwynedd would do fine on her own." She lifts her chin with an encouraging smile.

Mr. Yeats passes the mortar and pestle back to me. "Fine. I know when I'm not needed."

Trinity lets out a hearty laugh. "Mr. Yeats, you crack me up. You're like the parent who does homework for their kids, and they never learn how to do it for themselves."

"Mr. Yeats, stay and observe." Leslie gestures to the chair in the corner. "Gwyn, why don't you show me a quick protection spell for now?"

Oh, great. Put me on the spot. I pick up the glass salt container, and Mr. Yeats tries to grab it, causing the cork top to pop off. The salt flies in the air and sprinkles the front of his suit. Leslie and Trinity chuckle, and he leaves the room, transforming into his chimera cat persona. "Oops." I wrinkle my nose. "I'm sorry."

"Oh, don't worry about him," Trinity says, flipping her hand. "Been like that for years. Never gonna change either."

"Mr. Yeats has his quirks, but we mustn't dismiss his feelings. He has them," Leslie says.

"Are you returning from the Celestial Gardens?" I ask.

"Yes," Leslie says. "No evidence of the Host of the Unforgiven Dead or the Seelie Fae children."

"For now. Gotta be there at the right time, I think." Trinity pats my arm. "We believe you saw the Seelie Fae and the evidence of the Sluagh. Meanwhile, stay away from there."

On the walk home to meet Tyler for dinner, the permutations spin on a wheel in my head. It's like a game show called Pick a Fae. He's cooked a meal for us while I was "doing schoolwork." I'm not sure how long I can continue this facade. We chat about his job and a couple of dates he's had. I bite my tongue several times, keeping my prying-mom questions from spewing out.

"Grandma Wolfe wants us to visit for Thanksgiving," Tyler says. "Has she spoken with you?"

"Yeah." I puff air through my lips. "I'm not ready to deal with her yet. Why don't you go? Stay a couple of days and visit with Aunt Sammy, Uncle Drew, and your cousins. It might be more comfortable without me there."

Tyler rubs my shoulder. "You'd be alone for Thanksgiving, Mom. You shouldn't be by yourself this holiday."

"I'm sure I can eat with a member of the Fellowship. Plenty of options." I know exactly where I'll be spending Thanksgiving, and a smile sneaks onto my face.

"OK, but plan to chat." Tyler's eyes roll in his head. "I'm gonna need a respite from Grandma."

"Sure, as long as you're in a bedroom where I don't have to hear her." I hug him and muss his hair in jest. "Please don't worry about me. Enjoy your time in Virginia."

Out of nowhere, Audrey calls and invites me to dinner at the Raven Pub, saying she could use some "mom" time. It warms my heart so much she's reaching out. Not having a daughter, her need fills a void I never recognized I had. When my shift at Mystical Sage ends, I meet her at the pub.

We finish eating, and I sip a Scotch whisky, an acquired habit since dating Archie. Audrey loosens up with a glass of wine, sharing funny childhood stories and asking me to do the same. She becomes overly inquisitive about my parents. You'd think she was writing an article for a witch magazine titled the Life and Times of Bearsden Witches. She gets annoyed when I can't share much about their history. Rhys and Lowri kept everything hidden. To me, they were your average boring parental homebodies.

After dinner, we take a short stroll on Main Street until we arrive at Mitchell Hall, gloomy as ever in its rundown state. Tipsy from the wine, Audrey dances in front of the guardian of the fae house, hanging onto the iron fence like a stripper—a new look for her. "Hey!" she says drunkenly. "It's not that dark. Let's sneak into the Celestial Gardens."

Good grief. Why did you drink so much? "No, Audrey. Dr. Hughes and Archie gave us explicit directions not to go in there."

"OK! Suit yourself!" She flips her hand at me and skips into the gardens through the gate.

This leaves me in a pickle. Audrey has a higher level of witch skills than I do, but she's drunk. I can't let her go in there alone, and a good mom puts herself in harm's way for her daughter. Leslie and Trinity saw no evidence of anything. Maybe the fae children have left? I stop at the gate, and Leslie's orders ring in my head. If Archie or Leslie find out, there will be hell to pay. Damn you, Audrey. I push open the gate.

"I loved coming to the parties here!" Audrey sings as she skips through the gardens. "The Mitchells were such a happy couple. Always kissing each other, even into their 90s. Dancing out here at night was so much fun! They had fairy lights twinkling on all the trees and shrubs."

"It must have been magical."

I imagine a party full of guests, dancing and chatting in the moonlight's glimmer among the evergreen shrubs and colorful roses. An old, wrinkled man and woman with gray hair smooch like young lovers on the concrete bench under the romantic, emerald-green leaves of the hawthorn tree. Snapped back to the present, the tree stands barren, with bony limbs and thorns remaining—far from romantic. Eyeing the mound and hawthorn tree, I sense no presence of the Seelie or Unseelie Fae.

Audrey waves to me, inviting me to join her where she's sitting. "Gwyn, come here and look at this!" She shows me a small inscription carved into the concrete bench, faded from the outside elements. The lettering reads Alistair and Rose Forever with a heart under their names. How sweet. Audrey jumps off the bench and runs to read a plaque screwed to the high fence on the far side of the gardens.

Attempting to stand, I find my body unresponsive, and an overpowering sense of dread penetrates my body. A growl emerges behind me coupled with the low-pitched cawing of a bird. "Audrey!" I'm projecting my voice as much as I can, but she continues to read the plaque and dance near the fence. "Audrey!"

She turns around and gawks at me from the far side of the gardens. My face must have terror written across it, flashing HELP like a fluorescent neon sign, yet she stands there in a drunken stupor. In an instant, her expression changes, and she skips to me.

Audrey mumbles, slurring her words. "What are you yelling about over here?" Her head wobbles to and fro.

"I can't move." My stiff body won't budge, seized by the frightening moment.

She grasps my hand and pulls me off the bench without effort. "Well, you can stand now." She rolls her eyes.

Eyeing the creepy hawthorn tree, my thumping heart beats heavily in my chest. "I was glued to that bench." The menacing sounds are gone, but the eerie sense of dread remains. And the limbs of the hawthorn tree threaten with bird-like claws. I seize her by the arm and drag her out of the gardens.

Audrey whines like a six-year-old girl. "Stop pulling my arm. You're hurting me."

I scowl at her like an angry mom who caught her daughter breaking curfew. "We're not supposed to be in here. We're leaving."

When we reach the sidewalk, Audrey yanks her arm back and pouts. "Please, promise me you won't tell Dr. Hughes or Trinity or anyone else. I'm sorry. I drank too much."

I press my lips together and scatter my gaze. "Oh, all right. Please, go home and sleep this off."

"I will. Thank you, Gwyn. You're the best."

CHAPTER TWENTY
WHAT'S IN A DIRK?

By Thanksgiving, the lack of activity in the gardens reduces the worry of the Sluagh's presence, and the sense of dread is gone, replaced with the cheery sentiment of the forthcoming Yule. I know it's not an accurate assessment, but I can't tell them about my visit to the gardens with Audrey. I agreed to keep it our secret after all. With no more reports of unusual deaths, I'm confident I've made the right choice. A little white lie never hurt anyone.

The week before Thanksgiving, the Coven made plans to protest the demolition of the Mitchell's mansion in front of the Bearsden City Town Hall. Technically, the Coven already knows the outcome of the December vote because of the spell of influence. Optics still matter, I suppose.

At Elijah's request, a few Fellowship members serve dinner at the shelter on Thanksgiving. What better way to celebrate this holiday than by helping those in need and spending it with my new family? Most of the students are spending it with their relatives, but Spence is here with Tanner. Ronnie is meeting Derek's family, a huge step for her.

We're having a blast, joking around while dishing out the turkey dinner. The packed cafeteria has a diverse group of people, old and young. It's disconcerting how many children are homeless and need food in our small town. A city like Bearsden hosting a private college hoarding a bloated endowment shouldn't have any homeless. But the guests laugh and carry on like any gathering of family and friends—children giggling, drunk uncles guffawing, and moms coaxing their kids to eat their vegetables. I hope Tyler is having this much fun.

A few of the Fellowship members serve while others mingle among the guests, helping small children and those with disabilities. I scan the tables for Archie and locate him sitting next to an old woman. He's cutting her turkey because her twisted and misshapen fingers can't hold a knife. It warms my heart.

Trinity catches me eyeing my man. "You be careful with that one. He seems to have trouble with commitment. Just saying."

"I know about Courtney," I say, trying to assuage her fears. "He told me what happened."

"Uh-huh." Doubt lingers in her unwavering stare. "I care what happens to you, Gwyn. If you ever need anything, I'm here for you, day or night."

"I appreciate your concern, but Archie treats me so well." I glimpse him helping a child sit on a dining bench. He locks eyes with me and winks. "Everything is great."

Trinity presses her lips together. "Everything's always hunky-dory. Until it isn't."

Elijah sneaks up behind me, resting his large hands on my shoulders, and I let out a high-pitched yelp. He laughs and pats my back. "You OK, Gwyn."

Clutching my pounding heart, I chastise him. "Elijah, you can't do that. I don't have nine lives like Mr. Yeats." The children I'm serving giggle at my expense, and I return their teasing with a silly smile.

"You never know, Gwyn," he says. "Hey, Sebastian. How you doing?"

The older Black man waits for his cut of turkey and displays a thankful grin. No longer scruffy, Sebastian has a neatly trimmed, gray beard and a glimmer of renewal in his brown eyes. "I'm doing great! Been sober for a while now. I'm gonna make it this time. I know it."

"Good for you, Sebastian," I say, scooping potatoes onto his plate. "You can do it."

"Well, thank you, Miss Gwyn. I owe it all to Elijah." Sebastian shuffles down the line for peas and cranberry sauce.

"We all owe Elijah," Trinity says. "Keep the faith, Sebastian."

Elijah looks out at the guests, searching for someone. "Isn't Shane here?"

"He's here." As I slop mashed potatoes on the next tray, I notice the tiny boy barely reaches the height of the tray slide. "Enjoy your potatoes, dear. Shane's out there somewhere, helping the guests and chatting with them." Elijah and Trinity survey the area, and I gesture using my scoop. "He's over there with that group of old white men."

"Where?" Elijah's eyes zigzag across the room. "Oh, I think I found him. Couldn't tell him apart from the other men sporting long, white hair and beards."

Trinity laughs, holding her stomach. "Oh, my gods. You're right. He blends right in." We crack up, and Elijah walks over to join the conversation.

Spence comes out of the kitchen where he and Tanner have been cooking. "Who's being so loud out here?" Spence is wearing a Fellowship apron and a chef's hat. "You're not supposed to have this much fun without me!"

"Sorry, dude," I say. "You chose to sequester yourself in the kitchen. You can't hang with me all the time."

"Brazen and sassy!" Spence gawks at us with his arms crossed. "You've been hanging out with Trinity way too much!"

Trinity snaps with a hand on her hip. "Hey, you watch your mouth, son. You ever heard the phrase 'I'll wash your mouth out with soap?'"

"No, but it sounds naaasty." Spence grimaces, pretending to taste the fake soap.

"I wouldn't know. I wasn't like this before meeting any of you. So, it's the Cov...Fellowship's fault." I shrink with embarrassment, and my eyes dart to the potatoes.

Trinity whispers in my ear. "Gotta watch your tongue, Gwyn. Never slip up."

I've gotten too confident for my own good and everyone else's. "It won't happen again. I'll be careful from now on." I hate having to live this way.

Spence gestures to the kitchen doors. "Here come Tanner and Jamal with the cakes. I'll go get the cookies."

"I can't take all the credit." Tanner sets a cake on the dessert table. "Elijah has a fantastic crew of bakers back there, including Jamal."

"Thanks." Jamal prepares to cut the cake into small servings. "Glad you could help today, Tanner." A Black man with sepia-colored irises, he could be a model, but he works as a fitness trainer at Derek's gym. It was nice of him to volunteer.

The entry double doors break open with a loud bang, and two men carry in the body of a white man while yelling about a big, dark shadow in the sky. Undoubtedly drunk, they talk over each other. Archie, Shane, and Elijah dart to the men, advising them to place the man's body on the floor with care. The guests gasp, and parents cover their children's eyes. Trinity and I rip off our plastic serving gloves and rush to join them while Tanner and Spence continue to serve.

Archie and Shane squat to examine the poor man's body as Elijah tries to calm the dinner guests, suggesting they pick up their dessert and leave the cafeteria. The man lies on the floor in a bloody heap with mangled bones and a disfigured eye. I grab my stomach, getting queasy from the morbid sight as the image of Richard's bruised and broken body flashes in my head.

Archie puts his hand on my leg. "Are you all right?" I nod, but I'm not. Richard's lacerated and bloodied face continues to flash in my head over and over and over...

"It's Frank, and he's alive," Archie says in a muted voice. "But not for long, I'm afraid. Shane, can you stay with him? An ambulance should be here soon." He stands, a look of unease pinching his face. "Elijah, Trinity, let's question the men away from the probing ears of the guests."

"That's a sound idea," Shane says. "Maybe Tanner can help me until the EMTs arrive. I think he knows CPR." Shane motions to Tanner, and he dashes over.

I follow Archie, Trinity, and Elijah to listen while they interrogate the two men. Spence offers them black coffee and joins Tanner and Shane where Frank lies, fighting for his life. Elijah directs the men to sit on a cafeteria bench to question them. "Calm down and speak one at a time. What are your names?"

"I'm Harold. He's Chuck." Harold and Chuck are wearing tattered, dirty clothes, and they reek of alcohol.

With Harold appearing the most lucid, if you want to call it that, Archie asks him to speak first. "Take a deep breath, Harold, and tell us what you saw. Take your time and speak slowly."

"It was awful! Scary!" Harold waves his arms in the air. "We were drinking, you know, celebrating Thanksgiving and all, and a big, black shadow like a bird, but not a bird, swooped and snatched Frank with its gigantic claws." Sitting next to Harold, Chuck bobs his head. He's three sheets to the wind or in shock. Maybe both. "We chased after him as the bird flapped its ginormous wings." Harold raises his arms up and down like a bird in flight. "Screamed bloody murder we did until it dropped Frank flat on the pavement. Then it swooped in on him again! Plucked out his eyeball!"

Elijah pats Harold on the back. "Thank you for telling us, Harold. I know that must have frightened you something fierce."

A siren blares in the distance, increasing in volume until the ambulance and police car arrive outside the shelter. My stomach does somersaults over Harold's plucked eyeball comment while it replays in my head like a slow-motion film—"Attack of the Big, Bad Sluagh." A hot flash erupts, making me dizzy, so I stumble to one of the cafeteria benches.

"Anything you want to ask them, Trinity?" Archie rubs my shoulders as the room goes out of focus and my head spins like a top.

"Damn straight, I've got questions," she says. "Harold, what direction did the big shadow bird fly after it dropped your friend?"

"I don't know if I remember." Harold scratches his head through stringy brown hair. "I think it flew toward the end of Main Street." His hands tremble as he sips his coffee. "West. You know, toward the Mitchell's mansion.

Everyone forms a circle away from Harold and Chuck while I clutch the cafeteria bench. Poor Chuck. He's shaking so much he spills coffee on his pants.

Archie strokes my head. "Gwyn, why don't you put your head between your legs?" He guides my head toward the floor.

"Sounds like it's happened, for sure," Elijah says. "They're drunk but not hallucinating. So sad for Frank." He closes his eyes and lowers his head.

"I didn't believe his outlandish story before, but Frank was telling the truth," Trinity says. "I don't know about you all, but I've lost my appetite. And I really wanted a piece of Jamal's double-chocolate cake."

The dizziness has subsided, and I sit up. "Are you saying that thing...it's crossed over?" The director's cut of "Attack of the Big, Bad Sluagh" rolls in my head.

With a bang, the doors fly open and EMTs come running in with equipment. The woman takes over from Tanner and checks for a pulse while the man puts an oxygen mask on Frank. She uses the defibrillator, shouting "clear" while Shane, Tanner, Spence, and a few remaining guests observe.

Archie grips my hand. "We'll talk specifics after they've left, Gwyn. The Bearsden police officers will have questions for all of us."

"Harold," Trinity says, patting his back. "You tell the police exactly what you told us. They may not believe you, but tell them word for word what you said."

"They won't believe them." The room continues to spin as I massage my temples.

Elijah rocks his head. "That's the idea. I feel bad about it, but we're better off."

The EMTs place Frank on a gurney and exit the building. Shane turns his attention to us, shaking his head. Tanner has his arm around Spence, who isn't handling the violent incident too well. Shane walks over with the police officers to talk with Harold. Chuck still hasn't spoken one word.

It's nearly 6:00 p.m. before the Bearsden police officers finish questioning Harold and Chuck. A shelter assistant finds beds for the men while Officers Braddock Wilson and Quinn O'Connor discuss the ramifications of the bizarre incident with us. In the middle of this stressful line of questioning, I can't shake a nervous laugh. Officer Wilson must be over six feet six, and Officer O'Connor can't be over four feet eleven. The comic strip Mutt and Jeff pops into my head.

"There are similarities between the body of Frank Walker and the body we found on campus early in October," Officer Wilson says in a deep voice while taking notes on his tablet. "I've been in contact with Captain Malik Brown, and he says we need to approach this as a serial killer case. We need as many details as possible."

"Mr. Jackson, you run the shelter, I understand," Officer O'Connor says in a mouse-like voice. "You'll need to do your best to warn those in the shelter and on the streets to be on the alert."

"Will do, Officer. We'll get volunteers to roam the streets and alleyways to get the word out." Elijah types notes into his cell phone.

"So, you believe it's some sort of serial killer?" Archie asks, scratching his goatee. "Not a... What did Harold call it?"

"A Big. Shadow. Bird," Trinity says in a sardonic tone.

Officer Wilson grimaces. "No. They appeared to be drunk and in shock. The man named Chuck couldn't even speak, but they should both see a doctor. Their stories have little validity."

"I think that's all for now," Officer O'Connor says. "We'll follow up tomorrow. Try to enjoy the rest of your Thanksgiving."

Elijah gestures to the double doors. "I'll walk you out and lock the door behind you."

After the Bearsden Officers leave the shelter, Tanner and Spence shuffle over to our impromptu witch circle. Spence has a green face, as do I, and slides onto the bench next to me, wrapping me in a hug.

"It's not hypothetical anymore." Tanner rubs his palms together and frowns. "The Host of the Unforgiven Dead has crossed over."

Archie's eyes twitch. "No doubt about it. The question remains, where is it hiding?"

"You said it uses trees as hosts. A fucking lot of trees in Bearsden. Where do we even start?" Spence throws his hands up.

The Celestial Gardens, of course, but I can't bring myself to tell them. They'll figure it out somehow. "What about the Old Men oaks on campus? That's where I had a mishap, and the police found the first body."

"Unlikely. No other activity there since it happened." Shane has twisted the hair on his beard into a display of white ringlets.

Trinity shoves her cell phone into the back pocket of her pants. "I sent Leslie a text. Told her we have a serious problem."

"Thank you, Trinity. For now, I recommend we go home and do as the officer suggested. Try to enjoy the remainder of our Thanksgiving." Archie helps me stand, and we gather our belongings and leave for his home.

Staring out the window of Archie's Tesla, I flinch at every tree we pass. The Sluagh can hide in any of them, but I know where its favorite tree is. While Archie's in the bathroom brushing his teeth, I receive a text from Tyler on my cell.

Tyler: *Hope you had a Happy Thanksgiving, Mom.*

Me: *Thank you, dear. Hope you had a good one, too.*

Tyler: *Are you kidding? I was with Grandma Wolfe. It was a morbid turkey day.*

Me: *Sorry.*

If he only knew how far from happy it ended here. I put my cell phone on the nightstand, close my eyes, and try deep breathing exercises, anything to stop the construction worker from hammering nails into my chest. Archie approaches the bed and climbs in, sliding close to me. He reaches for my hand, placing his cold, freshly washed digits against mine.

"Hey." My eyes snap open. "Your hands are like ice."

He snickers while his hand heats with his internal energy radiating. "Not for long."

I yank my hand away, interlocking it with my other. "How can you even think of sex after what happened tonight? Even witch-energy sex won't help."

"Witch-energy sex?" Archie laughs out loud, and blond ringlets spill onto his forehead.

"Go ahead. Mock me." I stare at the smooth, white ceiling above me. "Won't change my mind."

"I'm sorry." He brushes the fallen locks behind his ear. "I hoped it might help reduce your stress. I do like your description, though." He caresses my cheek with the back of his hand. "I wanted to make you forget tonight's incident, if only for a while."

"I had a flashback to the night Richard died, seeing Frank's body." Every muscle contracts, and the pain in my lower back pinches and burns.

Archie continues to stroke my cheek. "I wish I could help you forget."

"I'll never forget." Studying the smooth ceiling, I search for the jagged crack that hangs above my bed at home, always there to remind me how damaged I am. A notification shows on my cell again. I assume it's Tyler, but it's not. It's a Bearsden City emergency alert. "Shit!" My hands are shaking like a rattlesnake. I pass my phone to him.

"What is it?" He reads the notification on my cell: *The bodies of two homeless men were discovered tonight. Please, be on alert and do not walk in the city or on campus alone. More details to follow.*

"I wonder where they found the other body?" Archie wraps his fingers around my hands in a fist-like grasp. "We will have to act as a coven to destroy the Sluagh. At the least, send it back to the Otherworld."

"But how do we kill it? It's a supernatural being."

Archie collects a key from a crack in the wood on the back of the headboard. He slides off the bed and opens the glass case, pulling the iron dirk from its leather sheath. "I'm going to tell you a secret." He lays the dirk on the cool satin sheets. "I've not told anyone in the coven. This dirk is more than a family heirloom and has a unique and specific purpose. For hundreds of years, my ancestors have used this dirk to protect our kind and Unremarkables from the evil fae."

"How will this single knife save us from a monstrous Slu-agh?" I pull my legs up into a fetal position, wrinkles folding between my eyes.

"You asked why it's made of iron. Iron can kill the Host of the Unforgiven Dead. This dirk has immeasurable powers, but only in the hands of ancestral witches." He wraps the fingers of his left hand around the dirk, lifting it toward the ceiling. Instantly, the aqua gem glows and his hand radiates with the amber glow seeping into the blade.

"Oh, my gods. The gem glowed like that on the night of Mabon. I saw it when I was falling asleep. I assumed I was dreaming."

Archie's eyebrows arch, and the corner of his mouth jerks. "I want you to hold it."

"I'm not going anywhere near that thing." Sitting against the headboard, I push his hand away. "It won't work for me, anyway. I know you all think I'm some kind of powerful Welsh ancestral witch, but I'm not buying it. If I were, I'd be better at magic. I could hurt someone by mistake with that dirk."

"You stubborn woman." Archie grabs my hand and forces my fingers around the handle of the family heirloom.

"Stop!" I try to release my grasp on the dirk, but it won't fall from my hand. In seconds, the gem shines as bright as a traffic light and triggers my witch energy, creating small beams of light to splay like electric tentacles from the blade. When I glimpse Archie's face, he's grinning from ear to ear.

I can only muster two words. "Oh, shit."

CHAPTER TWENTY-ONE
GUESS WHO'S COMING FOR BREAKFAST?

MYSTIC SAGE IS PACKED wall to wall like sardines on Black Friday, despite the Bearsden Police warnings of a possible serial killer in our midst. I rarely work on Fridays, but Shane needs the extra help. I'm a nervous wreck, one last straw from a full-fledged breakdown.

The customers shopping for ridiculous items give me pause. Who buys a friend or family member witch spells kits for Christmas? Around 8:00 p.m., the onslaught of customers dwindles to a sprinkling of shoppers. So tired from the day of shopping, they wander around the store like zombies. Dear gods, please tell me zombies aren't real?

Ringing up the last customer, I'm relieved Agnes Pritchard doesn't shop on Black Friday. I wipe the counter and knock over the skull mug loaded with pens. Shane shuffles in from checking the back rooms and notices me crawling on the floor.

"Let me help you, darling." He smells of cinnamon and rosemary. "You look so tired. Trouble sleeping?"

I place the skull mug on the counter, and Shane drops the pens in with a clink. "I tried. Last night was—"

"Traumatic? It's scary not knowing when the Sluagh will strike again. I wish I didn't know about any of it." Shane squats to pick up the trash from the floor. Black Friday shoppers are so disrespectful.

"Yes. I've already had my share of it." Unremarkable shoppers pass by Mystic Sage, and I'm envious of their *unknowing*.

"It can be quite a burden. Not even a month, and you're having so much of the secret world thrown at you." He dumps the trash into the bin and walks to me near the sales counter. "Remember, it's a shared burden. We gain our strength through our connections and convictions. No one expects you to cope in solitude. We're all here for you."

I lay a hand on his arm. "Thank you, Shane. I wish it helped more."

Shane gives me a fatherly hug, reminding me how much I miss mom and dad. What would they say about me joining the coven? Would they be angry? It's too late now. I can never go back to *unknowing*. I'm thinking I should sift through all their photos and mementos I stuffed in boxes when they died. And get someone to break open the rusted clasp on the steamer trunk they used as a coffee table, so I can sell it.

"Would you like a ride home, darling?" He folds t-shirts left in a pile resembling a teenager's floor hamper and has way too much work left to take me home.

"Nah. I'll stay on Manor Road until I get to my street." I slide on my puffer jacket and earmuffs. "I promised Archie I would text, but thank you for the offer. Enjoy your evening, Shane. You earned it today."

"You, too, darling." He locks the door behind me, and I wave goodbye through the glass door.

It's bitter cold, but the sky shines a crystal-clear, sapphire blue with a luminescent crescent moon. The stars glint with flashes of white and blue glitter. I text Archie while I sprint, but the thirty-degree temperature is too cold to keep my gloves off. Where is a flaming hot flash when you need one? Approaching Mitchell Hall, I cross the street to put space between me and the magical space. The sense of dread returns, and I quicken my pace.

Passing cars brighten the trek home, but the light fades as I approach Old Elm Road. After the stress of Thanksgiving and the long workday, I'll pass out as soon as my head meets the pillow. A high-pitched piercing noise sounds far off in the distance along with the guttural cawing of a flock of birds. Why didn't they fly south like the rest of them?

As I approach the turn onto Mulberry Lane, a flickering shadow in the moonlight distracts me. The shadow appears to follow me while the low-pitched cawing gets louder with each step. I panic and run to my house, scrambling to find the keys in my purse. Once inside, I lock the back door and scurry around the house, checking all the locks. And I call Archie.

"Hi, Gwyn," he says in a husky voice. "Miss me already?"

"What? No, I mean yes, but that's not why I called." I'm shaking from head to toe. "I'm in my house. The doors and windows are locked, so I'm safe. When I reached my street, I heard the low-pitched cawing of a bird or several birds. I couldn't tell. A shadow-like flicker in the sky appeared to follow me. I'm scared, Archie." As I grind my teeth on a thumbnail, it occurs to me I haven't done that since I was a little girl. "I'm too scared to leave the house. Tyler is at his grandmother's house in Virginia. Could you come here?"

"I'm on my way." Archie's call disconnects. Time appears to stretch from minutes to hours before he knocks on my front door, and I let him in. I wrap my arms around his torso, and my nails dig into his back as I press my ear to his chest. He kisses the top of my head. "I'm here," he whispers, but I can't let go.

The beating of his heart calms me. "Gwyn, if you don't let go, I can't lock the door."

"Oh, yeah." I release him from my grip of doom and knead my knuckles.

Archie locks the door and wanders around from room to room, checking the windows and listening for ominous clues. "I don't doubt you, but it appears to have gone, whatever it was. Did you get a good look at it?"

I'm trembling in my sweater and jeans. "No. Maybe I imagined it. I got so sick to my stomach when I saw Frank's body, and horrible images played in my head so vividly. I saw the attack on Frank Walker like I was right there with them when it happened."

"Why didn't you tell me?" Archie clasps my chilly hands.

I close my eyes, and my head quivers. "I don't know. All of this has been overwhelming. I'm afraid."

He wraps his arms around me again, and something hard pokes me from the inside of his jacket. "Why don't we try to sleep? I assume your bedroom is on the second floor?"

"Yeah. At the end of the long hallway." I motion toward the stairs.

Archie follows me to my bedroom, noting the paint peeling off the walls. "I could help you repair the walls. I did all the repairs in my house."

"Thanks for offering. Tyler plans to help. He's been after me to start the repairs and list the house with a realtor." I turn on the light, revealing my rundown bedroom with the mismatched bed.

"Do you want to sell?" he asks, removing his leather jacket.

"I think so. I didn't pick this house. Didn't like all the work it needed. Richard kept promising to hire people to do the repairs. After he passed, I didn't have the motivation to deal with it. Repairing the peeling paint seems to be a lower priority than finding and killing a murderous Sluagh. You know?"

"I do." Archie flattens his lips and scans the room. "The bathroom is in there?"

"Yes. Give me your jacket. I'll hang it in the closet." I hold out my hand as he pulls out his family dirk and sets it on a nightstand. He believes me.

Archie grabbed his toothbrush before coming. How can he be calm enough to remember his toothbrush? That gene didn't make it into my DNA. As he lies beside me, he molds his arms around my torso, sharing his calm to stop the tremors rattling my body. I fall asleep with the warmth of his body soothing my fearful heart.

Nightmare images of flapping shadows wake me throughout the night, invading the calm of Archie's embrace. When I awake, he has a firm hug around my shoulder. I shift onto my back, and his sensual smile relays a good morning. "I feel foolish now."

Archie caresses my arm. "Nonsense. I'm glad you called." He plants a wet kiss on my mouth.

"I guess I overreacted. Maybe I panicked and imagined all of it." Pushing against my headboard, I lean on the puffy upholstery material and relish in the velvety, warm coziness of my flannel pajamas and Archie in my bed. I haven't showered since Thanksgiving and can smell my body odor. How can he stand it?

"You didn't imagine it. Witches, especially ancestral witches, have an inner sense, empathic enough to absorb a person's potent emotions, and sometimes, even sense the future. Usually, it happens in the deep dream state. Odd it happened when you were awake."

The sense of dread I experienced at Mitchell Hall makes sense now. What other ancestral magic did I inherit? "I lack the coping skills to manage these new powers."

He draws a finger across my lower lip. "I know a sure-fire activity to reduce your stress." He ogles my chest and draws a finger down to the first button on my flannel top.

"Not happening. I'm gross and need a shower." I stretch my arms toward the ceiling and sigh at the crack. "That's it. I'm done with you." I jump out of the bed and walk to the door.

Archie pushes up on his elbows with a start. "Did I upset you?"

"Oh, no." I chuckle and gesture to the ceiling. "I'm done with that fucking crack on my ceiling. I'll be right back." After collecting a small tub of drywall mud and tools, I return and balance on the mattress while I slather the mud over the jagged crack in the plaster.

Archie talks like a foreman on a construction job. "You know you should put tape on the crack, right?" He rests his back on the upholstered headboard, clasping his hands behind his head. "And smooth it out." The flexing of his arms and pectorals is too much for me.

"I wanted to fill the gap first." Dropping on my butt, I bounce on the bed and lean over to give him a quick kiss. "I have so much to do to fix this house. On top of the repairs, I've got to go through all the closets, clean out the basement, and go through my parents' things. Didn't have the will to go through their stuff when they died." My eyes tear up a little. "I started going through a box before Thanksgiving but couldn't get through all of it without crying, so I stopped."

"I saw the open boxes and a steamer trunk in a bedroom. Nicer than the one I have." He runs his fingers through my hair and smooths my frizzy mop.

"Well, you're welcome to it, but the clasp is rusted shut." I fiddle with the hairs on his chest and ogle his pectorals.

His eyebrows tighten. "Don't you think you should check what's inside? There may be some important items in it."

"Oh, I doubt it. That clasp has been rusted shut for as long as I remember. It sat in front of the sofa so long there was a faded spot where the sun had bleached the carpet. It was a constant in my parents' house. I can't take it with me when I sell this house. It's too big and heavy."

"I'm sure." Archie brushes a finger across my lips.

Ogling his body reminds me I need to wash up. "I'll go take a shower and brush my teeth, and we'll continue this without my stink."

"I don't mind your stink," he says with a flirtatious smile. "I miss the smell of you when we're apart."

"You're pulling my leg." I poke him in the chest.

He snickers. "Maybe a wee bit. But I mean it when I say I miss everything about you when you're not with me."

It's about the closest he's gotten to saying those three important words to me. "I miss you, too," I say in a breathy voice.

Archie draws me to him and kisses me. "Go take your shower and brush your teeth." He grimaces and pats my butt.

"Hey. Not like you couldn't use a brushing yourself." I stick my tongue out and begin removing my pajamas, one sexy button at a time.

"So now you're going to tease me, are you?" He leans back against the headboard. "Not sure flannel pajamas do it for me."

While I continue to remove my old-lady jammies in a less sexy manner, Archie remarks on the style of my bed. "Why is your bed so modern, yet the rest of the furniture is cherry eighteenth century?"

"Not that it's any of your business what kind of bed I sleep in, but I had the four-poster bed Richard's father built. On the day of the funeral when Cassandra told me, you know, she also said Richard was going to give it to her."

"So, you sold it? Couldn't sleep in it after that?" he asks.

"No, I went out to the tool shed and got an axe. Lugged it up here and chopped it up." I pretend to hold an axe and swing it at the footboard.

"What?!" He laughs, grabbing his firm abdomen. "Remind me never to piss you off!"

I slip off my undies, throw them at him, and go into the bathroom to shower. He comes in to brush his teeth and splashes water on his face. I chuckle at the Horned God tattoo on his ass, a remnant of his youth. He blows me a kiss as he leaves the bathroom.

When I've finished, I dry off and slip on my purple, fuzzy robe, far from sexy, but it's what I've got. I strut to the bed, doing a seductive dance in my fuzzy robe, eliciting abdominal laughter from my gorgeous naked lover. I stop when a noise occurs downstairs, and I turn my ear toward the door.

"What's wrong?" Archie pushes up on his elbows.

"Nothing, I guess. Thought I heard a noise downstairs. Old, creaky house. Settling noises happen all the time in yours, too. Creeps me out." I walk over and get on the bed. "So, you don't think my purple robe is sexy?"

"No. Sorry. Not sexy at all," he says, rolling his head back and forth.

I climb over his torso and straddle him, pressing the warm, wet skin between my thighs against him. Desire burns in his clear-blue eyes. He pulls the tie on my robe and slides his fingers from the space between my breasts to my navel, exposing my bare skin.

"Well, well," Archie says, brushing his thumbs over my stiffening crests. "Now this is sexy." I lean forward to kiss his full, inviting lips, and the door to the bedroom swings open!

"Hey, Mom," Tyler says, walking into the bedroom. "Whose car is in the driveway?"

I shove the front edges of my robe together in a panic. "Oh, my gods, Tyler!"

"Shit!" Tyler turns around and heads back through the door. "I'm sorry, Mom. I'll leave and call you later." Before shutting the door, he says it again. "I'm so sorry."

"Agh." I hop out of the bed. "I've gotta get dressed and go talk to him before he leaves. You stay here." I collect some clothes and go into the bathroom to get dressed and comb my hair. When I come out, Archie has disappeared. "Archie? Where are you?" Voices echo in the stairwell, and I run to listen while my heart runs a mini-marathon.

Archie's baritone voice resonates in the foyer. "Hello. Tyler, right?"

There's silence, and Tyler's answer travels up the stairwell. "Yeah."

"It's awesome to meet you." I'm guessing some handshaking is happening. That's Archie's way. "My name is Archie Cockburn."

"Nice to meet you. Archie's not a name you hear often. My mom's guest lecturer the first week of school was called Archie."

My mouth falls, so low a train could easily tunnel right through it. I suck in all the air on the second floor and stamp down the stairs to warn them I'm approaching. I swallow and force the words through my lips. "Hi, Tyler. You've met Archie." I grin with every tooth showing, trying to appear innocent. Who am I kidding?

"Yeah. I should go. And come back later." Tyler looks away, suppressing laughter.

I stand speechless in the kitchen, with no foggy idea of what to say to my son. He turns toward the mudroom with car keys in his hand. Archie steps forward. "Stay, Tyler. I'm going to make breakfast. Please, join us." He gestures to a kitchen chair.

"Yes." I'm blushing like a high school girl who got caught screwing her boyfriend in the backseat of her parent's car. "Please, stay and eat breakfast with us."

Tyler's shoulders relax, and he chuckles. "OK. I can tell you about the fun times at Grandma Wolfe's." The awkwardness fades as Archie introduces a conversation about electric cars and the need for more charging stations in Bearsden. I can't slip in one word, but I don't care. They're talking like old friends.

When we've finished breakfast, I follow my son into the mudroom while Archie loads the dishwasher. "I'm sorry I put you in such an embarrassing situation."

"It's OK, Mom. I never walked in on you and dad having sex growing up, so it was bound to happen sometime." Tyler laughs and grabs his fleece jacket from a hook. "No need to get weird about it."

I gaze into the mirror image of my eyes. "Be honest. Does it bother you? Me being with someone?"

"Not at all, Mom." He zips his DUB fleece jacket and squeezes my shoulder. "This past year has been hell for you. You deserve to be happy. Does he make you happy?"

What a loaded question. Recently, it's crossed my mind I may have been better off never meeting him or any members of the coven. "Yes. I'm happy when I'm with him. He treats me like I'm the most important thing in his life." That's the first time I've said it out loud, yet how do I know for sure how he feels? He's never said those three words—I love you. But Richard said he loved me all the time, so maybe words don't matter?

Tyler wraps his arms around my shoulders in a tight hug. "That's what's important. Would you like to go Christmas shopping in a week or two?" He slips on his leather gloves. "Or whatever pagans celebrate. Yule? I could help you shop for Archie."

"You know, with everything going on, it hadn't even crossed my mind." Of course not. I have an evil Sluagh occupying my brain.

"I'll text you." He grimaces. "Find out what day works in your busy social calendar."

I frown and blink twice. "Don't be salty."

"You're hanging around Zillennials too much. Love ya." Tyler plants a peck on my forehead and heads for home.

When I return to the kitchen, Archie has finished cleaning. The countertops have never gleamed with such a reflection. The dishes and pans had piled up because of the pre-Thanksgiving school assignments and work. And the Sluagh shit. He pulls me to him, and his hands roam over my butt cheeks. "I think that went extremely well. Don't you?"

My eyebrows fall. "You're trying to be funny, right?"

"No," he says with a lopsided smile. "I'm not. I'm glad he knows. Aren't you?"

"Yeah. He's happy for me. I worried so much he would disapprove. Although I don't care what others think, Tyler's feelings matter." I finger the toned muscles on his back.

"And a fabulous young man he is, Gwyn. You should be proud. I look forward to visiting with him again." Archie kisses me tenderly. "Please, invite him to eat with us occasionally."

"I will." I peer out of the corner of my eye at the stairs.

Archie turns his head. "What are you looking at?"

"The steps. They lead to the second floor, which leads to my bedroom." I bat my eyelashes.

"The steps do ascend to the second floor." He kisses me again, teasing me with his tongue. "Shall we continue what we started?"

"Yes," I whisper with a breathy kiss. "Without my fuzzy robe."

CHAPTER TWENTY-TWO

A FAUX MOTHER'S BETRAYAL

ON THE SUNDAY MORNING after Thanksgiving, Ronnie sits at my kitchen table with her feet propped on a chair, waiting for her black coffee. Her crimson hair cascades over the back of the chair, a rippling river of wildfire, and she's wearing a sweater with a plunging neckline. It's easy to recognize how Derek found her so attractive. He appears so smitten with her bubbly, funny demeanor. I hope it works out for her.

After months of complaining, I gave in and bought a small slow drip coffee maker to make her the caffeinated fuel of champions she prefers. Thick like syrup, it's more like mud than coffee. It's death coffee. I retrieve an extra-large mug from the cabinet. "Meeting Derek's parents went well?"

"Fabulous." Ronnie checks her phone and sets it on the table. "His parents batted a few eyelashes over my age, but I think they're impressed I own a restaurant." She relaxes with her feet propped on the kitchen chair, as if there isn't a care in the world. How does she do it?

"They should be! I tell you all the time what a brilliant head you have for the business." I pour the black syrup into her mug and tip my head. "How the hell can you be so relaxed about the murders? Archie told me I shook all night in my sleep."

"My way of coping, I guess. And I wasn't there." Ronnie's eyebrows draw together. "So sorry you had to view the body. I didn't even hear about it until we got back last night. Trinity filled me in. Why didn't you call me?"

"I didn't want to ruin your weekend with Derek at his parents." I set the mug of death in front of her. "It was horrible. I looked at that man's missing eye and nearly threw up. A memory replayed in my head of Richard's body after the crash. I'm scared. Aren't you?" I join her at the table with a cup of Earl Grey.

"I am, but I have a lot of faith in our coven, Gwyn. Archie comes from a long line of ancestral witches, you know, but he hasn't had reason to show you the extent of his powers. Leslie, Trinity, and Shane have decades of experience. Elijah, Tanner, and Spence have natural abilities, including compassion and smarts. The rest of us? We're committed to doing our best. Your added power increased the group's potential exponentially. You get that, right? Archie's told you?"

"He did. I hope you're right." Her faith in their power comforts me. "How's the coffee? I don't make it much."

"It's delicious." She sniffs the swirls of the mud emanating from the mug. "Wouldn't it be great if I could inject it directly like a drug? Fat chance, though. We can't even get Delaware to pass a recreational marijuana bill. Good thing I have a secret source."

I fall back in my chair. "I never knew that! Why did you keep it a secret?" She knows I wouldn't care.

"Because you're a terrible liar." She drinks the last of her mud and sets the mug on the table. "I didn't want Richard to know. Mr. Goody Two-Shoes."

"We both know he was wearing the wrong shoes." I purse my lips and take a sip of my Earl Grey.

"That's for sure." Ronnie tightens a corner of her mouth and stands to pour herself another cup of death. "Things seem to be going well with Archie."

I grin from ear to ear. "They are. Tyler knows about him now." I chuckle, covering my mouth. "He walked in on Archie and me in bed."

"Oh, my gods." She cackles and nearly spills her coffee on the way to the table. "Was he upset?"

"Well, of course, at first. He caught his mother having sex, or about to, but he's OK with it. He wants me to be happy."

"I believed he would." Ronnie squeezes my hand. "I'm so happy for you. I like Archie."

"I never told you what happened the night of Samhain after Archie and I left the Pumpkin House." I'm getting cold feet, thinking about the walk back that night, but I want to tell her so badly. A naughty smile erupts, remembering our act of indiscretion.

Ronnie's blue eyes grow big and glassy, and she crouches over the table. I tell her every salacious detail from the sensual hand lovemaking to the heated moment against the bricks of Menzies Hall. Ronnie's jaw rests on the table, and I kindly push it closed before she drools into her mug.

"Gwyn! I'm so proud of you! Doing the deed outside your comfort zone. It must have shocked Archie."

"I think he was too busy ripping off my panties and losing them." I chuckle at the idea of some poor DUB student coming across my lacey lingerie on the walkway. "It was dark when we left. The Green was as empty as my fridge."

Ronnie guffaws like a hyena and almost knocks over her mug. "You have one over on me, lady. And who has time to grocery shop when there's sex to be had?" She clasps my hand and looks at me. "I'm laughing, but I am so impressed with how much you've grown in these last three months. I'm glad you found out about the coven and being a witch. It lifted an immense weight off my shoulders, too. I hated keeping secrets from you. Let's not keep anything from each other again."

Secrets. Like my visit with Audrey to the Celestial Gardens. If I tell Ronnie, she'd make me tell Archie. It's not worth the confrontation. Our stimulating discussion gets interrupted by texts on our phones. It's Archie. Their research at the Old Men oaks has shown no evidence of its use as a host by the Sluagh. He calls for a mandatory meeting at the Pumpkin House for all members to attend.

I lift my teacup to drink the remaining drops, missing my mouth completely, and the tea trickles down my top in a waterfall of Nervous-Nellie dribble.

On the walk to the Pumpkin House, Archie thanks me for not arguing with him over the escort. I should have worn a scarf to cover my face. It's more like a sprint than a walk, and the bitter wind scrapes across my cheeks with blades of icy air as I attempt to maintain his long stride.

When we arrive, the others are on the porch, shivering from the chilly air and apprehension. Archie unlocks the front door, and we flock like sheep to the back room, Leslie leading the way. I wait and lock the front door once the last members enter. We can't have Unremarkables walking in on this coven meeting. Somber expressions abound as we form a circle to discuss the murders on Thanksgiving.

Archie has a serious tone in his baritone voice. "Thank you all for attending this circle with minimum notice. By now, those of you not at the shelter on Thanksgiving have learned about the two additional murders of homeless men in the community. One was a frequent guest of the shelter named Frank Walker. The Bearsden Police have labeled the murders a serial killer case, but we know of the true killer. Elijah will explain what transpired at the shelter."

Elijah delivers details of the grim occurrence, prompting lots of groaning and gasps from the students who didn't attend the Thanksgiving dinner. He gets emotional talking about Frank and how scared the community has become, fearing the homeless are easy targets. Shane, Tanner, and Spence add a few comments about how the ordeal affected them and the guests.

"With the sightings by the two men who were with Frank Walker, we now have evidence the Host of the Unforgiven Dead has crossed over into our world," Leslie says. "We must discern two things. How did the Sluagh cross over? And how can we find it and send it back, or kill it?"

Congregated on one side of the circle, the young students sit speechless. I imagine making love potions, healing spells, and influencing corrupt politicians foretold of fun times when the coven leaders approached them about learning magic. Killing an Unseelie Court fairy that snatches its victims and dumps them hundreds of feet to their deaths wasn't on the job application.

The Bearsden witches talk over each other in a desperate, disorganized babble, like the heated public comment at the city council meetings. Prior coven circles never attained this level of a free-for-all. Trinity huffs, finding it impossible to interject a comment. "Enough!" Trinity stamps her stiletto heel. "All this jibber-jabber has gotten us nowhere. The person who knows the history of the Sluagh is Archie. What say you, leader?"

"Stories of the Sluagh passed down through my family for hundreds of years," Archie says. "What do we know for sure from family lore? We know the Sluagh can reach into our world through a host tree but cannot pass through in that fashion, and it can hide in a host tree to safeguard itself once it's here. And that is the puzzle, isn't it? It needed a portal to cross over and had to be summoned by a witch."

The burden weighs heavily on Trinity's brow. "We have too many unanswered questions at this point."

I have to tell them something. They need to check the Celestial Gardens again. Think, Gwyn, think. "Should you check the Celestial Gardens one more time? I know Leslie and Trinity checked there, but maybe it was in another tree that day."

"It's not a bad idea," Archie says. "Elijah, Shane. Let's check it out. We know the Seelie Fae children are coming through there."

"Can I go with you?" I rotate my earring as the sense of dread overcomes me, pulling me to the space.

Leslie taps her staff. "That isn't advisable. You are not level three trained. Elijah, Shane, and Archie will visit and report back. While we're assembled, the Nine will remain to prepare for the Monday council meeting."

"Yes, we have other fish to fry," Trinity says. "With the Celestial Gardens having some sort of portal, we have more important reasons to keep Mitchell Hall from becoming a parking lot. What would happen if they try to remove the mound? It sends shivers up my spine, thinking about it."

Archie ends the meeting, but Audrey remains seated with folded hands and an eager smile. He hasn't told her yet, always waiting until the last minute. There's no way I'm going to follow the order from Leslie now. I glance at Ronnie and Archie, pick up my purse, and head for the door. They can't stop me.

As I'm leaving, Leslie calls out to me in a strident voice. "Gwynedd, where are you going? You need to remain with the Nine."

I turn my head toward Archie, hoping for support. He glares at me and addresses Audrey. "I'm extremely sorry, but the coven needs Gwynedd's powers to ensure our success at the council meeting. Audrey, you may go."

Audrey glances back and forth at the Nine, and her bottom lip quivers. "Archie, you promised I would collaborate in this spell of influence. I worked damn hard to gain the skills needed to participate with the Nine." She screams something unintelligible and storms out of the room.

Dashing out after Audrey, I stop her before she exits through the front door. "I'm so sorry. I knew Leslie wanted this, but I tried to leave."

"Why didn't you withdraw?" Audrey sniffs, holding back the tears of disappointment.

I move closer to comfort her, but she steps back. "It's not my place to make these decisions. I've not even been a practicing witch for more than two months. The leaders have to decide what's best for the coven."

Audrey glares at me, clenching her teeth. "What a Faux Mom you turned out to be." She storms out of the Pumpkin House with a slam of the screen door.

I turn around and discover Archie has been listening from the hallway. "She will get over it." He offers his hand.

"You should have supported me," I say, clasping his fingers. "And I should have had more of a say. Do you let Leslie override every decision you make?"

"As Elder, Leslie has the final decision on certain matters." Archie brushes a hand through his hair. "She has her reasons for excluding Audrey but hasn't shared them with me. It's not my place to question it."

"There are certain dynamics about this coven I don't understand. I'm not sure I ever will."

When we're finished rehearsing the spell of influence, I approach Trinity, who's in a mood. "I have a question. Why bother with all this charade of applying for paperwork to give the mansion historical status? Picketing on campus?" I fling my hands in the air. "Why waste the time?"

"We make it look like we worked hard at changing their minds." Trinity crosses her arms and sways her head. "We can't go about using magic willy-nilly. It could blow our cover."

"Maybe we will convince them without another spell of influence."

"Maybe, but we can't take the chance. You see that, don't you? There is too much at stake."

All of it gnaws at my insides. The ethics of their actions. The threat of a raven monster crusher. And Audrey. How do I make things right with her? I wait for Archie on the porch with Ronnie, discussing the fiasco. "How do I improve our relationship? To her, I'm as bad as her real mom now."

Ronnie rubs my arm. "I don't know. Some people have too much baggage. Let her sulk a while. Eventually, she'll accept you had no say." She hugs me goodbye.

Tanner and Spence walk onto the porch with Elijah and Shane following behind them. "You still good for working Wednesday and Saturday, darling?" Shane asks.

"Sure, Shane. I have to continue with some kind of normalcy." I slip my gloves on my frigid hands.

"True dat." Elijah waves a hand. "Stay safe, everyone."

"Keeping a routine always helps me." Tanner winds his DUB plaid scarf around his neck like a corkscrew. "Although this has tested my cortisol levels. I need a swim."

"You all can go on about coping," Spence says, sliding on his mittens. "I'm going home and freaking out, thank you very much."

Tanner lays a tender hand on his back. "Let's go home, hon."

Archie and I walk back to his house and stop at my Prius in the driveway. "It's late. Why don't you stay tonight?" he asks.

"Not tonight. I have insurance work to complete tomorrow and need to be in my office to focus." I grab my car door handle with a beep-beep and yank it open. "And I've got schoolwork to complete. How the hell do Spence, Skye, and I concentrate on our presentation? I'm gaining a better understanding of my parents' decision to withdraw from this magical world. It's impossible to live a regular life."

Archie places both hands on my icy cheeks. "Tea. Lots of hot tea." He kisses me, warming my lips. "Search for the power inside. You will find the resolve. You have more strength than you realize."

I wish I had his confidence. My resolve tells me to go home, throw on flannel pajamas, and pull the quilt around my neck. And hibernate until spring.

Chapter Twenty-Three
The Ethics of Happiness

Restocking the shelves with herbs happens every Sunday at Mystic Sage. I don't mind, but the holiday onslaught of buyers has left the shelves of baskets and bottles in disarray. Not that I'm a poster child for organization.

A week has passed since the emergency coven circle. Because of the diligence of the shelter staff and the Bearsden Police, no more dead bodies have materialized. Of course, that doesn't mean the Sluagh took a coffee break. It could have dropped bodies in the local farm fields or woods in Maryland a couple of miles west of the DUB campus, and no one would discover them for weeks or months.

Archie, Shane, and Elijah visited the Celestial Gardens deep in the night. They remained for hours and saw no presence of either the Seelie Court Fae or the Sluagh. It makes no sense. I sensed its presence every time I visited the gardens. The obligation to tell Archie rips me apart inside, but I can't betray Audrey's trust.

My insides aren't the only parts falling apart. My hair needs coloring and a cut, and the dark circles under my eyes have returned, making my face appear as haggard as an old...hag.

Maybe today wasn't the day to go sans makeup? Shane eyes me while he stocks the holiday display of wood and iron puzzles. "Don't take this as an insult, but you look a little rough around the edges, Gwyn."

"I've not been sleeping well with everything going on," I say, dusting the bottles of herbs. "I'm on edge all the time."

"Sorry to hear that, darling. Maybe after we close the store, I can perform a healing spell. Refresh your body a smidgeon." He smiles, and his ruby-red lips peek through the white cloud of hair. "Or would you rather Archie do the healing?" He snickers under his breath while stacking the boxes of specialty games.

I throw him a look of really-you-went-there? "I don't think so, Shane. It's all the magic and supernatural mayhem that's making me feel out of sorts. I want normal right now. You know?"

"Oh, I do, darling. I do." He tidies the tarot cards and runes display where a rude customer had dumped the stones into a pile.

"Shane, do you ever wish you could go back to the time when you were an Unremarkable?"

"That would be a long trip! Late at night when I'm alone, my mind drifts back to those days." He has a twinkle in his emerald-green eyes. "In my twenties, I fashioned myself a haberdasher like my granddaddy. Then I met a woman. She had jet-black hair, enchanting blue eyes, and a figure to keep a man up at night if you get my drift."

I chuckle and wrinkle my nose. "I think so."

"She taught me about magic and the supernatural. Opened my eyes to everything. I came alive with that woman and credit her with my impeccable crystal skills. I miss her every day."

A sadness crawls onto my face, listening to Shane's story of longing. "Aww. Your wife, I assume?"

"Hell, no." He strokes his snow-white beard while he recalls bygone days. "My wife Judith was an Unremarkable 'til the day she died. Never knew I was a witch. Loved her and miss her dearly, though."

I tip my head. "Who was the witch with jet-black hair?"

"Cordelia. Turns out I was nothing but a plaything to her. Used me and left me for the wolves." Air hisses through Shane's teeth as he finishes with the games. "I met Judith not long after, and she was as sweet as pie. She provided normalcy, being Unremarkable. Gotta have a touch of normalcy to keep you grounded. You understand that, I bet?"

I shut my eyes for a moment, finding comfort in his story, and snap back to reality. "But you achieved your career goal, after all?" I blink twice and point to the Santa and Elf hat rack. "Haberdasher. Your granddaddy would be proud."

Shane lowers his bushy eyebrows, befuddled, and bursts out in boisterous laughter. "Good one, darling. Good one."

The door dings, and Elijah enters, appearing larger than normal in a gray puffer jacket and scarf. He looks like someone pulled out an air compressor and blew him up. "What's so darn funny?"

I clutch my abdomen, chuckling. "Shane. He's achieved his life goal of becoming a haberdasher."

"Isn't that glorious?" Elijah kneads his chilly hands together and warms them with his hot breath. "I doubt you'll get rich selling Santa and Elf hats all year round, though."

"Hardly," Shane says. "What can we do for you, Elijah?"

"I need your help. We've done a good job keeping tabs on the shelter residents except for one—Sebastian. He hasn't shown this week, and I'm worried."

Shane grabs his jacket from behind the check-out. "That's quite alarming. When did you see him last?"

"He stayed and ate at the shelter three nights ago. He's gone on benders before and could be passed out anywhere." Elijah rubs the nape of his neck, and his chest rises. "I hoped this time would stick. He was in good spirits. With this Sluagh flying around and hiding wherever the hell it is, I've got a bad feeling."

"Let's hit the streets then, friend. Gwyn, I didn't even ask. Do you mind closing the shop for me?"

"Sure, Shane. Go find Sebastian. And when you find him, tell him to come back to the shelter and eat lunch with Ms. Gwyn." Poor Sebastian. I don't want them to find him passed out on the street drunk, but that would be better than the alternative—a mangled, dead body missing eyes. Where is the Sluagh? How big is it? How does it lift a human body when it takes the form of a shadow? And why in the hell does it caw AND growl? Dog envy?

It's 5:58 p.m., and I decide to lock up early since the store was empty for the last hour. When I approach the door to turn the sign, eccentric Agnes Pritchard has her face pressed against the glass, one bulbous eye examining the inside of the store. Ugh. I move back from the door, and she enters with a ding. "I need ONE item." Agnes shuffles over to the herbs. Clutching two bundles, a mugwort and a St. John's Wort, she scoots to the counter and drops them on the counter.

"You have two items, Agnes," I say, frowning.

Her salt and pepper hair covers half of her withered face while she grumbles and scowls at me. "I need extra protection."

"Protection from what, Agnes?" I concentrate on her expression while I bag her items.

"Oh, you know what," she replies in a gravelly voice. "I don't need a receipt." She lays cash on the counter and exits the store. What else does Agnes know?

After closing Mystic Sage, I stroll home via Main Street with a plan to run the last mile. Shoppers pack the sidewalks from telephone pole to telephone pole, and I bump into the hurried consumers. The street glitters with white lights strung between the poles and gigantic, white snowflakes hang from each lamppost. The city has erected a large Christmas tree with red bows and a giant-size menorah, flickering with brilliant, fake flames. How I wish I could enjoy the Yule season.

On the way home, I think about Audrey. She's had a good amount of time to cool off, so I call her on my cell phone. Audrey answers but says nothing. "Hi, Audrey. It's Gwyn."

Quiet ensues, and I hope she didn't hang up. A whistle of air breaks the silence. "I know. Your number is in my contacts."

"Oh, right. I wanted to see how you're doing." There's another long pause, and my chest tenses.

Audrey sighs into the phone. "I'm over it, Gwyn."

My shoulders relax. "I'm so happy to hear that. Know that I cherish this relationship, Audrey. I never had a daughter, and your happiness matters to me."

"I value our relationship, too." Audrey is silent again for a moment. "I'll be there tomorrow night at the council meeting. The entire coven will be there for support."

"See you at City Hall." I swipe the red button on my phone and smile.

DUB students and members of the community are lining the front walk with various signs reading "Save Mitchell Hall" and "Vote NO for Alistair and Rose!" Most of the coven has arrived, and we choose to hang in the back behind the multitude of people. Mayor Manley and the council members listen intently to all community comments. The mayor displays his usual smug face.

Dr. Hughes speaks first, reminding the council they have filled out the paperwork necessary to have Mitchell Hall declared a historical landmark. Trinity and Elijah explain how permanent offices in a future community center would provide easy access for their community groups in need. Offices on Main Street would enhance services to underserved populations by providing job assistance that would lead to permanent housing.

Skye, Spence, and Zoe share how the Mitchells fostered an environment of acceptance, helping them to adapt to a campus atmosphere that wasn't always open to those who didn't fit the standard mold. Once the Fellowship has finished with their public comment, several Unremarkables line up to share their personal stories as students at DUB. Some community members share concerns over demolishing an iconic building that would change the architecture of Main Street.

The public comment goes on for two hours, and I doze off on Archie's arm. He nudges me, but I can't stop yawning. The council prepares to vote, and the Nine huddles close together while we chant inside our heads. Mayor Manley and two of his cronies vote yes to demolish the mansion, and the three council members on our side vote no like we expected. The final council member, Lindsey Hope, struggles like in the prior meeting, but this time she grabs her head as if she's experiencing intense pain.

"Someone is fighting against our influence, Trinity," Dr. Hughes whispers.

"Well, we'll fight a little harder." Trinity scans the room for a hidden malcontent but can't lock onto the source of the unwanted power grab.

Lindsey Hope comes through for us again and votes no against the demolition of Mitchell Hall, stating the importance of keeping the iconic, historical building. The room erupts with applause, whistling, and foot stamping, sounding like a herd of cattle on the run. Creating a community center was my idea, and it's come to fruition, no matter how unethical the means. When I view the Council Chamber doors, Audrey and Courtney leave without joining us in our celebration.

Mr. Yeats lounges in the corner chair of the magic room with his legs crossed, reading a book on the poets of the twentieth century. He's not supposed to be spying on me while I practice my protection spells. He tries to hide behind those antiquated spectacles and peeks at me over the leather-bound book.

"I see you, Mr. Yeats." I read the ingredients of the recipe out loud while I grind them. "A betel nut, ague root, a devil's claw leaf—" I read the recipe for the protection spell one more time and stop, remembering I can also burn curry powder while I work to keep evil forces at bay. I'd like to banish them to the Otherworld.

"You're forgetting the most important ingred-i-ents," he says in a condescending tone.

I huff at him. "I'm not done. Osha root and boneset make it complete." I grind in the remaining herbs, thinking I never worked this hard cooking dinner. It's so much like baking. I hate baking.

Mr. Yeats eyes my arm. "Quite a bicep you have there, Ms. Crowther. Much larger than most women your size."

"Thank you, I guess?" I love he noticed my hard work, but it's a little creepy he's been ogling my arms.

He insists on giving me directions while he flips the pages in his book. "You know you have to apply your witch energy to activate the spell or you will have wasted thirty minutes of work."

I pull out a sneer and whip him with it. "I'm activating it now." Summoning my witch energy, I apply it to my concoction and pray I don't ignite a fire. When the energy becomes hot like molten lava, I pull back and release it, leaving a bowl of nicely cooked herbs ready for a carry pouch. I grin with satisfaction. For the first time, I have confidence in my skills. "I'm a witch."

Mr. Yeats drops the poetry book in his lap. "You've only discovered this? What do you think you've been doing all this time?"

I chortle. "I didn't realize I spoke out loud. Of course, I knew I was a witch, but I didn't feel like one. At least, not a competent one." I scoop the protection spell, sift it into a small, purple velveteen pouch, and pull the drawstring closed. As I place it in my purse, I'm careful to insert it into a zippered section. With the Sluagh on the loose, I can't afford to have it fall out. I pray to the gods this protection spell works.

The mudroom door opens, and clicking footsteps approach the room. Mr. Yeats and I lock eyes and speak in unison. "Trinity."

"Whatcha doing?" Trinity's hair is clipped haphazardly with strands of burgundy hair seeking refuge near the curve of her neck. Mr. Yeats opens his mouth to talk, but Trinity throws him a laser glare. "Not you, Mr. Yeats. You're always up to no good, or in somebody's business."

He mumbles to himself, mocking her from behind his poetry book.

Trinity shakes a finger at him and grimaces. "Don't think I can't see what you're doing behind your book."

"I'm not working on anything now," I say, sweeping the table. "Finished a powerful protection spell to carry in a pouch. I improve with every practice session."

"Niiice!" she exclaims. "Leslie said you'd be here. I hoped we could shoot the shit about Monday night." Trinity leans back against the table, picks up one of Leslie's books, and turns the pages. "You left with a sour face the other night."

I return the mortar and pestle to the shelf and move next to her. "I still have mixed feelings about influencing the City Council vote. That being said, I am happy about the outcome. But I'm not sure how I feel about a coven deciding what is and isn't best for the community. Is it really our place?" She's too tall for me to meet her gaze, so I glance at Mr. Yeats, who has turned his ear to improve his eavesdropping.

"We've already talked about this many times. The sitting mayor and city council have a history of so much corruption, lining their pockets or the pockets of their friends." Trinity huffs and pushes up her lower lip. "And now I'm hearing rumors a big developer from Jersey bought votes to guarantee the contract on the planned parking garage. Do you think their plans are ethical?"

"No," I say, conceding her point. "I want all of us to be happy, but not at the expense of others. There's a line I won't cross if it affects the happiness of others."

Mr. Yeats interrupts and adds his two cents. "One should never increase their happiness at the expense of others. I completely agree."

"No one asked you." Trinity flashes him an evil eye. "Gwyn, you're not talking about the spells of influence. You're upset about Leslie's decision to choose you over Audrey to join the Nine at the last council meeting."

"Yes. I'm trying to be a foster mom to Audrey, and these decisions aren't helping me build the relationship. You, of all people, should understand her situation," I say.

"I do. I had the same mentoring when my parents kicked me out of the house, and I'll be forever grateful for it. It was Leslie's decision, and I'm sure as the sun rises and sets, she had a good reason." Trinity clasps my hand in hers. "I'll leave you with this. I live according to The Ethics of Happiness. It's Aristotle. Happiness is what we strive for, but it's not a means to an end. To get there, we must be rational, smart, and good people and become creatures of habit, doing these things rationally and of our own free will. So, I get what you're saying."

"I hope so." I notice Mr. Yeats bobbing his head as he inspects the ruffle in his bow tie. As if we need his approval?

Trinity pats my back when I turn toward the worktable to finish cleaning. "I'm glad we talked, 'cause we got bigger problems than the city council's corruption right now. The Bearsden Police found a fourth body in a back alley behind one of the campus buildings."

Mr. Yeats sits upright, adjusts his spectacles, and slams his book shut. My head snaps around. "Shit. Another homeless person?"

"Yeah." Trinity tears up. "Elijah identified the body, crushed and both eyes missing. It's Sebastian."

The Ethics of Happiness. I bet the evil Sluagh never read Aristotle.

CHAPTER TWENTY-FOUR
ATTACK OF THE SLUAGH

ARCHIE SENT ME A text, begging me to stay at his house and not walk alone at night. He called me a "stubborn woman" when I turned him down. I own it. The problem with a murderous Sluagh? It doesn't care if I've got classwork due the next day, but Dr. Hughes does. With a couple of weeks of class left, we have to push on, but I've got the motivation of a sloth.

The Bearsden Coven has decorated the Pumpkin House with evergreen festoons and colored lights. A Yule tree stands tall in the corner next to the oak fireplace, covered in strings of twinkling white lights. Envelopes containing gift wishes for needy children hang all over the tree.

There are less than two weeks to Yule, but the coven has a more pressing matter. With four bodies found so far, the Bearsden Police Department has issued official warnings to the community of a possible serial killer. We have to foster this alternate reality for the sake of the Unremarkables.

The meeting begins with the students, angry and shaken, demanding to know if a plan has been formulated. Have the elders discovered where it's hiding? How did it cross over into our world? Zoe whimpers. "I'm scared. I don't think we have enough magic skill to battle it."

"I wouldn't have become a witch if I'd known about any of this," Courtney whines. "None of this is worth putting our lives at risk." For a quiet girl, I find it interesting she's being so verbal now. Her friend Audrey says nothing.

Spence and Skye sport faces the color of chili peppers. Tanner is out of fucks and rants. "If any of you have more to reveal, you need to speak up. This is bullshit, being forced to fight supernatural beings with no preparation. And now, we have to do something as a coven to save the community from this Sluagh."

During this meltdown, the older witches remain silent, allowing the younger witches to vent their frustrations. And the guilt of my secret knowledge burns like acid in my stomach. Ronnie notices my fingers tapping like I'm sending Morse Code. "Do you need to pee, Gwyn?"

"No." I stop and fold my hands. "I may know something about the Sluagh. I think I know where it's hiding."

Ronnie gapes at me. "Humph. You need to tell them. And now."

Archie spies our conversation from across the circle and stands to address the coven. "I hear all of you. I understand your grievances, and they have validity. We always weigh the importance of being transparent, but the elements of the supernatural world are many. We train you for the elements as they present themselves. Anything more would be overwhelming."

"Thank you, Archie." Leslie stands with a grip on her staff. "Direct your complaints to me. I decided long ago too much information can inhibit neophytes, which does nothing to strengthen the coven. The success of the coven outweighs your need to know."

The coven erupts into a thunderous chatter with the students losing their shit. Ronnie elbows me. I'm about to speak when Trinity stands to talk.

"You can bitch and moan about what shoulda been, but it's history now. There is something very evil and dangerous, killing people in our community. You wanna bitch and lodge complaints after we've killed the thing or sent it back to the Otherworld? Fine. But for now, stop your whining and offer solutions. Or you know where the damn door is." She squishes her face like a pug dog and points her thumb at the door.

"These are MY people," Elijah says with tears in his eyes. "I eat with them, cry with them, help them through the DTs. And now four of them lie at the morgue. I know this all scares you. Scares the shit out of me, too, but I have faith you can pull through and help us fight this monster."

Ronnie mutters under her breath. "Now is the time. Why are you waiting?"

Why? Because the entire coven will chastise me, and I'm not looking forward to the condemnation. I survey the circle of witches and stop at Audrey. Another betrayal will kill our relationship for good. Better than getting killed by a Sluagh, I suppose.

"I have something to share. I think I may know where the Sluagh is hiding." Staring at Archie, I brace myself for his backlash. "It's using the hawthorn tree in the Celestial Gardens."

Archie's eyes twitch. "Why are you only telling us now?" He's really asking, why didn't I tell him before now?

Trinity leans back in her chair, flinging her hands. "Gwyn, we checked out the space. You know that. And the men checked it again last week. Nothing."

"Trinity, she's certain because she's been there since you examined the area. I'm correct, am I not?" Archie glares at me with steely eyes.

Trinity snaps. "What the hell, Gwyn?!"

"You defied our orders to stay out of the gardens," Leslie says with a stare so cold it makes me shiver. "No witch in this coven has ever defied our orders."

The others shake their heads, rumbling utterances I don't want to discern. Archie's angry gaze stakes me in the heart.

"I didn't want to. Audrey drank too much with dinner and ran in there. I couldn't allow her to be alone in case the Sluagh returned. It was the night I found out there may be a presence in the tree." I glance at Audrey, and she lowers her eyes. Nausea churns deep in my stomach, and I swallow over and over.

"Audrey can take care of herself, Gwynedd." Archie shifts in his seat, but his steely eyes remain fixed on mine. "We will deal with your disobedience and Audrey's at a later time. For now, you need to share what happened."

As I explain, Audrey stares at the floor. She won't forgive me after this. When I finish, I try to redeem myself. "Please understand. I supposed I imagined it. And when I sat on the bench, unable to move, I was sure I'd had a panic attack. No other explanation seemed rational. I'm sorry." The coven's faces remain sullen—my apology met with the sting of their contempt. My adopted family appears ready to throw this newbie witch out on the street.

"I understand how you feel, Gwyn," Tanner says calmly. "But it wasn't your choice to decide what is important. You're part of a coven now. You can't decide one witch has more importance than the coven and the town. Archie's right. Audrey can take care of herself."

"I believe you were trying to do right by Audrey," Elijah says, scratching his head. "Yet if you had told us all sooner, maybe Sebastian would be alive."

That. Hurt. I get it. I fucked up, but Sebastian's death is NOT my fault. Instantly, I want to bolt out of there before they kick me to the curb.

Leslie raises an open hand to the coven, and their buzz of disapproval dissipates. "We shan't lay blame. We succeed as a coven, and we fail as a coven. Without Gwyn's return to the gardens, we could have searched for weeks trying to discover the Sluagh's host while more community members lost their lives." The others relax their tight faces, including Archie.

"The Sluagh's choice of the hawthorn tree as a permanent host aligns with the lore," Archie says. "But it still doesn't explain how it crossed over."

Shane hypothesizes while he pets his beard. "The mound in the gardens allowed for the Seelie Fae children to cross. Gwyn's interactions with the mischievous Seelie prove the crossover. Could the Sluagh have crossed through the mound as well?"

"Not according to the lore," Archie says. "It must cross through a much larger portal."

Spence perks up, snapping his fingers. "We opened a portal. On Samhain!"

Trinity grimaces. "While I don't doubt it's a possibility. I think we would have noticed a big, raven shadow flying through it."

Audrey squirms in her seat, like she's sitting on a pinecone, and scans the others for their reactions. Did she notice something? I wait for her to speak up, but her lips are sealed. I think back on Samhain recollecting the phenomenon that changed my life forever. "Samhain was an emotional night for the entire coven. If the Sluagh had to cross over through a large portal, we have to assume it entered our world that night."

I glance at Archie, and his face has relaxed to more of an observer collecting information for a hunt—a big, bad Sluagh hunt. The younger witches shift in their chairs and babble about what they remember from the ritual. Leslie sits with her hand on her Elder staff, collecting the morsels of each conversation.

Some say it was invisible. Others suggest it sneaked in when Richard appeared. We're wasting precious time. Leslie taps her staff three times, and their words fade into silence. "I appreciate the energy all of you have put into deciphering this mystery. In the early days, this coven opened the portal, and I witnessed an astounding event. I saw nothing unusual occur the evening of Samhain."

I cut her off. "No, but I think I did." An insignificant memory proves to be not so trivial. "Everything was a shock to me on Samhain. In an instant, I knew I existed in a different world than I'd known all my life. After I pushed my hand toward the portal, I saw the blue haze dissipate. And something near the ceiling moved. A black shadow, slithering like a snake as it vanished into the wall."

Ronnie presses her lips together. "I sure wish you had remembered that sooner."

"I'm doing the best I can, Ronnie." I grind my teeth.

Tanner wipes his sweaty hands on his pants. "So, how do we send this murderous thing back if it came through the Samhain portal?"

"Exactly," Spence says. "How many people will it kill by next October?!"

Skye talks with a quiver in her voice. "We can't wait that long. The Unremarkables will eventually discover the Sluagh. Would cause a helluva problem."

Archie trades glances with Leslie, unspoken witch communication, and makes an announcement. "We open the portal now."

The coven creates a rumble with a lot of "whats" and "hows" prattled about, but I'm too upset to offer suggestions. And what do I know?

Leslie waits for the witches to quiet down. "It's difficult to open a portal outside of Samhain, but some covens have been successful. Archie and I would need to reach out to other covens and ask for representatives to strengthen our group and guide us through it."

"We'll petition the city to use the gardens for our Winter Solstice celebration," Archie says. "It has an eight-foot fence, and it's where the Sluagh resides. We do it there." He intercepts my gaze and holds it captive, and I can't breathe. "Leslie, Trinity, and I will make plans and send them to all of you. In the meantime, please be vigilant."

With three taps of her Elder staff, Leslie dismisses the coven. The younger witches dart out while Tanner and the older witches gather to discuss the parameters of renting the space. They also discuss the most important question. Who summoned the Sluagh through the portal and why? I slide on my jacket and make my way to the front door. I'm not about to stay at Archie's after he embarrassed me. Leader or not, he could have been more understanding.

As I'm leaving, Archie grabs my arm like a Scottish brute. "Gwyn, where are you going?" He glares at me with those steely eyes, and I'm not having it.

"I'm walking to my car and going home." My eyes spasm as I yank my arm from his grasp.

Archie clenches his jaw, and his nostrils flare. "I'm the leader of the coven, Gwyn. You put me in a difficult position by keeping your wee visit a secret."

"I. Don't. Care." I shove the door open and step onto the porch. I see Ronnie and walk to her, where she's waiting for Derek to give her a ride home.

"I'm sorry, Gwyn." She extends her arms to me. "I know you're pissed. I should have been more supportive, but I'm not happy with you either. Why didn't you tell me about your sneaky visit to the gardens? We vowed not to keep any more secrets. It's upsetting you couldn't trust me."

My brain floats in a dense fog, and I mumble. "I'm sorry. But I don't like how Archie treated me in the meeting."

"As the leader, he's responsible for all of us." Her chest deflates, and her arms drop to her sides. "What did you expect? Would you like Derek to drop you off at your car?"

"No," I say curtly. "I'm gonna walk on the Green. It's lit well enough and has lots of nooks and crannies to take cover. I'll be fine."

Ronnie pleads with me through soulful eyes. "Call me soon?"

"I will." The corners of my mouth struggle to rise. It's all I can force out of this body full of knots.

I glance back through the front door. Archie is talking with Elijah and Tanner. They're probably talking about me, but I don't care. I want to get home to the sanctuary of my bed, and the heavy cotton quilt calls out to me as I cross the street to the Green.

Empty like an Egyptian tomb, the clicking of my high-heeled boots echoes off the red-brick buildings, creating a creepy stalker vibe. I stop and turn around to a vacant Green. Too angry and too tired to be scared, I trudge along. Click, clack, click, clack. I turn around again. I'm sure I heard muffled footsteps but deduce it's the resonance of my boot heels.

The lampposts provide plenty of light as I approach the Old Men oak trees. I veer off to the angled paver walkway leading to the left side of the Green. I'm not making THAT mistake again. For all I know, the Sluagh made those trees its first host to take me out. I stop. "Take me out." All at once, it dawns on me. What if finding me was its objective all along? I panic, and my head becomes foggy again, and a sense of dread seizes my body.

In the distance, I notice two men running toward me, one of immense height and build, the other thin and not so tall. The deep caws of a bird and the growling of wolves echo off the buildings on the Green. They're behind me. No. To my right. To my left. No. Above me!

I bend my head back to observe the crescent moon, illuminating the Green, and panic at the sight of an approaching monstrous, flapping figure—an enormous, black raven, glimmering in the moonlight. It's a shadow, but not a shadow, with thousands of smaller ravens, creating the illusion of one gargantuan bird. It's heading straight for me, its beak opened wide enough to swallow me whole!

I raise my hands to summon my witch energy, but it won't surface! I remember the pouch is in my purse and chant the words to the protection spell, but they get jumbled in my head. It's too late. The Sluagh's colossal claws reach out to snatch me, and I cover my face, screaming.

Elijah and Tanner shove me to the ground. They chant and stretch their hands toward the sky with fireballs of amber in the palms of their hands. They throw the balls of fire at the Sluagh with the force of missiles, sending it off against the backdrop of the white glow of the crescent moon.

"Are you OK, Gwyn?" Elijah and Tanner ask, helping me off the ground.

My body trembles as I spit out the answer. "Yes. I'm so grateful you both happened by." My teeth are chattering so loud they must hear them.

"Archie decided it would be a good idea," Tanner says. He strokes my back while Elijah calls Archie on his cell phone.

"What?" I ask. "Archie sent you to stalk me?" The white mist of our breath creates a ground-like cloud of protection around us.

Tanner wraps his arm around me. "We weren't stalking you, Gwyn. Archie had a right to be concerned." Tanner glances at Elijah. "Does he want us to wait here with her?"

"No," Elijah replies with a frosty breath. "He wants us to take her to his house and wait there. You have a key, Gwyn?"

"Yes, I have a key."

When we get to Archie's, I offer them hot chocolate, but they tell me I should find a seat and calm down. I sit on the loveseat, and my body trembles like the aftershocks of an earthquake, not knowing when they'll strike. After a few minutes, Tanner returns with hot chocolate for all of us.

"Be careful," Tanner says, passing us the mugs of comfort. "The water came to a full boil in the microwave."

I take a sip, singeing my tongue and throat, but I'm numb to it. The front door opens, and Archie enters, motioning Tanner and Elijah to the foyer. He thanks them for their help, but I can't make out the rest. I set the mug on the steamer trunk. The mantle clock strikes 9:00 p.m., and the dings begin. I don't want to talk to him, but I'm too shaken to go home. "I'm going to bed."

Archie gazes at me with his icy blues that melt even the coldest heart, but not tonight. I throw off my boots and stamp up the stairs in my socks, determined not to speak to him. After stripping to my bra and panties, I climb into his bed and pull the covers close to my chin. The vision of the Sluagh violates my inner thoughts, and I can't stop quivering.

The shuffle of Archie's footsteps resounds in the house while he checks the locks on all the doors and windows. The stairs creak, and he enters the bedroom, emptying his pockets onto the dresser. I face the wall away from him, and the glass door to his dirk case opens. There's a rustling of his pillowcase as he slides the dirk under his pillow. He climbs into bed next to me, never uttering a word. I don't want him to touch me. Yet he wraps his arms around my upper body, still quivering uncontrollably from the attack of the Sluagh.

CHAPTER TWENTY-FIVE

A SLUAGH HANGOVER

I ROLL MY HEAD and find Archie absent from the bed. I touch the dented spot where he slept, nestled against my back all night, and it warms the palm of my hand. The memory seizes me. I cry out from visions of gigantic claws piercing my skin. They dig deep into my muscle and drag me along the abrasive concrete pavers, painting them garnet-red, the color of the azaleas in my garden. A numbing chill crawls up my vertebrae, stopping with a violent shudder at the nape of my neck, and I take a minute to draw air back into my lungs.

The dirk rests safely back in its locked case, and the aqua gem gleams from the sun peeking through the window shade. My feet hit the cold wooden floor, and I hug my arms to limit the rising hair on my arms. I run to the toilet for my morning pee and pluck Archie's black thermal robe from the hook on the creaky bathroom door. The robe smells of his woodsy cologne, and I press my nose to the material.

Archie's loading the dishwasher, wearing the t-shirt and lounge pants he slept in. I fall into a chair and lay my groggy head on the palm of my hand. I feel like shit—a Sluagh hangover. He turns around, sporting a complacent face, and dries his hands on a tea towel. I expect him to chop my head off and rub my face in it.

"How are you?" he asks, a warmth radiating in his eyes. His soft, Scottish accent calms me like always. "You look a wee bit peely-wally. You whimpered in your sleep and shook all night."

I peer at him through droopy eyes. "What is peely-wally?"

"Oh, it means pale, tired." Archie tosses the towel on the counter and leans back.

Yeah. That's me. "I had nightmares about the Sluagh. I was running, and it kept getting closer no matter how fast I ran. Each time I turned my head, the claws grew larger, and the caws and growls rang louder in my head. Its claws dug deep into my body, and it dragged me away, leaving streaks of blood as it pulled my body along the walkway." I stop to fill my lungs and let the air out as I count in my head. "I know that's not what happened, but it appeared real in my dreams."

"It's possible you inherited heightened empathic skills, experiencing the attack through the eyes of a victim. Sensed it from the Sluagh as it approached." Archie's brow creases. "You said you've had other dreams. Let's hope your nightmares have empathic connections and aren't warnings about future events."

"Well, that sucks." I recall the two dreams from my Unremarkable days, and my head throbs. Does acetaminophen cure a Sluagh hangover?

Archie sets a cup of hot tea in front of me, sits, and takes my hands in his. "Gwynedd, I am truly sorry you felt attacked by the coven last night, and me. However, if given identical circumstances, I would react accordingly. As coven leader, I am responsible for the welfare of every witch in it. Rules, like laws, are established for a reason—order and safety. Your actions, and Audrey's, put the coven at risk. More importantly, it put the community at risk."

He's right, of course, but I stand my ground. "I didn't want to betray Audrey's trust. As a mom, I'd do it again."

"True enough, stubborn woman." He scratches his goatee. "But know consequences follow unwise decisions."

"So, what is my punishment? Do I get spanked?" I quip.

A wicked grin emerges on Archie's face. "It's NOT the standard punishment, but I'd be willing to consider it a substitute."

I flatten my lips. "Seriously, what consequence exists for disobedience in the coven? I'll abide by it."

Archie cups my pale face with his tender hand. "You've suffered enough. No other sanctions are necessary. I hope you have learned from it."

"Getting attacked by the Sluagh? Or the ire of the coven?" I ask.

"Both, but you needn't worry about the Fellowship." He goes to the fridge to get eggs. "I sent a text to everyone, letting them know of the attack. They expressed their concern to you directly, but you mustn't have checked your phone." The tightness in my chest loosens a bit as he continues. "I've told everyone to stay away from the gardens until the Winter Solstice." He glares at me with tight lips and drops a pan on a burner with a clink.

"I will. I promise." My index finger swipes back and forth on my chest. "Cross my heart."

Archie's eyes narrow. "You know, it's a Christian expression and means nothing to a pagan."

I chuckle and bat my eyes. "You'll have to trust me, I guess."

He stares at me with a lopsided smile and cracks an egg open in the pan. As the egg sizzles, my mood changes from teasing to the reality of the frightening situation.

"How will we send it back? And not get hurt or killed in the process?"

"That's the million-dollar question, isn't it?" Archie flips the omelet in the pan. "Leslie has called the covens in the area and asked for their help. We haven't heard back from them yet."

My hands shake, and the idea of facing the Sluagh again overwhelms me. "I don't think I can do this. I believed I could until I saw the monster raven." My body stiffens, craving the solace of my bed and an Unremarkable life. I can't hold back the torrential deluge. "I wish...I wish I were Unremarkable again, living a boring, depressing life as the widow of a cheating husband. And I need to tell Tyler what happened, but I can't. I hate keeping secrets from him. He needs to know."

Archie turns off the burner and rushes to me, taking me in his arms. His gentle hand presses my head against his chest. "I worried the joking was a deflection." He strokes my tousled, faded hair while my wet cheeks dampen the front of his shirt. "I forgot how frightening it is to witness the first monstrous being. I came close to driving my car straight into a loch the first time I saw one. Was raised a witch but never saw something so scary as the Bean Nighe I saw as a wee lad. About thirteen, if I remember correctly."

I lift my head and search his face for comfort. "You were scared?"

He wipes the tears from my face. "Hmph. Pissed my pants!" He bursts out laughing, and the crow's feet around his eyes fold out like a hand fan.

"I can't believe you told me that." I'm laughing, my face a soggy mess.

He cups my face again. "I never told anyone. You're the first." He hands me a tissue. "Told my family I fell in the loch. I jumped in to cover the fact I'd pissed myself." His story makes me laugh out loud. "You have an infectious smile, Gwyn." He strokes the side of my mouth. "No matter what you say or do, I can't help myself when I see your smile." He kisses me, and my trepidation melts away, if only for this Sluagh-free moment in time.

"Some powerful ancestral witch I've turned out to be," I say through sniffles.

"You're stronger than you think." He blots the tears of terror from my peely-wally face with the tissue. "Although I jest, I don't make light of your fear. The Sluagh has supernatural power and presents a danger to all of us. We must send it back."

"And if we can't?" I place a trembling hand on his unshaven cheek.

Archie presses his lips together, and his eyes spasm. "I must kill the Sluagh with my family's dirk. Only a strong ancestral witch can summon enough of its power to eliminate the evil fairy."

"I don't want you to get hurt." Or die, but I can't say it out loud or it may come true.

"Let's not fret over that sliver of possibility." He caresses the underside of my chin with a feather-like touch. In an awkward attempt to pick me up, he knocks his head on mine. "I'm sorry. It was supposed to be romantic. I wasn't expecting you to be so heavy!"

"Ouch. Are you saying I got fat?" I ask.

"Naw." He lifts me easily on the second try. "It's the muscle you've added. I should have expected it, but I've not tried until now. Why don't we go back to bed?"

"What about breakfast?" I whine.

He smiles. "It will be here for lunch."

Archie tells everyone to go about their lives as normal. How do I do that when I'm *in the knowing*? The attack of the Sluagh haunts me in my sleep every night, and I wake drenched in sweat.

Skye and Spence have lost patience with my lax work ethic. During Tuesday's class, they flip out on me, saying I need to "get it together" for our final presentation. So, I push everything aside to finish my portion of the presentation. By the time our last Thursday class rolls around, it's done and our presentation is well-received. Dr. Hughes commends us on our unique findings, but what began as an enjoyable class ends with a cleansing sigh of relief.

"I'm so sorry I caused you both so much stress." My fingers twist and pull at an earring while I apologize. "I'm so anxious about the Winter Solstice."

Spence rattles off. "You and me both, Gwyn." He yanks at the jammed zipper on his backpack as he grits his teeth, gives up, and swings it over his shoulder in a huff.

"Well, let's be happy we're done and can concentrate on the ritual." Skye lowers her chin to her chest and talks in a deep, husky voice. "Or should we call it—THE PURGE?"

"The Purge? I like it. It's optimistic." And I could use a generous dose of that right now. I wave bye to them and almost make it out of the room without talking to Dr. Hughes, but she flags me down.

"Mr. Yeats reports you haven't been practicing your magic." Leslie has an air of scolding in her voice. "It's more important than ever with the Winter Solstice Ceremony days away."

"I understand. Believe me when I say I'm committed to the Winter Solstice, but I'm not so sure about after." I glance at the passing Unremarkable students in the hallway, and envy pinches my heart. "I'm beginning to understand why my parents withdrew from all of this. They wanted me to live a regular life. I'm not sure I want to continue this alternate existence."

Leslie tilts her head and her silver swept bangs slide back to expose her indignant face. "You do not know the entire story behind your parents' departure."

I glare at her. "Well, maybe someday, you'll tell me."

Leslie's silver eyebrows plummet to her eyes. "Indeed—but not today."

The next seven days pass in a blink of an eye while the coven prepares for the Winter Solstice. We rehearse the chant to open the portal every day. The preparation builds confidence, but the banishment frightens me to the core of my being, and the younger witches share my apprehension. Audrey hasn't spoken to me since the last meeting. Better to wait until after the Winter Solstice to heal those wounds.

Leslie and Trinity managed to sweet-talk the council into leasing the Mitchell's Celestial Gardens but had to pay for liability insurance for the evening's celebration. What could go wrong?

Experienced witches from other covens say we'll have a limited amount of time to open the portal. Volunteers will join us to strengthen our circle and guide us through the portal spell while a few of the Bearsden witches create a trap for the Sluagh and send it back through the opening.

Despite the angst surrounding the Winter Solstice, I'm excited to celebrate Yule. Archie wakes me with a kiss on my cheek. "Good morning and Happy Winter Solstice."

"How can you be so cheerful, knowing what we have to do tonight?" I ask.

"How about we enjoy the holiday for now?" He slides out of bed. "I'll be back straight away."

I receive a text from Tyler wishing me a Happy Yule and hoping I have fun at the Winter Solstice Celebration. If only he knew. When Archie returns, he hops into bed holding two packages wrapped in recycled brown paper with string for a bow and a purple ribbon with the symbol of the triple moon.

"Open them," he says, hopping on the bed.

I'm grinning like a child who received a package from Santa Claus. "Thank you. I wasn't expecting anything with all the nonsense going on."

"I bought them a while ago. Something practical and something personal." He taps his fingers on the sheet, and his eyes widen. "Open them. Open, open, open."

"OK, OK. I'm opening it." I tug at the string on the bow with the pace of a tortoise.

Archie beams with the excitement of a little boy, moving around on the bed and fluffing his pillow. "You're moving slowly on purpose."

"Maybe I want to make the moment last." I give him a quick kiss, rip the brown paper, and open the box to find a black mortar and pestle with white, etched filigree around the edge and a tree of life symbol on one side. My fingers roll the smooth pestle in the palm of my hand.

"I knew you didn't have one of your own. Figured it was time you did. To continue your family's legacy." He kisses me on the cheek.

I smile and stroke his face. "It's beautiful. Thank you." It's so pretty I can't imagine grinding herbs in it and dulling the shine.

"Now, the personal gift. I hope you like it." Archie hands me the package with an air of arrogant satisfaction.

I take care, unwrapping the dainty package to avoid tearing the paper. The box contains a silver necklace with a hanging dragon's body. It's curved into a half-circle, creating a dragon crescent moon. I slide my fingers over the silver dragon, touching the scales on its body. "Oh, Archie. I love it." I grasp the nape of his neck and lean in to kiss him.

A longing smolders in his eyes. "I bought it because of your Welsh heritage. The dragon has such prominence for the Welsh. From the dragon, may you find inner strength."

"I feel awful. I have nothing for you to open," I say with a sexy pout.

He sports a devilish grin. "You already have what I want."

He rolls me on top of him and lifts my chemise over my head. Cupping my breasts and kissing them, he takes a nipple between his teeth. I flinch and grasp his rounded shoulders, pressing his head against me. He hesitates for a moment and draws my forehead to his.

"Gwynedd," he says in a hot, breathy voice. "You are all I need."

Chapter Twenty-Six

Haunts of
Witches Past

Archie checks the leather sheath of his family dirk on his way down the stairs, making sure it's attached to the belt in his jeans. I'm already at the front door, dressed in multiple layers for the expected frosty temperatures. A glance at the mantle clock over the fireplace tells me it's almost 8:30 p.m. "Archie, can you get a move on?" I slide on my insulated gloves and wrap a scarf around my neck. "I'm getting hotter than the fringes of hell in all these clothes. It's gonna trigger a hot flash."

Archie slips his arms into the sleeves of his wool coat. "No wonder! I can't imagine how you'll move in all those clothes."

"You know I can't stand being cold. I've got on a bra and panties, long underwear, jeans, a turtleneck, thermal socks, boots, and my puffer jacket. I plan to stay warm. We don't know how long this banishment will take."

"True, but you'll move none too easily." He slips on his leather gloves and cap, examining me with serious eyes. "Are you all right? Ready for this?"

"Yes!" I'm as sure as a lawyer with a whiplash case. I tip my head, and my mouth falls open to the left. "I've wondered if this thing has been after me all along. Like, why does it only show up when I'm around?"

Archie cocks his head. "Why haven't you mentioned this before?"

"I thought I was overreacting, but after it attacked me last week? It seems like an unlikely string of coincidences. If it is after me, for whatever fucked up reason, I will not react like a whimpering, middle-aged Unremarkable. This bitch plans to fight back."

Archie has a more pronounced twitch in his eye. "I'm not sure whether to be pleased with your change in attitude—or alarmed."

"Let's go banish this Host of the Unforgiven Dead," I say, smacking him with a kiss. "Before I change my mind."

It's a bit surreal passing the holiday decorations of red, green, blue, and white. The nippy temperature doesn't hurt too much until the biting winds sting my face. Witches from the local covens are already in the back room of the Pumpkin House, conferencing with Leslie and Trinity, by the time Archie and I arrive at a quarter to nine. The rest of the coven chats about the dangers ahead except for Audrey and Courtney, who sit in a corner alone, sulking. Zoe hasn't arrived.

The volunteer witches from the other New Castle County covens move to a corner of the room. Archie joins Leslie and Trinity to discuss the plan. When they're finished talking, Leslie moves to front and center, wearing a black wool cape. She taps her Elder staff.

"We will begin early," Leslie says. "I want to introduce the representatives from our neighboring covens who are taking part in tonight's circle. I thank each of you for your support in this dangerous endeavor. One day, I hope we can reciprocate." She lowers her head in thanks, and the local witches respond in kind.

Leslie continues. "Please stand when I call your name. Gareth Thomas comes to us from the Coven of New Castle, Brayton Harris from the Coven of Wilmington, Riley Shaw of Middletown, Elizabeth Wang of Greenville, and Laura Lovelace from the Coven of Hockessin."

The two men appear young, tall, and muscular. The petite woman, Riley Shaw, has white hair and appears one breath from an ICU bed. Elizabeth Wang, a woman in her forties, has exquisite beauty with impeccable makeup. I don't recognize any of them until Laura Lovelace stands to identify herself. She's the former DUB doctoral student who spoke to Archie at the Raven Pub when we had dinner. Why didn't he tell me she was a witch?

Laura Lovelace remains standing and walks over to Trinity. She whispers into Trinity's ear, and Trinity's eyes open wide like an owl's. When Laura Lovelace shares the information with Leslie, her face turns cherry red. Archie moves in my direction with a look of irritation in his eyes but never veers his gaze from Laura Lovelace.

"What is this about?" Ronnie mumbles in my ear. "Her name spells trouble always. Didn't Archie tell you about her?"

"He said she was a former doctoral student. I saw her speak with him in passing at the Raven during dinner." The beginnings of knots entwine and wrap around my insides.

"She's also a former witch recruit." Ronnie bites her lip. "They also had a fling. I expected he would have told you. It ended about the time he recruited me. Didn't last. He didn't tell you he dated her?"

I frown as my heart does jumping jacks. "No. He did not." Am I really that dense? She kissed all over him. Grabbed his phone and typed into it. It was probably her phone number. "Why are you saying she's trouble?" Trinity's announcement cuts our side conversation short.

"My fellow witches of Bearsden," Trinity says. "The visiting witches look forward to aiding us in the banishment of the Host of the Unforgiven Dead—a dangerous threat to all of us. However, we have to address a problem before they agree to proceed. A witch in our coven has contacted them with accusations of moral improprieties. I invite her to come to the front and formally address the group."

Courtney Davies marches to the front holding a red folder in her hands and an arrogant expression engraved on her face. Her blond ponytail flips back and forth as she pounds the floor in her brown hiking boots. Archie stands a few feet away next to Ronnie, agitation contorting his face as he strokes the tip of his goatee.

"What the hell is she up to?" Ronnie mutters. "I can't believe she's gonna speak to the coven. She rarely puts two words together during coven meetings."

"I don't know," I say, "but she looks pissed." I'm startled when I find Spence standing next to me. "What are you doing?"

Spence puts his palms up. "I don't know. Trinity sent me a text and told me you may need me. I don't question my superiors, especially not before a Sluagh fight."

Courtney announces in an accusatory tone. "A witch in our coven has been using his affections to recruit new witches. I know of at least two witches in our Bearsden Coven, but also others in the local covens. The accused person is Archie Cockburn."

I groan, exasperated. Courtney's been a problem since the beginning—jealous of my flourishing relationship with Archie after their hookup went nowhere. He said she was obsessed with him, but I didn't think she'd go this far. The coven is rattled, but not convinced, according to the murmurs of comments. Archie shakes his head, and the winding knots in my torso tighten a little more.

Spence rests his hands on his hips. "She's a fucking mess. Archie better do something."

"I bet Laura started this," Ronnie says. "She's been after Archie since they stopped dating. Don't let this bother you, Gwyn. It's all bullshit."

Archie shifts to the front of the circle. He's going to address the accusations. "According to the policies of the Regional Coven Book of Shadows, I have a right to defend myself." Archie crosses his arms over his bulging chest, as it rises and falls in erratic intervals. "And we have more important issues at hand. We must prepare for the Sluagh banishment."

Leslie taps her Elder Staff. "Archie speaks the truth. As a member of the Bearsden Coven, he may defend himself no matter how severe the accusations appear. However, I have agreed to allow this in exchange for their help."

"That's encouraging," Ronnie says.

"Yaaas," Spence exclaims under his breath. "Archie gets to clap back."

My heart thumps like a generator running out of gas while I wring my hands. Why has Courtney chosen now of all nights to spew these lies? To embarrass Archie? Get revenge? What a spoiled brat she is.

Courtney sneers. "I haven't finished." She tugs at a stack of papers inside the red folder, removes them, and throws the folder on the floor with a plop. "I have letters signed from other women in local covens who were recruited while at DUB as students or employees, or through local coven events. They attest Archie recruited them, shared affections, and made false promises of love to lure them into becoming witches."

The knots in my stomach tighten while Courtney reads the names of the accusers. One after another, she tosses each letter into the air. I stop counting after several letters fly like little paper airplanes, crashing onto the wooden floor.

Leslie addresses Archie while the coven witnesses the accusations in disbelief. "Archie Cockburn, do you deny the allegations?"

"I do not." His shoulders fall, and a piece of me falls, too. "However, the statements contain inaccuracies. I admit I dated some of these witches. The relationships were always consensual, and I never made promises of love or commitment to any of them. You asked me to move here to recruit. I completed the task. Sometimes relationships developed, but like many casual relationships, they didn't last. I never treated those women with anything but the utmost respect."

"Wow, Archie," Spence says, snickering. "You're a fuckboy."

"Spence!" Ronnie slaps him with the back of her hand and wraps an arm around me.

Archie peeks at me, and I'm huffing like a steam engine. "I can't listen to any more of this, Ronnie." I have eyes of a woman twice burned, and he must see them.

As I'm darting out, Leslie gives orders. "Archie Cockburn, you will wait outside while the coven discusses the evidence at hand."

My hand's already on the front doorknob when I decide I can't leave. It's not fair to the coven to expect them to follow through with one less witch for the banishment spell. And damn. I left my jacket, gloves, and scarf in the backroom. Footsteps resound in the hallway, becoming louder until they end behind me. As I stare through the etched glass of the Victorian door, I contemplate what I should say. I turn around to face him, but my lips won't move.

"Are you going to speak to me?" Archie asks. He gazes at me with his magnetic-blue eyes while I wrestle to keep the anger inside. "Please, talk to me, Gwyn."

"How do you want me to respond?" I snap like a mad dog. "You lied to me. All this time, I believed I'd found a nice man to treat me with respect. Instead, I find out you're no different from Richard."

"I am NOT Richard." His fingers brush his blond locks. "I have never cheated on you, Gwyn. You're the only woman I'm seeing, the only woman I want. Have I ever been disrespectful to you?"

"Well, no, but you never told me about all those women, the witches you recruited and slept with." And how many more are there you aren't telling me about?

His shoulders relax while he kneads his jaw. "Gwynedd. I'm forty-four years old. Do you think I've not had other relationships? Slept with a few other women?"

My eyes drop to the wooden floor. "Of course, I expected you to have been with other women, but Archie...there were so many." My eyes veer back to meet his icy-blue gaze.

He snickers, stroking his goatee. "Aye. I was a wee bit shocked myself."

I lay my hands on my flushed cheeks. "You think it's funny?"

"You have to admit," he says in a sardonic tone. "It is a wee bit."

"Oh, my gods." I moan as I wipe my face and squeeze my eyes shut. "I believed we had something special." I gaze into his eyes, my fraught heart aching. "I know we haven't talked much about how we feel. It's only been a few months, but I'm gonna say it. I love you, Archie. I think I've loved you since the first time I saw you. Well, not the actual first time, because I only saw your ass, but the first time you recited Robert Burns."

A smile peeks through his goatee, and he moves closer while I spill the tea.

"I know you're gonna say there's no way I could have those feelings yet, but I do. How do I know? Because it hurts. I ache when you end a phone call, and I no longer hear your sexy Scottish accent making love to me on the phone. An emptiness grips me in the pit of my stomach when you aren't lying next to me in bed. I ache when the warmth of your skin tears away from mine. That's how I know I love you."

Archie shifts even closer with his hands in his pockets. "Gwynedd, I care deeply for you. When I told you all I need is you, I meant it. You're the only woman I want. I don't know what more you want me to say."

"Hmph." I break his magnetic gaze. "And that's the problem."

Archie's mouth flattens, and he turns his head.

I close my eyes, and the memories of the past few months play in my head like a drawn-out miniseries. Our first meeting in class. Our first kiss in front of his fireplace. The first time we made love on Mabon. The evening of Samhain. I want to go back to those moments in time and hold them forever, but that's not how miniseries progress. When I lift my eyelids, Archie is staring at me, his eyes drawing together. "After tonight, I want a break from all of this, the coven and you."

"Gwyn, don't." Archie runs a shaky hand through his wavy hair. "We need you." He offers me his hand. "I—I need you." His transparent eyes appear genuine, but how can I be sure?

"I want more from a relationship than being needed," I say. "And I need a break from the insanity of this alternate world. I need normal again."

Archie shakes his head. "You can never be Unremarkable again. You will forever be *in the knowing*."

"True, but I can choose not to be a witch." I glare at him. "Or the plaything of a womanizer."

Archie scowls while he rants. "I cared about each of those women. Many of them initiated our dating. And I did not sleep with all of them. Most of the letters of judgment were full of false statements. Once Leslie and the coven representatives investigate using a verity spell, the truth will come out."

"That may be true, but it doesn't explain all of it. You obviously hurt some of those women, whether it was intentional or not, and you don't appear to have any remorse at all."

"I understand how you'd think that." Archie scratches the whiskers on his chin. "I wish you would reconsider, but I will honor your request. If that's what you want."

The door to the backroom opens, and Spence shuffles up the hallway to us. "The verdict is in, witches!" He motions us to return.

We follow Spence back into the room where the coven and the visiting witches wait in bitter silence. Courtney has returned to the circle with an air of winning about her. The Bearsden witches sport scowls. Archie walks to the front of the circle, where Leslie announces the decision. Laura Lovelace stands nearby displaying a look of defeat.

"Archie Cockburn," Leslie announces. "After investigating the authenticity of the letters using the spell of falsehoods, we have found them to be fraudulent."

The Bearsden Coven witches stamp their feet on the floor, creating a rumble. My feet remain glued to the wooden floor, and Ronnie notices.

"Gwyn," she whispers. "This is good news. Why are you sulking?"

"I don't think Leslie has finished," I reply.

"There is the question concerning the ethics of your behavior," Leslie says. "Although you have violated no policies in the Regional Book of Shadows, we have decided sanctions are in order."

"May I enter a formal Expression of Defense?" Archie asks, folding his hands.

Leslie raises her chin. "You may speak."

"When you came to London and asked for my help, begged for my help, I might add. I resisted, explaining how difficult it would be to recruit in an area with so few witches and possibilities for fresh blood to build upon. You said I could use any means available to me. I accomplished what you asked, and I won't apologize for being a man, looking for relationships among the only viable options. Regardless, I will accept whatever sanctions you determine are proper."

"Indeed, you shall," Leslie affirms with the tap of her Elder staff.

The Bearsden Coven witches yell "it's not fair" and "Archie deserves the right to address his accusers." Courtney and Audrey remain silent.

"Going forward," Trinity says, "we will consider your Expression of Defense, but you will need to make better choices. Sanctions will be determined after we banish the Sluagh."

"I accept your decision." Archie bows his head and returns to the circle between Elijah and Skye.

Leslie pushes her silver bangs aside. "We still have the task at hand. We must determine how we will lure the Sluagh into the gardens if it has left for the evening skies. Suggestions?"

I raise my hand, and Leslie gestures to me. "The Sluagh has been in my presence several times, including the attack." I turn my lips inward. "I have a weird feeling it's been coming after me."

"You mean like it's stalking you?" Spence asks. He waves a finger at me. "That's messed up."

Archie eyes me, mouthing "no" over and over. I shut my eyes and suck in air, holding it for a second. "If the Sluagh isn't resting in the hawthorn tree when we arrive, use me as bait."

Stepping into the circle, Archie shouts and makes a fist. "That is NOT a solution! Gwyn does not have the skill to defend herself against a Sluagh." Archie's eyebrows collapse, and the corners of his mouth pull down. "She will be lost." It's comforting to watch him fight for me, but it's too late. I've made my decision. It's the only logical solution.

Leslie purses her lips. "It's not your decision to make, Dr. Cockburn."

"Gwyn?" Trinity crosses her arms and stiffens her back. "Are you really OK with this?"

"Yes, I am. It will work, and I'll be fine. You'll all be there with me." As upset as I am with all of them, I trust they will do everything in their power to keep me safe.

The visiting witches are getting restless and itching to get on with it. Except for Audrey and Courtney, the Bearsden witches shout over each other with concerns for my safety.

"No way, you should do this," Spence says, waving a finger back and forth. "This sucker could snatch you up and fly away with you before we're able to stop it. Tanner and Elijah could have lucked out the other night."

Elijah stands, and everyone averts their gaze to his commanding stature. "I'm with Gwyn. She knows we might have dealt with this sooner had she alerted us to the Sluagh's whereabouts. I believe she is making amends, and we need to let her do it."

My mouth quivers, locking eyes with Elijah, and Ronnie notices. "Gwyn, I don't want you to do this. You don't have to."

I clasp her hand and tear up. "Yes, I do." I know if we do nothing, the situation will get worse, and the Sluagh could attack Tyler. I can't let that happen. Archie stares at me from across the circle, pressing his lips together. I sense his distress, but I've dug in my boot heels.

Leslie taps her Elder staff. "It's decided. There will be no more discussion. Let us form the circle and prepare. We only have a couple of hours to get this right."

The front door slams and the thud of weighty boots heads to the backroom. The witches remain silent as mice, and their eyes hop around the circle. Who is this uninvited guest? The door swings open with a bang, and Zoe rushes into the room with a perplexed look on her round face.

"Please tell me I'm not late?" Zoe's anxious eyes scan everyone in the room, searching for confirmation from someone. "I put 9:30 p.m. in my phone alarm."

"Zoe." Spence covers his mouth with both hands and air slips through his lips. "It started at 9:00."

"Oh, I'm sorry." A look of chagrin spreads on her face. "Did I miss anything?"

CHAPTER TWENTY-SEVEN

THE PURGE

A BITTER WIND BLOWS through our bodies while we march to Mitchell Hall under an indigo sky with wisps of gray, gloomy clouds. I focus my attention on the skies above me, scanning for shadows in flight, when I notice the tall Scot beside me.

"Gwyn," Archie says. "If you must position yourself as bait, remember to chant and invoke a fresh protection spell. I don't know if it will prove effective, but you should do it." His eyes narrow. "As the leader of the coven, I'm advising you."

"I'll take it under advisement then," I say, grimacing.

"I understand you're angry with me, but you have to suspend those emotions for the present. You must remain focused on the task. Whatever you think of me, you must be ready for whatever happens, for the sake of the coven and the community. Can you do that?"

"Yes," I reply. "Of course, I will put the community first." I hate conceding the point, but he's right. As upset as I am, I have to bury it for now.

We arrive at the mansion and proceed through the gate to the Celestial Gardens, forming a circle to prepare for the banishment spell. Riley Shaw of Middletown and Elizabeth Wang of Greenville approach the statuesque hawthorn tree and join hands to sense the resting place of the Sluagh.

Riley proclaims in a delicate voice. "The tree is barren. The Host of the Unforgiven Dead is in flight!"

"I sense no presence." Elizabeth Wang assists Riley back to the circle. "We must implement a spell to attract the Sluagh, using Gwynedd Crowther as bait."

"We shall proceed." Leslie moves to her position. The chilly wind blows her silver hair, and she raises her black hood. "Gwynedd, enter the circle."

I scurry to the center of the circle and wait for the other witches to summon the Host of the Unforgiven Dead. The winds increase, scattering the remnants of the fallen leaves and other plant debris, and send my chestnut strands flying. The earmuffs I'm wearing block the clarity of their chant, so I take them off, releasing the wind's full force on my long hair.

The calling of the Sluagh continues while my eyes sweep back and forth across the dismal night sky. A bird's low-pitched caws sound in the distance, and I check for the protection-spell pouch in my jeans pocket. I peer at Archie, and his icy blues are glued to me. I try not to think about the other witches he's bedded and focus on the Sluagh.

The coven and visiting witches change their chant, repeating words to open the portal to the Otherworld. The increasing gale causes my hair to dance like the snakes on Medusa's head. Snakes for hair prove hard to tame as I bat my hands at them without success. I glimpse an odd movement of a gray cloud in the distant sky, and the others view the billow of doom, too.

Riley Shaw of Middletown shouts above the hissing of the wind. "The Host of the Unforgiven Dead is near! We must invoke our combined energies to force the portal open!"

The visiting witches position themselves among the Bearsden Coven to guide them through the spell. They raise their hands, and amber glows of energy radiate like sparklers from their hands. In the blackness of the gardens, a tiny bubble of blue haze forms with arm-like rays, pushing out from the center and growing exponentially. Glancing back at the skies over the Green, I discern a single, rogue cloud. The Sluagh has camouflaged itself, flying with the illusion of a pearlescent facade, nothing but another gray cotton puff of gloom to the community of Bearsden.

My fellow Bearsden witches call out to me in overlapping cheers of support. "You can do this!" Archie says nothing, but I sense the foreboding on his face. Leslie and the visiting witches are too preoccupied with opening the portal to worry about li'l ol' me.

The shimmering, flapping cloud of gloom transforms into the body of small ravens—interconnected and working in tandem to form the impressive black raven shadow. It doesn't appear as intimidating this far away, but the memory of its expansive open beak petrifies me as I quake in my boots.

"We must work harder to expand the portal," Elizabeth Wang of Greensville shouts. "It must be larger to push the Sluagh through!"

The combined amber glow of witch energy intensifies, creating beams of light toward the portal. I'm taken aback by the incredible beauty, and I forget what I'm supposed to be doing. The Sluagh is only minutes away, and I remember the protection spell. I check for the pouch in my pants pocket again and chant to summon my witch energy. The amber glow fans out from my hands with such intensity it breaks through the cover of my gloves.

Leslie raises her raspy voice to break through the roaring hum of the portal. "The Sluagh is only a few hundred feet away. We must increase our combined energies to the maximum you can bring forth!"

With one last push, the witches' combined energies spark with blue lightning, forcing the ball of blue haze to open while the suction of air pulls debris into the massive hole. In a matter of seconds, the Sluagh arrives with massive flapping wings of tiny ravens working in tandem. I chant over and over, and my breathing stops and starts. Remembering Tyler, I regret my offer to bait this monster. What was I thinking? How will he ever forgive me for making him an orphan?

The witches holler at each other to keep the portal open as the Sluagh heads straight for me, and the white vapors of my breath surround me while the Sluagh swells in size. I chant the protection spell as the Host of the Unforgiven Dead swoops with its extended claws, aiming to snatch its prey—me. My inner thoughts shout at me to run, but intense fear has glued me to this spot. I squeeze my eyes shut, clench my teeth, and prepare for the pain of the claws to dig in, knowing my nightmare will come to fruition! And nothing happens.

I open an eye to find the Sluagh has turned and flown straight into the dark abyss of the midnight sky cutting through smoky, cotton-candy clouds. It caws and growls while it flies overhead, invisible to our eyes until we observe the glistening black of its gigantic shadow wings. It dives like a hawk, opening its beak so wide, I swear I see the souls of the dead homeless men screaming inside. Instinctively, I splay a hand, projecting my energy outward like a glass-blown, amber barrier. The Sluagh voices an ear-piercing shriek and reverses gear.

The witches whoop and holler at my success. "Well done, Gwynedd of Bearsden!" Riley Shaw of Middletown yells.

"Keep it up, Gwyn!" Trinity cheers. "It's deflecting the Sluagh's attack!"

As I scan the coven for other feedback, Archie catches my gaze and smiles. He shouts to the others over the hum of the gateway to the Otherworld. "This time, let's deflect it toward the portal!"

"Come again, asshole." I turn my rage-filled gaze toward the sky. "I'm ready for you."

The sinister cloud emerges before transforming into the shadow of ravens. I lift my open hand again to prepare for the attack, and the Sluagh swoops at me with a vengeance, blasting us with a shriek so loud the ground rumbles and quakes. The Host of the Unforgiven Dead avoids the suction of the portal and dives into the hawthorn tree, transforming into a terrify-ing tree of evil, spreading with long, thorny, arm-like limbs.

The Sluagh lashes out like a toddler having a tantrum, swinging its arms at random. Without warning, it stretches its arms to the circle, grabbing a witch—Ronnie! She screams, flailing her arms about, and tries to break free but doesn't have the strength. Her crimson hair stands out like burning fire against the blackness of the hawthorn tree, and blood trickles on her face and hands.

"Roooniiieee!" I dash toward the Sluagh tree, but Archie and Elijah grasp my arms, stopping my foolish gesture of hero-ism.

"Gwyn," Archie shouts over the roar of the wind and portal hum. "It will kill you!"

Elijah bellows into the frigid air. "Archie is right! You can't save her by yourself!"

"We have to do something!" I cry out as warm tears roll down my freezing face.

"The portal should have sucked in the Sluagh!" Archie sweeps the hair from his face while his eyes bounce around the circle. "A witch must be controlling the Host of the Unforgiv-en Dead!"

The Bearsden Coven witches scrutinize each other with outrage and distrust, realizing it could be any of them. The young witches accuse the visiting witches of Greenville,

Hockessin, Wilmington, New Castle, and Middletown, while the Sluagh continues to crush Ronnie's body.

Leslie comes to their defense. "These are long, trusted friends of the Bearsden Coven! It is NOT them!"

Ronnie cries and calls out with ear-piercing shrieks. "Help me! Please, help me!"

My heart races from the adrenalin pumping through my body while I spin inside the circle to examine each witch in the Bearsden Coven. "What if it's no one here?! Could it be Agnes Pritchard?!"

"Agnes would never do this!" Shane says. "She may be a loner, but she's not malevolent!"

The hum of the portal muffles Leslie's raspy voice. "Agnes has no reason to call for the Sluagh! It is someone in our midst!"

I scan the group again, inspecting the faces of each Bearsden witch for a culpable expression, and stop at Courtney. She has guilty-as-charged stamped on her face, a billboard advertising wicked witch for hire. What would Audrey say about her friend? I search the circle for her reaction. "Where is Audrey?"

Every witch searches the circle, and they discover it, too. Audrey is missing. Ronnie's cries continue to cloud my thinking, and the hum and whir of the portal muddle my brain while I stand helpless in the grasp of Archie and Elijah.

Trinity breaks from the circle and approaches Courtney Davies with a jade-green glare, demanding the whereabouts of her friend. She forms a ball of amber energy and places her hand at Courtney's throat. "Where. Is. Audrey?" As she bears down on Courtney's neck with a robotic pinch, the other Bearsden witches roar at her using profanity.

Courtney screeches, struggling to spit out the words. "I swear. I don't know!"

Trinity glimpses the flickering of blue light in a second-floor window of the mansion and releases her clamp around Courtney's neck. The other witches spy the blue glow and demand we send witches to stop her.

"Courtney Davies," Leslie says. "Stand aside." Courtney removes herself from the circle and waits for her judgment.

"I never trusted that girl!" Elijah says, fuming. "I'll take care of her!"

"I'll go with you, Elijah!" Archie says. "You may need help if she's truly an ancestral witch!"

Ronnie writhes in pain as blood seeps into her clothes, and my brain wanders from thought to thought, searching for a solution. She will die if we don't get her out of its thorny, crushing arms soon.

Archie hands me his family dirk. "Elijah and I will deal with Audrey." He removes my glove and wraps my fingers around his family heirloom. "Your skin must contact the handle to empower it. When she releases the Sluagh, you must pierce the tree with all the strength you have. The Sluagh will extricate its grip on Ronnie and flee from the tree, and hopefully, get drawn into the portal."

Crying and shaking, I grip the dirk. "I can't do it!" I stare into Archie's eyes, so clear and genuine.

"Yes, you can, Gwyn." A glimmer of faith shines in his eyes. "I believe in you. You have an untapped power. Summon it now using strong intention to save your friend." He places his warm lips on mine, still quivering, and presses hard against my teeth.

"How will I know when Audrey's control of the Sluagh breaks?" I ask.

He lays a gloved hand on my pink cheek. "You'll know."

"We need to go, Archie!" Elijah waves his arm. "Before she realizes we've discovered her!"

Archie leans his forehead against mine. "I have to go. Monitor the window for activity. You'll sense the release."

He darts to the back entrance of the house with Elijah. Opening it with a spell, they head for the second floor. My fingers, already numb from the icy temperature, clasp the dirk at its base. Ronnie's crying has subsided. Her body has collapsed over the arms of the Sluagh, and crimson-red curls hang from her limp torso as the Sluagh lifts its higher, thorny limbs in defense.

"Look at the fairy mound!" Zoe squeals. "It's lit like a stage!"

As I turn to view the mound, the two Seelie Fae children appear, giggling and running, until they see Ronnie trapped in the limbs of the Sluagh. Their mint-green eyes open wide, tearing with glistening droplets of translucent green, and they point to Ronnie.

In my peripheral vision, I catch sight of a fireworks display in Audrey's hideout on the second floor. A gust of wind blasts us, sending my snake-like strands behind my head. I raise the dirk, summoning my witch energy to ignite its power, and it radiates with the brightness of the sun's rays. Fearing it will hold me back, I rip off my puffer jacket and brave the bitter cold.

The Seelie Fae children skip to me. They each grasp an arm and drag me to the Sluagh tree. The Bearsden witches cheer me on, encouraging me to attack with the dirk. I try to get close enough to impale one of the arm-like limbs, but the Sluagh whacks me with one of its higher limbs, sending me flying and landing on a grassy area in a heap.

Zoe rushes to help me stand, and I wince at the pain. Now, I'm pissed. The Seelie Fae jump up and down, pointing their fingers to the Sluagh, urging me with their mint-green eyes to try again. A drop of liquid trickles between my eyes and slides down the side of my nose. I wipe the fluid with the back of my hand and a vivid shade of red appears.

The Bearsden witches' rowdy voices bleed through the hum of the portal. "Go again, Gwyn!" "You'll get it the next time!"

"You can do it!" "We're ready for it!" Leslie commands me to go again. "Gwynedd! Do not hesitate! You must succeed!"

Suddenly, the wind shifts, and the portal contracts, like the drawstring on a duffle bag. Elizabeth Wang points at the opening. "The portal is closing! You must do it now!"

As I smear the remaining blood on my chin, I plan the path of my next attack. I sprint to the Sluagh with all the vigor my legs can muster. It swipes at me with a free limb, but I drop on my butt and slide on ice to the tree, slashing a limb with the dirk. Ronnie falls limp to the frigid ground, and the Sluagh shrieks with a growl-like roar, fleeing from the tree.

The hawthorn tree explodes with blue liquid squirting in all directions. Casting their witch energy into a single stream, the visiting witches chant the spell of banishment over and over in a loop. The draw of the portal nabs the Host of the Unforgiven Dead as it closes, sending it back into the closing void.

The Seelie Fae children grin as they run to help me. I touch Ronnie's pale, frigid face, but the warm skin under her jacket tells me she's alive. Trinity, Tanner, and Shane run to us and help me check her body for wounds.

"She's alive," I say in a cloud of white mist.

"We should call 911 for an ambulance." Shane warms her body using the amber glow of his hand. "She won't last long. We don't have the ingredients or the time for a healing spell for her injuries."

"Do it," Trinity says. "We will deal with Audrey. Keep her alive however you can."

Behind me, the coven continues to chant, ensuring the portal remains closed. I walk over to the Seelie Fae children, where they are hugging each other. The Seelie Fae little girl speaks to me in a sweet, angelic voice. "The Sluagh scared us. Thank you for sending it away."

"You're welcome," I say with a friendly smile.

The Seelie Fae little boy stares at me, a bewildered expression on his face. "Where is Momma Mitchell? She always meets us in the gardens. It has been so long since she's played with us."

I squat in front of them and grasp their tiny fairy hands. They're as warm as a summer's day. "Momma Mitchell doesn't live here anymore. She grew old and her time here ended."

Twinkling tears of mint green leak from their eyes. "But you'll be here for our visits, Aunt Lowri?" Their faces gleam with the radiance of sunshine.

"Aunt Lowri?" My frosty breath slithers in the air between us. "You knew my mother?"

The Seelie Fae boy and girl gape at each other. "You're not Aunt Lowri?"

"Lowri was my mother." My lower lip quivers. "And she's gone, too, but maybe I can visit you sometimes."

The Seelie Fae children grin at me with their mint-green eyes and skip to the mound. They wave to me and vanish into their world.

Archie and Elijah have returned with Audrey, and Trinity heads over to join them. Hanging over Elijah's shoulder, Audrey pounds his back and kicks her feet like a two-year-old.

"Put me down! Put me down!" She squawks like a spoiled child.

"As you wish!" Elijah drops her ass on the chilly gravel walkway.

Audrey wails. "Owww!" She stands and flicks the tiny pebbles from her pea coat.

The young witches hurl obscenities at her, calling her a traitor and a vile, selfish witch. Forming an impenetrable circle, the remaining witches of Bearsden join them, but the visiting witches stand back and observe.

Archie approaches Audrey, a piercing stare flaring. "You need to explain yourself."

Audrey eyeballs the witches in the circle. "I can't. A spell was cast to stop me from divulging my intentions." She smirks and scans the circle. "You think my capture wasn't considered before sending me here to your pathetic coven?"

I'm practically speechless, freezing in my blood-soaked clothes. "But why hurt Ronnie? She did nothing to you."

"I called on the Sluagh to eliminate you," Audrey says. "I didn't expect your suppressed powers to grow so strong. So, I chose the next best thing—kill your best friend." She sneers at me. "And you took Archie's affections from my friend. It broke her heart."

I peer at Archie out of the corner of my eye. "Well, she can get in line." He averts his gaze from me, and I turn to the other members of the coven. "What happens now? What do we do with her?"

"There is not much we can do, Gwynedd," Leslie replies. "I had my suspicions about Audrey early on. The mishap Mr. Yeats observed in your training confirmed it. It's why I didn't allow her to join the Nine."

Trinity moves toward Audrey again. "I say we use magic to remove the cloaking spell."

"Removing the cloaking spell could kill her," Leslie says matter-of-factly. "You are aware."

"What?" I move between Trinity and Audrey. "I can't let you harm her. We don't know who has control over her. We could kill an innocent person. If you have any hope of me returning to this coven, you can't do it. I won't let you."

Audrey howls with laughter as her hands spread like claws. "You're pathetic."

I stare at her, emotionless, recognizing she's under someone's control.

"We will expel Audrey from the coven and send a warning to all covens across the region," Trinity says. "At least she won't have the membership of a coven to enhance her powers."

Audrey straightens her coat and walks to the gate but turns toward us. Summoning her witch energy, she blows on the amber light, shooting a flame of fire that stops short of singeing us. She laughs and exits through the gate.

Leslie raises a hand to the visiting witches before they depart. "I want to give undying thanks to our neighboring witches for their help in this endeavor. We are in your debt! Be safe on your journey home."

I dart back to Ronnie where Shane has been using half-assed healing spells to keep Ronnie alive. My puffer jacket covers her bloodied, battered body while I shake and jerk from the icy chill. An ambulance siren wails in the distance.

"Thank you, Gwyn," Zoe says, becoming weepy. "I hope Ronnie will be OK."

"Me, too, Zoe," I say, laying my numb, icy hand on Ronnie's bloodied face. I stand and walk toward the gate, stopping to give Archie his family dirk, covered in blue sap from the Sluagh.

"Where are you going, Gwyn?" Archie's wet eyes hop from one bloody wound to another on my face and body. "You should go to the hospital with Ronnie. You're hurt. At least let me heal you."

"I'm going home," I say with a snippy tongue. "I care about all of you, but now I understand why my parents wanted me to have an Unremarkable life. Being a witch has been exciting and adventurous, but also dangerous. I don't know if I want this kind of life anymore."

"Don't go, Gwyn," Skye says. "I've learned so much from you."

"You can't go." Spence rests his hands on his hips. "You haven't finished your training."

The others beg me not to go, pleading with me to stay and make things better, but Tanner understands. "Let her go," he says. "Gwyn needs to decide her future."

I smile through tears at my Zillennial friends as Leslie approaches me. Her silver hair flits in the chilly breeze as she lifts her chin. "You can't remove yourself from the coven. This is your destiny."

"Fuck destiny." I glance at Archie one last time and those magnetic-blue eyes emanate a familiar yearning I once found irresistible. I close my eyes, snap out of the mini-trance, and pivot for home.

I run the entire mile with no jacket while my teeth chatter and enter my house through the mudroom. After ripping off my blood-soaked clothes, I throw them into the washing machine to soak and trudge upstairs in my bra and panties, craving a hot shower to clean my wounds. With a flip of the light switch, I view myself for the first time.

I gasp. "Fuuuck." Lacerations cover my extremities, torso, and forehead, and blood dribbles on my face, arms, and legs. My disheveled hair has blood-drenched bangs and bloody ice cycles dangling. Not my sexiest look. My cell phone rings, and I leap toward the ceiling. It's Tyler. "Shit, shit, shit." I swipe the green circle, tap the speaker icon, and try to calm my chattering teeth. "Hi, dear."

"Hey, Mom," Tyler says. "How was the Winter Solstice Celebration? Did the Fellowship accomplish everything it planned?"

I remove my bra and panties with shivering hands. "Yeah. We did. What do you want, dear? I'm home and getting ready for bed."

"I figured you were at Archie's. I wanted you to know I'm gonna stop by the house for a few things in my old room. Didn't expect to see you."

"No, no—no, no, no!" I exclaim while my heart rushes into tachycardia mode. Rotating the shower handle, I hope he hears the rushing water against the tile. "I'm about to get in the shower and go to bed, dear. I'm exhausted."

Tyler snickers into the phone. "You don't have to make excuses, Mom. If Archie's there, I won't stop by."

"He's not here, Tyler." I scramble over the pile of words in my head, searching for what to say. "I'm not gonna see Archie for a while. Or attend Fellowship meetings."

"Oh, Mom, I'm sorry. Did something bad happen tonight?" he asks in an elevated voice.

I stare at my bloodied body and swallow. "You could say that." I want to tell him so badly. "I don't wanna talk about it right now. OK?"

"Sure." The hiss of Tyler's breathing fills the quiet moment. "Are you all right, Mom?"

I inspect my bruised and bloodied body again. It's real, not healed by magic. "I'm OK. How about we plan on having a secular Christmas celebration like we used to have with Nain and Taid? Only the two of us?"

"Christmas alone would be great. I love you, Mom."

"I love you, too, Tyler." I swipe the red button on my phone and step under the spray of hot, cleansing water.

It's amazing what a hot shower does. It's like hitting the refresh icon on your laptop. I gaze at the ceiling and search for the dagger-like crack, a remnant of my Unremarkable days, but it's hidden now under layers of drywall mud. Somehow, I know Ronnie will be OK, but how will the coven explain what happened in the Celestial Gardens to the city? And it occurs to me. It's not my problem.

Chapter Twenty-Eight

CLEANING HOUSE

I DON'T LEAVE THE house for the next three days except to retrieve my Prius from in front of Archie's house when he's at school. Tidbits of the Winter Solstice fallout show in my social media feeds—gossip surrounding an outlandish pagan celebration and unapproved fireworks obliterating an old, beloved hawthorn tree in the gardens of Mitchell Hall, leaving one of its members injured and hospitalized. I send Shane a text, telling him not to expect me to work for a few months, and he says, "Take all the time you need, darling."

The attempt to have a normal, Unremarkable holiday fizzles with Tyler's mention of the scratches on my face and hands, and the absence of his father. He doesn't press me for an explanation of my wounds, but his face tenses with worry over the news of the Winter Solstice "mishap." It's not fair to put him through this. I want so badly to tell him the truth, but I can't. And I stress over the obvious. What if he's inherited my mom's ancestral powers?

Devastated over Ronnie's near-fatal wounds, Derek didn't leave Ronnie's bedside for days. But I couldn't bring myself to visit her in the hospital while she slept in a drug-induced coma. Over a week has passed, and he calls to deliver the fantastic news the doctors have brought her out of the coma. He says she's aware and talking "gibberish" about the attack of a monster bird tree and begs me to visit her.

Other members of the Fellowship have been visiting to comfort Derek during her sedated state, and the guilt hits me like a wrecking ball while I stand outside her hospital door. What kind of person doesn't visit her best friend in the ICU? I enter to find Derek standing next to Ronnie, grasping her hand.

She lifts the other when her eyes intersect mine. "Gwyn, I'm so happy you're here."

I hug her as close as I can with all the tubes and wires protruding from her arms and chest.

Derek kisses Ronnie's forehead and smiles faintly at me. "I'll get some lunch while you two girls chat. Love you, babe." He whispers "thank you" to me when he passes.

"What the hell happened?" Ronnie asks. "Derek can't tell me. And I haven't spoken to anyone else yet." She snickers through the pain. "He told me I woke up spitting nonsense about an evil bird tree crushing me."

"It worked," I say, exhaling. "I slashed a limb of the Sluagh. It fled from the host tree and got sucked into the portal, right before it snapped shut."

"I'm so relieved." Ronnie blows air through puckered lips. "You did it, Gwyn. If you could kill a Sluagh, think of the amazing things we can do going forward."

Sharing the events of the evening brings back all the emotions—Audrey's infiltration and the unanswered questions of her purpose, the Seelie Fae children, the attack of the Sluagh, and its banishment. I turn my gaze to the sprinkles of snowflakes falling on this New Year's Day, anxious about the future. "Ronnie, I left the coven."

"What? Why?" Ronnie grimaces as she tries to clasp my hand, pulling at the tubes in her arms.

"I don't think I want to live like a witch anymore. My parents raised me as an Unremarkable for a reason. I may never know why, and Leslie won't tell me." I return my gaze to her battered face.

"But how can you say goodbye to them? They're friends now." Ronnie peers at me through sagging eyes. "You can't stop being a witch, Gwyn. You are a witch."

"I can go back to an Unremarkable life and continue as if I don't know any of the coven witches like my parents did. Or I go back to the coven, knowing the unethical things they do to shape our community and put it at risk." I pause, contemplating my options. "I'm so screwed."

Ronnie cackles, holding her ribs. "But you have a third choice."

"What do you mean?" My eyebrows gather in a questioning clump. "There is no third choice."

"Sure, there is," she says, batting her eyes. "You go back and help shape the coven in your image." She glances at the heart monitor briefly and looks back at me. "I'm almost afraid to ask. What about Archie?"

My eyes swell up, and a tear spills out. "I left him, too."

"Oh, Gwyn. I'm sorry. I swear I didn't know about his history." Ronnie winces in pain and struggles to move, and I help her shift in the bed.

"I believe you. Archie said he would honor my wish to stay away, and he has. He seems to care for me, but I need to clear my head about him without his presence. I had one philandering husband. I don't want another."

"Do you believe him? That he never cheated on you?" she asks.

"I don't know. How do you believe someone who kept secrets about so many prior relationships? And being a witch in a coven?" I'm not sure of anything. The coven. Practicing witchcraft. Archie...

"Secrets aren't a great basis for a relationship. That's for sure. But sometimes they're necessary to protect the ones you love." She squeezes my hand, and I think of Tyler.

The door to Ronnie's room opens, and Derek enters with three paper cups in a cardboard tray. "Hot chocolate for a nasty, frigid day, ladies?"

"Mmm. It's delightful," I say. "Be careful Ronnie. Maybe you should use a straw. Let it cool a bit."

"What I want is a fucking mirror!" she demands in a snit. "Loverboy wouldn't give me one to see how bad I look." She winks at Derek, and he chuckles.

"And you believed denying her a mirror would assuage her fears?" I pull a mirror out of my purse. "Before I give it to you, I want you to know you look like shit."

Ronnie grimaces and snatches the mirror from my hands. "Oh, shit. Guess I should be happy I'm alive with those fireworks going off by accident." She winks lightly at me. "Wait. What's this?" Ronnie inspects the clump of white hairs growing at her hairline.

"The doctors said the shock of your injuries may cause some hair to turn white. I don't care, babe. I think it's mysterious, almost magical." He kisses her on the lips.

"Liar. I could dye it, but I think it could be sexy." She winks at Derek, and he puckers and blows her a kiss.

"OK, you lovebirds." I chuckle at their flirty interaction. "I'm gonna leave. Ronnie needs to rest." Her eyes dart around the room, and I lay my hand on hers. "Don't worry. I'll always be here for you. I love you, friend." A quick hug sends me out the door, with Derek trailing close behind.

"Wait, Gwyn." Derek follows me into the hallway. The dark circles under his eyes have aged him. "When Ronnie came out of sedation, she cried about an evil bird or tree, unexplainable blather. Now she says it must have been a dream, but it sounded eerily like the nightmarish talk of the homeless men who were killed. I have this odd feeling she's not telling me everything. Do you get that vibe?"

"What are you saying, Derek?" I blink several times and avert my eyes.

"Agh, I don't know." He shakes his head. "So, you can't tell me what happened at the Winter Solstice?" He hikes his dark eyebrows. "I don't believe for a millisecond it was just fireworks."

I try to weave my way around the truth. "The Fellowship rituals date back many years. Their practices bind us to keep silent. But she loves you. Give her time to heal. She'll confide in you when she has a better grip on her recovery."

Derek lays a rugged hand on my shoulder. "Thanks, Gwyn. You'll come back tomorrow?"

"Of course, I will."

January brings lots of snow and ice, turning cars into projectiles. The hospital moved Ronnie to a rehab facility, and I visit her three times a week to encourage her progress, not that she needs it. Pledging not to practice witchcraft, I ponder the path ahead of me. I miss the magic, the incredible rush of power flowing through my body, and I miss my witch friends. I even miss Mr. Yeats and his shenanigans. And I miss Archie.

Tyler and I visit his father's grave on the anniversary of his death, acknowledging the grief and disappointment of his poor decisions, and I cancel my spring semester registration to concentrate on the sale of the house. The amount of work overwhelms me, but Tyler says not to worry. We'll pummel through it like ninja house warriors. He called around for vol-

unteers to help, so I'm not surprised when the doorbell rings.
I'm excited to see his friends after so long.

"I'll get it!" I run to the foyer with a hammer in my hand.
When I open the door, I'm stumped by the faces on the slushy
granite stoop—Spence, Tanner, Skye, and Zoe. "Why are you
here?"

"I told you it was a bad idea to come." Zoe crinkles her brow.

Spence points a finger at my raised hammer, and his eyes bug
out. "Are you planning on using that?"

"Yes," I say, lowering my hand. "I'm patching the walls."

"We're here to help with the house, Gwyn," Tanner says.

I'm overcome with emotion and swallow to hold back tears.
"I don't understand. Who asked you?"

"Me," Tyler says, strolling into the foyer. "Don't make them
stand in the frigid air, Mom. Please, come in. Nice to meet all
of you." Tyler passes fist bumps all around.

I'm befuddled, and my mouth opens and closes, stuttering.
"How...how did you find their phone numbers?"

"In your cell phone." Tyler laughs and punches my arm
playfully. "You should pick a more difficult pin, Mom. 1-2-3-4
is hardly cryptic."

Skye grasps my arm and squeezes. "Is this OK? Us helping?
We don't have to stay." She leans toward me and whispers. "I
promise. We won't mention the Fellowship. We're here to help
a good friend."

My eyes hop around the foyer. "Of course. I appreciate your
help." I motion for them to follow me. "Tyler, let's show them
the damage."

We're busy bees over the next couple of weeks. Like clock-
work, my young friends descend on my house. A harder working group of young people, you will not find, but I knew that
already. Cracks in the plaster exist in every room, and water
stains blotch the ceilings. Tanner and Spence convince me to
buy paint in bulk, and we give every room a fresh coat of white.

Skye discovers a knack for painting woodwork, a tedious job I hate. Taking a liking to Tyler, Zoe hangs out with him on every project, including moving furniture. The tiny woman has hidden strength. I knew that, too.

By the end of January, the house gleams, but I have packing to complete as well as sifting through my parents' belongings. I dread those mementos the most. At Tanner's suggestion, the Fellowship crew stops by one last time to help stage the house, and my heart aches at the idea of never seeing them again. The day shines bright with skies the color of summer cornflowers, not a day to say goodbye.

"Hugs." Spence swaddles his arms around me. "Even if you don't return to the, you know, text me. You're still fam. I can't stand goodbyes. Tanner, give me the keys. I'll warm up the car."

"Thank you, Spence," I say. "Good luck with the spring semester."

"Have you called a realtor yet?" Tanner's eyes roam the exterior of my house. "Selling a house is daunting, but I could help you through the process. I've saved a bit of money for a few years now. I've been thinking...maybe it's time to buy a house and settle down."

I goggle at Tanner. "With Spence?"

"As much as Spence will ever settle down." Tanner grins as he glances back at the house. "After doing so much work on it, the place seems like home. You know? Call me when you're ready to settle." He hugs me and walks to his car.

Tanner waves goodbye and Spence throws air kisses from the driver's side of the SUV as they drive off. I walk over to join Skye at her car, where she's waiting for Zoe to finish talking with Tyler at his sedan.

"What's going on there?" I ask.

Skye squints and observes the interaction. "Looks like they're entering phone numbers. What do you think of that, Mom?"

"I don't know. Do I have a say?" I grind my teeth and moan.

"Probably not," Skye says, laughing.

Tyler hollers from the car. "Bye, Mom! I'll call tomorrow to discuss the realtor."

Zoe approaches and wraps my torso in a tight squeeze. "I'm gonna miss you, Gwyn." She smiles with her signature wide-toothed grin.

Tears fill the bottom of my eyes as Zoe drops into the passenger seat of Skye's two-door hatchback. I can't keep Tyler away from my witch friends. And I love Zoe.

"Don't feel pressured to come back. You don't owe anyone anything. Live your life the way you want. The coven will survive." Skye caps my hugs for the day and gets in her car. They wave one last time and drive off.

Back inside my refurbished home, I envision a house full of extraordinary possibilities, but they won't be mine.

CHAPTER TWENTY-NINE
SAY HELLO TO YESTERDAY

PURGING AND PACKING ALLOW no time for regrets since the March settlement looms. I throw on a grungy t-shirt and jeans, clip my hair, and throttle full steam ahead to empty every closet, dresser, and bookshelf, displacing dust bunnies and their kin. Tyler helps me clean out his father's tools and man cave in the basement. I couldn't do it alone. Too many terrible memories. And I relive the last conversation with Richard on that revealing Samhain—the night I learned I was a witch.

The only remaining items are my parents' boxes and the steamer trunk with a rusted clasp. It pains me to get rid of it, but there's no room to store it in Tyler's small apartment. I sit on the trunk and sort through the cardboard filled with mementos, finding books on Wales, Mom's collection of Welsh love spoons, and family photo albums. Flipping through the pictures evokes magical memories. Not all magic is supernatural. I take note my three-year-old pictures are missing. They must have been too busy transitioning their lives to snap photos.

I tear up, sorting through the holiday cards I'd given them, and save a few cherished ones. When I reach the last box, I sigh. It has years of old federal tax returns, so I can throw those away, for sure. Rhys and Lowri covered their tracks well. They intended I never discover the truth about them—and me.

Procrastination has robbed me of half the afternoon when I finish. Rising from the trunk, I rub my aching back and tie the recycling bags. I gaze at the beat-up trunk and contemplate. If I can loosen the rusted clasp, I could sell the old thing. Maybe I should try? I pick up my toolbox and find a couple of screwdrivers. The rust on the clasp sticks like superglue, and my hands don't have the strength to force it open. I grab a hammer and hit the hell out of the end of the large screwdriver, and it gets lodged.

"Damn." I puff at my fringe of bangs.

A crowbar is the only choice left, so I position it under the screwdriver and push with the power of the bitch I've become. It flies straight up, embeds in the ceiling, and I fall on my ass. The clasp lifts, shooting sparks of light! Glimmering particles gather to form a floating hand above the metal clasp, and it closes it with a clink!

"Shit!" I burst into laughter and delight. "No wonder it was stuck." I pause for a minute, considering the conundrum of my magic sobriety. "Oh, screw it."

I summon my witch energy and chant using the single spell I can remember to break into an object. The amber glow heats the clasp, raising it an inch until it snaps shut. The glimmering, floating guardian of the trunk materializes and points its index finger at me, swaying back and forth, and disappears. I need magic advice. Ronnie's still in rehab, so I won't bother her with this. If I contact any of my fellow witches in the coven, they'll get the idea I'm practicing witchcraft again. With no alternative, I give up and call Skye.

She squeals. "That's lit! What have you tried? I don't think I know any more than you. You caught up with my training level."

"I've cast the spell I learned, but the silly hand keeps admonishing me. Thanks anyway. I didn't want to contact anyone else and raise their hopes I'm performing magic again."

"Well, you are," she says with a husky laugh.

"You got me." By all means, call me out, friend.

"I gotta get to class, but you know what? Don't try so hard. Instead of making a demand, ask for permission to unlock it?"

I tap my chin while I consider her suggestion. "I'll investigate that. Enjoy your class."

Chanting with a new spell, I ask the guardian to release the metal clasp. "Please, with a cherry on top?" The glimmering hand materializes, grasps the edge, and pulls it toward the ceiling. With its job complete, the magical protector disintegrates into minuscule, shimmering halos of light. "Thank you."

I lift the trunk's lid with anticipation. It's musty and full of cobwebs, and I sneeze and cough. The tray holds three folded, black capes with Bearsden embroidered in small, yellow script and ritual pamphlets for pagan ceremonies. Below it, I discover a trove of witch materials. There are bottles of herbs and animal bones, crystals, runestones, used candles, divination cloths, and more. I'll need days to inventory the contents, but I don't have the time before I move.

I notice the corner of a brown leather notebook with frayed, worn edges, the kind you find in antiquarian bookstores. The cover has no title, only a strap tying it closed. I open the fragile memento and discover page after page of handwritten Welsh, including detailed pictures of herbs. I assume they're directions for spells and how to prepare them for successful application, but I'll have to get them translated to know for sure. As I flip the delicate paper, the handwriting changes several times until I recognize my mom's penmanship. The pages after are blank.

I find a photo album marked "Gwynedd's Year Three." The scrapbook has photos of pagan celebrations, including

Mabon, Samhain, Yule, and Ostara. Family hikes in the local parks and walks on DUB's campus depict joyous occasions. There's a picture of a much younger Leslie with me saddled on her hip tickling my tummy. A three-year-old me giggles.

When I flip to the middle, an envelope falls to the wooden floor. My heart thumps, skipping a few beats. Gwynedd is written across the front in bold black ink. It's Mom's script. I've waited so long for this explanation from my mom, but my fingers tremble on the edge of the paper as I pull the letter out. I suck in a pocket of air and unfold it. The top of the paper reads "Dear Gwynedd," but the rest is blank. My shoulders collapse. "Shit. I guess she meant to write it, but died before she had the chance." I toss the unfinished letter into the tray insert.

The sun's rays from the window shine on the letter's surface, and I notice a shimmer of light. I grasp the paper with creases and hold it to the sunlight, tilting it from side to side. Nothing, but I saw what I saw. I close the trunk and lay the charmed letter on top. I can't use the full force of my magic on it. It might burn, and then where would I be? I summon the amber glow and pass my hand over the hidden words. Faint writing fades in and out, but not enough to read it. Mom cast a spell on it.

I'm relieved she left me an explanation, but now I have to research effective witchcraft to unlock the spell. I don't know of an incantation to call on the hand to secure the clasp. With no immediate solution, I store my mom's charmed letter along with everything else and close the lid.

I need to buy a lock.

I relax on the cool, granite stoop in front of my house and admire the buds emerging, tiny folds of emerald-green petals pushing to break free. Tyler comes out with a brown box, drops it, and sits next to me. He receives a text and starts typing into his cell phone. I stop myself from asking, and most likely it's Zoe, another reason to mind my business.

"What did you do with the steamer trunk?" Tyler asks. "I see it's gone."

"Oh, you didn't have room for it. It's at Ronnie's house. Derek came by and picked it up." It's safer there than in his apartment.

"Awesome. I was dreading lifting it." He checks his phone. "How's Ronnie doing?"

"She's home now. Still on crutches, but she won't need them much longer." The wind blows, and I zip up my hoodie.

"Phew. You guys were lucky." He rolls his eyes and chuckles. "I can't believe you set off fireworks in there. What were you thinking?"

"We figured we could contain it." My eyes hop to the barn-red cape cod with a white picket fence across the street. "Can we change the subject?"

Tyler's phone vibrates. He checks his texts and smiles. It must be Zoe. He turns his head and glances at his bedroom window.

"Do you remember the day we moved into this house? You ran upstairs and picked your bedroom?" I ask.

"Yeah, I do. I said, 'I want this room. It has the most windows.' In high school, you had to buy darkening shades, because the sun blinded me in the morning. Dad came in on Saturdays at 7:00 a.m. and pushed them up, yelling 'Rise and shine! Don't leave the day behind!' Used to piss me off." He laughs and glances at the spongy moss, growing in the cracks of the gray paver walkway. "Do you think Dad would be sad we're selling?"

"No." I take his hand in mine. "He'd say it made sense."

Tyler peers through strands of longer hair. "Is it OK I'm heartbroken he's gone?"

My eyes swell up with tears of regret, and I squeeze his arm. "Oh, Tyler, of course. I understand you were angry after learning of his infidelity, but he cheated on me, not you. He was a great dad. Cherish the good times you had with him. And remember, he was a man. All men have flaws. Even you." I elbow him.

He sucks in his lower lip. "Have you made peace with Dad?"

"I think he knows how I feel," I say, thinking back on Samhain.

"Speaking of flawed men." Tyler hesitates. "I ran into Archie at the Raven Pub on Thursday night."

"What? He had no business bothering you." My chest tightens, and I fidget with my dangling earring.

"Chillax, Mom." He punches my arm in jest. "I approached him. I've seen how unhappy you've been, and you won't talk about it. So, I kinda stuck my nose in it. I wanted to see what Archie might share to enlighten me."

Payback's a bitch, especially when it's your son. "What did he say?"

"He was cordial. Shook my hand and invited me to have a Scotch whisky with him. We talked about the weather, work, and fixing up the house. He asked how you were doing."

"What did you tell him?" The chilly air fills my lungs, and I hold tight for the answer.

"The truth. I told him you were busy packing and getting your life in order." A cool wind gusts, and Tyler wraps an arm around my shoulders to warm me. "Archie said nothing about what happened, but he looked sad."

"Good." I snicker but immediately regret it.

"He still cares for you, Mom. When he asked about you, his face lit up like a security light. You don't have to answer me, but did he cheat on you? Treat you badly?"

"No, I don't think he did, but it's more complicated than that." My son's questions irritate me, but he keeps going.

"I've never seen you so happy as you were with Archie. I guess you have to ask yourself, would you be happier alone or with him, a man who cares for you, despite his shortcomings? As long as he puts you first."

"When did you become such a philosopher?" I squint at him. "Does Zoe have something to do with that?"

He chuckles and rolls his eyes. "I'm not answering that question."

A silver metallic Tesla slows and parks in front of the house. My heart palpitates and butterflies flutter inside while I fiddle with the zipper on my hoodie. Archie gets out of the driver's side and stares in our direction for a minute. He catches my gaze, and a corner of his mouth lifts. He's so handsome in his tweed jacket and jeans, and the wind toys with his blond, wavy locks like tiny fae children. I grasp Tyler's arm as we stand.

"Don't be mad, Mom. He said he needed to talk to you. I sent him a text, letting him know we were here." Tyler waves at my former lover as he approaches us. "Hi, Archie. I'll check the rooms in the house one last time." The storm door closes behind him.

Archie steps toward me, displaying his charming smile. "It's so good to see you, Gwyn. Is this all right? Talking to you now?" He slides a hand into the pocket of his jeans and brushes the wind fairies from his hair.

I gasp a pocket of air and swallow. "Yes. It's fine." His Scottish baritone voice soothes me, and I can't take my eyes off his icy blues.

A broad grin stretches the whiskers of his goatee. "You look well. Refreshed. The last time I saw you—" He averts his eyes and runs a hand through his hair again.

"I feel fantastic. Looking forward to settling on the house. They're so many bad memories from the past year in this home. But a few cherished ones, too." Like the morning he woke in my bed.

Archie returns his gaze to me. "Tyler says Tanner and Spence are purchasing your house. That's wonderful." He extends his hand, an instinctive action to touch me, but pulls it back.

I chuckle. "Well, Tanner is buying it. Spence has no money." It's so awkward, and I search my brain for something to say. "They helped me renovate, and the home grew on them. Skye and Zoe chipped in, too."

"I'm sorry I wasn't here to help as I promised." His chest rises and falls as he holds my gaze captive.

"It's OK. It's done." My insides wrestle with the urge to talk to him about everything. The Winter Solstice. The Bearsden Coven. Us. But I'm not ready. "Is work going well?"

Archie shoves both hands in his pockets, and his body stiffens. "I asked to step down as chair."

I angle my head. "Are you upset about it?"

"Hell no. Hated being chair of the department. You know that." He chuckles, and his shoulders relax. "I prefer the classroom. Can't wait to teach those eager minds in the fall."

"I'm happy for you. I know how much you loved teaching," I say. "And the students will line up to fill your classes."

A sudden burst of wind blows and displaces his blond waves again, causing a few strands to flitter back and forth, but his icy-blue gaze never falters. I wait for him to brush the locks in place, but he doesn't move. The longer he stares at me, the more I crave to grab his gorgeous face and plant a kiss on those inviting lips. Yet, I can't. There needs to be something more between us than magic.

"Why are you here, Archie?" I ask, kneading my chilly hands.

He reaches into his jacket and pulls out his family dirk, protected in its leather sheath. "I want you to have this."

My lips part, and my head quivers. "I can't accept this. It's too precious."

A look of foreboding seizes his face. "Aye, you can. The Sluagh is not dead. We banished it to the Otherworld, but it could return. If the Host of the Unforgiven Dead crosses over again through another portal, it may search for you. I could not bear it if... Please, take it. I need to know you're safe."

His eyes become wet, and I swallow my obstinance for today. "All right. If you ever want it back, it's yours." I open my hands and prepare them for the weight of the heirloom.

Archie lays the centuries-old dirk on my palms, wraps his fingers around mine, and presses. I missed the hot caress of his skin. He gazes into my eyes, trying to convey his longing with unspoken words. "Take care, Gwynedd." He tears his hand away and turns to walk to his car.

Tyler walks out onto the stoop and locks the door. He notices Archie walking to his car and frowns. "I thought maybe?"

"No. It's too soon." I stare at Archie's family heirloom, coddled in my hands. "He stopped by to give me something."

My son pulls the Scottish dagger from its leather cover and examines the blade. "Wow. This is ancient. It must be valuable."

"More than you can imagine." I slip the sheath onto the dirk and grip it, knowing how much it meant for Archie to relinquish such a cherished object.

"And he gave this to you? That means something, Mom. Right?"

As Archie drives away, I smile and embrace his gift of protection against my heart.

"We better get moving." Tyler picks up the box off the stoop, and I follow him to his sedan.

"Do you have any idea where you're going to live yet? You can stay with me as long as you need to, of course." He pops the trunk, drops the last remnants of the house into it, and slams it shut.

"I'm not thinking about tomorrow." I behold the purple crocuses and daffodils in the garden, the initial signs of spring and a reminder of Ostara's renewal. "For the first time in my life, I don't know what I'm doing or where I'm going. And that's OK."

ACKNOWLEDGMENTS

MANY THANKS TO MY entire family for their support through my author journey. You are my rock!

Special thanks go to my editors Christopher Barnes and Amy Cissell at Cissell Ink for their work and support on my debut novel.

To my book cover designer Charles Clark, thank you so much for all the iterations.

ABOUT THE AUTHOR

J.C. YEAMANS is an author of paranormal fiction. A former public school teacher based in Lewes, Delaware, she writes about all things witchy to find the inherent magic in life's journey of discovery and love—all while making blunders along the way. Her prior career revolved around the performing arts. As the owner of Reed Shore Press, she also publishes fiction and nonfiction works for others. She is married and has two adult children. When she's not putting pen to paper (or more aptly, fingertips to keys), she spends time biking, hiking, and weightlifting.

Sign up for J.C. Yeamans's newsletter at jcyeamans.com to download a free backstory and stay in the loop!

OTHER BOOKS